FALCONE STRIKE

Professionally Published Books by Christopher G. Nuttall

Angel in the Whirlwind
The Oncoming Storm

ELSEWHEN PRESS

The Royal Sorceress
The Royal Sorceress (Book I)
The Great Game (Book II)
Necropolis (Book III)

Bookworm
Bookworm
Bookworm II: The Very Ugly Duckling
Bookworm III: The Best Laid Plans
Bookworm IV: Full Circle

Inverse Shadows
Sufficiently Advanced Technology

Stand Alone
A Life Less Ordinary
The Mind's Eye

TWILIGHT TIMES BOOKS

Schooled in Magic
Schooled in Magic (Book I)
Lessons in Etiquette (Book II)
Study in Slaughter (Book III)
Work Experience (Book IV)
The School of Hard Knocks (Book V)
Love's Labor's Won (Book VI)
Trial By Fire (Book VII)

The Decline and Fall of the Galactic Empire
Barbarians at The Gates (Book I)
The Shadow of Cincinnatus (Book II)

HENCHMEN PRESS

First Strike

FALCONE STRIKE

ANGEL IN THE WHIRLWIND

CHRISTOPHER G. NUTTALL

47NORTH

Published by 47North, Seattle

www.apub.com

Amazon, the Amazon logo, and 47North are trademarks of Amazon.com, Inc., or its affiliates.

ISBN-13: 9781503951587
ISBN-10: 1503951588

Cover design by Ray Lundgren
Illustrated by Paul Youll

Printed in the United States of America

PROLOGUE

The Hall of Judgment was a towering structure, huge enough to hold a thousand witnesses comfortably as the accused made his long slow walk towards the judges seated in their thrones, right at the front of the chamber. It was almost empty now, Admiral Junayd discovered, as two Inquisitors shoved him through the heavy wooden door and onto the stone pathway. The only people in the room, save for him and his escorts, were the First Speaker and two Clerics, waiting for him.

He rattled his chains mournfully as he started his walk, smiling inwardly at the cold glares aimed at him by the Inquisitors. They would have been happy to give him a good kicking if they hadn't had to keep him reasonably intact to face his judges. No doubt that was why they'd left half the chains off, even though procedure insisted the accused had to be weighed down with so many iron chains that walking at anything more than a staggering crawl was impossible. They wanted him to be able to answer the charges when they were leveled against him.

Not that there's any hope of leaving this room alive, he thought bitterly. *Someone has to take the blame.*

He ground his teeth together, silently. Who could have predicted that the Commonwealth, asleep for so long, would have woken up *just* in time to organize an effective defense? Who could have predicted that one of their junior officers—a *woman*, no less—would get enough ships out of the trap to render the First Battle of Cadiz a tactical success and a strategic failure? And who could have predicted that the Commonwealth would have enough reinforcements in the vicinity to launch a counterattack that had severely embarrassed the Theocracy? Someone had to take the blame . . .

. . . and, as far as the Theocracy was concerned, failure was a sign of God's displeasure.

The weeks Junayd had spent in captivity had been far from pleasant. His interrogators had alternatively rooted through his life, searching for the secret sin that needed to be punished to please God, and praying at him to repent and hurl himself into the fire, to sacrifice himself for the Theocracy. There had been no point, he was sure; he had committed no sin deserving of punishment . . . save, perhaps, for losing. And now . . . he knew the Speaker would need to make an example of him. The Theocracy had to be seen to deal with failure harshly or it would undermine its position.

He stopped in front of the thrones and bowed his head, feeling the weight of the chains pulling him towards the floor. It was all he could do to remain upright, but he forced himself to hold steady. Going to his death bravely, even willingly, would make up for his sins and convince the Inquisitors to spare his family. His wives might be returned to their families, his children might be distributed among his relatives, but at least they would be alive. The alternative was unthinkable. Sin was so prevalent and the Inquisition so determined to root it out that they would happily kill his children if they felt he had not repented.

"Admiral," the Speaker said. His voice was very cold. "You have failed God."

"I served God willingly," Junayd said calmly. "If it was His will that the battle be lost, it was His will."

The Speaker looked at him for a long moment. "You have served God well, over the years," he said. "It is our considered judgment that your work was undermined by the presence of sinners within our fortress and our failure to weed them out cost us the opening battles."

Junayd blinked in surprise. He'd expected to be made the scapegoat, not . . .

"But the opening battles have still left us in a strong position," the Speaker continued, seemingly unaware of Junayd's shock. "We will still win the war."

If we can, Junayd thought. The Commonwealth's long-term potential was far greater than the Theocracy's. Assuming it survived the opening blows, there was a very strong prospect of the Commonwealth winning the war outright. Junayd had no illusions about just how few of the occupied worlds truly loved the Theocracy. Resistance movements might be hopelessly doomed as long as the Theocracy controlled the high orbitals, but they would distract the Theocracy from focusing on the war. *The Commonwealth may survive long enough to bring its greater strength into play.*

He realized, suddenly, just how precarious the Speaker's position *was*. It had been his daughter—again, a mere *woman*—who had defected, taking with her advance warning of the oncoming storm. Who would have thought that Princess Drusilla, the Speaker's own daughter, would take such a chance? No one had given any thought to her at all, beyond the simple fact that whomever she married would be in a strong position to become Speaker when her father died. Hundreds had died to keep the secret buried, but if it got out . . . the Speaker's position would be untenable. Who could condemn Junayd for failing to react in time, perhaps because of a long-buried sin, when the Speaker's own daughter had committed outright treason?

A flicker of hope ran through him. He had friends and allies . . . most of them might shy away after the failure, but not all of them would. Maybe, just maybe, there was a chance for survival.

"You will be reassigned, Admiral," the Speaker said. "Command of the striking fleets will be passed to someone else. You will assume command of the outer defense formations, protecting our borders against intrusions. In time, with God's grace, you will return to your old role."

Junayd nodded, hastily. The defense formations weren't highly regarded, not when serving on the striking fleets brought glory and wealth, but at least he wasn't being ceremonially beheaded, let alone hung, drawn, and quartered. He could build a new power base for himself, given time; indeed, with the Commonwealth no doubt seeking ways to strike back, there would even be chances for glory. On the other hand, the manpower would be poor and morale would be in the pits. Few competent officers were assigned to the defense formations.

But at least I will be alive, he reminded himself firmly.

"You will assume your new role at once," the Speaker said. "The guards will escort you to your ship."

So I can't talk to anyone along the way, Junayd thought wryly. Whatever deals had been struck while he'd been languishing in a prison cell wouldn't have taken his desire to see his family and friends into account. *Everything I send to my family will be carefully censored first.*

"Thank you," he said, instead. "It will be my honor to serve."

"Indeed," the Speaker said. "And may God defend the right."

CHAPTER ONE

"You know," Candy Falcone said, "you really should be on the dance floor."

Kat Falcone sighed as she leaned over the balcony, peering down at the guests below. Candy had a talent for inviting the best and brightest—or at least the richest and well connected—to her balls, but Kat had very little in common with *any* of them. Some were trust-fund babies, unable to do anything more complex than unscrewing the cap on the latest bottle of bubbly; some had built themselves reputations based on their family name and a certain willingness to exploit it for themselves. They would have been somewhere—anywhere—else, she was sure, if they'd actually lived up to their claims.

"I'm bored," she confessed, without looking around. "I shouldn't even be here."

"You're the guest of honor," Candy said. "Percy wants to meet you,

Katherine, while I believe Owen and Gayle were trying to work up the nerve to ask you out . . ."

"God forbid," Kat said. "What do I have in common with any of them?"

Kat groaned, loudly. Percy was a weak-chinned wonder, a walking advertisement for the dangers of making someone's life too easy, while Owen and Gayle were known hedonists. It was hard to find something edgy in the Commonwealth, not without breaking laws that would see even high-ranking aristocrats in jail or facing a firing squad, but these two seemed to manage it. And besides, she *was* in a relationship. Why her sister didn't seem inclined to leave her to have her own life was beyond her.

"You're an aristocrat," Candy said. "You have *that* in common with them."

Kat swung around to glower at her sister. Candy was tall and blonde, wearing a long green dress that showed off her chest to best advantage while hinting at the shape of her legs. They hadn't gotten on since Kat had grown old enough to realize that her older sister spent more time in pursuit of pleasure than anything else . . . and that she would eventually grow bored of a baby sister, no matter how novel she seemed initially. If Candy hadn't been hosting some of the most important balls on the planet, with some of the most important movers and shakers invited to attend, Kat would have declined the invitation. Right now, she wished she'd declined it anyway.

"I am a serving officer in the Royal Navy," she said sharply. It was something she was proud of, if only because she'd achieved it on her own. "How many of *them*"—she waved a hand down towards the crowds—"have ever served in the Navy, let alone commanded their own starship?"

"I believe that Tryon owns a pleasure yacht," Candy said. "Would that count?"

"No," Kat snapped. "A pleasure cruiser isn't *quite* the same as a heavy cruiser."

"Your ship crashed," Candy pointed out. "What else do you have to do?"

Kat gritted her teeth. *Lightning* was being repaired after the battle, and her crew were dispersed among a dozen other ships as the Commonwealth struggled to regain its balance after the war had begun . . . she shouldn't be wasting time at a party. But she knew, no matter how much she wanted to deny it, that there was nothing she could do . . .

"Something," she said finally. Maybe she should have asked her father to use his influence, once again, to get her a transfer. *This* time, she was sure, no one could have argued that she hadn't earned the post. The medals on her chest proved that beyond all doubt. "This party is just a waste of time."

"It isn't," Candy said, as she took Kat's arm and led her towards the stairs. "The men and women gathered here aren't *entirely* useless. They represent voting blocs in family corporations—small blocs, to be sure, but not useless. Keeping them confident that our ultimate victory is assured is quite an important part of the war."

Kat blinked in genuine astonishment. "Really?"

"Yes," Candy said. She leaned closer to whisper into Kat's ear. "You're not the only one capable of thinking tactically, you know. Some of us fight battles in ballrooms and bedrooms, not in deep space."

"Oh," Kat said. She knew socializing was important, but she'd never been very good at it, not when she'd been the youngest of ten children. Instead, she'd been allowed to choose her own path and walked straight into the Navy. It still galled her to know that her family name—curse and blessing mixed into one—had smoothed her path to command. "But surely they know they can't escape the war?"

Candy smirked. "How many of them have never experienced the world outside the towering mansions of High Society?"

She had a point, Kat was loath to admit. *She'd* never really experienced hardship until she'd gone to Piker's Peak. Even sharing a room with a single roommate had been tricky, back when she'd been used to having an entire suite to herself. And the less said about the food the better. But she'd earned her uniform and her position in the Royal Navy. The men and women on the dance floor had no idea of what life was like outside their mansions . . . and they wouldn't have any real comprehension of just how horrific life would become under the Theocracy. What enemy forces had done to Cadiz, since driving Kat and 7th Fleet away from the planet, proved they wouldn't even *begin* to hesitate in reshaping the Commonwealth's worlds to suit themselves.

"So you go chat to them and tell them everything you saw," Candy added. "And make it clear that victory is inevitable, if they keep pushing for it."

Kat didn't *quite* roll her eyes, but she saw her sister's point. If victory was inevitable, why strive for it? But if victory was *not* inevitable, why *not* consider some form of compromise with the Theocracy? It was impossible, she knew—the only way a sheep could compromise with a wolf was from inside the wolf's belly—but someone without direct experience of just how ruthless the Theocracy could be might think otherwise.

"I'll do my best," she promised as they reached the bottom of the stairs. "But the sooner I'm back on the bridge, the better."

Kat groaned inwardly as the crowd surrounded them, some staring at her attire—Candy had insisted she wear her white dress uniform—others eager to chat with Candy about nothing in particular. Kat looked at them, silently grateful her father had allowed her to go to Piker's Peak rather than one of the finishing schools that specialized in turning young men into chinless wonders and young women into brainless beauties. If things had been different, if she'd been less driven to accomplish something for herself, she might be one of the admiring throng rather than a starship commander. It was not a pleasant thought . . .

But Candy has hidden depths, she told herself. It was an odd thought, reminding her of exercises where she'd hunted for stealthed starships. A cloaking device could hide a starship in the vastness of space or convince prowling hunters that it was nothing more than a small asteroid or a cloud of dust. *How many of the guests have hidden depths too?*

It nagged at her mind as the party dragged on. Candy had a point: The vast majority of the partygoers might be unimportant, in the grand scheme of things, but collectively they commanded huge wealth and power. Kat toyed with a handful of scenarios; maybe, just maybe, their influence would be sufficient to change the Commonwealth's path if they wished. But she found it hard to believe they had any real influence. God knew *her* share of the family voting stock was minimal, even though she'd proved herself at Cadiz.

"Lady Katherine," a smooth voice said. Kat turned to see Lord Brenham standing just behind her with a glass in his hand. "Would you care to join me on the dance floor?"

Kat bit down the reaction that came to mind. Lord Brenham was notorious, so notorious that even *she* had heard of him. He was an unrepentant rake, a seducer who was reputed to have slept with every girl and half the boys in High Society. And, surprisingly, he wasn't hated by everyone else. High Society didn't give a damn what happened, as long as it happened between consenting adults in private.

"No," she said flatly. She supposed she should have been politer, but she was tired and cranky. Besides, she'd never lost herself in hedonism and she wasn't about to start now. "I'm required to mingle."

Lord Brenham merely nodded, then walked off. He didn't show any sign of anger at her rejection, somewhat to her surprise, but she supposed it made sense. A man so intent on chasing bright young things wouldn't have time to get upset. All he'd need to do was find someone else . . .

"Great between the sheets," Candy observed. If rumor was to be believed, *her* string of conquests was almost as long as Lord Brenham's. "But personality? Skin deep."

Kat scowled at her. "Is it wrong to want something more . . . *personal* than a quick fuck?"

"This is High Society, sweetheart," Candy said gently. "You know as well as I do that marriage, that intimacy, isn't a matter of *choice*."

"I know," Kat muttered.

It wasn't something she'd ever expected to have to handle, not when she was the tenth child of Duke Falcone. Peter, Ashley, and Dolly—the three oldest—were the ones whose marriages had been determined by their father, mingling the family bloodline with partners who would bring strength and other assets to the family. Kat's share of the family bloc was so low that she *could* marry for love, if she wanted. Maybe it was a flaw in her personality, but she was damned if she was entering a loveless marriage. There was something fundamentally wrong about a match where both partners *knew* the other was having an affair . . .

The smaller clusters of people started to blur together as Candy moved her from group to group, sometimes clearly showing Kat off, sometimes just listening as the gathered aristocrats discussed the war and its implications. One elderly woman bragged about her grandchild fighting on the front lines; one younger woman talked about her new baby and wondered out loud if he would be conscripted into the military. Kat rather suspected she would wind up feeling sorry for the baby, if she ever met the child; the mother had given birth only a month ago, she gathered, and yet she'd left the baby with the servants and ventured out for a party . . .

At least Dad spent some time with us, she thought. Duke Falcone had been a very busy man and his ten children had suffered, although he *had* tried to make time for them. Their mother had largely stayed at home, supervising the children as best as she could and commanding a small army of servants . . . which hadn't stopped Kat and her siblings from running riot, on occasion. *What will happen to the poor baby?*

"But surely there would be room for peace," a middle-aged woman was saying loudly. Her shrill voice grated on Kat's ears. "The galaxy is big enough for the both of us."

Kat opened her mouth to make a sarcastic reply, but an older gentleman spoke first. "The Theocracy attacked us first, Lady Ella," he said. "*They* clearly do not agree that we can coexist; everything we know about them tells us that they cannot tolerate a different society near their own. Their expansion would inevitably bring them into conflict with us, if only because we welcome the refugees fleeing their rule."

"Some of those refugees turned out to be spies," another man said.

That, Kat knew, was true. The Commonwealth had taken in everyone, debriefing them thoroughly . . . but a number of spies and operatives had slipped through the net. After the first attacks had died down, every refugee had been hastily rounded up and interned, the innocent as well as the guilty. The innocent would be cared for, she knew, but it would also undermine their faith in the Commonwealth. And, perhaps, the Commonwealth's faith in itself.

She pushed the thought aside, irritated. The Commonwealth Charter was many things, but it was not a suicide pact.

"You might be interested in this," Candy said, tugging her towards another group. "And you might even have something to say."

"Admiral Christian should have continued to press the offensive," a man said. "In choosing to withdraw from Cadiz, he wasted a chance to smash an entire enemy fleet."

Kat felt her heart sink as she recognized him. Justin Deveron was an armchair admiral, an amateur student of military history who had never, as far as she knew, served in the military. He was handsome, in a way; his suit was carefully tailored to look like a uniform, suggesting he had served without ever making a false claim. His brown hair was cropped close to his scalp in a spacer's cut, adding another layer to the illusion. Kat had regrown her long hair once she'd left Piker's Peak, but most spacers preferred to keep their hair short. It could get in the way when they were on duty.

She groaned, again, as Deveron recognized her. He'd made a name for himself as a gadfly, questioning the Admiralty regularly and posing as an expert; indeed, the fact he'd never served allowed him to claim to be giving disinterested advice and commentary. But it also meant that his statements, at best, were wholly theoretical . . .

"But I believe you were there, Captain Falcone," Deveron said. There was an easy confidence in his voice that got on her nerves. "Do you believe that Admiral Christian passed up the chance to smash an enemy fleet?"

"Yes," Kat said, "but . . ."

"The Admiralty saw fit to *reward* him for abandoning the fight," Deveron said, addressing the circle. "He ran from Cadiz and they rewarded him . . ."

Kat felt her temper flare. She *knew* Admiral Christian. More to the point, unlike Deveron, she'd actually *been* there when he'd made the decision. She knew his reasoning and she agreed with it. So had the Admiralty. Many people had been criticized, in the wake of the First and Second Battles of Cadiz, but Admiral Christian hadn't been one of them.

She pulled herself to her full height, as if she were standing on her bridge in the midst of combat. "I'm afraid that isn't *quite* correct, Mr. Deveron," she said. It was easy enough to channel one of her more sarcastic tutors from Piker's Peak. "Your analysis, while superficially accurate, fails to take a number of factors into account. This failure undermines it to the point where it loses relevancy."

Candy shifted beside her, warningly, but Kat ignored her, never taking her eyes off Deveron.

"You see, in war, there are operational concerns, tactical concerns, and strategic concerns," she continued, speaking each word clearly. "Operationally and tactically, the combined striking power of 6th and 7th fleets could have destroyed the enemy force. Post-battle analysis suggested, very strongly, that the enemy ships had expended all of their missiles, requiring them to either force a duel at energy range or to abandon the battlefield. *Yes*, there was a very good chance we could have smashed the enemy fleet or convinced it to withdraw."

She took a breath, then went on. "*However*, there was no way to know if that was the *sole* enemy fleet in the sector," she said. "We didn't know—we *still* don't know—just how many ships the Theocracy possesses. Attempting the complete destruction of one enemy fleet could have led to the combined force shooting *itself* dry, just in time for a second enemy fleet to arrive and scatter us. Or, for that matter, to seize other worlds in the sector. The combined fleet was the *only* deployable mobile force available. Risking it for a dubious goal was not in the cards.

"Retreating from Cadiz was not a cowardly decision. It was a *brave* decision, purely because armchair experts such as yourself wouldn't hesitate to *call* it cowardly. By the time the Admiralty had examined all the sensor records and collected testimonies from everyone on the scene, the opinions of you and the other armchair experts would have filled the datanet with claims that Admiral Christian fled the battlefield and that if *you'd* been in command no enemy ship would have escaped."

Deveron stared at her. "But . . ."

"But *nothing*," Kat snapped. She allowed her anger to color her voice. "You weren't there. You weren't the one on the spot, with everything resting on you, when the decision had to be made. All you can do is carp and criticize, doing it from, at best, a flawed understanding of just what actually happened. He had no choice! Admiral Christian did the right thing at the right time, combining the goal of striking a blow against the Theocracy with the urgent need to preserve his command intact so it could hold the line. And, as the Theocracy invaded three worlds and attacked two more, in addition to Cadiz itself, we know he was right. It's only people like you who say otherwise."

She turned and stalked off. Candy would probably seek to smooth ruffled feathers, but Kat found it hard to care. The folks on Tyre had assigned Admiral Morrison to Cadiz, then chosen to turn a blind eye to his conduct, even as the storm clouds loomed over the Commonwealth. No doubt Deveron would have praised Admiral Morrison to the skies, even though he'd done more than anyone else to weaken the defenses and make the Commonwealth vulnerable.

I may get in trouble for telling him the truth, she told herself as she made her way back to the waiting aircars, *but it was worth it.*

CHAPTER TWO

"I seem to recall that there were times when you misbehaved quite badly as a child," Duke Falcone said the following morning. "You wanted my attention, did you not?"

"Yes, Father," Kat said, feeling her cheeks burn with embarrassment. Her father had ordered her to meet him in his office as soon as she'd woken, without any time for breakfast. "I was feeling neglected."

Her father's face darkened. "And are you feeling neglected now?"

"No, sir," Kat said. She wasn't a child any longer; she was damned if she was going to tolerate an unsubtle suggestion that she was acting childish. "I'm feeling useless."

Her father quirked his eyebrows. "I would hardly call the serving officer who saved half of 7th Fleet and then countless lives on Cadiz *useless*," he said. "You're very much a heroine to the population."

"I am a serving officer in good health," Kat said flatly. "I should be out on the front lines, not stuck here raising the morale of the civilian population."

"It is that morale that must be maintained," her father said. "Should vast numbers of our people despair, should they come to believe that there is no hope of victory, the war effort would be fatally compromised. You standing up in front of a crowd and telling them that the Theocracy *can* be beaten is important."

"I know that, Father," Kat said. What was it about her father that he could reduce her to the mindset of a teenage girl with a handful of well-chosen words? "But I still feel useless."

Her father sighed. "I don't blame you," he said. "And I don't blame you for wanting to squash that gadfly. But he's a gadfly with powerful connections and some of them have already been muttering in my ear, warning me that your words might have unpleasant consequences."

"That . . . *gadfly* might have connections to whoever was backing Admiral Morrison," Kat pointed out. "Attacking Admiral Christian might be a way to draw attention away from Admiral Morrison."

"It's a possibility," her father said. He shrugged. "It's also possible that he really is nothing more than a loudmouth with a handful of political connections."

"He's a danger," Kat said tartly. "The news bulletins from the front aren't really censored, Father. It doesn't take much intellectual effort to see that we were caught flatfooted when the Theocracy came pouring over the border . . ."

"We weren't, thanks to you," her father said.

". . . and that Admiral Morrison was primarily to blame," Kat continued. Morrison had simply refused to even *consider* the possibility of an oncoming storm, let alone make preparations to meet it. She would have gleefully strangled the man at the time if she'd realized the true scale of the disaster bearing down on them. It would probably have cost her everything, including her life, but it would have saved countless more. "No attempt to cover up the truth is likely to work."

"You'd be surprised," her father said. His voice took on a more formal tone. "One might say that Admiral Morrison was guilty of nothing more than trying to do his duty under trying circumstances."

"One might say that," Kat said, "but one would be wrong."

Her father shrugged. "Be that as it may, you have been summoned to the palace," he said, rising to his feet. "The War Cabinet wishes to speak with you. Don your best uniform, then meet me at the shuttle-pad. And make damn sure you pin the Royal Lion to your chest. It should keep some of them from tearing a stripe off you."

Kat nodded—the Royal Lion was the highest award for bravery in the Commonwealth—and then hurried back to her suite to change. Her maid was already there, laying out her uniform on the bed; Kat sighed—she'd long since grown used to doing everything for herself—and hastily changed her casual wear for the uniform. The maid flustered around her, wiping imaginary dust off her gold braid and shoulder pads, and then stepped backwards as Kat glowered at her. These days, the thought of having someone tend to her felt more than a little absurd.

"You look lovely, my lady," the maid said. Kat tried to remember the girl's name and failed. "The very picture of a modern naval officer."

"Thank you," Kat said. "I *am* a modern naval officer."

The maid scurried away. Kat ignored her as she turned to face the wall and eyed herself in the mirror. The white uniform was deliberately designed to be uncomfortable, she was sure; she'd never met anyone who admitted to actually *liking* the Royal Navy's dress uniform. The combination of gold braid and her medals looked spectacular, she had to admit, but it didn't make up for the discomfort. Her blonde hair hung down her back; she tied it up into a long ponytail, then headed for the door. She knew from bitter experience that her father, at least, would not be happy if she was late. He was fond of charting out every last minute he spent awake, but his schedule for the day had already been ruined.

And that will make him look weak, she thought sourly. Countless meetings would have to be rescheduled; hundreds of people's lives would be disrupted. *His enemies will start to scent blood in the water.*

It was a bitter thought. She disliked politics as much as she disliked High Society, but she understood the basic principles. King Hadrian had placed an awful lot of power in Duke Falcone's hands when he'd made Kat's father the Minister of War Production, and his enemies would be watching carefully, looking for signs that he was either abusing his power or unable to handle the challenge. Kat's little outburst would have given them more ammunition to use against her father, if they chose to use it. And their forbearance would come with a price.

She gritted her teeth, feeling cold. She'd hoped to spend most of her life away from Tyre, perhaps assigned to patrolling the borders or defending worlds and trade routes against all threats. Instead . . . it struck her, suddenly, that her father's enemies might seek to exile her, as if sending her away from her homeworld was a *punishment.* It was an amusing thought, but also a limiting one. She knew, all too well, that her exile wouldn't be the only price her father's enemies could extract.

Pushing the thought aside, she walked through the corridors and down to the shuttlepad, where an armored shuttle was already waiting. It was overkill, she was sure, but commandos had launched dozens of attacks on Tyre as part of the Theocracy's opening gambit for the war. If there were any assault groups left, they might well take advantage of an opportunity to assassinate the Minister for War Production. And Kat herself was probably right at the top of their shit list, save perhaps for King Hadrian. Her lips quirked in bitter amusement. It was hard for her to comprehend that the Theocracy genuinely believed women to be inherently inferior to men, but if it made them feel worse about being defeated . . .

She shook her head as she climbed into the shuttle. Her father was already there, reading a datapad; beside him, Sandra, his personal assistant, had her head cocked as she scanned the datanet. Kat had never liked the woman and had a feeling that Sandra felt the same way about her too, although, as Kat was Duke Falcone's daughter, there was nothing Sandra could do about it. Unless she'd deliberately presented the Duke with a warped picture of public reaction . . . no, it would be an insane risk for anyone to take. Sandra would be lucky to escape treason charges if she did anything other than present the exact truth, no matter how unpleasant or embarrassing. Kat pushed the thought aside, then settled back in her chair as the shuttle took off and headed towards the palace. They'd be back on the ground soon enough.

"You'll be coming straight in with me," her father said, looking up suddenly. "I imagine they will make arrangements for your return to the mansion."

"Yes, father," Kat said.

Her father eyed her for a long moment. "Where is young Davidson?"

"He is currently on training operations," Kat said. She would have preferred to take her boyfriend to the ball, if only so she would have had someone to talk with that she actually *liked*, but the Marine Corps had found other work for him. Or had it been her father or Candy, seeking to ensure she'd *had* to socialize? "He's due back this weekend."

"Good," her father said.

He said nothing else until the shuttle had landed and all three of them had been carefully checked out by a handful of heavily armed Marines. Kat hadn't visited the Royal Palace very often, but she was quietly horrified by the sheer number of armored Marines and vehicles stationed around the low marble walls. The center of the government had become an armed camp, curled up and waiting for the next attack to begin. She had a feeling that most of it was just window dressing rather than serious preparations to handle an attack. If the Theocracy ever took the high orbitals, Tyre was doomed; the forces defending the palace could be obliterated from orbit if they refused to surrender or melt into the local population and vanish. Or, if the Theocracy didn't give a damn about civilian casualties, a nuke hidden somewhere in the city could do considerable damage to the entire structure without having to breach the defenses.

"Right this way, Your Grace," an equerry said. "They're waiting for you in Conference Room A."

Kat nodded, then eyed the young girl suspiciously. The uniform she wore drew the eye to her curves, but it was clearly cut to allow the wearer maximum freedom of movement. Kat would have bet half her salary that the young girl was an operative, probably an enhanced bodyguard; hardly anyone would take her seriously until she showed her true nature and by then it would probably be too late. She smiled, then pushed the thought aside. It was good to know the king was protected, even inside his palace.

They paused outside a wooden door, which opened slowly to reveal a conference room. A large table dominated the space, with five men sitting on the far side and a handful of wallflowers standing against the wall, under a large portrait of King Hadrian. Kat felt her blood run cold as she recognized the prime minister, the Leader of the Opposition, and Grand Admiral Tobias Vaughn, the First Space Lord. It was starting to look as though she was in real trouble. A room hadn't felt so ominous to her since she'd attended a court-martial, after the incident on HMS *Thunderous* . . . and she had been a witness, not the one facing the full weight of military justice. It took all the discipline she had to hold herself steady as her father walked forward, then bowed politely to the prime minister.

"Duke Falcone," Arthur Hampshire said. He looked at Kat. "Captain Falcone. Please, be seated."

Kat obeyed, feeling as if her mouth was suddenly dry. She was barely aware of Sandra stepping backwards until she was standing against the wall, joining the other wallflowers. She had to force herself to look at the prime minister, meeting his gaze as steadily as she could despite her growing nervousness. He looked back at her, his face expressionless, as she hastily tried to recall everything she knew about him. She didn't know him that well, although she'd met him at a couple of formal functions she would have preferred to avoid. He would have the confidence of the king, as well as the houses of Parliament; now, in wartime, he would have to gather and hold the confidence of the opposition as well.

"This meeting of the Commonwealth Defense Committee is called to order," the prime minister said. "I must state for the record, here and now, that while we are currently serving as an informal fact-finding committee, our decisions will have a very real impact on the war."

Kat had to fight not to clench her fists, silently cursing her family. Any other naval officer who shot their mouth off in public would be severely reprimanded by his or her superiors . . . or put in front of a court-martial, if the offense was serious enough to merit more than a verbal reprimand and a nasty note in their file. But she, the daughter of the Minister for War Production himself, couldn't be handled gently, not when she'd accidentally kicked a political hornet's nest. They needed to make it clear that she was being punished for her thoughtlessness before the opposition started feeling the heat from some of their supporters.

An informal committee, her thoughts mocked her. *Of course it will have an impact on the war.*

She glanced at her father, feeling suddenly out of place. If she'd been put in front of a court-martial, she would have known how to react; if she was being chewed out by her superior, she would have held herself steady and waited for him to run out of unpleasant things to call her. But this . . . the men in the room were the most powerful men in the Commonwealth, excepting only the king himself. They could wreck her career with a thought.

The prime minister met her eyes. "Perhaps, Captain Falcone, you could enlighten us as to what you were thinking last night?"

Kat winced inwardly. The Commonwealth Defense Committee couldn't have expected to be summoned to deal with her; hell, her father wouldn't be the only one whose schedule had been badly upset by the incident. But with a gadfly like Justin Deveron buzzing around, failing to deal with the problem as quickly and decisively as possible would cause all manner of problems. She'd been right . . .

. . . but she knew enough about High Society to know that being right was no defense.

"I was defending a fellow officer," she said, finally. There was no point in trying to deny anything, not when most of the guests would have been using their implants to record the entire party for later analysis. "Mr. Deveron's attacks on Admiral Christian were quite beyond the pale."

"They are also not taken seriously," the Leader of the Opposition said. "There was no need for you to defend the admiral."

Kat met his eyes. "If I had failed to rebut the accusations," she said, "it might have lent them credence."

The prime minister smiled, humorlessly. "There is little so conspicuous as a man ducking for cover," he said. "Your knee-jerk defense of a fellow officer might have lent credence to the charges against Admiral Christian . . . particularly, I might add, as you were trying to defend a position that seems flawed, even if it was entirely accurate. It was lucky, I suppose, that you didn't indict Admiral Morrison. *That* would have set the reporter among the politicians."

"It was not my intention to cause a political crisis," Kat said, after a moment. She had difficulty in believing that *any* political crisis could be caused by ticking off a gadfly, but politics was a funny business. Maybe Deveron had friends who needed to stick up for him, if only to avoid being thought fools for believing his armchair theorizing. "If I have caused a problem, I sincerely apologize."

"You have created a major headache," the prime minister said. "Do you have anything you wish to say in your own defense?"

Kat hesitated, then took the plunge. "Merely that I should be on the front lines, not here," she said. It was hard to keep the bitter frustration out of her voice. "I am profoundly unsuited to serve as a political or military spokesperson—or anything, apart from a starship commander."

The prime minister nodded, then looked at the First Space Lord. "Tobias?"

Grand Admiral Vaughn nodded curtly. "Captain Katherine Falcone," he said. "It is my obligation to inform you that your active duty career has been suspended, prior to a full investigation by a board of inquiry and possible court-martial proceedings. During this period of time . . ."

Kat barely heard him. The world seemed to fade out around her for a long moment, leaving her feeling dizzy and unwell. If she hadn't been seated, she knew her legs would have buckled. Her career was doomed. Even if the inquiry decided in her favor, she would never hold command again. Telling off a gadfly had cost her everything and . . . and the best she could hope for was either to find private employment or remain stuck on Tyre.

"That won't be necessary," a commanding voice said.

Kat glanced up sharply. One of the wallflowers had stepped away from the wall, coming into the light. But who would dare to interrupt the grand admiral?

"It is remarkably hard to blame Captain Falcone for pointing out the many flaws in Deveron's position," the wallflower continued. "I do not see any reason she should be penalized for it."

"Your Majesty," the prime minister said. "There are political concerns . . ."

Kat stared. The king? She'd seen King Hadrian a few times, but he'd always been wearing robes or uniforms . . . both of which had drawn attention away from his face. He'd been able to blend into the wallflowers easily, simply because it would never have occurred to her to think of them as anything other than part of the furniture. But, now that she knew who it was, it was easy to match his face to the portrait hanging from the wall. Her father rose and bowed; she followed hastily, then returned to her seat. She'd never met the king formally outside court!

"But those political concerns pale in importance compared to winning the war," King Hadrian said. He didn't seem concerned about the lack of protocol. "Victory salves many wounds, Arthur, while defeat renders them immaterial."

He took a seat at the end of the table, then smiled. "Captain Falcone, it is my very great pleasure to offer you command of Operation Knife," he said. "I believe it would be ideally suited to your talents."

CHAPTER THREE

Kat forced herself to think coldly and logically, despite the multitude of shocks. Her career had been ruined—she knew that for a fact—and then saved by the improbable appearance of King Hadrian himself. But she hadn't heard him enter the room after the door had shut, which meant he'd been watching her ever since the meeting had started. Had he planned the whole thing? And, if so, why? To see what she would do if confronted with the prospect of losing everything? Or merely to make it clear to her just how close she'd come to complete disaster?

"I would be honored," she stammered.

She knew nothing about Operation Knife but it had to be better than being put in front of a board of inquiry. It crossed her mind that the king might have planned matters so she'd feel obliged to accept, but he'd hardly need an elaborate charade to convince her to take the job. She'd been so bored on Tyre that she would have happily accepted a mission that involved returning to Cadiz or one of the other occupied worlds. Given how many times she'd pestered the Admiralty for a new assignment, the king had to know she wanted to be somewhere, anywhere, else.

"Very good," King Hadrian said. He looked at the grand admiral. "By the authority vested in me, under the War Powers Act, I am assigning Katherine Falcone to Operation Knife. We will, of course, play up the fact she is a hero to convince the grown-ups to keep any threat of a political crisis under control. I refuse to sacrifice an officer to a moron's delusions of grandeur."

"Yes, Your Majesty," the grand admiral said.

King Hadrian smiled, then winked at Kat. She couldn't help smiling back. King Hadrian was only two years older than her; indeed, he was one of the youngest monarchs ever to take the throne, wielding very real power. God knew her mother had sometimes whispered that Kat would make an ideal princess, then a queen, even though it was unlikely in the extreme. The king had obligations, after all; he would have to marry a commoner to keep the bloodlines strong and prevent inbreeding. There had been no real chance for a relationship even if they'd spent plenty of time together.

"Sonja," the king said. "Why don't you brief us on the current situation?"

Kat looked up as another wallflower stepped into the light. She was a tall woman, wearing a naval uniform without any rank insignia, suggesting she was almost certainly an intelligence officer. There was something about the way she moved that suggested she'd been seriously injured sometime in the past, as if her body had been completely regenerated and she had yet to recover all of her facilities. Or she might have actually been on active service, once upon a time, and had her body altered to meet certain specifications . . . Kat pushed the question aside, absently. There was no way she'd ever know.

"Your Majesty, Honored Sirs," Sonja said. Her voice was calm, perfectly controlled. "The war situation is bad, but not disastrous."

She tapped a switch and a holographic star chart appeared in front of them, hovering over the table. Kat felt her insides clench as she saw a handful of stars shaded red, including both Cadiz and Hebrides, homeworld of her former XO. It wasn't a pleasant thought. Commander William McElney had been reassigned shortly after *Lightning* had limped back to Tyre and she hadn't heard anything from him since, not even a brief electronic postcard relayed through the StarCom network. It suggested he was doing something secret . . .

. . . and, given what she knew of his family connections, she had a feeling she knew precisely *what* he was doing.

"The current situation," Sonja said. "There are five star systems currently under enemy occupation; six, I should add, if one counts Cadiz. In addition, two more star systems are under siege and enemy-raiding formations have struck deep into our territory. Our current analysis suggests that the enemy is intent on reducing the defenses of Castor and Pollock before proceeding any further, although it is possible they will eventually decide that neither world is worth the effort of conquering while the main body of our fleet remains intact."

Kat frowned. Neither Castor nor Pollock was an industrial behemoth, although she had to admit that Pollock had a sizable space-based industry to protect. The Theocracy might want to bring its religion to as many worlds as possible, but there was little point in wasting time and effort seizing two immaterial worlds while the Commonwealth was scrambling to tighten the defenses and launch a counterattack. *She* had a feeling the Theocracy was hastily preparing a second series of offenses to be launched as soon as it could.

"There is some disagreement among the analysts about the true state of the enemy's fleet train," Sonja continued. "One school of thought believes that the enemy wouldn't have launched a major offensive before assembling its supporting elements, while the other points to the data and claims that the enemy has been having major supply problems from Day One. What *is* clear is that the Theocracy has been moving supplies forward in heavily guarded convoys, as if it fears even minimal losses. My *personal* opinion is that the second school of thought is correct."

And we know they were caught on the hop, Kat added mentally. *They probably wanted to wait to launch the offensive; we merely caught them by surprise and forced them to jump their plans forward.*

"Overall, however, we are forced to remain on the defensive until we have completed our transition to a war economy," Sonja concluded. "This has obvious weaknesses, starting with the fact it leaves the initiative in their hands. They may overcome their problems before we overcome ours, and resume the offensive."

"Thank you," King Hadrian said. "Admiral?"

The grand admiral cleared his throat. "Operation Knife has two major objectives," he said. "First, to force the Theocracy to react to us for a change, diverting their strength from the front lines and buying us time to gear up for war. Second, to make contact with resistance movements within the Theocracy itself and provide assistance, as well as gather intelligence on the true nature of the enemy. We have very few insights into the enemy's sphere, as you know well, and we need to know more about them."

Kat nodded wordlessly.

"You will be given command of a small squadron of starships, mostly older models we can spare," the grand admiral added. He didn't use the word *expendable*, but Kat heard it regardless. "For this, you will be given the brevet rank of commodore, although I'm afraid you will not receive the salary or the staff. You will take your ships into enemy space and proceed as you see fit: attacking convoys, trading posts, industrial nodes . . . everything you can find, provided it belongs to the enemy. Your overall task is to disrupt the enemy's ability to resupply the front lines and go on the offensive, while gathering intelligence and making contacts we can use to continue to undermine the Theocracy and take the offensive into their territory. You will continue your operations as long as reasonably possible."

Kat glanced at her father, whose face was completely impassive. The operation would be a challenge, but it was one she would enjoy; it certainly wasn't a punishment. But, on the other hand, they would be deep within enemy space. If something went wrong, they would be trapped and unable to retreat . . . and no one would ever know what had happened to them, at least until the war was won. Hell, even *getting* into enemy space would be tricky. The Seven Sisters Hyper-Route was likely mined or guarded by now.

And if we run into formidable defenses, she thought, *we might be wiped out before we realize just how badly we've fucked up.*

"You will also be given a handful of fully loaded freighters as your fleet train," the grand admiral informed her. "We do not expect you to be able to maintain operations for longer than six months once you arrive on station, unless you manage to capture enemy weapons and turn them against their masters. Depending on your success rate, we may manage to ship additional supplies to you, but that may prove chancy."

Kat nodded. There would be no StarCom, no FTL transmissions; she would be unable to request supplies without actually sending a ship back to the front lines and demanding assistance. It was highly unlikely that any reinforcements would reach her in time to make a difference, even assuming they were dispatched as soon as the message arrived. She would have to be careful, very careful. If there was one thing both sides had learned from the Battle of Cadiz, it was that the consumption of missiles in wartime had been grossly underestimated; both sides had practically shot themselves dry. And it was unlikely she'd be able to adapt any enemy weapons to shoot from her missile tubes.

The Theocracy fired our missiles, but they parked them in open space, she thought. Firing the missiles wouldn't be a challenge; the trick would be luring the enemy to engagement range in the first place. *Maybe if we attach them to the hulls . . .*

She pushed the thought aside as the king spoke. "Captain Falcone, do you accept the mission?"

"Yes, Your Majesty," Kat said, quickly. If nothing else, it would get her away from Tyre and back into deep space. The prospect of death hadn't bothered her since she'd nearly been killed on her first cruise. Being captured, she suspected, would be far worse. The Theocracy wouldn't hesitate to kill her as unpleasantly as possible, then bombard the datanets with recordings of her final moments. "It will be my honor."

"You will receive formal orders tomorrow," the grand admiral said. "Until then, I suggest you remain in your mansion, away from the media. Publicly, you will have been sent to Hammersmith to assist in developing war-winning strategies. It will look like a punishment, I believe, to Deveron and his ilk."

"Thank you, sir," Kat said.

"You may return to your home now," the prime minister said. "Duke Falcone, if you would care to remain . . . ?"

"Of course," Kat's father said.

Kat nodded, then rose to her feet and saluted, formally, to the table. The king winked at her while the prime minister and the Leader of the Opposition merely nodded back as Kat turned and walked out of the room. An equerry met her as soon as the door closed and beckoned her to follow him into a smaller waiting room. Kat glanced around in surprise, then tensed automatically. It felt very much like a trap . . .

"Captain Falcone," King Hadrian said as he entered through another door. "It's a pleasure to talk with you in private, at last."

"Thank you, Your Majesty," Kat said. Up close, the king looked surprisingly normal, but there was an inner stubbornness that reminded her of herself. His short dark hair topped an angular face that was both handsome and charismatic, although she had the feeling he had yet to grow into his looks. The smile he gave her was both warm and rakish. "And thank you . . . thank you for earlier."

"The politicians are often too concerned with playing politics to realize where the true interests of the kingdom lie," the king said. He looked her up and down once, then smiled again. "Please, relax and have a seat. I don't bite."

Kat forced herself to sit down in one of the comfortable chairs. The king was both part of the aristocracy and above them, one of the few who could and would call out aristocrats for bad behavior. His position, as long as he enjoyed the support of the dukes, was almost untouchable, granting him vast power over the Commonwealth. And yet, there were strong limits to what he could do. Some of her father's enemies would not be amused at how he'd saved her from the consequences of not thinking before she spoke.

She cleared her throat, feeling like a little girl. "Aren't you meant to be in the meeting, Your Majesty?"

"It's mainly boring details concerning war production," King Hadrian said. He waved a hand, dismissively, then sat down facing her. "Not that they're not important, of course, but I cannot afford to get bogged down in the little details. I have to concentrate on the bigger picture."

He smiled at her again. "And the bigger picture suggests that beaching you for telling a particularly annoying halfwit to go bugger himself isn't a good idea."

"I didn't tell him to go bugger himself," Kat protested.

The king affected surprise. "Really? I was watching the morning news and *it* said that you slapped him across the face, breaking his jaw."

Kat groaned. "I didn't even *touch* him!"

"Stories do have a habit of growing in the telling," the king said. "And . . . well, a halfwit like him has enemies. They can indulge their fantasies of someone beating the crap out of him, safe in the knowledge that any actual court case will prove your innocence."

"I should sue for libel," Kat muttered.

The king smirked. "Is someone claiming you thumped him actually *libel*?"

He shrugged. "Not that it matters, in the end," he added. "The bigger picture says that the Commonwealth needs you doing what you do best, out on the front lines—or, in this case, well beyond them. A know-it-all-who-doesn't isn't particularly important, not when the fate of the Commonwealth itself is at stake."

Kat looked down at her hands. Months ago—it felt like years—she'd been horrified when her father had used his influence in her favor, granting her a command she knew she hadn't earned and one she realized everyone else would know she hadn't earned too. Now, she'd proved herself worthy of command . . . and the king had done her another favor, saving her from the consequences of her actions. And if someone believed the more exaggerated stories, they might think she'd been saved from more than a few ill-chosen words.

But he's right, she thought. *We do need to look at the bigger picture.*

"Thank you, sir," she said, finally.

"Think nothing of it," King Hadrian said. "We're quite alike, you and I."

Kat blinked. "I think no one is likely to mistake you for me, Your Majesty," she said. "I have blonde hair, for a start."

"Mentally, of course," the king said. "I was prepared to do an end run around politicians too concerned with maintaining their authority to consider the long-term view. You did an end run around Admiral Morrison to get 7th Fleet ready to fight, and, when the shit hit the fan, you took command and saved half the fleet from certain destruction. The Royal Navy has good reason to be proud of you, Captain Falcone. *I* have good reason to be proud of you."

He sighed. "Maintaining the balance that holds the Commonwealth together is all well and good," he added, "but right now . . .

well, there is a war on. I suspect we may have to reshape the Commonwealth completely before the war is over."

"Like finding more opportunities for spacers who weren't born on Tyre," Kat said. "Or even born before their homeworlds joined the Commonwealth."

The king gave her a sharp look. "Like your XO?"

"He should have held a command of his own long before I ever did," Kat said. "And I recommended him for command in my final report."

"We found a more important mission for him," the king said. "But you're right; devising ways to integrate such personnel is important, yet difficult."

Kat nodded. The patronage networks that pervaded Tyre had worked fine, as long as the kingdom hadn't tried to assimilate entire populations. But when it had, the system had run into problems. Newcomers had no links to preexisting patronage networks, so they tended to be denied promotions they'd otherwise earned . . . which, unsurprisingly, led to resentment and outright discontent. Her XO had to have regarded her appointment as a bad joke before she'd proved herself. *He* was old enough to be her father.

"Maybe you can make a start on it," the king added. He met her eyes suddenly. "We need a second victory, Captain. We need something we can sell to the people, something to prove we can win."

"I understand," Kat said. She paused. "Is there any chance of a negotiated settlement?"

"I am dead set against it," the king said. "We did throw the ambassador and his staff out after the first attacks on Tyre. But they are sending messages into the datanet, promising peace in exchange for submission . . . or even the surrender of the occupied worlds. I don't think there's any strong peace party, not yet, but that could change."

And you might be overruled, Kat thought. *Or impeached, if the houses of Parliament thought you were failing in your duties.*

The king shrugged. "I will ensure that Captain Davidson is assigned to your command," he added. He winked at her. "I trust that will meet with your approval?"

Kat blushed, furiously. "That's going to look awkward . . ."

"Looking good or bad is not the issue," the king said. He looked her directly in the eye. "All that matters is winning the war."

He rose to his feet. "And with that in mind, Captain, I suggest you start planning your operations," he concluded. "You will have complete freedom of action, once you cross the border, as we don't know enough about enemy territory to offer precise instructions. I strongly advise you not to waste your time—or your authority."

Of course, Kat agreed, as she rose too. It was independent command on a scale she hadn't expected, even with her father's patronage, for years. But if she failed and survived, she'd never be allowed to sit in a command chair again. *I won't get a second chance.*

"And don't tell anyone we met," he added, turning to leave. "It would only confuse their small minds."

CHAPTER FOUR

If there is a more wretched hive of scum and villainy than here, Commander William McElney thought as he strode through the asteroid, *I don't want to see it.*

He kept his face impassive, somehow, despite the urge to sneak back out of the asteroid and return with a small flotilla of patrol ships. There were countless warrants, he was sure, that could be settled overnight if the Royal Navy raided the asteroid cluster and captured the inhabitants. The Burton System existed on the very edge of civilized space, on the no-man's-land between the Commonwealth and the Theocracy; it was no surprise, perhaps, that the wretched refuse of both systems had congregated here, beyond the reach of either power. No one cared about the Burton System, save for those with nowhere to go. It was, after all, largely worthless.

Unless you're interested in smuggling goods from one power to the other, he thought. *Or if you wanted to find something you couldn't get anywhere else.*

He sighed as he walked past the stalls—offering everything from illegal drugs and stimulant programs to weapons that were banned even on Heinlein—and the prostitutes standing beside them, doing their very best to lure him into their arms for a night. None of them looked particularly appealing; indeed, he had a feeling that most of them had started life as penniless girls, tricked into slavery, if they hadn't been captured by pirates and sold to pimps. One of them, kneeling on the ground with her mouth wide open, had had her teeth knocked out, probably to keep her from biting her customers. William wanted to do something—anything—to help her, but what could he do? As far as they knew, he was nothing more than an independent trader, one of many who wanted nothing more than food, drink, sex, and supplies, perhaps not in that order. He shook his head, mentally, and looked away. There was nothing he could do.

"Hey," a voice called. "I have sims here, just for the discerning customer."

William recoiled as the man shoved his datapad in William's face. It showed a list of simulations, ranging from mild pornography to scenarios he hadn't believed physically possible until he'd left his homeworld for the first time. Fighting down the urge to punch the hustler as hard as he could, he shook his head firmly and walked on, checking his pockets out of habit. Someone could easily have used the moment of distraction as an opportunity to pick his pocket, despite the risk. The asteroid's rulers might cater to everyone who had money, but they policed their territory with an iron hand. Allowing their inhabitants to steal from clients was bad for business.

He gritted his teeth, then walked into the larger cavern. A dozen men, all clearly from the Theocracy, were buying up every starship component on sale, offering prices that were obviously inflated. William smirked, remembering what the Commonwealth had concluded about the Theocracy from earlier dealings, then walked past as another group of men started complaining loudly. The Theocrats were driving up the prices for everyone, not just themselves, and they might well put a few dozen ships right out of business. They might even have planned it that way, William considered. A few booths down, there was an agent hiring cargo vessels for an undisclosed master . . . and it almost *had* to be the Theocracy. Who *else* would be interested in hiring so many ships?

They'd be smarter to work for the Commonwealth, William thought as he stepped past the booth and walked towards the diner. *The Commonwealth won't behead them for bringing contraband into their space.*

He smiled at the thought, then stopped outside the diner. A naked girl, barely out of her teens, looked up at him, her smile turning into a frown as it became apparent she didn't recognize him. William sighed, then held out the message he'd been sent an hour ago. The girl glanced at it, then nodded and beckoned for him to follow her, twitching her bare ass in a ludicrously sassy motion. William wasn't quite sure where to look, so he fixed his gaze on her shoulder blades and kept it there until she stopped by a private booth.

"Bill," a voice said. "How nice to see you again."

The girl dropped to her knees. "Can I get either of you anything?"

"A bottle of Old Spacer," Commodore Scott McElney said. The smuggler chief—and black sheep of the family—smiled up at his brother as the girl rose and hurried away. "You can have her, you know, for a small gratuity."

William scowled, then sat down facing his brother. "This place . . . is terrible."

"If you have it, flaunt it," Scott said. "And if you have the power to make others flaunt it, make them flaunt it."

He leered cheerfully towards another waitress, who was equally nude, then smirked at William. "I must say I was surprised to hear from you," Scott said as he brought out a privacy generator and placed it on the table. "You're quite the war hero."

"Thank you," William said. The Royal Lion he'd been awarded, after the Second Battle of Cadiz, allowed him to claim a salute from everyone who *didn't* have the award. It was something he intended to exploit as much as possible. "And you're still a smuggler chief."

"Of course," Scott said. The waitress returned, carrying a heavy bottle and two glasses. "It's on me, of course."

His eyes followed the waitress as she sashayed away, then he turned back to his brother. "The last time we spoke privately, I offered you a chance to come work for me," he said. "Dare I assume you're interested?"

"No," William said flatly. "I wouldn't care to live here for the rest of my life."

Scott made a show of looking offended. "It may only be an asteroid where dogs eat dogs—and pussies too—but it's home to me."

"No, it isn't," William said. "*Home* is under occupation these days, as I'm sure you've heard."

His brother frowned. "*Home* kicked me out pretty comprehensively, unless you've forgotten," he said. "The priest read me out from the altar, remember?"

William winced. Hebrides had always been a closely knit society, but the strain of pirate attacks, before the Commonwealth had rediscovered the colony, had done untold damage to countless lives. Scott . . . had grown darker and darker until he'd finally crossed the line and been formally disowned, both from his family and the greater community. Most men would have cringed at the thought, but not Scott. He'd left his homeworld and become a smuggler chief.

"I don't believe you hate everyone we knew back there," William said. "What about Mary? Or Kate? Or Carolyn?"

His brother glared at him. "Low blow, Bill."

"Mary had children, three of them girls," William said. Scott had been friendly with Mary, or as friendly as an unmarried boy could be with an unmarried girl. "They would be in their teens by now, I believe. What sort of life do you think they're having under the Theocrats?"

He sighed, and then continued. "Kate is a teacher, remember? If they killed teachers on Cadiz, where some of the population would be friendly to them right from the start, what do you think they did to her? And Carolyn married Father Theodore. He'll be dead now, along with his wife and family . . ."

"Father Theodore never liked me," Scott snapped.

"Carolyn liked you," William said. Carolyn had been their second cousin, too close to them to be considered a potential wife. "She wanted you to chaperone her when she spoke with him, remember?"

"Maybe we should remember Harris," Scott said. "Or Brennan. Or James."

"They might be dead too," William pointed out.

"And good riddance," Scott snapped back.

He glowered at his brother, then leaned forward. "What do you *want*, Bill?"

"You helped us to find a passage into enemy space," William said. "We need to find ways to slip more ships into their territory and whatever intelligence you can give us on the internal layout of their space."

Scott eyed him, darkly. "Any fool could get that from the navigational service."

"Any fool wouldn't think the navigational service could do more than tell us where the stars are," William said, placing tight controls on his temper. Scott had always been good at getting under his skin. "Where are their bases, where are their production nodes . . . which worlds have resistance movements and which worlds are completely pacified, ground into the dirt by the bastards?"

"I see," Scott said. "And how much are you prepared to pay for the data?"

William gave him a long look. "Don't you care about our homeworld?"

Scott's eyes flashed with sudden anger. "You know why I like this place?"

William felt a matching surge of anger. "Because you appreciate the chance to live life without any restraints?"

"Because there are no lies here," Scott said. He waved a hand at one of the naked waitresses. "Here, no one tells themselves any pleasant lies to hide the dark truth. That poor bitch is here because she couldn't pay her debts, or sold herself into slavery, or was simply overpowered and forced to work for her master. The master too is owned by someone higher up the food chain; he dreams of climbing higher, then knifing his former master in the back and taking everything he owns for himself. Outside, there are men and women who made the free choice to drink or drug themselves into a stupor, and sim addicts who have indulged themselves for so long that they're no longer sure just what's real and what isn't."

"No rules," William said.

"None at all," Scott agreed.

William looked him in the eye. "Might makes right is a fine way to live, I am sure, as long as you happen to be the one with the might. What happens when you run into someone stronger?"

"Here, there would be no lies or evasions," Scott said. "Tell me; how many of our kinsfolk, mainly young girls, were sacrificed to the pirates back before the Commonwealth arrived?"

William shuddered. Scott's *girlfriend* had been sacrificed to save countless others. "Hundreds?"

"Maybe more," Scott said. His eyes flashed with bitter pain. "Matters were really quite disordered back then. How do we *know* the actual figure wasn't much higher? But tell me . . . those girls were the cost of our survival, sold into a ghastly slavery so that the rest of us could live. Why aren't we honest about the price we paid, the price they paid, for us to live?

"We're not honest. Nor were the priests. They were hypocrites. I brought in food and drink; they read me out from the altar, condemning me even as I saved their lives. Where was their god when they needed him?"

"People don't want to think about it," William said, quietly.

"Here, everyone acknowledges it," Scott said. "There's no attempt to come up with an extensive justification, no attempt to prove that one party has the right or the obligation or the desperate *need* to take something from the other party. They just *take* and, if they have the strength, that's the end of the matter."

Scott smiled. "You don't want to think about it either."

"Because it's horrible," William said. "You have neither laws nor morals."

"The powerful have been getting around laws since the day the first caveman decided it was a good idea to tie a rock to the end of his club," Scott said sweetly. "And morals are a social construction, which the powerful can avoid if they wish. Here . . . well, you can do anything if you have the strength, and you don't have to hide."

William shook his head. "Scott," he said slowly, "what will happen to this place if the Theocracy wins the war?"

"They have a use for us," Scott said. "They'll leave us alone."

He smiled, suddenly. "They're no different," he added. "There are over a thousand separate categories of forbidden items in the Theocracy . . . and yet their wealthy and powerful come here, or pay for us to smuggle the goods into their territory. The rules made for little people, supposedly enforced by God Himself, are ignored by those with the power to avoid punishment."

William frowned. "Are you sure? You're useful to them now, but how long will that last?"

Scott frowned back. "Are you saying they will lose the war?"

"They might," William pointed out. "And how do you plan to explain selling weapons and ships to the enemy when the Commonwealth catches up with you?"

"Money, dear boy," Scott said.

"I don't think that will be accepted," William said. "You know as well as I do, *brother*, that the Theocracy is in desperate need of freighters; hell, you brought it to our attention, back before the war. The Commonwealth will, at best, see you as willing collaborators."

"Assuming the Commonwealth wins the war," Scott said. "What sort of revenge do you think the Theocracy will take if *they* win the war?"

"Pick a side," William said.

Scott snorted. "And what, again, are you offering me?"

William leaned forward. "We want the data and, perhaps, your services," he said. "In exchange for the former, I am authorized to offer one billion crowns; half now, half upon the data being tested and verified."

"You have a great deal of faith in me," Scott said, amused.

"In exchange for the latter, we are prepared to offer the chance to go legit," William continued, refusing to allow his brother to distract him. "You and your crews can form a small shipping line and make profit legally, with your pasts officially forgotten. The fact you were shipping war materials, or items that could be *considered* war materials, will be buried so deeply no one will ever know. You will even have access to a line of credit intended to help you expand your operations at *very* low rates of interest."

Scott shrugged. "Do *you* expect them to keep their word?"

"I don't think the Commonwealth wishes to develop a reputation for breaking promises," William said. "It makes it harder to make new ones."

His brother considered it for a long moment. "And if we choose to only supply the data?"

"You will be paid, but there will be no promises for the post-war world," William said. "And if you try to make a deal after the war, you will be in a very weak position indeed."

"How true," Scott said.

William waited, saying nothing.

"I can offer you the data now, or I will, once it's compiled," Scott said. "There are some other routes into enemy space that are not well-guarded, although they're dangerous to fly if you're not careful. But the other offer? I will have to discuss it with my captains. They're not all keen on doing anything that might get them into the middle of a shooting match."

"They're *already* in the middle of a shooting match," William said. "How long will it be, you think, before someone sends a squadron out here to blow the asteroid?"

Scott's eyes narrowed. "Are you saying the Commonwealth is seriously preparing to kill innocent captives?"

"This is *war*," William said. "And war has a habit of washing away the little niceties. This asteroid is playing host to representatives of the enemy, men who are buying goods and signing up freighters to keep the war going. *That* makes it a legitimate target. Maybe they can't spare the Marines to take and hold the asteroids long enough to evacuate them, but they can smash them into rubble with a missile attack. Hard luck to the captives, of course . . ."

"Of course," Scott echoed. "But the decision to join openly is not one I can make alone."

"I know," William said.

Scott waved to the waitress, whose breasts jiggled as she walked over to them. "I will be back here in an hour," he said as he passed her a handful of untraceable bills. "Until then, I wish you to take care of my brother. Bill . . . could do with some rest and relaxation."

William shook his head firmly. "I'll be right here," he said. "I don't need anything else."

"Are you sure?" Scott asked mockingly. "I don't think you've been laid for years. Has everything gone rusty by now?"

"No, *thank you*," William said sharply. He'd spent time and money in the Royal Navy's brothels, but that was different. The girls were well paid, and troublemakers were ruthlessly evicted and, in some cases, charged with crimes. Here . . . he had a feeling he could beat the girl to death and no one would give a damn. "I'll wait for you here."

"Very well," Scott said. He gave the girl a slap on the rear that sent her scuttling off. "You do realize she'll be punished for failing to attract you?"

William glared. "This place is a nightmare."

"It is the only place I can be truly free," Scott countered. "I'll be back with the data in an hour, Bill. Feel free to call the waitress if you want anything."

He strode off, not looking back. William shuddered, then looked down at the table and closed his eyes. What had happened, in the time since Scott had left their homeworld, to turn him into a monster? He would have agreed with his brother, once upon a time, that their homeworld had too many rules, but the bad rules didn't actually mean that the good rules weren't necessary. But then, Scott had always been a wild child. He'd chafed more against the rules than anyone else in the family.

Once I have the data, I can go, he told himself, firmly. He hadn't been told anything officially, but he had a fair idea of what the Commonwealth Intelligence Service (CIS) wanted the data *for. By now,* Lightning *should be nearly ready to go back on active service. I can go back to the war.*

CHAPTER FIVE

Kat had managed to successfully avoid her father by the simple expedient of shutting herself up in her suite after her orders arrived, and reading through them carefully to determine precisely what resources had been assigned to Operation Knife. *Lightning*, it seemed, would be returning to active service within the week, but she was the only modern vessel assigned to the operation. Kat was mildly surprised the Admiralty hadn't added *Uncanny* to the flotilla, although it made a certain kind of sense. The ship already had a reputation for bad luck and assigning it to an operation that required a great deal of *good* luck was asking for trouble.

She ordered a shuttle for the morning, then went to bed and awoke feeling genuinely excited for the first time since she'd been unwillingly beached. Several messages had arrived in her in-box, including one from Davidson telling her that he'd been assigned to join her at the base, and a message from her father, ordering her to meet him for breakfast. Kat sighed, showered, and dressed herself in her uniform, then headed downstairs to the dining hall. Not entirely to her surprise, her father was the only person in the room.

"I suspected they would find a way to penalize you until the whole matter went away," he said as Kat sat down. "Taking you off active service would probably satisfy the grown-ups in the Opposition. I wasn't expecting the king to have his say."

Kat frowned. "They're sending me on a dangerous mission," she pointed out. The king *had* told her to keep their private conversation to herself, after all. "I don't think it will be particularly *safe*."

Her father snorted. "Look me in the eye and tell me you're not keen to take command again."

"I can't," Kat said. The orders had made it clear that Operation Knife would be dangerous, but she had no intention of refusing them. "And it will certainly look like I've been punished by being sent to a distant base, if the truth doesn't leak out."

"It won't," her father said. "That armchair admiral might not be able to keep a secret if his life depended on it, but the Leader of the Opposition knows which side his bread is buttered on. As far as anyone will know, you've been sent to one of those bases where disgraced officers go to drink themselves to death."

"Yes, father," Kat said.

"I wasn't expecting the *king* to join the conversation," her father said, again. "And for him to exert his authority in such a manner . . . it's odd, to say the least."

Kat nodded. "Maybe he thought I was in real trouble," she said. "Or maybe he just doesn't like anyone trying to push around one of his officers."

"Could be," her father said. He sighed. "You're a genuine war hero, Katherine, whether you recognize it or not. Having you here, drumming up support for the war, was always a good use of your talents. There *are* other starship commanders, but relatively few *heroes*."

"I could name a dozen others who deserve the Royal Lion without even trying," Kat said sharply. "I'm not *that* special."

Her father looked her in the eye. "Our system was designed to handle one planet, one star system," he said. "Expanding to include a number of other worlds, especially several that had different systems of government, was always going to put a strain on our society. Your XO, for example, might well have risen to command years ago if our system hadn't been focused on aristocrats and those with powerful patrons. If we'd had time to adapt to the influx, we might well have coped admirably . . . but right now, we have to fight a war. That's one of the reasons so many senior officers were prepared to throw you under the shuttlecraft. They really didn't have time to fight another political battle."

Kat winced. "I'm sorry . . ."

"So you should be," her father said, shortly. He looked her in the eye. "We need this war to end soon, Katherine, and the only way we can end it is through victory. Eat your breakfast, then . . . good luck."

Kat nodded. Her father had never been given to emotional displays, not to her. She'd always been the youngest child, the baby of the family . . . and the one who saw her father the least. To see him now, to see him regularly, felt odd. She pushed the thought aside sharply. She'd chosen a career that ensured she would only see her family while she was on shore leave, if they happened to be on the same planet as she was. There was no point in mourning, now, over what she could never have had.

Her father ate his breakfast in silence, then rose and left her alone. Kat felt strange, almost abandoned, in the giant dining hall; it was so empty, as now she was used to crowds. She finished her breakfast, collected her bag from her room, and walked down to the shuttlepad, half-wishing she'd had a chance to say good-bye to her mother before she left. But her mother was out, socializing, something she did every day. Kat shook her head, wondering just how someone could spend their lives in High Society without their brains turning to mush, then walked onto the shuttlepad and into the waiting shuttle.

"Captain Falcone," the shuttle pilot said. Her implants pinged, warning her they were being probed, her identity checked against the Navy's files. "Welcome onboard."

"Thank you," Kat said. The pilot looked to be a civilian, probably a reservist who'd lost the military veneer between his departure from the Navy and his recall. Middle-aged, if she was any judge, he'd probably done his time, then moved into the civilian sphere and better-paid jobs. "Do you have an ETA to our destination?"

"Seven hours, I'm afraid," the pilot said. "This craft isn't rated for hyperspace. Do you have any other baggage?"

Kat shook her head. Midshipmen weren't allowed anything more than a single carryall and she'd grown used to never having more, even though she'd been promoted at breakneck speed. Besides, anything she really *needed* could be found on the ship. She stowed her bag in the locker, then took a seat and opened her datapad. There would be additional orders and files waiting for her on the datanet, probably including personnel files. God alone knew what sort of crewmen would be assigned to a deep-strike mission.

The pilot didn't seem inclined to make conversation, thankfully. He merely returned to his seat, then toggled switches. A low hum echoed through the craft as its drives came online, then it shuddered and launched itself into the air. Kat smiled, remembering the first set of simulations she'd been put through at Piker's Peak, then turned her attention back to her datapad. Her father had uploaded a sample of news reports too, some centered on her and Justin Deveron. She couldn't help being amused when she noted that most of the media seemed to be solidly on her side, including a handful of Opposition outlets. No doubt Justin Deveron had made himself unpopular there too.

Or they're trying to come up with an excuse for not throwing a hammer at me, she thought sourly. None of the stories from the major outlets seemed to be particularly exaggerated, although one reporter seemed to think that the whole incident was proof that she was having an affair with Admiral Christian. Kat rolled her eyes at the thought, then closed the file. She hadn't even *met* Admiral Christian until after the First Battle of Cadiz and they had barely had time to prepare a counterattack, let alone have an affair. *And I was dating Pat at the time.*

She shrugged, then turned her attention to the other files until the shuttle finally slowed, beginning its approach to Hyperion Base. Kat put the datapad away and leaned forward as the gas giant came into view, surrounded by a network of orbital battle stations and automated weapons platforms. A good third of the system's industry orbited the gas giant, she knew; her tutors had drummed its importance into her time and time again. Hundreds of fabrication nodes, asteroid smelters, cloudscoops . . . everything the Commonwealth needed to turn out warships, gunboats, and war materials to hold the line. She glanced down at the scanners as the shuttle drew closer, sucking in her breath at the sight of dozens of starships under construction. The Theocracy wouldn't stand a chance if the Commonwealth lasted long enough to bring its full might to bear.

But if we'd started this earlier, much earlier, they wouldn't have stood a chance at all, she thought, grimly. She *thought* the Theocracy's industrial base was smaller than the Commonwealth's, but no one really knew for sure. *They may be able to defeat us before we even the odds and then outproduce them into the dust.*

"Incoming gunboats," the shuttle pilot said. "I hope those codes of yours are correct."

Kat nodded as three icons swept towards them on attack vector. "They're direct from the Admiralty," she said, remembering the first time she'd seen gunboats in action. Theocratic gunboats had been devastating against unprepared targets at Cadiz, although they'd been less effective against ships and crews who knew what to expect. Not, in the end, that it would matter; the gunboats approaching them would have no difficulty blowing the shuttle into dust if they had any reason to suspect trouble. "I'm *pretty* sure they're accurate."

She tensed as the gunboats closed in, then flashed past the shuttle and into the distance. The pilot let out a sigh of relief and then took the shuttle into the giant complex, following a flight path downloaded to him from the security office. Kat knew they wouldn't be allowed anywhere near some of the facilities, although she had a feeling that most of the *really* secret work was carried out somewhere in deep space, somewhere where no one would stumble on it except through an improbable dose of sheer luck. The shuttle glided onwards until, finally, the Knife Squadron came into view.

Kat took one last look at the scanner, then peered through the viewport, trying to soak in every detail. *Lightning* was exactly as she remembered; the repair crews had even replaced the paint coating her hull, making her look as though she'd only just left the yard for the first time. Beside her, there were fourteen other ships, all older designs. Kat recognized a handful from history files, but seven were completely unfamiliar to her. They looked old, too old. A modern warship could blast them out of space in moments.

Then we'd better make sure we don't encounter any modern warships, she thought. The UN had designed its warships to be modular and everyone else had followed their lead, but she was fairly sure there were hard limits to how far they could be upgraded without prohibitive costs. Freighters could serve for hundreds of years without ever going out of service; a warship had to keep up with the times or it would be nothing more than a target. *But they might serve as a distraction, if necessary.*

She pushed the thought to one side as the shuttle coasted down to the manned station and linked airlocks. Kat held onto her seat as the artificial gravity fields matched, then stood and removed her bag from the locker. The pilot saluted, then opened the hatch and waited for her to step through the airlock. Kat took a breath as the station's atmosphere started to flow into the shuttle—it smelled, as always, of too many humans and pieces of machinery in close proximity—then stepped through the airlock, into the station. No one was waiting for her outside the hatch.

Odd, she thought. She hadn't expected a formal greeting ceremony, but it was vanishingly rare for a new commanding officer *not* to be met by someone. *Where . . . ?*

A hatch banged open, revealing a dark-skinned woman wearing overalls and a rank badge—commander—on one shoulder. She seemed to be a froth of frantic energy, her eyes darting from side to side before locking onto Kat with unnerving intensity. The woman's lips curved into a smile, which faded as she cocked her head, clearly consulting her implants. Kat felt a flicker of irritation, but controlled it firmly. No one would be in command of a repair station unless his or her competence was considered beyond question.

"Captain Falcone," the woman said. She held out a hand, glanced at the oil staining her skin and hastily withdrew it. "I'm Commander Sasha. Welcome onboard."

"Thank you," Kat said, a little bemused. Clearly, Sasha was very much a hands-on commander. "I'd like to see the ships, if you please."

"Right this way," Sasha said, turning back to the hatch. "Or do you want to drop off your bag first? I assume you'll want to stay onboard *Lightning*?"

"We're scheduled to leave in two weeks," Kat said, more sharply than she'd intended. "I don't think I have time to stay anywhere else."

"Of course, of course," Sasha said. "*Lightning* is pretty much done, save for a handful of minor issues your chief engineer is handling. She's handling very well for a ship that went through hell only a few months ago. Shame it can't be said of some of the other beauties we have here. They really shouldn't be going back into space at all."

Kat stared at her back. "Is it really that bad?"

"We started with thirty ships so old that even pirates would refuse to use them," Sasha said without looking back. "Most of them were surplus from the UN before the Breakaway Wars; they belonged to a handful of systems that joined the Commonwealth and traded them in for newer warships. Too small to be converted into freighters, really; too common to go straight into museums. And really too pretty to be scrapped."

Kat frowned. "*Thirty* ships?"

"Ten of them proved to be completely beyond repair," Sasha explained. She opened a hatch by pushing her hand against a scanner, then motioned Kat to step through. "Five more had to be cannibalized to get the other ships operational. We upgraded everything we could, Captain, but they still have problems. I really wouldn't want to take any of them through the more turbulent regions of hyperspace."

The chamber was dominated by a holographic display, showing fifteen starships attached to the giant repair station. Kat carefully did *not* look at *Lightning*; instead, she studied the older ships, her implants accessing the local processor nodes and downloading data from each of the files. If anything, Sasha had been optimistic. Half of the ships under her command would be nothing more than targets if the Theocracy happened to get into range. Their armor was ancient, their targeting sensors were lousy, and their point defense was weak . . .

"It's not actually that bad," Sasha replied when Kat said that out loud. "We have managed to upgrade quite a few of their systems. Their sensors are perhaps the worst, but we did obtain some replacement components from the fabrication nodes and coated their hulls in sensor blisters. And we managed to double their missile loads . . ."

Kat frowned. Modern missiles were *much* larger than their counterparts from the Breakaway Wars. It was quite likely the ancient ships wouldn't have anything like the firepower of a modern ship the same size, let alone everything else. She rubbed her forehead and then turned her attention to the rest of the display. Maybe Justin Deveron would have the last laugh after all, she had to admit. Her squadron would be a joke if it were matched against a pair of Theocratic battle cruisers.

"Those are the ships," she said. "What about the crews?"

Sasha looked hesitant. "We have about half our assigned crews already here," she said. "The remainder have yet to arrive, because the Admiralty keeps reassigning people earmarked for us at short notice. Several of the ships don't even have commanding officers . . ."

"Clearly I will have to go through the files, again," Kat said darkly. The Admiralty probably considered the squadron nothing more than a forlorn hope; hell, she'd be surprised if they rated *that* high, given their weaknesses. "Maybe I can get away with leaving half of the ships here."

"They're *all* assigned to your command," Sasha said.

Kat looked back at the display. "Can they match *Lightning* for speed?"

"We did reconfigure the drives," Sasha said. "Their normal space velocity is superior to a commercial-grade drive, although inferior to most warships . . ."

"Oh, *goody*," Kat said sarcastically. It would be embarrassing as hell to go back to the Admiralty and report she hadn't managed to blow up a single enemy freighter because her ships had been *outrun*. After they'd finished laughing, they'd put her in front of a *real* court-martial board and dismiss her from the service for gross incompetence. "I assume there aren't any other surprises?"

"Not many," Sasha said in a manner that was clearly intended to be reassuring. "The files aren't quite up to date, but . . ."

Kat rolled her eyes. She'd been taught, time and time again, that there were files that needed to be updated because it was vitally important to know what had changed and files that needed to be updated because the bureaucrats would complain if they weren't. She had a feeling that the files Sasha was talking about fell into the first category. A ship that was a hodgepodge of old and new technology could become a right mess if the engineers literally had no idea of just what, if anything, had changed . . .

"Then we need to start work," Kat said tartly. She'd have to see how many of her old officers had remained on *Lightning*, then start pestering the Admiralty for replacements. "I'll put my bag on my ship, then you can show me around."

"Of course, Captain," Sasha said.

CHAPTER SIX

"That's the data, I believe," William said. "Everything *he* was able to scrape together."

Commander Janice Wilson eyed it doubtfully. "Do you trust him?"

William eyed her sharply. He hadn't been allowed access to her file, but he had a sneaking suspicion that Janice had never been in the field, no matter how capable she was as an intelligence analyst. Her questions weren't bad ones, yet they insisted on a degree of precision that anyone who knew anything about the real world would know better than to expect. The smugglers weren't an organized nation-state; they were, at best, an anarchic grouping of men and women who shared a more or less common interest. Expecting them *all* to pull in the same direction was naive.

"I think the data is accurate, or at least as accurate as he can make it," he said finally. "He would not want to develop a reputation for selling trash."

"I see," Janice said. She was a thin-lipped woman who seemed to be permanently disapproving of everything. "And will he join us?"

"I suspect he will consider it," William said tiredly. "However, you may have to make the offer a little sweeter to get him to openly choose a side."

"He won't be shot for treason when we win the war," Janice insisted. "Isn't that good enough?"

"We told him that he could go legit," William reminded her. "This is a particularly bad moment to try to change the agreement. He isn't the only smuggler we could induce into coming out of the cold, if agreement could be reached."

Janice's lips pursed. "It just seems . . . unpleasant to make deals with such scum."

"It is," William said. "But people who are as pure as new-fallen snow don't tend to become smugglers."

He shrugged. In some ways, he agreed with her; Scott might have been his brother, once upon a time, but he'd jumped off the slippery slope a long time ago. His charges against their homeworld weren't inaccurate, William had to admit, yet they didn't excuse Scott from his own crimes. He could have taken his resources back home and started struggling for reform long ago, before the war broke out. Now . . . there was a good prospect that the old power structure wouldn't survive the war, no matter what happened. The Theocracy would behead every priest they caught, just to make it clear that there was no other religion but theirs.

"He's your brother," Janice said. "Do you trust him?"

"I trust him to put his own interests first," William said. "And yes, if we offer him something in his interests, he will probably work for us. But he will want to do it on his terms."

"And that means kowtowing to smugglers," Janice said.

William snorted. "Would you prefer to kowtow to the Theocrats?"

He smiled coldly at her reaction. The Theocrats had occupied Cadiz and promptly started purging the planet's society of anyone who could pose a threat to them. Former resistance leaders, fighters, religious figures, and teachers—along with any women who'd held authority—had been marked for extermination. They hadn't even bothered to wait until they'd won the war! The only upside, as far as William could tell, was that it had been a sharp lesson to anyone who would prefer a negotiated truce, or even a surrender. Defeat didn't just mean humiliation; defeat meant the end of life as they knew it.

"They wouldn't let me live," Janice said flatly.

"No, they wouldn't," William agreed.

He shrugged again. "You don't get to argue about *legal* or *nice* ways to win the war when you're staring down the barrels of extinction," he added. "All you get to do is deploy every weapon that comes to hand and if some of them happen to be smugglers . . . well, you use them anyway and thank your gods you're not unleashing genetically engineered supermen or some other nightmare from the past."

Janice looked doubtful. William wasn't too surprised. Tyre had been a powerful state right from the start, when fourteen corporations had turned it into a base of operations and themselves into the first aristocrats. There had never been any significant danger to the world; hell, their declaration of independence from the UN had been little more than a formality. The Breakaway Wars hadn't even touched them. But Hebrides had had a difficult life, ever since the first break with Earth. They'd learned hard lessons Tyre's population had never had to learn at all.

Until now, he told himself. *Will they learn those lessons in time?*

"That's as may be," she said finally. "Do you believe you can be of further assistance?"

"Not unless you want me to go back to Scott," William said. "And, frankly, I'm not keen to do anything of the sort."

"He's your brother," Janice said, again.

"Yes, I *know*," William said. "To me, Scott's the one who ran away from his obligations; to him, I'm the one who serves a distant power instead of fighting to reform the planet. We don't have much in common these days."

And he chooses to wallow in depravity because he can't see any way to keep others from doing it, he added silently. *Or maybe that's just what he tells himself, to keep from realizing what a monster he's become.*

"I used to fight with my brother," Janice said brightly. "But I don't *hate* him."

"I pity Scott," William said. He rather doubted Janice's brother had run off to become a smuggler, although fleeing to the naval academy seemed more likely. "Your brother probably had a very different life."

"Probably," Janice said. She looked him in the eye. "It is my belief and the belief of my superiors that there isn't any more work for you with us, at least at the moment. As you have proved you can be trusted to keep your mouth shut, you have a couple of options."

Definitely no field experience, William thought. Janice didn't realize, honestly didn't realize, just how offensive she was being. *She'd get into real trouble if she went out of a secure base and into the real world.*

"The first one is that you can go back into the general personnel pool," Janice said. "As an experienced XO, you would be snapped up very quickly. The second option, which may be more to your liking, is a return to your old post, XO of *Lightning*. Which one would you like?"

Command, William thought. But it was unlikely command would be offered to him, not when there was no shortage of officers with better connections. *And they might want to drag me back here on short notice.*

"*Lightning,*" he said, after a moment's consideration. At least he *liked* Captain Falcone, once she'd proven herself. A little rough around the edges, perhaps, but a worthy commanding officer. And she'd shown incredible nerve before the war had officially started. "When do I leave?"

Janice blinked. "You don't want any shore leave?"

"I've been crawling through sewers," William snapped. Maybe the asteroid had been clean, but morally it stank to high heaven. "I'd be happier on a starship than shore leave right now."

"You could have a couple of days in any one of the entertainment complexes," Janice pointed out, perhaps driven by an impulse to look after one of her agents. "I don't think it would make any difference."

"I don't think I could cope with it," William said. Part of his mind told him to relax, to take all he could get, but the rest of him wanted something *clean* to do. "Being back on a starship would be much more relaxing."

Janice eyed him for a long moment, then cocked her head, consulting her implants. "A shuttle will be leaving here in five hours, heading to Hyperion," she said. "You'll have a seat on it, Commander, and orders that will arrange for your transfer to *Lightning*. Good luck."

"Thank you, Commander," William said.

"I am also obligated to remind you that everything you've done here is classified," she warned. "You must not discuss your work with anyone, without prior permission."

William nodded, impatiently.

"There *is* a swimming pool in the residency complex, as well as some simulators," Janice added. "Feel free to use them, if you can't get to sleep."

William nodded. He'd been surprised, the first time he'd visited the unnamed asteroid, that it had so many facilities, but it was clear that most of the staff rarely left; hell, they probably endured longer deployments than any starship crewmen, even though they were in the Tyre System. He rose to his feet, then shook Janice's hand when she gravely extended it to him before turning and stepping through the hatch. Outside, he turned and walked down towards the residency complex where he'd been assigned a small cabin. His implants blinked up warnings as he passed secure compartments, reminding him he wasn't allowed to try to open the hatches. If he tried, he'd been warned months ago, he'd be lucky to see freedom again.

His cabin was small, not much larger than the one he'd enjoyed as a newly minted lieutenant on a starship. He lay down on the bed and forced himself to relax, then swore under his breath as his orders flashed up on the bedside terminal. *Lightning* was apparently orbiting the gas giant, but there was nothing else, not even warning orders for a future deployment to the front lines. Had the damage been greater than he'd realized? Or had the mission orders, whatever they were, been classified? He hoped, prayed, that it was the latter. Being stuck orbiting a gas giant would be maddening, with his homeworld occupied and the enemy pressing his comrades hard.

He gritted his teeth, realizing that sleep would elude him for the rest of the night, then sat up and accessed the latest intelligence reports. There wasn't much from Hebrides, but what there was didn't seem encouraging. The Theocracy had landed a large army and seemed to be engaged in massive counterinsurgency campaigns; the locals, meanwhile, had taken to the mountains and were raiding the enemy whenever they got a chance. Long-range scans from prowling recon starships noted that the occupiers were calling in kinetic energy weapon strikes regularly, almost on a daily basis. He couldn't help feeling pride, even as cold fear for his friends and family threatened to overwhelm him. At least they were going down fighting.

But they could still lose, he thought. *Scott and I might be among the last survivors.*

It wasn't a pleasant thought, so he contemplated it morbidly as he changed into his swimming trunks and headed down to the pool. It was deserted, save for a couple of intelligence analysts swimming laps around the edge of the water. He took a shower, then dived into the water and swam until he felt his body starting to tire. There was no point in trying to talk to either of the analysts, he knew; they rarely had anything interesting to say. They might have done so before—it did happen—but they would probably be under strict orders not to talk to their friends let alone someone in a swimming pool. He smiled at the thought, then climbed out of the pool, showered again, and then walked back to his cabin. An update, blinking away merrily on his display, told him that the shuttle departure time had been moved up. He shook his head in wry amusement—clearly, they were keen to be rid of him now that he'd outlived his usefulness—and then changed back into his uniform. It felt good to be wearing a proper uniform once again.

Janice met him as he left his cabin for the final time, his carryall slung over his shoulder. "I took the liberty of adding a note to your file about your work for us," she said, falling into step beside him. "Your career won't suffer for it."

"Thank you," William said dryly. Given his lack of aristocratic connections, it wasn't likely a link with intelligence could do any more harm. But at least it would *look* as though he hadn't spent the last six months twiddling his thumbs instead of overseeing *Lightning's* repairs or simply being assigned to another ship. "That's very considerate of you."

Janice beamed. "Your commander may be in some trouble," she added. "Telling truth to someone who has no power can be more dangerous than telling truth *to* power."

William shrugged. Kat Falcone had, arguably, defied her superior officer's orders at Cadiz and gotten away with it. The scale of the offense had been so great that even being *right*—and she *had* been right—might not have saved her career if she'd been anyone else. It was unlikely she'd be in *real* trouble, unless she'd punched the king in the face. Striking the monarch was pretty definitely treason . . .

"I'm sure I'll hear about it on the news," he said. He hadn't been interested in domestic affairs, merely news of the war. Even though it was sanitized, he knew enough to be able to read between the lines. "Is it likely to cause real problems?"

"Matter of opinion," Janice said. They paused outside the shuttle-bay. "Good luck, William."

"You too," William said. He wasn't blind to the *true* reason Janice had escorted him off the asteroid personally. She'd want to make sure he left, even though it was impossible for someone to remain in the complex without being noticed. "Be seeing you."

He stepped through the hatch and into the shuttlebay, where a large shuttle waited for him. It would be at least nine hours to Hyperion, he was sure; there would be no swift jump through hyperspace for *him*. But he'd have a chance to get some sleep, thankfully. He'd need to be on alert when he boarded *Lightning* for the first time in six months.

The pilot greeted him curtly, showed him where to stow his bag in the cabin, and then returned to the cockpit, leaving William alone. He sighed, then glanced at the other passengers: three men wearing black uniforms and a woman wearing civilian clothes, her hair falling down to her shoulders. Her face would have been attractive, he was sure, if she hadn't been sneering at the datapad in her hand. He sat down and opened his datapad as he felt the shuttle power up its drives, then put his device aside. It would be better to get some sleep before it was too late.

He must have fallen asleep quickly, because the next thing he knew, the pilot was announcing the approach to Hyperion. William took the opportunity to go to the fresher and splash water on his face, then he followed the others off the shuttle as soon as it docked. A grim-faced officer pointed him towards another shuttle, one designed for shorter hops. William sat next to the pilot and watched as he flew towards a large repair station. *Lightning* was clearly recognizable, but the ships hanging next to it were ancient. It made no sense to him.

Unless she's in real trouble, he thought. *Those ships might be her next command.*

Captain Kat Falcone met him at the airlock as soon as the shuttle docked with *Lightning*. She looked older than he remembered, although her face was unchanged; she held herself like an experienced officer rather than someone doubting her fitness for the command chair. Her long blonde hair, tied into a ponytail, hung down her back; William couldn't help wondering why she'd allowed it to grow longer while she'd been on Tyre.

"Captain," he said.

"Welcome back," she said. Her lips twitched humorlessly. "The good news is that I've been given command of a squadron."

William felt his eyes narrow. "And the bad news is it's composed of the ships out there?"

"Yeah," Captain Falcone said. She looked tired, all of a sudden. "Put your bag in your cabin, then join me in my office. I have some briefing notes for you."

"Understood," William said.

Lightning felt different, somehow, even though it was barely nine months since Kat had left the yards and entered active service. It wasn't just the atmosphere, which had lost the scent of newness that had once pervaded it like a shroud; it was the sense that she'd seen *real* action, that enemy fire had struck deep into her core. William checked his cabin—larger than his cabin on the asteroid, but equally bare—stowed his bag in the locker under the bed, and then walked back to the captain's office, next to the bridge. She was standing in front of a coffee dispenser, pouring them both something to drink.

"I don't have a steward yet," she said by way of explanation. "We have plenty of engineers, mostly conscripted civilians, but shortfalls in almost every other category. It's not going to be easy to depart on schedule."

William nodded as he took his coffee and sipped it carefully. *Lightning* had carried a full crew when she stumbled back home; there was no way the Admiralty would allow so many trained officers and crewmen to sit on their hands when there was work to do. The crew he and the captain had known had been split up and scattered over a dozen starships, save for a handful of engineers. It wouldn't be easy to assemble and work up the crew before they had to depart.

"And they want us to leave soon," he mused. "What do they want us to do?"

"Raid the enemy," Captain Falcone said. She outlined the mission, quickly and concisely. "I expect we will have a great many problems to solve."

"At least they're honest problems," William said, seriously. He considered it for a long moment. "If I work on the personnel issues, do you want to handle the engineering problems?"

"I may need you to command one of the ships," Kat said. "But yes, for the moment I need you helping with the personnel. It won't be easy to get them to blend together."

William smiled. "Then we'd better get on with it," he said. "But I would be astonished if we leave in less than a week. That would be a bloody miracle."

"Tell me about it," Kat said. She ran her hand through her long hair. "The Admiralty is insistent, William. They need us out there as soon as possible."

CHAPTER SEVEN

"Kat," Marine Captain Patrick James Davidson said as he sat down next to her. "Do you want the good news or the bad news?"

"The good news is that I'm going to shoot the next person who says that," Kat said. "And the bad news is that I will probably enjoy it way more than I should."

Davidson smiled. "The good news is that I have managed to scrape up enough Marines to fill a single company, although most of them have never actually trained together before," he said. "The bad news is that the rest of the groundpounders are even worse."

Kat cursed under her breath. When the Admiralty's personnel department hadn't been giving her hell over her demands for experienced officers and crew, they'd been denying her requests for several companies of Marines. She knew they were in short supply—everything was in short supply these days—but she needed a solid bloc of Marines to allow her to capture freighters or engage targets on the ground. A full company was more than they'd wanted to give her, yet it was much less than she *needed*.

"I don't think I want to know," she groaned. "What's wrong with them?"

"Well," Davidson said, "there're five hundred of them in all, mainly drawn from local defense forces. A relative handful has experience boarding starships; the remainder have none. Indeed, quite a few consist of refugees from the Theocracy who escaped as children and have now joined the military. They're quite eager to tear into their enemies, but their experience is lacking."

Kat rested her head in her hands. "Are they serious about the mission?"

"The Admiralty?" Davidson asked. "There actually aren't that many Marine units that aren't earmarked for local defense or ship-to-ship operations. Getting a full company made out of dribs and drabs wasn't easy. We're lucky to have that many. As for the others . . ."

"Train them," Kat ordered. "Train them *hard*."

"Believe me, I shall," Davidson said. "You want to hear the *real* joke?"

"No," Kat said.

Davidson ignored her. "The ones who *do* have experience are ex-military police . . . former redcaps, shore patrolmen, and customs officers," he said. "You have the making of an instant feud between them and your crewmen right away."

"Fuck," Kat muttered. Fistfights between the shore patrol and groups of roving starship crewmen were depressingly common and grudges tended to run deep. Davidson was right; if anyone found out, it was likely to cause problems. And what was a minor matter on a planetary surface might be far more dangerous in deep space. "Tell them to keep that to themselves."

"I've already done so," Davidson said. "Officially, they're ranked as part of a reserve formation that was activated over the last few months.

There shouldn't be anything to tip off our more observant spacers that the groundpounders used to be redcaps."

"Good," Kat said. "And their training?"

"I'm running them all through the simulators, as well as a heavy program of combat exercises," Davidson said. "However, we don't have the time to train them up to Marine standards. They might not be *bad*, on the ground, but in space . . . it's a whole different ballgame."

He leaned forward. "And the refugees want revenge," he added. "They may do something stupid at the wrong time."

Kat frowned. "And can they be *trusted*?"

"They've been vetted thoroughly," Davidson assured her. "I think the oldest was six years old when his family fled the Theocracy. They were checked for any form of programming, which came up negative. I don't think it's even *possible* to program a young boy."

"I hope not," Kat said. If there was any interstellar power that could, it would be the Theocracy. Imagine being able to program children to do precisely as they were told, worship whom they were told to worship. "But what about his family?"

"They were vetted too," Davidson admitted. "They're clean."

"Good," she said. But it wasn't *all* good. The laws on using interrogation technologies without due cause would have been bent, if not broken outright. God alone knew what that would do, in the future. There was always someone willing to play stormtrooper. "In that case, train them, but keep them aware that we don't have time to deal with rogue operatives."

"Of course," Davidson said. He pulled a datapad from his belt and held it out to her. "I'm planning to keep half of the trained Marines on *Lightning* and detail the others to serve on training missions, at least while we're *en route* to enemy space. It will be at least two months before we get there, so there should be plenty of time to knock the edges off. I can rotate them through the simulators here so everyone gets a chance to test themselves . . ."

He paused. "I do have some ideas regarding deployment, if you wish," he added. "It wouldn't be hard to deploy Marines from either *Oliver Kennedy* or *Henry Crux*, according to the engineers. They're both heavily modified light cruisers, with shuttlebays; hell, we could deploy the shuttles to the hulls and then use a tube to scramble the Marines, if necessary."

"I wasn't planning to launch a full invasion of an enemy world," Kat said, amused. "And anything else probably wouldn't require a scramble."

The thought made her smile. She knew very well she didn't have the firepower, not if the Theocracy had invested time and effort building up the local defenses. The intelligence staff had been unable to decide just how much enemy forces would have invested, pointing out that they would have seen advantages and disadvantages in defending worlds that weren't part of their core territory. On one hand, they'd get to keep the locals under control if they lost control of the high orbitals; on the other hand, the locals might manage to snatch control of the defenses and turn them against their builders. *That* would be awkward for the enemy!

"It would also give them a great deal of experience," Davidson pressed lightly. "And they do need it."

"Then see to it, once we're underway," Kat said. "Did you even manage to get extra assault shuttles?"

"After a long argument with the bean counters," Davidson said. "Luckily, we were able to lay claim to a dozen extra shuttles, as the Corps isn't currently planning any opposed landings."

"Good," Kat said. She looked down at the datapad, then up at her lover. "What do *you* make of it? Honestly?"

"I think they've given you a right bitch of a job," Davidson said flatly. "The only good news is that no one is going to make much of a fuss if you lose any of the older ships."

"I think three of them don't have any better use than decoys," Kat admitted. Sasha might have been determined to get all of the remaining ships into service, but Kat had decided that several of them weren't worth the effort. They were too weak even to soak up incoming enemy fire. "We might be able to get *something* out of them . . ."

She shook her head. The engineering problems were bad enough, but the personnel problems were a minor disaster. If her XO hadn't been there to take over, she knew she would have managed to get into worse trouble. He simply had far more experience in sorting through files and separating out the decent officers from the troublemakers, the ones that every other captain wanted to lose. And he really *should* have been granted one of the ships . . .

I'll have to make sure he gets a proper command, Kat promised herself. *God knows he has the experience.*

Her intercom bleeped. "Captain, this is Lieutenant Ross," Linda Ross said. Kat was mildly surprised her communications officer hadn't been snatched away, but she wasn't about to complain. "We have a personnel shuttle inbound. One of the occupants has requested to speak with you immediately after boarding. There was no name attached to the request, but they do have a priority code."

Kat exchanged looks with Davidson. A senior officer or politician would have announced his impending arrival . . . unless he hoped to catch her by surprise. Who else could it be? A reporter . . . no, a reporter might not have announced himself, but the Admiralty would have made damn sure she knew one was on his way. And, given the secrecy of the operation, it was unlikely the Admiralty would allow a reporter to join them anyway. If one *had* managed to somehow get onto the shuttle, he was going to spend the rest of his time on *Lightning* in the brig.

"Understood," she said. "Please have the . . . *occupant* escorted to my office, once they have been checked by the duty officer."

"Aye, Captain," Linda said.

"Odd," Davidson said as Kat closed the connection. "Your father, perhaps?"

Kat shook her head. She couldn't see her father leaving Tyre for at least a day, probably longer. He'd never taken a vacation, as far as she knew, since the day he'd assumed control of the family assets. Hell, he'd never even managed to attend most of her birthday parties . . .

"I doubt it," she said. One of her brothers? The grand admiral? No, none of those seemed likely either. "I'll just have to wait and see."

Davidson rose to his feet. "If you don't mind, I'll return to Marine Country," he said. "Or do you want me to remain here?"

"No, thank you," Kat said. She glanced around her office, making sure that anything classified was out of sight, then checked her appearance in the mirror. "I'm sure it won't be anything serious."

She watched him go, then bent her head over the latest set of engineering reports. Sasha might have complained hugely about updating all of the reports and paperwork, but at least they now had a good idea of what they'd actually done to the flotilla . . . and what needed to be done, if only to make themselves more of a threat to the enemy. Some of the engineers might have been civilians or spent years in civilian service, but they'd put their time to good use, coming up with all sorts of innovative improvements to the older ships. At the very least, the Theocracy would get a few nasty surprises . . .

Sure, her own thoughts mocked her. *Right before they blow our starships to bits.*

The buzzer rang. Kat hesitated, then keyed the switch. "Enter."

She lifted her eyebrows as the newcomer stepped into the office. It was hard to be sure, but she looked to be at least ten years older than Kat, with brown hair tied up into a stiff bun and a face that looked as if she was permanently chewing on something sour. She wore a long dress rather than a military uniform; it spun around the deck as she walked forward. Kat rose to her feet and held out a hand, hastily checking the woman's face against the files stored in her implants. They didn't find a match.

"Captain Falcone," the woman said. She shook Kat's hand firmly, then smiled in a manner that suggested she was out of practice. "My name is Rose. Rose MacDonald."

"Pleased to meet you," Kat said. Who *was* this woman? An off-worlder, she was sure; her accent didn't match anything she'd heard on Tyre, although there was *something* oddly familiar about it. And how had she obtained a priority code? "I was not informed you were coming."

"I was told that it was a secret," Rose said. "No doubt they assumed the priority code would be enough to gain your attention. As it happens, I am the Observer to Sandy McNeal, the Most Honorable Representative of Hebrides to the Commonwealth. My current assignment is to accompany you on your voyage and report back to my superiors."

Kat blinked. Hebrides? That explained, at least, why the accent was familiar; her XO's accent was lighter, but it was definitely similar. And she *had* heard of Sandy McNeal, although she'd never met the man. A Most Honorable Representative commanded considerable political clout . . .

But his homeworld is under occupation, Kat thought. *Does he still command any authority?*

She pushed the thought aside ruthlessly. "Might I enquire as to *why* you have been assigned to *my* command?"

"The Most Honorable Representative was concerned about the preparations being made to liberate his homeworld from the Theocracy," Rose informed her. Kat could *hear* the capital letters slamming into place. "It is my task to report on your deployment and reassure him, or raise issues to be debated in public, should he not be reassured."

Kat frowned, motioning for the older woman to sit down. Someone was playing games, but who? And why? Kat had no intention of taking her squadron anywhere near Hebrides, not when the latest intelligence reports had suggested there were at least two enemy battle squadrons hanging in orbit around the occupied world. Hell, at the very least, Rose would be away from her political superior for at least four months . . .

Maybe that's what he wants, she thought, with droll amusement. Rose looked, very much, like a strict auntie, someone who wouldn't allow *any* fun on her watch. Kat had met the type from her family's plethora of relatives. *A chance to get rid of her for months . . .*

She gritted her teeth, then frowned. She'd never let any of those joyless matrons ruin her fun and they'd *all* been related to her. Rose most definitely *wasn't*.

"This squadron will not be going to Hebrides," she said slowly. Officially, the deployment was to the border with Marsalis. It would get her well away from Tyre, but nowhere near the war zone. "If you're hoping to observe a raid on the planet, you would do better to attach yourself to Admiral Christian."

"This squadron also includes a sizable percentage of men and women who do not come from Tyre," Rose stated. "It represents a chance to observe their integration into the Royal Navy and their progress through the ranks."

Kat sighed. "I will have a cabin earmarked for you," she said. "Until then . . ."

She scowled, thinking it through. No, the *first* thing she'd do would be to complain to the Admiralty and demand an explanation. Had someone decided it would be better for Rose to accompany a squadron going into the heart of enemy territory . . . or did they believe the cover story? If so, had they sent Rose to *Lightning* on the assumption that she would be safe, if bored, on the far side of the Commonwealth from the war?

"It is imperative that I observe your crewmen from start to finish," Rose informed her. "I do not exaggerate to say that my observations may determine the future of the Commonwealth."

"There's a war on," Kat said, feeling her patience start to snap. "It is *imperative* that my crews complete their work without being observed or distracted. Should you prove a nuisance, I will not hesitate to put you in the brig for the rest of the deployment. We will discuss precisely how you will carry out your observations later, once the ships are ready to depart."

And after I've gotten in touch with the Admiralty about this entire godforsaken mess, she added silently. Maybe she could convince the Admiralty to pawn Rose off on someone else. She'd be a pain in the ass, at least, while the squadron was on its way. *Or maybe they'll tell me to put up with it.*

"That will be suitable," Rose said. Her voice grew louder. "However, I would like to begin my observations as soon as possible."

Kat tapped her buzzer. Moments later, Emily Hawking, her new steward, stepped into the office.

"Please escort Miss MacDonald to one of the spare cabins and assign it to her for the moment," Kat ordered curtly.

"Yes, Captain," Emily said. "Miss MacDonald?"

Rose nodded, then turned to follow the steward out of the cabin. Kat watched her go, remembering all the times she'd made rude gestures at her aunts when their backs were turned, then shook her head in disbelief. She'd asked the Admiralty for more officers and crewmen and they'd sent her an observer, someone who would be peering over her shoulder whenever she was trying to think. It was unbelievable.

She keyed her terminal. "Record," she ordered. "Private message to Admiral Hanson."

Her console bleeped. Kat ran through a short explanation, then asked for a set of official orders or permission to remove Rose MacDonald from her ship. It beggared belief that *someone* would have given her the priority code without informing Kat in advance, but it wouldn't be the first time one part of the government hadn't known what another part was doing. She might just wind up having to take Rose MacDonald with her anyway . . .

As an afterthought, she sent a message to the XO, asking him to meet with her as soon as possible. He probably didn't know either Rose MacDonald or her superior, not personally, but he might have an idea of how best to handle them. No doubt there were politics involved, somewhere. Perhaps the diplomats thought it was actually a *good* idea . . .

A message flickered up in front of her. Kat read it, then cursed. Rose MacDonald *had* been granted permission to accompany the squadron, permission that had come straight from the War Cabinet itself. There would be no hope of convincing them to change their minds, not now that they'd taken the plunge. She'd been right. It *was* political.

She sent another message to her father, then sighed and started to draw up the first set of deployment plans. No doubt there would be another crisis, then another, then another . . . she'd be lucky if she managed to stay ahead of them all. But at least she'd be able to rest once the squadron was in hyperspace. There wouldn't be any way to change her orders after they'd departed . . .

Unless they find a way to mount StarComs on ships, she thought darkly. *That would be the end of independent commands.*

CHAPTER EIGHT

The spy couldn't help feeling a hint of trepidation as the shuttle landed neatly in the heavy cruiser's giant shuttlebay. He'd hoped—prayed—that he wouldn't be assigned anywhere sensitive, but God hadn't been listening to him. No doubt the billions of believers in the Theocracy cancelled out one young man who'd never taken religion very seriously. Now . . . he had his orders and he knew what would happen if he disobeyed. His sister, his sole relative, would be brutally killed once her captors knew he'd betrayed them. And it was already too late to go to the counterintelligence services. They'd want his scalp too when they found out the truth.

He stood with the other crewmen and walked out of the shuttle, the group forming a loose line in front of the waiting XO. The man looked older than the spy had expected for an officer who had served in the Navy for years rather than transferring to the reserve, but he was clearly not someone to irritate. His gray eyes flickered over the crewmen, one by one, then fixed on a spot just above their heads. The spy couldn't help wondering if he'd already realized that not all of the crewmen were completely devoted to the Commonwealth. Quite a few of them had had problems that would have mandated their dismissal if there hadn't been a war on. They weren't likely to cause too many problems, he hoped, but it only took one idiot acting idiotically at the wrong time to cause a disaster.

"Welcome onboard HMS *Lightning*," the XO said briskly. "I'm afraid you're all going to have to hit the deck running as we are scheduled to depart tomorrow. Your department heads will see to it that you are assigned berths and timetables, then you will join the rota for department-based drills and exercises to bring your skills up to par. We will be very busy right up until the moment the mission actually begins."

The spy kept his face expressionless with an effort. He'd been recalled to active service a month after the start of the war, but his skills had been so outdated that he'd had to go through an emergency tactical course at Piker's Peak before he could be assigned to anything more advanced than an asteroid mining station. It hadn't been hard to *complete* the course, even though it was constantly updated as the Navy learned from successive engagements with its first true foe, but he'd hoped to be assigned somewhere harmless. Indeed, he *had* been assigned to a deep-space monitoring station and then reassigned, two days before he'd been due to leave. All he'd been told, when he'd received his new orders, was that he'd been tapped for something important.

"The full details of the mission will be disclosed once we are underway," the XO informed them, forestalling any questions from men and women who had been civilian reservists only a few short months ago. "Suffice it to say, for the moment, that it is quite important; your skills will be pushed to the limit. Indeed, some of you are uniquely qualified for your roles on this ship and the accompanying squadron."

That didn't sound likely, the spy thought. *Lightning* was a modern heavy cruiser . . . and he'd been in the reserve years before she'd left the shipyard for the first time. Unless, of course, the XO meant to say they were expendable. The spy had few illusions about his skills compared to someone who had spent a lifetime in the Navy. *They* would have the chance to broaden their skills indefinitely, while *his* work had been limited to civilian tech. Unless they *did* plan to work with civilian-grade computers. It was possible, he figured, but unlikely. He rather doubted that *anything* civilian could match military-grade technology.

"I have one final thing to say before you are dismissed to your berths," the XO said. "For some of you, I suggest you consider this a fresh start; for others, a reintroduction to military life. I do not have time to coddle people with behavioral problems. If you cause trouble or render yourself unfit for duty, you will spend the rest of the cruise in the brig, eating stale bread and drinking recycled water. And when we get home, I will make damn sure you're not only dismissed from the Navy, but dumped on a penal island."

He didn't look to be joking, the spy considered. Most of the reservists he'd met at Piker's Peak had been decent people, but some of the shuttle's passengers had been drunkards or others with clear problems. The spy wondered, absently, if any of them could be used . . . then dismissed the thought in some irritation. He might be doomed, when the truth finally came out, but there was no reason to drag anyone else down with him.

His implants blinked up a message as two data packets were downloaded from the ship's datanet: one assigning him to a berth and showing him how to reach his department, the other ordering him to report to the department head within twenty minutes. He scanned the files absently, then nodded. It wouldn't be hard to get there in time, as long as he dumped his bag into the sleeping compartment rather than unpacking it piece by piece. No one would touch it, by long tradition. The Navy couldn't have endured otherwise.

"Dismissed," the XO said.

The spy saluted, then joined the others as they headed for the hatch.

◆ ◆ ◆

William shook his head in tired disbelief as the last of the newcomers walked through the hatch and out into the ship. Reservists . . . reservists and civilians and crewmen who really should have been discharged years ago. He'd barely had an opportunity to read their files, but it had been alarmingly clear that most of them were either out of date or regarded as problem children. The former might be an advantage, with so many old starships assigned to the squadron, yet the latter might be actively dangerous. He'd briefed the department heads carefully, warning them to take immediate action against any troublemakers, but he knew it wouldn't be easy. The Marines might have to intervene if the shit hit the fan.

He cursed under his breath, then walked through the hatch himself and back up to the bridge, where a handful of new crewmen were running exercises on the tactical computers. It looked as though they were doing well, although William knew that the settings had been jacked higher than reality would allow. The enemy missiles on the simulators were several times as fast and accurate as anything they'd seen from the Theocracy, at least for the moment. In theory, it would ready the crew for any real threat; in practice, William wasn't so sure. There was a fine line between feeling ready for anything *realistic* and outright overconfidence.

"Carry on," he ordered, once the simulation had finished. "I want you to tighten up your point defense formations. You're running the risk of allowing the enemy to overload your defenses and punch through to the flagship."

Midshipman Travis blinked in surprise. "Sir," he said, "I thought it was impossible to identify the flagship."

"We managed it at Cadiz," William reminded him. The case of hidden flagships was another prewar certainty that hadn't lasted long, once two reasonably capable interstellar powers had started shooting at each other. "And for us, it will be blindingly obvious which ship is the flagship."

He scowled up at the near-space display. There was only one modern ship in the formation, *Lightning* herself. The Theocrats might be fanatics, but they weren't stupid; it would be easy to deduce that *Lightning* was the flagship. She was both the only modern ship in the formation and the only one with a hope of surviving a close engagement if the enemy got lucky. He'd toyed with the idea of moving fleet command to one of the older ships, but the disadvantages outweighed the advantages. Besides, none of them were set up to serve as a flagship.

And neither are we, he thought as he walked over to the captain's office and pushed the buzzer. *We had real problems commanding 7th Fleet when we led the remaining ships back to Cadiz.*

The hatch opened. William stepped inside, catching sight of Captain Falcone chewing a strand of her hair as she bent over a set of reports on her desk. It made her look absurdly young, although there was a harder edge to her movements these days. She glanced up as he entered, then waved a hand at the chair facing her desk. William stepped over to it and sat down, waiting patiently for her to finish the report. There would be time enough to discuss his concerns with her once she was done.

"Commander," she said, tiredly. "Do you know Rose MacDonald, Observer to Sandy McNeal?"

"No," William said. "Well, I know McNeal by reputation, but I've never heard of MacDonald at all."

The captain gave him an odd look, then flushed with embarrassment as she realized her mistake. William frowned inwardly; they might have shared a homeworld, but he'd never actually *met* McNeal, let alone spoken with him. There were untold thousands of emigrants from Hebrides who'd fled to the Commonwealth in hopes of a better life. But for the captain, who'd grown up in the aristocracy, it wasn't implausible that she might know the prime minister and his cabinet personally. She'd certainly be familiar with them.

"She's been assigned to us as an observer," the captain explained, picking up one of the datapads and passing it to him. "Apparently she's here to observe how the different nationalities interact as part of the squadron."

"It isn't as if we have time to worry about where people come from," William said, scanning the datapad quickly. Rose MacDonald—she might be related to the MacDonald family he knew, although the clan was large enough that the connection might be meaningless—had permission to go anywhere and watch anything, although she had no formal authority over the mission. "And if all she wants is to observe . . ."

"It's a complication," the captain said. "And one I could have done without, at the moment."

William nodded in bitter agreement. They'd been sent the dregs of the service, either because they were rated as expendable or because their former commanding officers didn't have a clue about Operation Knife. Some of them would shine, given a chance; others would need to be thumped, then dumped into the brig if they didn't grow into trustworthy crewmen. And quite a few of them were newcomers—men and women who hadn't been born on Tyre . . .

"We're not going to be the poster child for integration," he commented sourly. "Apart from me, there aren't many officers who *don't* come from Tyre."

"I know," the captain said. "I've tried explaining that to the Admiralty, but the department that wants her to accompany us doesn't know what we're doing and the department that planned the operation doesn't have the authority to tell them to go to hell. I did try suggesting she go to the front and observe 6th Fleet . . ."

Her voice trailed off. "She's going to be a problem," she added after a moment. "I'd like you to take personal charge of her, but you have too much else to do. She needs to be supervised by someone senior enough not to be pressured into making poor decisions."

William thought about it quickly. He didn't know Rose MacDonald, but he *did* know she'd have no trouble finding evidence that integration wasn't working very well if she chose to look. The latest classes from Piker's Peak included quite a few officers who hadn't been born on Tyre, yet it would be years before the Tyre-born no longer dominated the upper ranks. Hell, his *own* career suggested that integration was a major problem. He should have had a command years ago.

But I wasn't trained at Piker's Peak, he thought. It wasn't a pleasant thought, but it had to be faced. He lacked the training all Commonwealth officers were given as a matter of course. *I was an adult before the Commonwealth discovered my world.*

"I could spare time for her once we're underway," he said reluctantly. "Maybe not much, but enough to keep her happy. If she's from Hebrides, she'll understand that the world can't bend to her will."

"She's a politician," the captain said. "They *all* believe they can bend the world to their will."

William smiled. "Does she actually know where we're going?"

"Not from what she told me," the captain said. "Officially, we're on our way to the other side of the Commonwealth, as far from Theocratic space as possible. She may be under the impression she will have time to observe us away from the fires of war. Only a handful of people know the truth, so I doubt she's learned any differently since."

"Then I will take her in hand once we depart," William said. "I'm sure she won't be much of a problem once she understands where we're actually going. She won't even insist on being dropped off somewhere."

"Not that we could," the captain said. She cleared her throat. "And the newcomers?"

"We should have everyone we're going to get now," William said. "I've spread out some of our experienced crews to train up the newcomers, so we should be up to speed by the time we reach the border. The improved tactical exercises have been sharpening their skills, Captain; the only real danger is too many officers and crew believing the cover story. I've had to speak sharply to a couple of officers who were slacking off on the assumption we wouldn't be seeing any action."

The captain nodded. "Any disciplinary problems, so far?"

"Nothing major, Captain," William assured her. "A couple of minor incidents during basic training; I dealt with them at once and I doubt they will recur. I've also ordered all illicit stills to be shut down for the duration of the voyage, apart from the one the chief engineer is running. There won't be any other source of alcohol while we're underway."

The captain looked disapproving, but nodded reluctantly. William didn't blame her; alcohol had caused too many problems on the Navy's starships, yet there was no way to prevent enterprising crewmen from setting up their own stills. Having one semi-legal still operating in the hands of someone who could be trusted to ensure that no one got enough to get smashed out of their minds would be safer than banning it completely. He had no illusions about just how well stills could be hidden if someone decided it was worth the risk of setting one up. Crewmen tended to be *very* enterprising when money and alcohol was involved.

"And the minor incidents?"

"A handful of reservists objected to working on the older ships because their skills would be out of date," William said. He'd heard that some people only joined the Navy to develop skills and then take them into the civilian market, but it was the first time he'd ever heard anyone blatantly complaining the Navy was giving him or her the wrong training. "I dealt with them curtly and the matter should be settled."

The captain smiled. "Thank you," she said. She glanced down at another datapad, then looked back up at him. Her blue eyes met his. "Do you want command of any of the smaller ships?"

William hesitated. If he'd been offered command a year ago, or even a month ago, he would have accepted at once. He knew he had the skills to handle it. But now . . . now, he couldn't help wondering if the captain needed him more on *Lightning* than commanding one of the older ships. It was galling; he could have command, if he wanted it, at the cost of leaving a commanding officer he'd grown to respect without a strong right arm.

"I would probably be better suited to remain here," he said reluctantly. If *that* ever entered his file, he could kiss good-bye to any hope of independent command. "Do you have commanding officers for them?"

"Mostly younger officers," the captain said. If she was disappointed by his refusal, she didn't show it. "A couple of commanders; the rest are lieutenant-commanders . . . all of whom will be called captain, as long as they're on the ships. It should look good on their files when we get home. I'm going to host a dinner for them once we're underway where we'll discuss the mission itself."

"Unless they've already guessed we're up to more than just patrolling a friendly border," William pointed out. The Commonwealth's neighbors weren't likely to cause problems for the Commonwealth while the war was underway. They would prefer to keep the Theocracy as far from them as possible. "It isn't as if we *need* to watch our backs."

"The Theocracy could send a fleet the long way around," the captain said, "although it would be unlikely. They'd have to be out of their minds."

William nodded. It would take at least six months for an enemy fleet to sneak around the Commonwealth's borders, then fall on the undefended rear worlds like wolves on sheep. In that time, Admiral Christian might punch through the weakened Theocratic defenses and advance directly towards the enemy homeworld itself. They'd have to be insane to take the risk of detaching a significant force; hell, the Commonwealth was up to something similar and *they* hadn't been able to spare more than a single modern cruiser and a handful of older vessels.

"They're fanatics," he said after a moment. His homeworld had had too many problems with fanatics in the past. "They might consider anything possible, as long as it was done in the name of God."

CHAPTER NINE

Despite herself, Kat couldn't help feeling a flicker of excitement as she strode onto the bridge and sat down in her command chair. Getting the squadron anywhere near ready to depart had been a hassle, but now they were finally ready to get on their way. She glanced at the near-space display, showing the fifteen older starships and three freighters assigned to Operation Knife, then keyed a switch on her console, opening a link to engineering.

"This is the captain," she said. "Are we ready to depart?"

"Yes, Captain," Zack Lynn said. Her chief engineer sounded confident, at least; she'd taken the time to go over the repairs with him, and he'd assured her that the ships were practically as good as new. "All systems are operating within acceptable parameters."

Kat nodded, then glanced at her helmsman. "Set a course for the nearest suitable jump point," she ordered. "And then copy it to the squadron."

"Course laid in, Captain," Lieutenant Samuel Weiberg said. "Copying it to the squadron now."

Kat smiled. She'd been surprised when he'd returned to the ship, along with several other experienced officers, but he *had* spent the last few months at Piker's Peak, sharing what he'd learned with the new recruits. Maybe someone in the personnel department had had an unaccustomed fit of common sense and realized it would be better for him to go back to *Lightning* rather than a new ship. Or maybe it had just been a stroke of luck.

"Communications," she said. "Contact Shipyard Command and request permission to depart."

"Aye, Captain," Lieutenant Linda Ross said. There was a pause as she worked her console. "We are cleared to depart, Captain. Shipyard Command wishes us luck."

"Send a copy of our final status report to the Admiralty," Kat ordered. She felt another flicker of excitement, which she ruthlessly suppressed. "Helm, take us to the jump point."

She sat back in her command chair as she felt a dull thrumming running through the ship, slowly increasing in power as *Lightning* moved out of position. The rest of the squadron fell in behind her, keeping their formation spread out to minimize any chance of an accident. Kat had never heard of one starship ramming another by mistake, but their early exercises had made it clear that the older ships were far from reliable. It was better, she reasoned, to avoid taking chances while her crews were still getting used to them. Even with the latest weapons and drives crammed into their hulls, some of them still maneuvered like wallowing pigs.

"All systems check out, Captain," Lynn said.

"The squadron seems to be operating at acceptable levels," the XO added from his console. "They should have no trouble navigating hyperspace."

Until we try to slip through the border, Kat thought. She'd seen the star charts the XO had bought from his brother. The route into enemy space might not be *quite* as bad as flying through the Seven Sisters, but it was going to be bad enough. *We might lose a ship or two there.*

She sucked in her breath. It wasn't going to be easy, not with ships that hadn't been designed to brush up against energy storms. The men who'd started to chart hyperspace, back in 2109, had been *brave.* They'd gone out willingly, knowing the odds of a safe return were poor. She couldn't help admiring them, even as she appreciated the advancements in modern technology. As long as *Lightning* didn't try to fly right *through* a storm, she was safe in hyperspace.

"Good," she said, glancing at the display. "Transmit details of the first waypoint to them."

"Yes, Captain," Linda Ross said.

"Captain," Weiberg said. "We have reached the first jump point."

Kat nodded. Trying to open a gateway so close to Hyperion would be asking for trouble, if not outright disaster. No one had managed to *completely* account for the relationship between hyperspace and real-space, but everyone agreed that trying to jump out close to a planet was akin to diving right into an energy storm. She might have risked it, if she'd been desperate, yet the price would have been high. There was no need to take the risk now, not in a secure star system.

"Open the gateway," she ordered. "Take us into hyperspace."

The gateway opened, revealing the shimmering lights of hyper-space. Kat's stomach clenched as the ship dived into the vortex, a reflex she'd never been able to suppress even though she knew it was purely psychometric. Others, natural-born groundhogs, weren't able to cope, seeing the vortex as a gaping maw or a mouth filled with sharp teeth and hyperspace itself as a profoundly unnatural realm. She felt a dull shiver run through the ship, a sensation that it was no longer flying through empty space; she pushed it aside, irritated. It wasn't as if it was her first time in hyperspace.

"Mr. XO," she said, formally. "Squadron status?"

"All eighteen ships made it through the gateway, Captain," the XO reported. "They're reporting no problems; I say again, no problems."

"Inform their commanding officers that they are invited to join me for dinner at 1700," Kat said, glancing at her chronometer. It was 1400, plenty of time for any problems to crop up before the officers left their ships. "I expect their responses shortly."

She leaned back in her command chair and studied the readouts. Everything seemed to be fine, save for odd fluctuations in the drive nodes. The engineers were already on it, checking and rechecking something that *looked* like a case of faulty tuning. Kat hoped they were right. Losing one drive node would be irritating, losing three would cripple *Lightning* if she had to take the ship into battle. It was probable that the tuning hadn't been quite perfect—it was hard to tune a node without actually running it—but if it was something worse . . .

We might have to halt long enough to actually cut the node out and replace it, she thought sourly. Doing such an operation in deep space would be an absolute nightmare, but it would have to be endured. *We don't dare drop into a fleet base as it would betray our true vector.*

She looked at the near-space display and frowned. Tyre was the busiest system in the Commonwealth, with thousands of ships coming and going every day, and it was quite likely that *some* of those ships were actually spies. *Kat* would have established spying bases, if she'd been planning a war; it wouldn't have been hard for the Theocracy to set up spy rings as well as insert commandos into enemy territory. Hell, she *knew* they'd inserted commandos; they'd caused a great deal of disruption during the opening hours of the war.

And now, she thought, *are unfriendly eyes tracking our departure?*

There was no way to be sure, she knew. Sensors were unreliable in hyperspace; an enemy ship could be right on top of them before she saw it coming, or watching her from a safe distance, effectively invisible. It was no consolation to know that the Theocracy would have similar problems, that their sensors couldn't be *that* much better than anything possessed by the Commonwealth. All she could do was fly an evasive course and hope that hyperspace allowed them to avoid their opponents before it was too late.

"The commanding officers have responded, Captain," the XO said. "They *will* be attending your dinner."

Kat smiled. As if there had been any doubt . . .

There might have been, she had to admit. Her subordinates were commanding ships that hadn't seen real service for decades, if they were lucky. Something *might* have cropped up that would have forced a CO to remain with his ship, even if he had been invited—ordered—to attend a dinner. She wouldn't have penalized a CO for that either. It wouldn't have been a deliberate snub, but a reasonable response to a serious problem.

Not that Candy would have understood, she thought as she rose to her feet. *If she invites someone to her parties, that person had better go. And if they're on their deathbed, they should bring their deathbed with them.*

"You have the bridge," she said, addressing the XO. "I'll be in my office."

She stepped through the door, ordered coffee from her steward, and sat down with the latest set of intelligence reports. There was actually a considerable amount of data, but she lacked any context . . . and the intelligence officers, suffering from the same problem, had spent hours crafting complex reports that managed to hide their basic ignorance under a mountain of bullshit. She rubbed her forehead; it was useful to know that the CIS had identified fifty-seven separate enemy super-dreadnoughts, but there was no way to know just how many super-dreadnoughts the enemy actually *had*. Had they sent all of their mobile firepower forward or had they kept half of it in reserve?

Her steward appeared from the side door, carrying a large mug of coffee. Kat took it, nodded her thanks, and looked back at her data-pads. It took her a moment to realize that Emily Hawking, instead of withdrawing as silently as she'd arrived, was waiting patiently to be acknowledged. Kat sighed inwardly, then looked up.

"Captain," Emily said, "the observer has requested permission to attend the dinner."

Kat frowned. Her first inclination was to refuse, but it would be undiplomatic. Rose MacDonald presumably had no way to know that they *weren't* heading away from the war, yet it wouldn't be long before she found out the truth. It would probably be better, all things considered, for her to attend the dinner. If nothing else, half of the officers Kat had recruited to command the older ships were newcomers to the Navy. Some of them had more relevant experience than anyone from Tyre.

"Tell her she would be welcome," Kat said. It was a half-truth, at best. "Have the cooks include her in their calculations."

"Aye, Captain," Emily said.

She saluted, then withdrew. Kat looked back at her paperwork and then opened the report from the XO's brother. Unlike the intelligence analysts, it was clear and remarkably concise, although there were very definite gaps in what the smugglers knew about the Theocracy. It seemed they rarely went anywhere near the core worlds, fearing certain death if they were caught. Given how badly the Theocracy treated innocent spacers who had been *invited* into their space, Kat wasn't remotely surprised. At least the smugglers didn't bother to play games; they either knew something or admitted it when they *didn't*.

Her terminal bleeped, alerting her to the time. Kat sighed, then stood and hurried down the corridor to her cabin, where she showered and changed her uniform. There was no point in getting into her dress uniform, she decided; it wasn't as if she was hosting an admiral. She glanced at herself in the mirror, tied her hair back into a bun, and then walked down to the officers' mess. The other commanding officers had already assembled, looking torn between eagerness and fear. Very few of them had any *real* command experience before they'd been offered the chance to command a set of expendable vessels.

"At ease," Kat ordered as she stepped into the officers' mess. "Take your seats"—she smiled as she realized the cooks had put a chair out for the observer—"and relax. We have a great deal to discuss."

She took her seat at the head of the table, then nodded to the XO as he sat at the far end, facing her. It was an odd arrangement, she had to admit, but he was effectively second in command of the entire squadron as well as her XO. She was surprised he'd turned down one of the ships himself, yet she was grateful. It wouldn't have been so easy to get the squadron organized without him.

"We will eat first, I think," she added. "This may be the last decent meal we have for some time."

The stewards brought in the first course, then withdrew. Kat watched as her officers drank their soup, all seemingly unwilling to start a conversation. She didn't really blame them; they *were* very junior officers and it was unlikely that any of them had taken part in a formal dinner before, at least outside Piker's Peak. And it wouldn't be the same, not really. There, someone would correct their mistakes; here, a mistake could blight their careers. Kat recalled just why she detested formal parties, even though she was the daughter of a duke. A single mistake could have High Society sneering at someone for years.

She waited until they'd finished the dinner and the stewards had poured coffee, then leaned forward, tapping her fork against her glass. "As some of you may have realized," she said without preamble, "we are *not* heading to a peaceful border. In fact, our mission is to strike deep into the Theocracy and raid their supply lines."

There was a long pause. Several of the officers looked excited or resigned rather than shocked; they'd seen her insistence on stocking up on everything from missiles to spare parts and deduced she expected to see action sooner rather than later. And the Admiralty had raised no objection either. With missiles in such short supply, they would have raised a fuss if she'd tried to take several thousand missiles away from the front. The signs had been there for anyone who cared to look.

"We are not going to seek open combat," Kat said after a moment. She might as well head *that* idea off at the pass. "We're going to find their weak points and wreak havoc, blowing holes in their system, just to buy time for the main body of the fleet to regroup and prepare to take the offensive. And believe me, we need to buy time."

Lieutenant Slater of HMS *Checkmate* leaned forward. "Are you saying we're losing the war?"

"No," Kat said. Slater, according to his files, was too cynical to be promoted much further, which she suspected meant he had a habit of asking too many questions. It wouldn't be the first time someone had come up with an excuse for blighting an officer's career out of personal dislike. "I'm saying we need to buy time to strengthen our defenses and complete the switch to war production."

Rose MacDonald coughed. "You mean . . . we're going to war?"

"Yes," Kat said. "We're going to be operating deep within enemy space."

She concealed her amusement at the observer's sudden discomfort. "There's a full tactical brief available in the datanet," she said. "You'll have a chance to study it over the next month, while we approach enemy space, and then suggest possible targets for our first set of raids. We know little about the Theocracy's inner structure, so collecting intelligence is one of our first priorities. Ideally, we want to get a complete map of their space."

"That won't be easy," Commander Millikan said. "Everything I've heard about the Theocracy suggests that their people are kept in complete ignorance. Even starship officers never learn anything other than their own specialties."

"Which makes you wonder, really, how they maintain their society," Commander Kent said sarcastically. "We cross-train our people for a reason."

"There are limits to how far people can be cross-trained," the XO pointed out. "And really, would you be able to navigate a starship using only the information in your head?"

"I'd want to be sure I could repair the navigational systems myself, if necessary," Kent countered. He turned to look at Kat. "If we could kill or capture their engineering personnel, Captain, it could cripple their economy."

"Maybe not that much," Commander Millikan said. "Their worlds are apparently largely pastoral. It doesn't take much advanced knowledge to operate a farm."

"Unless you happen to want to increase your yield," the XO said. "Hardscrabble farming is just that—*hard*."

Kat tapped the table sharply. "I intend to make a formal announcement tomorrow," she said flatly. "We will not, of course, be docking at any fleet base before we cross the border, so there should be no risk of the secret getting out. However, I expect you to inform your subordinates that the Quiet Storm protocols are now solidly in effect. I do *not* want any unsecured data being stored, let alone transmitted, without clear authorization from me personally. This will cause problems, I know, but they have to be handled. We cannot risk any form of security breach."

She paused. "Are there any questions?"

"It will cause . . . *issues*," Commander Millikan warned. "No one *knew* they were signing up for a dangerous mission."

"They joined the Navy," Kat said flatly. "They knew the job was dangerous when they took it."

She kept her expression blank with an effort. The Quiet Storm protocols included everything from personal terminals—frowned upon, but not actually forbidden—to paper diaries. If someone *had* been earmarked for a secret mission, they would have been told not to bring anything along those lines. Yet she'd known she couldn't risk letting anyone know the truth before they left. The protocols *would* cause problems, which would just have to be handled. There was no other choice.

"I will be holding another dinner once we cross the front lines," she concluded. "At that point, we will pick our first targets. By then, we should also have a better grasp of our strengths and weaknesses."

She finished her coffee, then smiled. "I will withdraw now, in line with protocol, but feel free to stay here as long as you wish," she added after a moment. Protocol dictated that the senior officer was always the first to leave. "Thank you for coming."

Rose followed her as she slipped out of the hatch. "Captain!"

Kat turned to face the older woman. "Yes?"

"We're really going to war," Rose said. "It's not a joke, is it?"

"No joke," Kat said. It wasn't nice, but part of her was enjoying Rose's discomfort. "Once we cross the border, we will start looking for things to kill."

CHAPTER TEN

"Well," Lieutenant Cecelia Parkinson said as the tactical staff assembled in their compartment, "this is a surprise, isn't it?"

The spy cringed inwardly. He'd been told that they were going *away* from the war, not towards it . . . let alone carrying it deep into enemy space. He'd hoped he would have an excuse for doing nothing, for not breaking one set of oaths in hopes of saving his sister's life, but it seemed he was to be deprived of any excuse at all. The Theocracy would expect him to do his utmost to help them or they would kill his sister . . .

. . . and he had a priceless opportunity to do just that.

We're going to be unpredictable ghosts, he thought. *Moving from star system to star system, picking our targets at random . . . they would have to get very lucky to have a battle squadron in position to catch us when they have too many stars to cover. But I could tell them where to place their ships.*

He fought to keep his expression under control, cursing the Theocracy's luck. Maybe there *was* something to their religion after all. Random chance alone couldn't have accounted for it, unless he'd just been very unlucky. But he would have needed to be unlucky at least three times over: the Theocracy had captured his sister; they'd discovered she was related to someone on active service; and now he was in position to actually *do* something for them, something that would betray all his oaths. And yet . . . what else could he do?

"We'll start new tactical exercises in an hour," Lieutenant Parkinson said. The spy hated her—she was blonde, bubbly, and too young for her post. But then, she *had* done well at Cadiz; she'd probably deserved her promotion. If there were any dark secrets in her past, she'd hid them very well. "By then, I expect you all to come up with imaginative ways to use the resources at our disposal."

Sending them all into a sun would probably work, the spy thought darkly. *But then, no one would ever know what I'd done.*

He looked at the tactical display, wishing he dared trust either side. If the Theocracy gave up his sister, they wouldn't have anything more to hold over him . . . apart, of course, from the fact he'd committed treason. It was in their interests to *keep* his sister as long as possible, even if she was unhurt; they had no reason to return her just because he'd had enough of working for them without a clear reward. But the CIS would be worse; they'd take him, use him to feed the enemy false information . . . and if his sister happened to be killed in the process? Well, they'd be regretful, and they'd say all the right things, but it wouldn't make any difference. The only hope for his sister's life was to work with the Theocracy . . .

. . . and that meant betraying the Commonwealth, once and for all.

◆ ◆ ◆

Kat had privately expected more trouble as the ragtag formation moved steadily towards the front lines, carefully evading most of the major shipping lanes, but—somewhat to her surprise—the problems they encountered were swiftly ironed out by a crew that had become remarkably motivated after they realized where they were going. The only real problem had appeared when one of the ships suffered drive node failure, which could have been disastrous, but *Lightning* had taken her in tow until the engineers had replaced the failed nodes. Overall, she had to admit, everything had proceeded much more smoothly than she had a right to expect. By the time they started their approach to the border, she couldn't help feeling that the handful of ancient ships had become a viable squadron.

"The course through hyperspace isn't going to be easy," the XO said. "I can see why the smugglers like this route, but the Theocracy will probably like it too."

Kat nodded, studying the holographic star chart. It wouldn't be *quite* as bad as the passage through the Seven Sisters, but it would be quite bad enough, even without the occupational hazard of enemy ships patrolling their side of the border. The Commonwealth had kept a close eye on the sector before the war, knowing that smugglers, refugees, and spies used it to cross between the two powers; now, most of the patrol ships had been withdrawn. But was that true on the other side? Eighteen starships were much more visible than a single starship trying to hide. They might cross the border and run straight into trouble . . .

Or a minefield, she added mentally. *They mined quite a few of the routes in and out of their space.*

"We'll make it through," Davidson said confidently. "The real challenge will come once we're on the other side."

Kat nodded. There were some worlds that should, logically, be bases for enemy operations . . . and others, she suspected, that were profoundly unimportant. And yet, did the logic even hold up? The Theocracy wasn't interested in building an economic powerhouse, but a religious state. They might keep their industries well away from restive worlds . . .

And we have no idea what we're going to be jumping into, she thought. *We could run slap into something we can't handle.*

"I was considering options," the XO said. He cocked his head, using his implants to send orders to the room's processor. The star chart changed its position, zeroing in on a star system close to the border. "This might be a good place to start operations."

Davidson frowned. "UNAS-RD-46785? We've been there."

"That's where we met the freighter convoy," Kat recalled. "Why *there?*"

The XO smiled. "They used it as a place to route ships across the border," he said. "I'd bet good money they're still using it to route ships towards the front lines."

"That makes no sense," Davidson said. "They'd be better off just forwarding the ships directly to the front lines."

"You're thinking like a Marine, not a bureaucrat," the XO said. "To a bureaucrat, the established routine is the holiest of holies. That system is used for routing ships over the prewar border? It's *still* used for routing ships towards the war front. And it does make a certain kind of sense. They wouldn't want to send freighters into a war zone, so they'd want to have a place to halt and collect the latest pieces of information before advancing onwards. Why not the system they're already used to using?"

"There's nothing there," Kat pointed out.

"That's the beauty of it," the XO countered. "There's no one there to watch them, so they can carry out their operations in perfect secrecy. And the system *is* centrally located along the border stars; they can draw food supplies from five other systems, assemble there, and then advance to the war front."

Kat considered it for a long moment. "It seems a good place to start as you stated, Mr. XO," she said finally. "And we can detach a couple of the destroyers, send them to probe other star systems for potential targets."

"Or even raid two of them, if we see a chance," Davidson offered. "Give them something else to think about, apart from us. We could even run drones through the system claiming to be superdreadnoughts."

"Then they'd wonder why the superdreadnoughts weren't launching missiles at them," the XO growled. "It wouldn't take them long to deduce that they're nothing more than drones."

"They'd still have to take the threat seriously," Davidson said. "Or we could just keep springing their tripwires until they don't take *any* threats seriously . . ."

"And then stick a knife in their ribs," Kat said. She studied the star chart for a long moment, then looked at the XO. "Is there any halfway reasonable chance of contacting the local smugglers?"

"Perhaps," the XO said. "However, if they do have bases within enemy space, it's quite likely they do so with the blessing of the local authorities. They may not be inclined to work with us."

Davidson lifted his eyebrows. "The Theocrats *allow* the smugglers to have their bases?"

"The Theocrats ban everything that makes life worth living," the XO said. "If my brother is to be believed, whatever central authority may say, the local authorities have always had a cozy relationship with the smugglers. They'd be in deep shit if they were ever caught, of course, so they've learned to be very careful. It suits both sides to keep everything firmly under wraps."

Kat shook her head in disbelief. "It sounds insane."

"Tell me something," the XO said. "How many things are there, on Tyre, that are banned outright? That the mere possession of is considered a crime?"

"Not many," Kat said after a moment's thought. "Why?"

"If you wanted to drink yourself to death, no one would stop you," the XO said. "If you wanted to lose yourself in a simulated world, or wire your brain for pleasure, no one would stop you either. There simply aren't many things that are considered criminal, let alone sinful. The

Commonwealth doesn't judge as long as people keep their vices in private and non-consenting people are not harmed.

"But the Theocracy? Everything is forbidden unless permitted. Taking a drink could earn you a whipping. Questioning religious leaders could get you burned to death. Having sex outside marriage could result in castration or worse; a woman committing adultery could expect to be executed for defiling her marriage bond. There are far more ways to push the limits in the Theocracy and far more demand for forbidden items."

"Because there are so much more of them," Kat mused.

"Exactly," the XO said. "There's much more opportunity for sin—and, once you're committed, you may as well keep going. You won't be forgiven if the Inquisitors find out."

He shrugged. "I've been told you can make yourself rich for life by shipping mild euphoric drugs into the Theocracy," he added. "Or, if you want to live dangerously, books or datachips that haven't been vetted by the Inquisition. Or even something as simple as bottles of alcohol. There's no lack of demand."

Kat smiled. "We'll have to see what we find," she said. "Are there any other problems?"

"The observer has spent most of her time in her cabin," the XO said. "I did take her on a tour of *Thundergod*, which has the most integrated crew in the squadron, but she didn't seem interested. It's unusual, Captain. I'd expect a woman from my world to be more accepting of danger."

"She *is* a politician," Davidson said.

"I looked her up," the XO replied dryly. "Apparently, she worked for several ministers before she was assigned to Sandy McNeal; she knows, or she certainly *should* know, the dangers of the real world. She didn't grow up on a nice peaceful planet that didn't face any real threats. It's quite possible she may have been sent here to get rid of her."

"I did wonder about that," Kat said. "Is she not popular?"

"She isn't *meant* to be popular," the XO said. "Once elected, our politicians serve only a single five-year term, then retire from public life. Civil servants such as herself are meant to support the elected ministers, not try to become popular and run for office themselves. It's quite possible she pushed too far . . . or that she accepted the assignment under the genuine belief that she was heading away from the war, where she could carry out her observations in peace."

"How unfortunate for her," Davidson observed.

Kat shrugged. "I'll try and make time to speak with her, when I have a moment," she said, reluctantly. "However, as long as she isn't causing trouble, what she does in her cabin isn't likely to be our concern."

The XO nodded. "I've had to alter the training schedules a couple of times," he said. "A handful of the older ships are having problems keeping a crew on duty at all times; I think we may have to concede that we're not going to be able to obey regulations, not now."

"As long as the mission is a success, no one will care," Kat predicted. Ideally, she needed at least two hundred additional crewmen, but she knew she'd been lucky to get enough personnel to provide each ship with a skeleton crew. "We can fudge the figures, if necessary, and time our attacks so our ships have a full crew."

"Aye, Captain," the XO said. He looked down at his datapad for a long moment. "With your permission, then, I will return to my duties."

"Granted," Kat said. "And thank you."

The XO nodded, then rose to his feet and left the cabin. Kat watched him go, then turned to Davidson. "Pat?"

"No major problems, so far," Davidson assured her. "Except, of course, that *someone* hasn't been keeping up with her exercises."

"If only I had the time," Kat said. She missed sparring with him too, although she knew he went easy on her. It wasn't as if she had the time to actually become a true martial artist, or the inclination to try. "How are you coping with the refugees?"

"Most of them are very motivated, although a handful are of two minds about the whole thing," Davidson said. "On one hand, they grew up with tales of the evils of the Theocracy; on the other, they're trying hard to blend into Commonwealth society and they don't want to remain a separate subculture."

Kat nodded. Tyre had always been welcoming to immigrants, but it had insisted on doing this on its terms. Immigrants were expected to blend into the mainstream within a single generation; an immigrant community that tried to remain isolated would eventually be broken apart by pressures from the mainstream or simply deported. She could understand why the refugees wanted to keep something of their old society, but Tyre could not allow them to do so. They were harming their children by clinging to the past.

"As long as they are prepared to fight when the time comes," she said. It was, no doubt, a problem that would solve itself, in time. The first generation would pass away and the second would be less motivated to keep itself together, while the mainstream was reaching out a welcoming hand. "Are they?"

"Oh, yes," Davidson said. "Several of them are in line for Marine training; they will probably get their chance, if they survive this mission. Proper experience is a right booster when the supervisors start taking a look at applicants."

Kat nodded. The Royal Tyre Marine Corps had been far better than anyone else at absorbing recruits from new member states; it made sense they'd be better at taking in the refugees too. But then, the Marines broke their recruits down to the bare essentials and then rebuilt them into Marines. It wasn't something that could be done on a large scale . . . after all, she reflected, everyone who volunteered for boot camp had known what they were getting into and they'd done it anyway.

"Then all we can do is wait for the first chance to put them to the test," she said. She paused; they hadn't had an opportunity for a proper chat since before she'd had her . . . disagreement . . . with Justin Deveron. They'd both been far too busy. "How did you cope with Tyre?"

"I don't think I like High Society," Davidson said. "How did they manage to produce you?"

Kat sighed. "There are three types of aristocratic brat," she said. "There are the firstborn children: the heir and the spare. They're taught to carry on the family business; the heir will inherit, everyone assumes, while the spare will be there to take over if necessary. After that, you have the middle children; the ones who will inherit smaller parts of the family's holdings but never claim any real power. They tend to get married off to seal deals; no one gives a damn what they do as long as they're reasonably discreet. And then you get the youngest children, the ones like me. They get trust funds; they'll never want for anything, but they won't have any power and they're largely worthless on the marriage market."

She sighed, again. "I got to choose my own path," she said. "I could have vanished into the Navy and been quite happy, if I'd been allowed."

"You make it sound . . . inhuman," Davidson observed.

"It is," Kat said. There was little room for true romance in High Society. Candy's string of partners hadn't changed her life in any way. "The system was designed to keep the original corporations in power— and, at the same time, make room for talented newcomers. But right now there are more talented newcomers, like William, than can be reasonably absorbed. It was never designed to cope with the combined stress of becoming the Commonwealth *and* a major war."

She shook her head. Davidson too was a talented newcomer, even if he'd been born on Tyre. Her father wouldn't have raised any objections if she'd wanted to marry him, then bear his children. Or, rather, combine his sperm with her eggs in an exowomb. But, at the same time, it wasn't a life he would have chosen for himself. She was far more tempted just to walk away, cash in her trust fund, buy a freighter, and vanish. It wasn't as if anyone needed her on Tyre.

Perhaps after the war, she thought as she checked her timetable. She'd been careful to ensure that they had an hour together before they started preparations to cross the border. It wasn't a whole day together, but it was more than she'd hoped for when she'd started planning. *We could go off together and forget everything.*

"There isn't much time," she said, reaching for him. His body, as always, felt rock solid against her fingers. "But we should have just long enough."

CHAPTER ELEVEN

Like many of the other oddities in hyperspace, no one had been able to come up with a reasonable explanation for the Horizon Reach. It wasn't a terrifying region of high-energy storms, but a zone where eddies and flows in hyperspace pushed ships off course and confused sensors so badly that it was hard, even with modern systems, to navigate safely. Indeed, it was easy, according to the files, for a starship to be deep within the Reach before discovering that it was surrounded by hyperspace distortions. It simply made no sense at all.

Unless it's actually a living thing, Kat thought, as *Lightning* and her squadron picked their way through the Reach. Keeping the fleet together was a minor nightmare, even without the threat of enemy starships patrolling the other side of the disturbance. *Reaching out for us and toying with our ships, then letting us go.*

She pushed the thought aside as two of her ships blinked off the display, then reappeared seconds later. They'd known there was a danger of losing contact, of having to meet up at the rendezvous point on the far side of the border, but it still chilled her to the bone to watch her ships seem to vanish. Another wave of distortion swept over the squadron, blurring her sensors for a long moment, and then fading away into nothingness. Ahead of them, she knew, was enemy territory.

"There's another disturbance moving towards us," Lieutenant Nicola Robertson warned. The navigation officer looked tired; she'd stayed at her station for hours, even though the rest of the crew had been rotated to ensure they remained fresh. "Suggest altering course to evade it."

"Do it," Kat ordered.

"Aye, Captain," Weiberg said. *Lightning* shivered slightly as she altered course. "We may be unable to avoid brushing up against the edge of the disturbance unless we reverse course completely."

Kat gritted her teeth. The sooner they were out of the Reach, the better. But if they reversed course, it was likely their passage would cause more disturbances, perhaps an outright energy storm. *That* would be far more dangerous than any minor disturbance.

"Try to avoid contact for as long as possible," she ordered finally. "But if we have to go through the disturbance, take us straight through."

She sucked in her breath. There were people—idiots, in her view—who delighted in trying to surf the edge of hyperspace distortions and storms. They tended not to come back, which didn't seem to have any effect on the sport's popularity. She'd wondered why it wasn't banned, but Davidson had pointed out that it was a twisted form of natural selection. Those who were stupid enough to risk their lives didn't deserve to breed. Even bare-knuckle fighting in a pit was safer than riding a hyperspace storm.

Another shudder ran through the ship. "The disturbance is growing stronger, Captain," Nicola warned. "But it looks to have very limited staying power."

"Understood," Kat said flatly. Had she made a mistake? It was too late now. "Take us straight through."

The ship shuddered one final time, then broke free. Kat let out a breath as her squadron followed *Lightning* through the disturbance, heading right into enemy space. She looked at the tactical display, which was slowly recovering from the Reach. There didn't seem to be any sign of prowling starships on the far side, but she knew her sensors were unreliable in hyperspace. A single ship could be holding position, close enough to the Reach to watch for intruders while far enough to be difficult for her to see. And there was no hope of using a cloaking device in hyperspace. If they were seen, they were seen.

"Local space appears clear, Captain," Lieutenant-Commander Christopher John Roach said. The tactical officer looked tired as well, but alert. "There's no sign of any enemy presence."

Which leads to a simple question, Kat thought. *Did they decide there was no point in guarding the Reach, now there's a war on, or are they strapped for ships?*

She pushed the thought aside as she leaned forward. "Do we have a solid link with the entire squadron?"

"Aye, Captain," the XO said. "They made it through the Reach."

Kat nodded in relief. She'd planned for losing contact with one or two ships, for having to wait at the RV point for any stragglers to catch up with the rest of the squadron, but it looked as though she wouldn't have to stand by. The first piece of real luck, she figured, since she'd realized just how important the mission actually was. She smiled at the thought, then looked up at the star chart. There was no *objective* difference between hyperspace on one side of the border and the other, but it *felt* different. They were within enemy territory.

You've been here before, she told herself firmly. *It isn't anything special.*

"Lay in a course to our destination," she ordered. They'd fly an evasive course, avoiding the most logical shipping lanes within enemy space, although that wouldn't make it impossible for the enemy to detect them if a Theocracy ship got lucky. "Mr. XO. Are any of the ships reporting problems?"

"No, Captain," the XO said. "They're ready to follow us to the target star."

"Good," Kat said. "Helm?"

"Course laid in, Captain," Weiberg said. The display changed, showing a course from their current location to UNAS-RD-46785. It looked rather like a roller coaster, Kat had to admit, but there was no need to make a beeline for their target. "We're ready to depart."

"Take us there," Kat ordered. She glanced at the display again. "Remember, evade even the slightest *hint* of an enemy starship. We don't want to risk detection before we're in a position to do some damage."

"Aye, Captain," Weiberg said.

Kat sighed, cursing the oddities of hyperspace under her breath. They might detect a starship, only to discover that it was a sensor glitch or a reflection of something thousands of light years away. The only advantage was that any prowling enemy starship that caught a sniff of the squadron *might* assume it was a glitch, although Kat knew she couldn't take that for granted. If *she'd* been in charge of defending a border, *she* would have made it damn clear that all sensor readings were to be checked, just in case.

But if we happened to run across a lone freighter, we could grab it before the crew could make their escape, she thought sourly. *It just isn't worth the risk.*

She settled back in her command chair as the minutes turned into hours. Local space seemed to be surprisingly clear, both of hyperspace distortions and enemy starships. If Kat hadn't *known* they were in enemy territory, she wasn't sure she would have believed it. The Theocracy was a space-faring society, so where were their ships? But it was also a highly regulated society. They probably didn't have half the problems that the Commonwealth had in setting up a convoy system and making it stick.

But convoys tend to be delayed, Kat thought. It hadn't been *that* long since she'd been forced to study basic economics, even though she'd been bored out of her mind. *A lone freighter crew can lose their ship if they fail to make delivery on schedule, even though it wasn't their fault there wasn't an escort ship available. And if they go on their own and run into raiders, they will lose their ship anyway.*

Her father had gone on about it, she recalled, during one family dinner. He'd pointed out that the bigger corporations had been blocking any legislation that would absolve smaller shippers of any debts incurred because they'd had to wait for a convoy. The Falcone Corporation could eat its losses, if necessary, but a family-run freighter, living hand-to-mouth, couldn't afford to miss even a single payday. Even now, with a war on, it was a problem the Commonwealth had yet to solve. Any proposal to change matters was blocked in committee.

She pushed the thought aside as she rose to her feet. "Mr. XO, you have the bridge," she said. "I'll be in my office. Inform me if we run into any problems."

"Aye, Captain," the XO said.

Kat nodded, stepped through the hatch, and sat down at her desk. The next set of reports was already waiting for her, although they were nothing more than brief updates on the older ships after their passage through the Reach. Nothing seemed to have gone badly wrong, she was relieved to note; one ship had had problems matching its drive field to cope with the distortion, but the crew had managed to compensate. She silently thanked them for their service, then checked the reports from different departments. The tactical department had several suggestions for later targets, but they couldn't guarantee anything. Kat shrugged and filed them away for later consideration. No one, in her experience, could guarantee *anything*.

Her communicator bleeped. "Captain," the XO said, "the observer has requested a meeting with me after I finish my shift. Would that be permissible?"

Kat sighed. The XO had three more hours, just long enough for her to take a catnap and then return to the bridge. "That should be fine," she said, closing the terminal. There was no point in reading her reports now, not when there was nothing marked *urgent*. "I'll relieve you on the bridge beforehand."

William frowned inwardly as he stopped in front of the observer's hatch and pressed his hand against the buzzer. He hadn't thought much of Rose MacDonald when they'd first met and he hadn't seen anything, since then, that suggested his first impressions were wrong. She was a political appointee, plain and simple, and even though she came from a planet *renowned* for being plain and simple, she was still a political appointee. Hell, in many ways, she was more dangerous than a politician. *She* had never had to stand for election.

And if she doesn't have to stand for office, he thought as the hatch opened, *she doesn't have to leave either.*

He stepped into the room and glanced around. Rose was sitting behind a desk, her dark eyes peering down at a datapad in her hand. William couldn't help flashing back to the days he'd spent in school, with grim-faced matrons patrolling the desks, willing to rap the knuckles of any boy they caught concentrating on anything but schoolwork. He honestly couldn't say he'd learned much at school, but at least he'd mastered the basic skills he needed to become an apprentice and then a spacer. It was easy, somehow, to imagine Rose as a teacher.

"Commander," Rose said as the hatch closed behind him. "Thank you for coming."

"You're welcome," William said, warily. He had no idea what Rose actually *wanted* and that worried him. Admiral Morrison's political games had been bad enough, but at least he'd played them during peacetime. This was war. "What can I do for you?"

"I've been reviewing the records," Rose said. She looked up at him suddenly. "Why weren't you offered your own command? You are very well qualified to command one of the ships out there."

She waved a hand towards the bulkhead, her dark eyes never leaving his face. "You have over thirty years in the Navy," she added. "Why don't you have your own ship?"

William swore inwardly. Was there any right answer? "I was offered one of those ships," he said truthfully. "However, I believed it would be better for me to remain as XO on *Lightning* and combine those duties with those of a fleet coordination officer."

"Which leads to a different question," Rose said. "Why doesn't your commander have much of a staff?"

"This whole operation was put together at breakneck pace," William said. Reading between the lines, he had a feeling that Operation Knife hadn't been meant to depart for at least another month. Captain Falcone's indiscretion on Tyre might have forced the departure date forward. "Furthermore, the entire Navy has a colossal personnel shortfall. We were, quite frankly, lucky to get as many officers and crew as we did. A full staff was probably too much to ask."

Rose tilted her head slightly, then returned to the original subject. "Your commanding officer joined the Navy in 2408 and entered active service, as a lieutenant, in 2412. In 2416, she was promoted to commander and became XO of a battlecruiser; in 2420 she was promoted to captain and placed in command of HMS *Lightning*. By my count, she has spent no more than twelve years in the Navy. Less, in fact, if you count from the year she actually graduated from Piker's Peak and entered active service."

Her eyes were suddenly very sharp. "So why haven't you been placed in command of a starship?"

William cursed under his breath, fighting to keep his expression under control. If he told the truth, he would be disloyal to the Navy; if he lied, he would breach his own sense of personal honor as well as making himself look a fool. The hell of it was that he'd had similar objections himself to Kat Falcone, when he'd discovered she'd been promoted over his head, only to lose them when she proved herself. What did he say? What *could* he say?

Rose spoke before he could come up with an answer. "I have been reading through the records," she said. "It is clear that there is a strong bias in favor of candidates from Tyre, graduates from Piker's Peak, in the promotions board. You should have been given your own command years ago, but you were constantly pushed back by newcomers from Tyre."

"I don't think that's quite fair," William said crossly. Was she going to make him defend a system he despised? "There are certain factors you are not taking into account."

"Oh," Rose said. She fixed him with a gimlet stare. "And those factors would be?"

William took a breath. "Tyre was settled by fourteen corporations with a staggering amount of wealth, industrial knowledge, and suchlike between them," he said. "By the time the Tyre Development Corporation was folded into the Kingdom of Tyre, Tyre already possessed shipyards, planetary defenses, and a growing industrial base. It proved adept at recruiting talented outsiders and giving them a stake in the system, allowing it to grow outwards at terrifying speed. In short, by any reasonable definition, it was a success. They were so quick to establish themselves that they have never known danger, hardship, or want."

"Until now," Rose said.

"Until now," William agreed. Tyre had never suffered a terrorist campaign, not until the Theocracy had taken the war onto the streets. "We, on the other hand, lacked most of those advantages.

"Hebrides was intended to be a low-tech colony right from the start. Modern technology was kept under strict control. We would be farmers, we thought; our society would consist of hamlets and small towns, scattered across the planetary surface. Our government would have very limited power; the church would provide what moral leadership we needed; and our people would become tough, spurred on by hardship. We never wanted to be considered a significant world."

"And then we were attacked," Rose said. "I know this as well as you, Commander."

William nodded. "I shall be blunt," he said. "The Commonwealth needs to integrate newcomers carefully, to make sure they actually fit in. I may have served in the Navy for thirty years, but I never went to Piker's Peak. Nor did many others who were absorbed into the Navy, after we joined the Commonwealth. This actually hampered their ability to rise in the ranks, because the Commonwealth had problems knowing just what they could do."

He took a breath. "However, those of us who went through Piker's Peak—which can only take a small number of candidates every year—rise through the ranks without problems . . ."

"But not as fast as your captain," Rose pointed out.

"The captain handled herself well," William snapped. He would not have insulted the captain behind her back under any circumstances, but he didn't *want* to insult her. "Her rise does, however, indicate another problem. Because Tyre was so predominately powerful within the Commonwealth, their political system gives their personnel advantages. Many of them are already linked to politicians and aristocrats, others have the opportunity to make useful connections . . . opportunities that are largely denied to mustangs or candidates from out-system."

"That problem needs to be fixed," Rose said, sternly.

"Yes, it does," William said. "The problem, however, is simple. Can it be fixed without weakening the Navy?"

Rose eyed him for a long moment. "*Can* it be fixed without weakening the Navy?"

William sighed. "Seeing we have a war on, we have a need for hundreds of new officers," he said. "You could suggest pushing for an expansion of Piker's Peak. We already have basic training camps in each system for crewmen; there's no reason we cannot expand Piker's Peak, perhaps even set up alternate campuses away from Tyre. And with more slots open, we could get more candidates from newer systems."

"That isn't an immediate solution," Rose said.

"I don't think there *is* an immediate solution," William said. He forced himself to meet her eyes. "Creating divisions within the Navy's ranks, pitting officers from Tyre against officers from everywhere else, will cause short- and long-term problems. The only way to avoid such a disaster is to expand the training academy, perhaps even have representatives select candidates from their homeworlds. It won't be easy, but it has to be done."

Rose nodded slowly. "I will so advise my superiors," she said. "But I don't think I have to tell you that this is causing problems back home."

William shook his head. "I think they have worse problems right now," he said. "Hebrides is a *religious* world. The Theocracy probably targeted us because they saw Hebrides as competition, even though we didn't seek new believers. Right now, if we don't win the war, Hebrides is doomed."

CHAPTER TWELVE

"Transit complete, Captain," Weiberg said.

"No enemy vessels detected," Roach added. The display flickered, then started to fill up with a handful of tactical icons. "There's no hint they may be under cloak."

"Take us into cloak," Kat ordered. The UNAS-RD-46785 system might be useless—apart from the red star itself, the only items on the display were a handful of comets and asteroids—but if the Theocracy *was* using it as a waypoint, there might be an observer or two watching the system from a safe distance. "Mr. XO?"

"The squadron reports ready, Captain," the XO said. "They're going into cloak now."

Kat nodded, feeling something churning in her stomach. They could be wrong . . . and if they were, they were going to waste at least a week, a week they could be using to wreak havoc elsewhere. On an interstellar scale, a week probably didn't really matter, but it was still worrying. The best guesses of worlds important to the Theocracy were just that, guesses. She might as well start pulling names and targets out of a hat.

"Hold position here," she ordered. She briefly considered deploying drones, then decided it might alert any prowling enemy ships to their presence. So far, it didn't *look* as though they'd been detected, but that could change at any moment. "Keep a sharp eye on the passive sensors and inform me if anything appears."

She keyed her console, then brought up the XO's report on his discussion with the observer and read it for the third time. The observer was going to be trouble, Kat knew, even though she had a point. Maybe she would do something relatively harmless, even beneficial, by urging the expansion of Piker's Peak . . . or maybe she would press for something far more dangerous, something that would tear the Navy apart. She cursed under her breath, then brought up her own report to her father and read it once again. There was no hope of sending it home unless she detached a ship, but at least it would be ready.

The day passed slowly. Kat handed command to the XO, slept for several hours, and then returned to the bridge. The XO ran training and tracking exercises for the crew, reporting to her that gunnery competitions between the tactical officers were keeping them all on their toes. Kat allowed herself a smile, then told him to make sure he got some sleep for himself before the shit hit the fan. God alone knew how long it would be before the next convoy came along, assuming they weren't completely wrong about the enemy still using UNAS-RD-46785 as a waypoint, but they'd need to be alert when the time came.

It was four days before the tactical officer sounded the alert.

"Captain," Roach said, as a red icon blinked into existence in front of her. "A courier boat just popped out of hyperspace."

Kat frowned. "Just one?"

"Yes, Captain," Roach said. "It's hard to be sure, but I'd say she came over the border."

The former border, Kat thought. Cadiz was now firmly in enemy hands and, even though the inhabitants had resisted the Commonwealth with bitter determination, she couldn't help feeling sorry for them. The Theocracy was a far worse enemy. *And are they here to meet someone or what?*

"Sound yellow alert," she ordered. It was unlikely a courier boat could detect the squadron, unless they got *very* unlucky, but its presence strongly suggested that someone else was on the way. "Do *not* do anything that might imperil the cloaking device."

"Aye, Captain," Roach said.

Kat studied the courier boat as it held position, drifting in orbit around the red star. It was really nothing more than a giant drive section with a tiny crew compartment at the front; indeed, it was clear the Theocracy had merely copied and updated a UN design that had been brought into service before the Breakaway Wars. *She* wouldn't have cared to serve on a courier boat, where there was barely enough room for two crewmen to swing a cat. In her experience, their crews tended to be a little weird. Some were lovers, enjoying their privacy as they flew from system to system; others hated each other so thoroughly that they couldn't stand to be in the same room once they reached their destination. And yet they kept flying together . . . she shook her head, pushing the matter aside. No doubt an overpaid psychologist would come up with an elaborate theory to explain it if anyone asked . . .

Maybe they just know the other is reliable, she thought, after a moment. She'd learned the difference between someone reliable and someone likable very early on and, in her training, the former was always preferable. *They rely on each other even though they detest each other.*

An alarm sounded. "Captain, a hyperspace gate is opening," Roach said. "I'm counting seven starships . . . no, twelve. Three destroyers, one cruiser, and eight freighters."

Kat tensed as the display updated. "Sound red alert," she ordered. Alarms howled through the ship. "Bring the ship to battle stations, but keep the cloak in place."

"Aye, Captain," Roach said.

The XO hurried onto the bridge and took his console. "All ships report ready, Captain," he said after a moment. "They're red and hot."

Kat nodded, running through possible options in her mind. The cruiser looked to be modern; the destroyers were probably refitted . . . and the freighters were very much a mixed bag. It was unlikely, though, that any of them lacked a hyperdrive. They'd be grossly inefficient if they needed to travel without a larger ship to open the gateways into hyperspace for them.

But that might suit the enemy fine, she thought, recalling just how many ships had limped across the border. *You can't run away if you're restricted to STL speeds.*

"Lock weapons on the enemy warships," she ordered. If the cruiser happened to be looking for trouble, they *might* detect the cloaking fields. "Target secondary missiles on the freighters. If they start preparing to escape, I want them destroyed."

"Aye, Captain," Roach said.

Kat nodded. "Take us into firing range," she ordered. "And prepare to fire."

"Aye, Captain," Weiberg said.

"Watch them carefully," Kat added. "If they sweep us, fire at once; don't wait for orders, just fire at once."

"Aye, Captain," Roach said again.

Kat smiled, then keyed her console, hastily checking her calculations against the tactical computers. How long would it take for the enemy to recycle their hyperdrives and jump back out? Long enough for them to be caught by her missiles? It wasn't standard procedure to keep the drives warmed up, not when it put a great deal of wear and tear on the system, but this was wartime. She could see advantages in keeping her drives ready to open a gateway, even if it meant they would have to be replaced sooner rather than later. It all depended on just how paranoid the enemy was feeling.

"Entering firing range," Roach reported. "There's no sign they've detected us."

Unless they're very cool customers, Kat thought. A cloaked ship couldn't raise shields without breaking the cloak. If someone had picked up the flotilla on passive sensors, they might *just* wait until the ship slipped into point-blank range and then open fire before the incoming ship could realize it was under attack and raise its shields. *But would someone with that sort of nerve be left running convoy escort missions?*

She took a breath. "Attack pattern beta," she ordered. "Fire at will."

Lightning shuddered as she unleashed the first spread of missiles, aimed right at the enemy cruiser. The display updated rapidly as the other ships fired too, launching enough missiles to overwhelm an enemy force twice the size of the one facing them. Kat hadn't been inclined to take chances, but as the enemy ships struggled to react, it rapidly became clear that they'd been caught completely by surprise. Their point defense was barely effective and they didn't even launch a single missile in response.

If nothing else, they'll be more paranoid after this, Kat thought. *And the wear and tear on their sensors will make it all worthwhile.*

Cold hatred burned through her gut as the enemy cruiser twisted in a desperate attempt to escape the inevitable. Seven missiles slammed into its shields, knocking them down before they could even solidify; three more slammed into its hull, blowing it apart into an expanding ball of plasma. Kat watched the cruiser die, then turned her attention to the destroyers; one of them, with a captain and crew who were clearly on the ball, managed to launch a broadside of their own before they were smashed to atoms. But they'd had no time to target the missiles properly, let alone set up a tactical assault program. The entire spread was wiped out before they could even lock onto their targets.

"All four warships and the courier boat have been destroyed," Roach reported. Kat hadn't seen the tiny starship die. "Missiles locked on enemy freighters."

"Communications, send the surrender demand," Kat ordered. "Tactical, prepare to open fire if they try to escape."

"Aye, Captain," Nicola said. Roach echoed her a moment later. "Message sent."

Kat rolled her eyes. She'd originally intended to record the surrender demand herself, but Davidson had pointed out that the Theocracy's soldiers and spacers wouldn't want to surrender to a woman. It sounded absurd to her—her gender had no bearing on her ability to command a starship—yet if it prevented unnecessary bloodshed, she could cope with it. And besides, if the enemy was so foolish as to deny themselves the talents of half of their population, she might as well take advantage of it. There was a certain kind of advantage in being constantly underestimated.

Princess Drusilla certainly took advantage of it, she thought with wry amusement. *They never anticipated she could actually steal a freighter, let alone make a run for the Commonwealth.*

"No response," Nicola said.

"Two of the freighters are powering up their drives," Roach added.

"Target them with active sensors," Kat ordered. She didn't need to refine her targeting data any further, but even civilian-grade equipment couldn't fail to pick up the sweep. It was a threat, a clear warning that she was prepared to open fire on a defenseless freighter. But then, defenseless or not, it was part of the enemy's war effort. "And repeat the surrender demand."

"No response," Nicola said.

"Target the two runaways," Kat ordered. They'd make their escape into hyperspace if she hesitated any longer. "Fire!"

"Aye, Captain," Roach said. He tapped his console. The freighters, protected only by civilian-grade shields, were rapidly blown into atoms. "Targets destroyed."

"The remaining freighters are signaling their surrender," Nicola said.

Kat allowed herself a sigh of relief mixed with concern. It was possible that the enemy ships had chosen to surrender, but equally possible they were planning a trap. A crew of fanatics wouldn't hesitate to blow their drives once her Marines were onboard, killing everyone and leaving her with fewer troops. The safest course of action would be to simply kill all of the remaining freighters, but she needed the ships and their computers intact. And besides, destroying surrendering ships would be cold-blooded murder.

"Inform the Marines that they are cleared to depart," she ordered. "Communications, inform the enemy that they are to cut their shields, drives, and active sensors. If they comply with our orders, they will be taken into custody and transferred to a POW camp, where they will be held until the end of the war. Any resistance, however, will be met by the destruction of the offending vessel."

The XO opened a private channel to her implants. "They may not be safe when they return home if we take them as POWs," he said. "We may want to offer them a permanent home."

Kat frowned. The idea of butchering one's own personnel was strange and alien to her, but it fit in with the Theocracy's system. They wouldn't want anyone who'd seen a different society to return to the mainstream, certainly not a society as irreligious as the Commonwealth. No, the XO was right; it was much more likely that returning them to their homeworld would sign their death sentence.

"See to it, if they're willing to cooperate," she sent back. "The Marine intelligence officers can interrogate them, then make a few offers."

She closed the channel, then turned to watch as the Marine shuttles slipped closer to their targets. None of the freighters seemed anything but conventional; Kat couldn't help feeling nervous as the Marines closed in, then docked on the hulls. A single mistake now could lead to disaster. She would have preferred to deal with the freighters one by one, but the Marines had different ideas. The enemy couldn't be allowed time for second thoughts, let alone a chance to put those thoughts into action. Rigging a freighter to blow, unlike a warship, would take time.

Unless they already have a self-destruct system, she thought. *It would be just the sort of thing they'd have.*

There was no point in trying to issue orders, she knew, as the Marines swarmed into the enemy ships. They'd treat everyone they encountered as a potential enemy, at least until they knew better; the crew would be bound, stacked against the wall . . . or stunned, if they tried to put up a fight. At least the Marines might avoid the horrors she'd seen on pirate ships. Kat forced herself to wait, despite her growing nervousness, as one by one the Marine units reported in. The enemy ships had been secured.

"Captain," Davidson reported, "two of the ships are crammed with janissaries."

Kat sucked in her breath. "Can you control them?"

"They're unarmed and unarmored," Davidson assured her. "We can keep them under control, if necessary; hell, they were practically being treated as prisoners anyway."

"Good," Kat said. "Do you have a head count?"

"Five thousand on this freighter; I'm presuming a similar figure on the other ship," Davidson reported, after a moment. "Fucked if I know how they fit so many into a handful of holds."

"It's astonishing how many people will fit into something if you squeeze," Kat muttered, recalling evacuation drills during her first cruise. Officially, shuttles were rated to carry no more than twenty people, but more could be crammed in if there was no other option. It was uncomfortable, to say the least, yet if there was no choice . . . they'd just have to cope with it. "Can you handle them long enough for us to come to a decision?"

"I believe so," Davidson said. "The system here is set to drop sleeping gas—or outright poison—into the compartments, so we can put them to sleep if necessary. It's more like they're transferring prisoners than soldiers."

The XO entered the conversation. "They train their soldiers to be extremely violent," he said softly. "Perhaps they fear to let them off the leash when they're away from occupied worlds."

Kat winced, remembering the reports from Cadiz. Davidson was a hardened Marine, yet he'd still had nightmares over what he'd seen as the Theocracy occupied the planet. Anyone who refused to cooperate was beaten, raped, or killed; the enemy soldiers had carried out their orders with gusto, using extreme force against even minor targets. As a terror tactic, she had to admit it was workable, yet it needed to be controlled. What was the point of using terror as a weapon if you couldn't turn it off on command?

"Or maybe they just know they have too many people crammed together," Davidson said tartly. Boot camp tended to separate those who could handle close confines from those who couldn't. "I'd be surprised if they didn't have a riot or two."

He cleared his throat. "Orders, Captain?"

"Keep the soldiers on the ships, for now," Kat ordered. Ten thousand enemy soldiers, assuming the estimate was accurate: keeping them would be a major headache, but slaughtering them all would be cold-blooded murder. "What do the other ships hold?"

"Weapons and food supplies, mainly," Davidson reported. He sounded more than a little perplexed. "One of them is apparently crammed full to bursting with ration packs. There's enough food on the freighter to feed a small army."

Kat exchanged a glance with the XO. Ration packs? It made no sense. There wasn't a world in the Commonwealth that couldn't feed itself, or support an occupation force if necessary. If the Theocracy was tying up a freighter with ration packs, it was wasting space it could be using for weapons, ammunition, spare parts, or anything else an advancing invasion force might need. It definitely made no sense.

"Transfer the crews to our ships, then the techs can go to work," Kat said. They'd have to move the freighters before the enemy realized what had happened and sent a battle squadron to the dull red star, but her most pessimistic estimate suggested it would be at least a week before the enemy could react. "Tell your intelligence staff to offer them a chance to switch sides, if they like. They don't have much of a future in a POW camp, no matter who wins."

The XO grinned at her, but said nothing.

"Aye, Captain," Davidson said. "I think we managed to take some data from the ships; a couple of crews purged their databases, but the others remain intact. The techs can give us a better idea of just what we're facing."

"Good," Kat said. "And pass a message to your men from me. Well done."

She closed the channel, then looked at the XO. "Pass the same message to the rest of the squadron," she added. "They did *very* well."

"The next time will be harder," the XO reminded her. "They'll realize we're out here soon enough."

"I know," Kat said. Surprise had given them a one-sided victory. A squadron of modern destroyers would be hard for the squadron to handle, even with *Lightning's* heavy firepower. "But let them enjoy it, for the moment."

CHAPTER THIRTEEN

William wasn't sure what he'd expected when he boarded the Theocratic freighter. A smelly death trap, like the pirate vessels he'd seen, or a starship held together by spit and baling wire, like far too many commercial ships whose owners were running short of money. Or, perhaps, something akin to the Royal Navy's fleet train. Indeed, his first impression was that there really wasn't any difference between one fleet train and the other. But the more he explored the hull, the stranger it became.

"They've placed religious slogans everywhere," the Marine said as he led the way onto the bridge. "They're even written on the command chair."

"I see," William said. The bridge was larger than he'd expected for a freighter, but the command chair looked hideously uncomfortable. A pair of inspection hatches had been removed, allowing the Marine techs to access the enemy computer system. "Have you found anything useful?"

"Quite a bit," one of the techs said. She was a young woman, wearing a uniform that marked her as an Electronic Warfare specialist. "They wanted to purge the system, but they made the mistake of basing it on a commercial design; the purge was simply ineffective and they didn't try to destroy the datacores physically. Any *military* system would have been reduced to dust in seconds."

She smiled as she sat upright. "I don't think they had *much* beforehand, to be fair, but they do have quite a few pieces of data," she added. "This ship moved between a dozen worlds before it ever left enemy space, which it first did a couple of days after the Battle of Cadiz."

They outran their fleet train, William thought. Intelligence had suspected as much, but it was nice, if a little pointless, to finally have confirmation. *They had to call a halt long enough to rearm their ships and make repairs.*

He shrugged, then peered down at the datacore. "Can you tell us anything useful about enemy space?"

"I'm hoping we can put it together, in time," the tech said. "Anywhere this ship went, I think, has to be important. They were carrying weapons, so it's probable they picked them up at their *last* destination"— she activated the star chart projector—"here. Logically, that star system is either a supply dump or a manufacturing center."

"Probably the former," William grunted. The Theocracy wouldn't want to risk placing a production node so close to the front lines. Hell, the Commonwealth had wanted to follow the same logic. "Is there much else?"

"There's a great many religious texts," the tech said. "I honestly couldn't find anything resembling manuals, let alone teaching aides; I think they were only ever expected to eat, sleep, and study religion while they were off duty. I'll forward everything we get to the intelligence staff, sir. They'll probably be able to draw more from it."

"Carry on," William said as Davidson stepped onto the bridge. He turned to face the younger man, who saluted. "What can you tell me about the crew?"

"All male, all largely uneducated," Davidson said. His eyes darkened with disapproval. "I don't think they could actually *repair* anything, if they ran into trouble. The best they could do is swap one component for another—and God help them if they didn't have a replacement on hand. I had a look at the ship's paperwork and it's long on exhortations and short on anything actually *practical*. Honestly, sir, if I saw this lot applying for a spacer's certificate, I'd probably die laughing."

William wasn't surprised. A spacer's certificate required a technical education, which required an understanding of the basis of science and engineering. It contrasted oddly with the Theocracy's insistence on religious education, where questioning was flatly against the rules and probably harshly punished. They'd squared the circle, William realized slowly, by making the system as simple as possible, which would work as long as the crew had spare parts on hand. The idea of making a *missing* component would not only be beyond them, it would likely be beyond their comprehension.

"They must have a repair crew with better education somewhere," he mused out loud. "A group who can actually produce newer and better pieces of equipment."

"Or maybe they don't," Davidson said. "Is our tech better than theirs or not?"

"I'm not sure," William said. "The general intelligence briefings suggested that we have better sensors, but there aren't many other advantages."

"That will change," Davidson predicted. "We simply have a much larger base of trained personnel to draw on, people who may produce the next great invention. They may have determined on war because another ten years of solid advancement would render us invincible, at least to them."

William gave a trademark shrug. "Are any of the crew worth keeping?"

"The captain and a couple of his officers were a little better educated than the rest," Davidson said. "I've taken the liberty of separating them from the others, so we can draw intelligence from them without contamination. The others would be in deep shit if they actually had to fend for a living."

"Good," William said. "Do you have a manifest?"

"Here," Davidson confirmed. "Weapons, mainly; I think they were meant to be mated with the janissaries as soon as they reached their destination. I've taken a few samples for study, but it doesn't look as though they've produced anything new."

"That's something, at least," William said. "Can we use them?"

"Not yet," Davidson said. "But we will see."

William nodded. "I'll check out the rest of the ship, then get back to *Lightning*," he said flatly. "The captain will be calling a meeting at 1800; you're expected to attend."

"Of course," Davidson said. "It will be my honor."

"If the data is to be believed," Lieutenant (Intelligence) Sandra Byzantium said, "this convoy was *en route* to Cadiz. They were meant to make a stop here, as predicted, so the courier boat could confirm that it was still safe to proceed. If they were told to wait, they would fall back to here"—she tapped a location on the star chart—"and await orders. This star system—it's called Aswan—is apparently a forward deployment base."

"Probably where they massed one of their attack fleets," the XO muttered.

"Probably," Kat agreed. It wasn't much, but at least they were starting to put together a map of enemy space. "Do we know much about it?"

"Very little," Sandra admitted. "The UN Survey Service swept through the system in 2270, but they found very little beyond a couple of Mars-class worlds and a single gas giant. There was never any attempt to settle the system, according to the records. I think there were too many Earth-class worlds in the nearby region."

"So no local population," Kat mused. "Could the Mars-class worlds have been terraformed?"

"Probably, but someone would have had to make the investment," Sandra said. "There's no record that anyone actually *did* until the Theocracy absorbed Aswan within its borders."

She paused, then continued. "I have also identified a handful of smaller worlds," she said. "This one"—she tapped a point on the display—"is apparently a penal world. The Theocracy has been sending people there for daring to disagree with its policies rather than simply killing them outright. There's no explanation in the files, but according to the prisoners the world is borderline habitable and the Theocracy is hoping the prisoners will make it *more* habitable or die trying. One of the freighters we were forced to destroy was a prison ship, according to the prisoners; it dumped its passengers there, then joined the convoy into occupied space."

"To take more prisoners," Davidson said. He gave Kat a sharp look. "Captain, they could be dumping POWs there."

Kat nodded slowly. "So we should try to rescue them, if possible," she said. "How long would it take us to get to the penal world?"

"Five days, assuming we fly a straight-line course," Sandra said.

"Which we can't, because we may need to evade enemy ships," Kat said. She looked down at her hands for a long moment. Cold logic suggested she would be better hitting a major world, but she couldn't leave POWs in enemy hands. "What sort of defenses does it have?"

"Unknown," Sandra said. "There's almost no tactical data stored in the captured datacores at all."

"They do have a mania about security," Davidson agreed. "Even a maggot with a couple of weeks at boot camp would know more than the enemy spacers."

"Then we'll have to sneak into the system and find out," Kat said. "Do we have any update on how long it will be before they realize they've lost a freighter convoy?"

"The courier boat was meant to head directly to Aswan, once it passed on its message," Sandra said. "I'd assume no more than five days, perhaps less. They would have been expected to fly like the clappers."

"Of course," Kat said. There would be some leeway—even the Theocracy had to understand that keeping schedules on an interstellar scale wasn't easy—but how much? Better to assume the worst. "We'll leave here as soon as reasonably possible."

She looked at Davidson. "Which leaves us with a dilemma," she added. "What do we do with the prisoners?"

"Transfer them to the janissary ships, then send them all back home," Davidson said. He ticked off points on his fingers as he spoke. "We can't keep them asleep indefinitely, not with the gas their masters use; we can't butcher them; and we can't abandon them in deep space . . ."

"We could abandon them on the penal world," the XO suggested. "At least they'd have a *chance* to survive. Sending them back to Admiral Christian's forward base runs the risk of having them intercepted in transit."

Kat considered it briefly, then frowned. "Can we hope to extract any useful information from them?"

"Probably not," Davidson said. "Most of them are utterly ignorant of anything we might consider useful, and the janissaries, at least, are outright dangerous. Better to wash our hands of them as quickly as possible."

"Then we drop them on the penal world," Kat decided. "As for the remaining ships, we'll move them to the first RV and hold them there. They might come in handy."

"Aye, Captain," the XO said. "We could probably use the transport ships to spring POWs from the penal world."

"Yep," Kat agreed. She took a breath. "I'll want to see a breakdown of everything we know about enemy space, now that we've captured some data."

"Of course, Captain," Sandra said. "I'm preparing a complete download now."

"Good," Kat said. "Dismissed."

She waited for the lieutenant to leave, then looked at the two men. "Our first strike was a complete success," she said. "But where do we need to improve?"

"We were quite lucky," the XO said. "Not just in our choice of targets, but in the escorts they attached to their convoy. We might not get so lucky the second time."

"There were some glitches with the boarding parties, which will be extensively detailed in my report," Davidson said darkly. Kat knew he'd want a chance to fix the problems before anyone else get involved. "At least we know where to concentrate, now that we've got a real success under our belts."

Kat nodded. "Detach one of the patrol boats and send it to Aswan," she ordered. "I don't expect any heroics, but I want some good passive sensor sweeps of the system. If it *is* a forward base for the enemy, I want to know if we can hit it or if it's too strong for anything smaller than a superdreadnought squadron."

"Aye, Captain," the XO said.

"Once that ship is underway, take the rest of the squadron and our prizes into hyperspace and set course for the first waypoint," she added. "Once there, we can set course for the penal world. If we run into something bigger than us . . . well, at least they won't be able to recover those freighters."

The XO saluted cheerfully. "We'll be costing them more and more freighters as we continue the attacks," he said as he rose to his feet. "If nothing else, they'll need to pull ships back from the front line to chase us."

"That's the plan," Kat said. "Let me know once we have an ETA to the first waypoint."

She ran her hand through her hair as the XO headed to the hatch and stepped through it into the corridor beyond.

"It could have been a great deal worse," she said softly. There weren't many people she would confide her doubts to, but Davidson was definitely one of them. "We could have run into something much bigger than us."

"Of course," Davidson said. He didn't seem inclined to worry about it. "But you would have broken contact, if you'd been detected at all."

He took a long breath. "The interrogations didn't reveal much useful information," he added, "but some background data was quite worrying. Our captured prisoners told us about the propaganda the Theocracy is putting out. Apparently, the Commonwealth not only started the war; it's butchering prisoners on sight and sacrificing them to the devil."

"*They* clearly didn't believe it," Kat observed. The Commonwealth hadn't had much opportunity to take prisoners, but mistreating anyone taken into custody was strictly forbidden. "Or they would never have surrendered."

"They took a chance, after we proved ourselves willing to shoot anyone who tried to escape," Davidson said. "Kat, I've got intelligence teams working with the prisoners, trying to put together a picture of enemy society. It isn't very reassuring. You know we thought things were bad on Cadiz? It's far worse on worlds that have been part of the Theocracy for decades. Much of the population accepts, like sheep, that what they've been told is true, that there's no point in actually thinking for themselves . . ."

"We knew that," Kat pointed out.

"It's a nightmare," Davidson said. "You know, as well as I do, just how modern technology can be used for population control. Everything they tell us makes it clear that the Theocracy keeps its population under very tight control indeed. Men are given a very basic education, mostly centered around religion, then pushed into jobs or the military; women are kept at home, then married off to have the next generation of babies. Their population density is unbelievable."

"Perhaps we shouldn't believe it," Kat said. "They could be lying."

"We have them under constant monitoring," Davidson assured her. "Even a heavily augmented operative would have problems lying successfully—and these men do not have any augmentations. No implanted weapons or senses, no booster caches; they don't even have basic neural links or any other form of implant. I don't think they're trying to lie to us.

"The commander of the first freighter to surrender is the seventh of fifteen boys; apparently, he has five sisters he rarely saw before they were married off. His oldest brother has seven children; his second-oldest brother has nine. These aren't members of the aristocracy, I think; they're common citizens."

Kat frowned. *She* was the youngest of ten children, but large families weren't normal on Tyre, at least outside the aristocracy. Raising children cost money, after all, and not everyone was wealthy enough to give ten children a reasonable upbringing. She vaguely recalled, from history texts, that large families had once been the norm, when the planet was being settled, but that hadn't lasted more than a few decades. If the Theocracy had started with a couple of thousand settlers, and each of them had had five children and each of their children had had five children more . . .

She ran through the math in her head, then cursed. "No wonder they started to expand," she said. In the days before spaceflight, large families had been a defense against disease and deprivation, but modern medicine ensured that all children grew to adulthood. "They needed more living space."

"So it would seem," Davidson said. "They take the concept of having dozens of children quite literally."

He sighed. "And that explains, I think, their high level of social control," he added. "They don't dare relax their system for fear of an explosion. If their population started to question their leaders, all hell would break loose."

Kat shuddered, remembering stories of Earth's last days. The UN had been a poor master; too large to be effective, too powerful to be trusted. No wonder that so many people had fled Earth . . . and no wonder that the colonies had fought desperately to avoid being occupied by the UN. In the end, they'd seen no alternative other than the complete destruction of humanity's homeworld. Billions had died in one day, leaving Earth a scorched wasteland of destruction. And now . . .

"If we lose the war, it will mean the end of everything we hold dear," Davidson warned quietly. "But if we win, we will have a horrific mess to clean up."

"I know," Kat said.

She shook her head slowly. "Go see to your people," she ordered. Part of her wanted him to hold her, but she knew her duty. "I need to sit down and think."

Davidson nodded, rose to his feet, and left the compartment. Kat sighed, then felt the gentle tremor as *Lightning* slipped back into hyperspace. Defeat was unthinkable; defeat meant the end of everything. But victory . . . ? How did one solve a problem like an overpopulated planet? Would it settle down, once the Theocracy was crushed, or would the issue fester for uncounted generations?

Not that it matters, she thought grimly. She could just imagine some of the solutions that would be put forward, ranging from sensible programs to outright genocide. What would the Commonwealth be prepared to do after a long and bitter war? How many laws would fall by the wayside as hatred grew stronger, overriding decency?

She shook her head, tiredly. *We have to win the war*, she told herself firmly. *There will be time to decide what to do with the consequences of victory after we win.*

CHAPTER FOURTEEN

Despite herself, Kat considered the problem of just what to do with a victory for five days while the small flotilla made its way to the penal world. Her father had told her, more than once, that idealism wasn't something a corporate head could allow himself, but she'd always had more idealism than she cared to admit. The thought of imposing her will on an entire population was fundamentally wrong—it was what the Theocracy did—yet was there any choice? It was no comparison, but she couldn't help wondering if the Theocrats felt the same way. By the time the squadron reached the penal system and slipped out of hyperspace at the edge of the system limits, she had reluctantly decided that the issue would have to be left until after the war.

"I'm not picking up any signals from deeper within the system," Linda informed her. "The entire system appears to be as dark and silent as the grave."

"No trace of any starships either," Roach added. The tactical officer scowled down at his display. "There are a handful of rocky worlds and little else; no gas giant, nothing to sustain a modern industrial base."

"No wonder they turned it into a penal colony," the XO commented. "The system isn't worth the effort of establishing a proper settlement."

Kat nodded. The Commonwealth used the same principle, although she preferred to believe that most of the prisoners trapped on isolated worlds were guilty of much more than merely seeking freedom of religion. If they survived and prospered, she'd been told, their children would one day be admitted back into the Commonwealth; if they died, or killed each other, it was no skin off the Commonwealth's collective nose. Everything she'd seen about penal colonies suggested, quite strongly, that shooting the prisoners outright would be kinder.

"Cloak us, then set course for the penal colony," she ordered, leaning back in her command chair. There was no need to skip through hyperspace, not when the system appeared to be deserted. She had plenty of time to assess the target before deciding how best to assault the world. "ETA?"

"Seven hours, Captain," Weiberg said.

"It is unlikely they've detected us, unless they set up a network of sensor platforms," Roach added. "We were careful to scale our vortex down as much as possible."

"True," Kat agreed. It was unlikely the Theocracy would waste resources on establishing an early-warning network, not in a system it deemed worthless. Even the Commonwealth only set up such networks in wealthy systems and production nodes. "Helm, take us towards the planet, best possible speed."

She forced herself to relax as the seconds slowly ticked away. It was just possible that the enemy naval base at Aswan knew, already, that they'd lost a convoy to raiders. What would they do? Kat knew *she* wouldn't send a fleet to defend a penal world—and even if they did, it was unlikely one could arrive in time—but the Theocracy might have other ideas. Even so, they wouldn't have dumped prisoners they regarded as supremely dangerous, would they? The Commonwealth executed prisoners who were just too dangerous to be allowed to roam free, even on a penal colony. Or maybe the Theocracy would just see it as a poke in the eye, one that could not be allowed to go unanswered.

"Captain," the XO said. "Observer MacDonald is requesting permission to enter the bridge."

Kat hesitated, but she couldn't think of any reasonable grounds for refusal. At least Rose MacDonald was smart enough to *ask* before entering the bridge, unlike some of the other politicians she'd had to handle. If only she'd been in command of *Thunderous*, when they'd played host to a small group of committee members. Her family name might have allowed her to keep them in line instead of having them prowling around the ship poking their noses into everything. They'd been lucky, from what she'd seen, that one of them hadn't accidentally walked out an airlock.

"Granted," she said finally.

Kat looked up as the observer entered, then returned her gaze to the display and brought up the latest analysis from the intelligence staff. They hadn't been able to fill in too many details, but they *did* have several new tidbits drawn from the prisoners. Five worlds within fifty light years had large local populations, some of whom were probably restive. But the Theocracy would have made damn sure to keep control of the high orbitals. As long as they were in a position to rain down KEWs from high overhead, no revolt could hope to take and hold ground.

"Captain," Rose said. "Why are we creeping towards the planet?"

Kat blinked, her surprise almost overriding her irritation at being questioned on her own bridge. A moment later, she realized that Rose, for all her political experience, wouldn't have any real understanding of interstellar distances. Few did; politicians should know it took a month to travel from Tyre to Cadiz, but they rarely grasped it. The StarCom FTL network spoiled them.

"I would prefer to know in advance if we're about to run into trouble," she said. "They'd have some additional warning if we were to jump through hyperspace and open a vortex on top of them."

Rose frowned. "Do you think they know you're coming?"

"I hope not," Kat said. If the Theocracy *had* set up an early-warning network, or if their sensors were far better than intelligence thought, the flotilla might be about to run into a nasty surprise. "But it's better to take precautions than be caught by surprise."

The observer nodded, then started to putter around the command deck, never approaching any of the consoles too closely. Kat couldn't decide if she was concerned about distracting someone at a crucial moment or if she was just trying to see what would draw a reaction from the crew. She'd seen politicians do the same in the past, before the war; now, a distraction at the wrong time could prove disastrous. Thankfully, Rose thought better of it after a few moments and headed for the hatch, walking off the bridge. Kat exchanged a glance with her XO, then sighed. The woman was going to be trouble. She knew it.

"Six hours, thirty minutes to the penal colony," Weiberg said.

Kat nodded. "Rotate the crews," she ordered. The alpha crew could get at least five hours of sleep before the attack began, unless the squadron was caught by surprise. "Mr. XO, make sure you get some sleep."

"You too, Captain," the XO said. "You too."

◆ ◆ ◆

Jean-Luc Orleans swung the pick at the ground, cursing under his breath. A year on the hellworld, a year since he'd been captured throwing bombs at an armored convoy, had left him hard but powerless. There was no hope of escape, no hope of doing anything but eking a minimal supply of food from the ground; hell, he didn't even have any hope of finding a wife and raising a family. The settlement had no women, none at all. There had been some on the transport ship that had taken him to his new home, but they hadn't been dropped into the settlement. He didn't want to *think* about what might have happened to them.

"You need to break the ground harder than that," Perrier said. He was one of the old sweats, a man who'd survived more than five years on the ground. Jean-Luc had no idea what kept him going; Perrier, like the rest of them, had nothing to live for. "We need loose soil to plant the next set of seeds."

"It's pointless," Jean-Luc snarled. He glared down at the patch of dirt, then slammed the pick into it hard enough to hurt his arms. "There's no damn point in planting more crops."

He sighed. The hellworld—he had no idea if anyone had bothered to give it a name—was right on the edge of the habitable zone, so cold that it wasn't uncommon for frost to kill their crops before they could be harvested. The handful of native plants that could be eaten were hardier, but there simply weren't very many of them. If he hadn't had a great deal of genetic engineering in his background, he had a feeling he would be dead by now. The native crops had to lack some of the nutrients humans required to stay alive.

"Where there's life, there's hope," Perrier said. He lifted his own pick, then struck the hard ground with practiced ease. "We may yet survive."

Jean-Luc stared at him, then turned to peer towards the settlement. It was nothing more than a primitive village, a handful of makeshift huts surrounded by a dirt wall. Somehow, he couldn't imagine it becoming anything more, not when they had to fight every year to harvest enough food to keep themselves alive. And even if they managed to stabilize themselves, what would they do then? It wasn't as if they could have children without women!

"Hah," he grumbled.

"Johan went out naked," Perrier said quietly. "Do you want to join him?"

Jean-Luc sighed. Some prisoners just gave up living—and when they did, they stripped themselves naked and walked out into the cold.

They never lasted long; their bodies, if they were recovered, were buried in shallow graves and left to rot. He'd known that Johan was too depressed to carry on for long, but he hadn't expected him to commit suicide so soon . . .

"I don't know," he said finally. There were days when he just felt like sitting down and waiting for the cold to claim him. "I just don't know."

"That's why we keep going," Perrier said. "Because while there is a spark of life left in our bodies, Jean-Luc, we don't let ourselves lie down and die."

"Hah," Jean-Luc said. He looked up at the darkening sky. "We don't have anything to live for, do we? There isn't even a hope of revenge."

The stars would come out soon enough, he knew, and one of them would be the Theocracy's orbiting station. He hadn't seen much of it, when he'd been hastened off the transport and dumped into a one-way landing pod, but he knew it was there. Perhaps the women were there too, serving as slaves or worse. It was just another reminder that he was helplessly trapped, forced to struggle to tame a world that had killed hundreds of people so far. If they'd killed him instead, when they'd captured him, it might have been a mercy.

But they're not concerned with mercy, he thought. *Merely with making us work.*

◆ ◆ ◆

"It's a fairly basic orbiting station, Captain," Roach said as the squadron closed in on the planet. "I'd place it as a modified Type-III UN colony station. The only real difference is that there don't seem to be any shuttles attached to the hull, but they may have fitted an internal shuttlebay instead."

"Or they just don't have any," Kat mused. There were no shortage of stories and movies about criminals who'd escaped penal worlds by capturing shuttles after luring them down to the ground. It wasn't as if they had much to lose. "It wouldn't do to check on the prisoners after they were dumped on the planet."

She frowned as she studied the display. "Any defenses?"

"There's a remote weapons platform here, orbiting below the station," Roach said. "I'd guess it's designed to fire down at the planet, if necessary. There doesn't seem to be anything capable of standing off a single destroyer, let alone the whole squadron. The station itself may not be armed."

The XO leaned forward. "No weapons blisters?"

"None," Roach said. "But they could have easily hidden them under the hull."

Kat considered it briefly, then shrugged. "Target the remote weapons platform," she ordered. "The Marines are to capture the station once we have killed the platform."

"Aye, Captain," Roach said. He keyed his console, then looked back at her. "Missiles locked on target."

"Transmit the surrender demand as soon as we fire the missiles," Kat ordered, addressing Linda. "I don't want them to have a chance to consider blowing the station."

Because that would be inconvenient, she thought coldly. *We couldn't get the prisoners down to the surface without the landing pods. We'd have to leave them on the freighters or dump them all into space.*

"Aye, Captain," Linda said. "The message is ready for transmission."

Kat nodded, tensing. Everything *looked* safe; everything *looked* as though she had all the cards in her hand, but she knew all too well just how quickly things could change. The enemy might be on the ball; the enemy might have seen them coming; the enemy might already have signaled for help . . . the only advantage, as far as she could see, was that there was no StarCom. Even if the Theocracy had a courier boat in the system, it would be several days before it could fetch help.

"Fire," she ordered.

Lighting shuddered as she fired two missiles towards the remote weapons platform. The enemy, taken completely by surprise, didn't even have a chance to raise shields before the missiles struck home, vaporizing their target. Kat smiled in savage glee, then glanced at the communications console. A message was already going out, filling the airwaves with a cold—masculine—demand for surrender. If the station was unarmed, the crew had to know they didn't have a hope of survival unless they surrendered. But what if they tried to blow the station . . .

They might have a self-destruct system already powering up, she thought grimly. The Marines were already on their way, four assault shuttles heading towards their target. *They might wait until the Marines dock, then trigger the bomb.*

"Captain," Linda said, "I'm picking up a message. They say they're willing to surrender in exchange for guaranteed survival."

Kat's eyes narrowed. Did they believe the Commonwealth ritually butchered prisoners and used their remains in satanic orgies? Or did they have some other reason for demanding guarantees?

"Tell them that they will survive as long as they surrender promptly," she said. Davidson's shuttle was on its final approach now, far too close to the station for her comfort. He would insist on leading from the front, wouldn't he? "They are to hand the station and its control codes over to the Marines once they dock."

There was a pause. "They've surrendered, Captain," Linda said. "They're opening the hatches now."

Kat frowned as the Marines swarmed into the station, ready to deal with any resistance. It didn't look as though there *was* any; indeed, the station, which would normally have had a crew of at least two hundred, seemed undermanned. They took thirty-seven men into custody, then searched the station. And then they broke into the hold.

"They kept some prisoners, all women, Captain," Davidson said. His voice sounded cold and dispassionate, but Kat knew him well enough to pick up the underlying shock and rage. "They're not in a good state."

No wonder they wanted guarantees, Kat thought angrily. She expected such behavior from pirates, not the Theocracy. But then, if one had a society that regarded even *believing* women as chattel, it wasn't a stretch to start enslaving prisoners and turning them into whores and sex slaves. And being trapped on an isolated station wouldn't have helped. *Those men would be killed by their own people, let alone us.*

"Let the medics deal with them," she ordered tartly. There was nothing the Marines could do for the women, not now. "Move the enemy prisoners to a storage bay, then see if you can get the pods ready for deployment."

"Aye, Captain," Davidson said. There was a pause. "With your permission, I'd like to deploy an intelligence team too."

"Granted," Kat said. She doubted there would be anything important in the station's database, but even a prisoner manifest would be useful data. At the very least, they'd know what the prisoners were supposed to have *done.* "Ask the prisoners if any Commonwealth POWs were dumped here."

"Aye, Captain," Davidson said.

We can dump the station crew on the planet too, Kat thought as the channel closed. If she hadn't offered guarantees, she could have killed them out of hand. *They'll have their lives and a better chance than their former prisoners.*

"There are at least seventy small settlements on the planet's surface," Roach observed. "I think the largest isn't much bigger than a couple of hundred personnel, although it's impossible to be sure. I'd honestly rate the planet as uninhabitable and leave it at that, at least without trying to set up a greenhouse effect . . ."

Kat nodded. The penal colony was too cold to sustain life for long, unless the food crops were genetically modified to survive. Even so, it was hard to imagine *anyone* willingly immigrating to the planet unless there were some *very* strong incentives. And what could anyone offer, she asked herself, that would match the opportunities on warmer worlds?

"Set up a shuttle schedule, based on the assumption that we will spend no longer than five days here," she ordered. "I want each of the settlements visited; if the prisoners want to leave, we make plans to pick them up once the freighters are empty."

"Aye, Captain," Roach said.

"They will need medical support," the XO offered. "Hell, if they don't want to leave, we could drop the ration packs on the surface."

Kat shrugged. "I think they'll all want to go," she said. She found it hard to imagine anyone actually wanting to *stay*. "The only real question is where we take them."

Her console bleeped and a voice came online. "Captain, this is Davidson. I've downloaded a copy of the prisoner manifest. There's no trace of anyone from the Commonwealth."

"Thank you," Kat said, disappointed. It would have been nice to rescue POWs. "Copy the intelligence over here, then continue with your operations."

"Aye, Captain," Davidson said.

CHAPTER FIFTEEN

"There's a shuttle inbound," Talien shouted. "There's a shuttle!"

Jean-Luc frowned as he pushed the blankets aside and scrambled to his feet. He'd seen the explosion in orbit, where he assumed the orbiting station had been, and pieces of debris burning up as they fell into the planet's thin atmosphere, but he hadn't allowed himself to hope that they were about to be rescued. It was far more likely, he told himself, that the Theocracy's crewmen had done something stupid. Or that one of their prisoners had managed to cause an explosion that had destroyed the station.

He stumbled out of the hut and peered into the distance. There *was* a shuttle inbound, heading towards the settlement and dropping down to land just outside the walls. He stared in disbelief—he hadn't seen a shuttle since the day he'd been shipped up to orbit and thrown into a holding cell—and then joined the others as they ran towards the walls.

The Theocracy had never sent anyone to check up on them, not since they'd been abandoned. Whoever was flying the shuttle, he was sure, wasn't one of their jailors.

The hatch opened, revealing a man in powered combat armor. Jean-Luc felt a flicker of fear, recalling the Theocratic stormtroopers who'd broken countless resistance cells, then relaxed as he realized the markings on the armor were different. He had no idea whom he was staring at, but at least he didn't work for the Theocracy. Were they being rescued? He couldn't help feeling a flicker of hope, his first in a year. They might survive after all!

"Greetings," the figure said. There was an odd accent to his Galactic Standard, but it was understandable. "I represent the Commonwealth of Tyre. We have smashed this world's defenses, but we cannot remain here for long. How many of you wish to leave?"

"All of us," Perrier said.

The figure nodded. "How many of you are there?"

"Fifty-seven," Perrier said. "When can you pick us up?"

There was a long pause. Jean-Luc had a moment to feel that, perhaps, there were too many of them to be uplifted, then the figure spoke again.

"A shuttle will be assigned to pick you up tomorrow morning," he said. "If you have personal possessions, declare them to the Marines. You may not be allowed to take them with you."

Jean-Luc snorted inwardly. Personal possessions? There were no personal possessions in the settlement! It was why the suicidal stripped naked before giving themselves up to the cold. Someone else could use their ragged clothes . . . there was nothing, not even the shirt on his back, that truly belonged to him. They had achieved an equality he couldn't help feeling the communists on his homeworld would have envied.

"We understand," Perrier said.

"I have some food supplies for you, along with basic medical gear," the figure stated. "You are welcome to them, but please be prepared to leave as soon as the shuttle arrives. We may not have much time."

Jean-Luc barely heard him. They were saved! Wherever they were going, he was sure, had to be better than the penal colony! And who knew? There might be food, drink, women, and warmth! He'd give up the first three for the fourth.

He watched as the shuttle crew unloaded a pallet of supplies, then returned to their ship and took off. Perrier elbowed him, pushing him to join the men running towards the pallet and digging it open. Inside, there were a hundred ration packs and a handful of medical kits. It looked very much like manna from heaven.

"Don't eat too much at once," Perrier warned. "You'll get sick."

Jean-Luc knew he was right, but, as he tore into a ration pack, it was hard to resist the urge to just eat and eat until he burst. Real food! And they were going back into space . . .

"This is the best day I've spent here," he said, grinning. He wasn't the only one. Everyone was grinning like an idiot. "And tomorrow we're leaving for good."

◆ ◆ ◆

"Most of the female prisoners were either kept on the station as slaves or dumped in an isolated colony," Doctor Katy Braham said. "They're not as badly off as . . . well, pirate prisoners, but they were treated pretty badly. Most of them managed to survive, however, with their sanity intact. I expect them all to make a full recovery."

William winced. "And the ones on the ground?"

"They're worse off," Doctor Braham told him. "If they hadn't received regular food shipments from orbit, I think most of them would be dead. Hell, even *with* the shipments, quite a few just died of despair or nutritional problems. They didn't have a hope of growing enough food to feed themselves."

"Then this was never intended as a breeding colony," William observed. The Theocracy never failed to find new ways to horrify him. "They were *all* intended to die out within a generation."

"Or someone changed the plan," Doctor Braham said. "Several of the sex slaves admitted they served willingly, in exchange for food being sent down to the surface. And it was, apparently. They might have changed the plan to hide what they were doing."

"Seems flimsy," William said.

He shook his head. Set up a penal colony, dump prisoners . . . and then not give them what they needed to establish a permanent settlement. It looked more like an exercise in sadism than anything else, except the Theocracy had lavished resources on the penal world. They could have been sadistic without shipping the prisoners away from their homeworlds. No, it made no sense at all.

"I looked through the manifests," Doctor Braham added. "We think there's around seven thousand prisoners on the planet's surface, mostly from Verdean. However, the manifests state that over twenty *thousand* prisoners were dumped onto the surface. That's a hellish loss rate by anyone's standards."

William shivered. "How does it compare to ours?"

"I don't know," Doctor Braham admitted. "As far as I know, no one has ever actually studied the development of our penal colonies. But then, most of the prisoners are guilty of appalling crimes. For all we know, the truly bad ones get killed shortly after they're dumped on the surface."

"Probably," William agreed. The worst of criminals were often killed by their fellow inmates, even in a secure jail. He doubted any of them would survive for long on a penal colony, not if their crimes were common knowledge. "It's not the same, is it?"

"No," Doctor Braham agreed. She cleared her throat. "A number of prisoners are suffering from various diet-related illnesses despite considerable levels of genetic engineering. Luckily, regular food will help them recover, but they'll be weak for some time to come. The remainder should be fine once they've had a chance to relax and eat; there's more than enough food for them, thanks to the captured ships. Long-term, of course, they may manifest other health problems. We don't have time to do a full medical check on each and every one of them."

"I'll inform the captain," William said. "Is there anyone we can *use*?"

"You'll have to check the manifests," Doctor Braham said. "I wasn't interested in anything other than their health."

"Understood," William said. It was unlikely the Theocracy would choose to maroon trained spacers, not when it had ways of making them obedient, but it was possible. He'd check the manifests before reporting to the captain. "Do you think any of them will pose a *threat*?"

"There may be some extreme behavior," Doctor Braham said, slowly. "For better or worse, most of them believed they'd been dumped to die—quite rightly, given the evidence. They had no hope of doing anything more than living as long as they could, then dropping dead. Now that they're free, or at least have real hope, they may act out in unpredictable ways. And if any of them were loyal to the Theocracy . . ."

"Or conditioned," William interjected.

"Or conditioned," Doctor Braham agreed, "we probably won't know until it blows up in our face. All we can really do is keep an eye on them and hope nothing goes badly wrong."

William nodded. He couldn't imagine anyone remaining loyal to the Theocracy after being dumped on an icy hellworld, but people had remained loyal to unworthy governments in the past, despite being treated like shit. It was just something else the crew would have to watch—and watch carefully. A single person who'd been conditioned, without *knowing* he'd been conditioned, might explode like a time bomb at the worst possible moment. He wouldn't set off any alarms because he wouldn't *know* he was lying. Only a deep mind probe would find the truth . . .

And such a deep probe would do more harm than good, William thought sourly.

"I'll report to the captain," he said. "And thank you."

Doctor Braham nodded curtly. William left Sickbay and walked to the intelligence section, where a team of staffers was already going through everything pulled from the station's computers and matching it against what they already knew. There was little direct data, he saw, but quite a bit that could be mined for useful intelligence. Later, once the former prisoners were on the freighters, they would be interrogated too. The oldest of them had been on the planet no longer than six years. They'd have more up-to-date information than any second-generation refugee.

He pulled up the prisoner manifest and ran through it. The Theocracy hadn't bothered to compile a proper manifest; most of the prisoners, he saw, had been classed as insurgents, questioners, or heretics. He was surprised the latter had remained alive long enough to be dumped on the icy world, but perhaps there *was* a certain sense to it. The Theocracy would assume that mere death wasn't good enough for the heretics, not when they needed to suffer first. And, judging by the vast numbers who'd died on the penal colony, they'd succeeded magnificently.

Bastards, he thought savagely.

There didn't seem to be anyone immediately useful, much to his irritation. He wasn't sure he would have trusted any former prisoner with military-grade technology, but it would have been nice to have some extra crews for the captured freighters. Shrugging, he made a copy of the data, then checked the latest updates from the surface. The captured soldiers had been dispatched to the planet's surface in landing pods, while the first prisoners were being brought up to the ships now.

He shrugged, then walked through the ship to the captain's office and pressed the buzzer once. The door slid open, revealing the captain studying the fleet readiness reports from the rest of the squadron. William had to smile; how long would it be, he wondered, before the other ships started complaining that they weren't being given a chance to take a swing at the enemy? But then, they *had* fired on the convoy escort ships . . .

"Captain," he said, saluting. "I have the report from the doctor."

He outlined what he'd heard and then leaned forward. "Most of them are from a single world," he said. "There's clearly *something* going on there."

"I know," the captain said. She tapped a switch, then motioned for him to take a chair as a holographic image sprung to life. "Verdean. Settled in 2300, according to the old UN files; apparently, the original settlers were a French offshoot who had no real interest in settling on the official French-ethnic worlds. The files don't go into details on why, or how they managed to remain separate from New France, but they convinced the UN to give them a settlement grant and a colony ship. They were quite well established by the time the Breakaway Wars began."

She shrugged. "Like us, they took no official part in the conflict," she added after a moment. "And that's the last we heard of them until now. They were already behind the Theocracy's borders by the time we realized we needed to gear up for war."

"They couldn't have been occupied for very long," William said thoughtfully. "Not if there's a resistance movement still in existence."

"No, they couldn't have been," the captain agreed. She gave him a mischievous smile that almost made him wish he was younger and out of the chain of command. "And they're barely twenty light years from our current location."

William smiled back. "You intend to attack?"

"I certainly intend to scout out the system," the captain said. Her smile widened. "It occurs to me that we have several thousand former resistance fighters, a great deal of captured weapons, and a restive world. Dumping both the fighters and the weapons onto Verdean might give the Theocracy a few nasty headaches."

"Or they might simply wreck the world from orbit," William said. He didn't disagree with the captain, but it was his job to point out the downsides. "They're not likely to restrain themselves if they feel their grasp on the world is weakening."

"The resistance may have to choose if they wish to fight or not," the captain said. "All we can do is give them the opportunity."

"They could stockpile the weapons and build up their forces," William suggested. "When we liberate the system properly, they could hit the bastards on the ground."

"Their choice too," the captain said. "I've asked for two representatives from the resistance to join us."

"What they know will be out of date," William warned.

"I know," the captain said. "But it's the best we have."

♦ ♦ ♦

Jean-Luc couldn't help feeling bitter envy as he and Perrier followed the Marine through the starship's corridors and into the captain's office. If Verdean had had such ships, it would never have fallen when the Theocracy arrived; it would never have known the humiliation of submission to an alien religion and an alien way of life. But Verdean had never been wealthy, never been able to afford more than a pair of destroyers to ward itself against outside threats. The formal battle for his homeworld had lasted, he'd been told, less than an hour.

He blinked in surprise when he saw the starship's captain. She was young, so young he would have classed her as no older than himself; beside her, the grizzled older man looked far more like a commanding officer. But there was no mistaking the gold star on her collar, or the simple fact she was sitting behind a desk. Perrier hesitated, then snapped a salute; Jean-Luc, unsure of what to say or do, merely nodded. The captain didn't seem inclined to take offense.

"Welcome aboard," the captain said. Her voice was sweet, all the more so for being the only female voice he'd heard in a year. "I'm Captain Falcone of the Royal Tyre Navy; this is Commander McElney, my XO. Thank you for coming."

"Thank *you* for coming," Perrier said. "I don't think I have the words to say just how grateful we are."

The captain nodded. "I'll get right to the point," she said. "The Commonwealth and the Theocracy are currently at war. Our king has stated his intention of eventually taking the conflict into Theocratic space, liberating the worlds currently held in bondage and occupying their homeworld in hopes of preventing a resurgence of the war. Our mission is currently to make their lives as miserable as possible, buying time for a major offensive to be prepared."

Perrier smiled. "Sounds like a good idea to us," he said. "How may we be of service?"

"It is my intention to scout out your homeworld, then plot a raid," the captain said. She must have sent a command, somehow, for a holographic star chart appeared over her desk. "You'll notice that we're not actually *far* from Verdean. Assuming we can break the defenses without risking major losses, I will do so—and then hammer the enemy positions on the surface. I *then* intend to insert you and your men onto the ground before the enemy can rally a counterattack."

"Interesting," Perrier said. "You don't intend to hold the system?"

"I don't have the firepower if the enemy comes in force," the captain admitted. "I may hang around long enough to lure them into a trap, but that will be tricky. There's very little leeway to do anything but get out before they pin us down."

Jean-Luc coughed. "So you can get us down, but not help us?"

"You would need to decide if you intend to continue the fight or remain underground until your world can be liberated completely," the captain said. "We couldn't force that choice on you."

Perrier considered it for a long moment. "We were slowly being strangled when I was captured," he said. He glanced at Jean-Luc. "I don't think the situation has gotten any better since."

"Oh, no," Jean-Luc said. He forced himself to feel anger. Anger was far better than the helpless despair that had convinced him to throw himself at the janissaries, fully expecting that they would kill him. "It was dire when *I* was captured. They killed my family for nothing, after they'd had their fun. It's a fucking nightmare."

"Language," Perrier said quietly.

"I've heard worse," the captain assured him.

She gave Jean-Luc a smile tinged with sadness. "We will spend the next couple of days going through everything you know, then we will start preparing you for the insertion," she added. "If we don't, or we can't complete that objective, for whatever reason, we will find another option. You'll have your chance to make them pay for what they've done."

"Thank you," Jean-Luc said. "But when will our world be liberated?"

"I wish I could give you a timetable," the captain said. "We need to keep them off balance while we gather our forces, then take the offensive and ram straight into their territory. I hope it won't be long, but . . ."

"We understand," Perrier said. "Any help you give us will be very welcome."

Beside him, Jean-Luc nodded in agreement.

CHAPTER SIXTEEN

It had been years since Admiral Junayd had visited the Aswan System, back when he'd been supervising the border defenses before the Theocracy started preparing for war in earnest, and he hadn't been too impressed at the time. Aswan existed as little more than a forward operational base, a minor shipyard and industrial node; too far from the border to support the offensive, too close to be transformed into a major industrial base. Even now, with a war on, it didn't seem to have been improved. A single squadron of superdreadnoughts held station orbiting the planet itself and another squadron drifted near the shipyard, while several dozen smaller ships flitted around the system or dropped in and out of hyperspace at will.

He stood on the bridge of the light cruiser *God's Faithful* and felt cold anger congealing inside his heart. Aswan hadn't been one of his responsibilities while he'd been planning the offensive against Cadiz, but he'd been expecting better from the commodore in command of the base. It was depressingly clear that he'd allowed standards to lapse: the light cruiser, which had dropped out of hyperspace twenty minutes ago, hadn't been challenged, even though it was on a direct course towards the planet itself. The superdreadnoughts, which should have been on alert, seemed to have been stood down. He hoped he was wrong, but experience suggested otherwise.

It's Cadiz in reserve, he thought. He had no idea why Admiral Morrison had cared so little for even basic precautions, but he would make damn sure that the commodore got the punishment his Commonwealth counterpart had earned. *And if the enemy attacked, all hell would break loose.*

"Admiral," Captain Erith said, "we are being challenged."

"Finally," Admiral Junayd snapped. "Send them my command codes, then inform Commodore Malian that I wish to see him the moment I board."

"Yes, Admiral," Captain Erith said.

Admiral Junayd ignored him, concentrating on the display. The defenses *looked* formidable, at least, and the sensors were active . . . but why hadn't his ship been challenged? Had they been so confident that he was friendly? Or were they merely being idiots? If Admiral Junayd could take a spy ship into enemy space, there was no reason the Commonwealth couldn't do the same. He ground his teeth with anger. It was bad enough that he'd been made the scapegoat for the Theocracy's failure to close the trap properly, a problem caused by Princess Drusilla, but to have to cope with incompetence . . .

He swore under his breath, then turned to look at the captain. "Order my staff to be ready to board the station as soon as we dock," he said. "I don't want to waste any time."

A dull shiver ran through the ship as it docked. Admiral Junayd steadied himself, then walked down to the airlock, ignoring the sharp glances Captain Erith threw at him. It wasn't hard to guess that Erith was worried about his career too, but Admiral Junayd found it hard to give a damn. Right now, he had a far more important problem to worry about. Unless his guess was very wrong, those superdreadnoughts were in poor repair.

And should be at the front, he thought as he stepped through the airlock. The thought of what he could have done with an extra squadron of superdreadnoughts—let alone two—was thoroughly unpleasant, but unavoidable. He could have trapped and destroyed both Commonwealth fleets, then ripped through the defenses of a dozen worlds. *But there's no point in worrying over what might have been.*

A small party met him at the airlock, led by Commodore Malian and his cleric. Admiral Junayd studied both of them for a long moment; the commodore looked alarmingly fat and happy, while the cleric had the dimwitted expression common to men who'd been promoted above their level of competence. Junayd felt another surge of hatred and then fought it down; he believed, but he hated men who thought their belief made them more competent than those who had studied war for decades. There was no point in making a second enemy right now.

"Admiral Junayd," Commodore Malian said. "Allow me to welcome you . . ."

"You will take me to your office at once," Admiral Junayd said, cutting him off. He had no interest in an extended series of welcoming speeches that would be long on flowery religious references and short on anything useful. "The rest of your staff can return to their duties."

The commodore gaped at him, then hastened to obey. Admiral Junayd muttered orders to his staff, then followed the commodore through a series of twisting corridors and up to his office, which was surprisingly luxurious. A warrior was meant to have a bare office, Admiral Junayd had been taught, but the commodore had clearly gone soft. The bulkheads were decorated with paintings, the chairs were sinfully comfortable, and the desk was made of real wood. What had his cleric been doing? Maybe the idiot was smart enough to understand his own ignorance, but surely he could have noticed everything in plain view? Or had the commodore merely convinced him that it was vital for the war effort that the CO was allowed to decorate his own office?

"Sit," Admiral Junayd ordered. "Explain. Now."

Commodore Malian stared at him, his eyes wide. "Explain what, sir?"

"Your command failed to challenge my ship until we were already alarmingly close to the planet," Admiral Junayd said. "Your starships appear to be concentrated here, rather than on patrol or scattered over the numerous potential targets in the sector. Your superdreadnought squadrons look to be in very low readiness; indeed, the only area where you can reasonably be said to have lived up to regulations concerns planetary defenses. Explain."

He lowered his voice. "And you can also explain," he added, "why I shouldn't be sending you back in chains, charged with corruption and gross incompetence."

"I am not incompetent," the commodore protested.

"This system reminds me of Cadiz," Admiral Junayd said coolly. "It is important to learn from our mistakes, but learning from the enemy's is a great deal cheaper. Explain."

The commodore took a long breath. "Admiral," he said, "I was ordered to keep my forces concentrated here."

"You were?" Admiral Junayd asked. "Ordered by whom?"

"The War Council," Commodore Malian said. "They believed that my ships would serve as a reserve force, to be deployed to the front if necessary. I couldn't deploy them at a moment's notice if I had them spread out over the sector."

"I imagine not," Admiral Junayd sneered. "But why did you allow the superdreadnoughts to fall into such disrepair?"

"Most of my repair crews were sent forward," the commodore said defiantly. "I am forbidden to train new ones, while all my requests for replacements have fallen on deaf ears."

"I see," Admiral Junayd said coldly.

He took a long moment to study the older man. Malian had had a decent record until recently; indeed, no one had realized there were problems at Aswan until now. But if Malian hadn't had the tools to fix the problems, he couldn't really be blamed for them. How could Junayd himself resent his own treatment at the hands of the War Council and blame Malian for his failures at the same time?

"Then we will have to work on your problems," he said. "Give me a breakdown of your smaller ships. I intend to use them to patrol the sector."

Malian blinked. "But they might be called forward at any moment!"

"Only an idiot"—*or a cleric*, he added silently—"would expect them to be ready to depart at once," Admiral Junayd said firmly. "We do have a network of courier boats here, do we not? I can use them to recall the smaller ships if necessary. In the meantime, we will begin repair work on the superdreadnoughts. I do have the authority to conscript repair crews and to train others."

"There are regulations against it," Malian pointed out.

"This is war," Admiral Junayd countered. The repair crews wouldn't be left alive, not after the war was over, but for the moment they were needed. "Get a training program sorted out, then start looking for recruits. I'll send a request back for other repair crews on the StarCom."

"But they'll know there's a problem," Malian whined.

"They will also know that your repair crews were summoned to the front," Admiral Junayd pointed out with heavy patience. "I dare say they will be understanding of any requests you made for replacements—and, also, why *I* made a request as soon as I took command of the station."

"Yes, sir," Malian said.

"Good," Admiral Junayd said. He sat down behind the desk, silently resolving to have the chair replaced with a properly uncomfortable design as soon as possible. "Now, I am willing to let your previous conduct go unpunished, provided you give me your all. Do you understand me?"

"Yes, sir," Malian said. It was better than he could reasonably have expected and they both knew it. "I won't let you down."

"Glad to hear it," Admiral Junayd murmured. He cleared his throat loudly. "Now, I want you to draw up a schedule for a series of patrols through threatened systems—and for courier boats, in the event of us needing to recall the ships at short notice. Let me see it before you issue any actual orders."

"Yes, sir," Malian said.

"It would be much easier with a set of StarComs," Admiral Junayd mused. "We could send messages from system to system practically instantly, not rely on courier boats away from communications nodes."

He sighed. If he'd needed proof the Commonwealth was considerably *richer* than the Theocracy, he didn't really need to look very far. They'd managed to give just about every inhabited system, even Cadiz, a StarCom, even though they were staggeringly expensive. The Theocracy hadn't managed to do nearly as well; there were only three StarComs in the entire sector, despite the fact it was on the front lines. He would have traded one of his superdreadnought squadrons for a dozen StarComs and the freedom to choose their locations for himself.

Given time, they will outproduce and overwhelm us, he thought. *We have to win the war within the next two years, or . . .*

It was called defeatism, he knew, to even *suggest* there was a possibility of anything but triumph. No one would spare him, this time, if he openly discussed the prospect of losing the war. Everyone knew that God favored them, that He granted the Theocracy the help it needed to win the war . . . if they remained faithful and devout, praying every day for victory. And yet . . . while the Inquisition preached that God was on the side of the faithful, Admiral Junayd had long since come to realize that He was on the side of the big guns. The only real question was who had the *bigger* guns.

He shook his head, dismissing the thought. "I will review the rest of your records," he added flatly. "You will report back to me in two hours. By then, I'm sure we will have a great deal more to discuss."

Commodore Malian bowed low, then retreated from the room. Admiral Junayd sighed, then glanced at the latest set of reports. All seemed well in the sector, but that proved nothing. A dozen worlds were permanently on the verge of exploding into hopeless rebellion against the Theocracy, draining troops and ships from the war front. If he'd been in command of the enemy's forces, he would have taken a leaf from the Theocracy's plans for war and supplied weapons to the insurgents on worlds that had yet to bow the knee to God. It was unlikely any of them would actually be able to *win*, but they would provide a distraction at a crucial moment.

The sooner we start regular patrols, the better, he thought. *We need to keep our finger on the pulse of the sector.*

The intercom chimed. "Ah . . . Admiral?"

"Yes," Admiral Junayd said. The voice sounded young and nervous, unsurprisingly. No doubt the speaker was on his first posting. "Report."

"The courier boat for Convoy CAD-362 is overdue," the speaker said. "It's probably nothing, but . . ."

"Nothing is ever nothing," Admiral Junayd said. It was something he'd been taught in training, back when he'd spent his days memorizing tactical formulations and his nights reciting religious texts from memory to please the clerics. "When was it due to arrive?"

"Two days ago," the speaker said. "Ah, there was a period of leeway before it could be declared overdue."

"I know the procedure," Admiral Junayd said patiently. CAD-362 . . . it would have headed directly to Cadiz, once it met up with the courier boat. It was possible, he had to admit, that the courier boat might have had an accident somewhere along the way, but he disliked the thought. A convoy heading into a war zone would be a very tempting target. "Did we receive confirmation that it had departed?"

"Yes, Admiral. We were sent a message via StarCom from Cadiz, confirming the courier boat's departure."

We might have outsmarted ourselves, a little, Admiral Junayd thought. *He* hadn't devised *that* procedure, thankfully, but that might not be taken into account when the investigation began. Someone was *always* at fault. *And if something has happened to the courier boat, what happened to the convoy?*

"Send a signal to Cadiz, asking them to inform us the moment the convoy arrives," he ordered. It didn't seem likely that the convoy *would* arrive, but he had to hope for the best while preparing for the worst. "And detach a pair of destroyers. They are to fly directly to the convoy's RV point and investigate; no, one of them is to investigate, the other is to hang back."

"Yes, Admiral," the speaker said.

"Good," Admiral Junayd said. "Inform me the moment the destroyers are on their way."

He sat back in his chair, then closed the channel and brought up the star chart. As he'd suspected, CAD-362 had been due to meet the courier boat at UNAS-RD-46785 before proceeding to Cadiz, while the courier boat headed onwards to Aswan. But the courier boat hadn't arrived, which suggested . . . what? Accident? Or deliberate attack? And if the latter, what had happened to the convoy?

At least it happened before I took formal command, he told himself. *The sooner we start reestablishing patrols, the better.*

◆ ◆ ◆

Lieutenant Lars Rasmussen hadn't expected to earn command after five years in the Royal Navy, certainly not of anything larger than a gunboat. Indeed, when he'd been told that there might—*might*—be a prospect of command if he transferred to a secret mission rather than being posted to a battle cruiser, he'd been half inclined to believe his CO was playing a complicated joke on him. And when he'd laid eyes on his new command, he hadn't been able to keep himself from wondering if someone had deliberately set him up.

No, he told himself firmly, as HMS *Mermaid* drifted through the Aswan System. *That isn't fair at all.*

HMS *Mermaid* was an odd duck, a strange cross between a military-grade warship and a cutter intended for nothing more than customs duty. He'd actually checked her file and discovered she was the sole representative of her class, a design that was neither fish nor fowl and had never worked well in practice. But as a spy ship, once some of her older equipment had been replaced, he had to admit she was matchless. The Theocrats didn't have the slightest idea she was there.

"That's definitely a second superdreadnought squadron," Midshipwoman Grace Hawthorne reported from her console. Her voice was very quiet, as if she thought the enemy could hear her words. "Either they're keeping the drives stepped down for some reason or they're in desperate need of repairs."

"Not that we want to tangle with them anyway," Lars said, peering over her shoulder. "A single superdreadnought could swat the entire squadron, minus *Lightning*, without breaking a sweat."

"*Lightning* wouldn't last much longer," Grace agreed. She frowned as more data poured into the starship's sensors. "I'm thinking this place is definitely the center of operations in this sector."

"It looks that way," Lars said. The POWs had said as much, yet it never hurt to check. "But it also looks like they're preparing to deploy forward."

He paused. "Do we *know* those superdreadnoughts?"

"Not as far as I can tell," Grace said. Her brow furrowed as she bent over the console, comparing the sensor readings with her records. "Their drive fields aren't recorded in our database, but they might have retuned the drives. It wouldn't be too hard for them to change the drives enough to give them a completely new profile."

Lars nodded, slowly. According to the files, which he had only been allowed to read after they crossed the border, the Commonwealth had recorded the unique characteristics of nine enemy superdreadnought squadrons. Assuming that no one had messed with the drive signatures, he was looking at two more . . . and no one had any idea of just how many *other* superdreadnoughts there were, waiting for their chance to attack the Commonwealth.

Unless they have been modified, he thought. *Or is that wishful thinking?*

"Keep us on course," he ordered. *Mermaid* would slip through the system, then jump back into hyperspace once they were well outside sensor range. "Captain—*Commodore*—Falcone will be delighted to have this information."

"If only to know this system shouldn't be attacked," Grace said. Her face twisted with grim amusement. "I wouldn't care to attack those defenses without a superdreadnought squadron of my own. And they have a StarCom, worse luck. They could call for help."

"That does raise a different question," Lars said. If Aswan was the local Sector HQ, where *else* would the enemy base ships? "From where?"

He looked back at the display, then shrugged. They'd find out soon enough.

CHAPTER SEVENTEEN

"It looks as though Aswan is far too dangerous for us," the XO said.

Kat nodded in agreement. Two superdreadnought squadrons were overkill, as far as her puny flotilla was concerned; the smaller ships alone would be a major headache. Perversely, it was the smaller ships that posed the greatest threat; even a relatively low number could cost her dearly if she ran into them at her next target. They could be moved from star to star quickly, if necessary, spreading out to blanket all possible targets.

She sucked in her breath. The intelligence staff might believe the superdreadnoughts were in poor condition, but a single superdreadnought with half its missile tubes out of commission would still be able to smash her entire flotilla. She wouldn't care to visit Aswan without a superdreadnought squadron of her own—and, as the enemy could be trying to lure her into close combat by pretending to be weak, she would have preferred at least three superdreadnought squadrons, if not four. Having a two-to-one advantage practically guaranteed success.

"Yeah," she said. There was no point in plotting an attack, not with the firepower at her command. "We'll have to send the data back to Admiral Christian, if he feels like cutting loose enough firepower to raid behind enemy lines."

"He won't," the XO predicted. "The situation along the front lines is too insecure for him to risk anything of the sort."

"I suppose," Kat agreed. "Still, the chance to smash two enemy superdreadnought squadrons should not be missed."

"If it didn't cost us the war," the XO said.

Kat nodded, reluctantly. Sending a fleet—any fleet—away from the front lines risked the enemy making major gains, while the dispatched fleet had absolutely no idea what was happening behind it. The fleet might return to discover that its base had been destroyed, or that the enemy had punched through the weakened border defenses and started a drive towards Tyre itself. No, the XO was right. No matter how tempting the target—and the target might have been *designed* to look tempting—it couldn't be risked. It was why the Commonwealth had sent only a handful of older ships—and *Lightning*—to raid behind enemy lines.

"Never mind," she said, closing the display. "Are we ready to move to Verdean?"

"Yes, Captain," the XO assured her. "The prisoners who are in no state to join the resistance, or unwilling to do so, have been transferred to one of the freighters, which is currently holding station at the RV point. Everyone else is being given enemy weapons and taught how to use them, along with ammunition and enemy supplies. Apparently, their ration packs are even worse than ours."

Kat had to smile. Complaining about rations was an old tradition, but the Royal Navy's ration packs weren't actually that bad. The Theocracy, on the other hand, seemed to think that even eating rations should be a test of one's endurance. She wouldn't have been surprised to discover their captains were allowed to flog crewmen, or that devout believers engaged in self-flagellation every Thursday at nine. It made no sense to her—life in space was hard enough without making it worse deliberately—but she wasn't about to look a gift horse in the mouth. Anything that weakened the enemy worked in her favor.

"As long as they're edible," she said.

"Oh, no; they don't serve *those* kinds of meals," the XO said. "Perish the thought!"

Kat laughed—it was a punch line from a sitcom she'd detested as a young girl—then tapped the console, bringing up the star chart. Verdean glowed red in front of her; the prisoners had been able to tell her a great deal about the system itself, but next to nothing about the Theocracy's deployments. There would be an automated weapons platform—perhaps more than one—guarding the planet itself, but what else? Normally, a spacefaring society would have started mining the gas giants and asteroid belts, yet the Theocracy seemed unwilling to risk moving *any* form of industry into occupied systems. It was quite possible the local industrial base had been completely destroyed.

It's inefficient, she thought crossly. *Are they so determined to keep control that they're willing to swallow the extra cost of shipping everything from their heartlands to the edge of their territory?*

She shook her head in disbelief. Maybe she hadn't paid as much attention to her lessons as she should, but she understood the problems involved in shipping thousands of tons of goods across space. The Commonwealth had invested billions of crowns in building up local industries purely to boost the economy and keep prices down—and, just incidentally, convince the newcomers that the Commonwealth didn't intend to exploit them. But the Theocracy seemed determined to keep its worlds firmly in bondage.

The XO coughed. "Crown for your thoughts, Captain?"

"They're inefficient," Kat said, and explained her reasoning. "No wonder they're having supply problems."

"But they consider the trade-off worthwhile," the XO pointed out. "If the locals had control over an industrial base, even a small one, they'd have a disproportionate amount of influence over the Theocracy itself. They might be able to leverage that into better treatment from their masters, if they didn't manage to gain outright independence. Keeping everyone crawling on the ground, after the invasion, suits the Theocracy better. And it works in our favor too."

"Because they need to ship their supplies over a much longer distance," Kat mused. She shrugged. "They'll probably start expanding Aswan sooner or later."

"It'll take them years," the XO predicted. "Years they're not going to have."

"I hope you're right," Kat said. She looked back at the star chart for a long moment. "It's a three-day trip to Verdean from here, so we'll leave in an hour and use the time to prepare for the offensive. *Mermaid* can repeat her feat of slipping into the system when we arrive, with *Juno* and *Max Mercury* backing her up. Unless there's something there too large for us to tackle, we'll attack at once."

"Yes, Captain," the XO said.

Kat smiled, tiredly. "Are there any other issues of note?"

"Some minor disputes amongst the former prisoners," the XO said. "They were fighting over who did what during the first invasion and its aftermath, then over who should have overall command of the resistance. I don't think it will be a major problem, at least at the moment, but Verdean will not have a peaceful future after they're liberated for good."

"They can sort that out afterwards," Kat said firmly. She shook her head. "Are they trained on handling the communicators too?"

"We're doing that now," the XO assured her. "They should be able to maintain communications with a stealthed platform even after we leave the system. They'll be on their own for long periods, but they will still be able to leave messages for us . . . when, of course, we manage to slip a spy ship back into the system."

Kat nodded. It wasn't the best way to communicate, but in the absence of a StarCom there was no other choice. The Commonwealth would take the offensive, sooner or later, and when it did they'd need to make contact—again—with the resistance on Verdean. It might make liberating the system for good a far easier task.

"Then make sure you get some rest, once we're on the way," she ordered. "It won't get any easier from now on."

She keyed the console again. This time, it showed a pair of expanding message spheres: one centered on UNAS-RD-46785, the other on the unnamed penal world. The first sphere had already overlapped Aswan, while the second was only a couple of days from the Theocratic fleet base. It was quite likely the Theocracy had already realized they'd lost a convoy. She'd had the prisoners interrogated until they'd spilled everything they knew, but none of them had been quite sure just how much leeway was built into the system. The Commonwealth would wait at least a week before panicking—ships could be overdue without running into pirates or raiders—yet was that true of the Theocracy? They might start sounding the alarm if the courier boat was even an hour overdue.

But that would be stupid, she told herself. *Even without enemy interference, a courier boat could be delayed by any number of problems. A freak storm in hyperspace might even blow her light years off course.*

She ran through the problem in her own head. Assuming Aswan realized the courier boat was overdue at the earliest possible moment, without any leeway at all, warning messages could already be on their way to Verdean. She knew she didn't dare assume otherwise, even though logic told her there would be *some* leeway. Verdean might well be ready for her when she arrived.

They don't know what we have, she thought, grimly. *Nothing escaped the ambush, unless they had a covert satellite watching for trouble . . .*

"We'll revise departure and leave in two hours," she said instead. There was no point in worrying too much; she'd assume the worst, probing the system before she committed herself and backing off if it looked like too much of a challenge. "I'll want to speak to the patrol boat commanders before we go."

"Aye, Captain," the XO said.

"And make a note in the logs," Kat added. "The commander and crew of HMS *Mermaid* are to be commended for the first sweep of a Theocratic fleet base. They'll be in line for a medal when we return home."

The XO nodded, then saluted and left the cabin. Kat looked back at the display, unable to stop a cold hand clenching at her heart. The enemy had to know, now, that something was wrong. Her squadron's presence would no longer be a secret. Hell, she'd never *meant* it to remain a secret indefinitely—the idea was to force them to react to her presence—but she couldn't help feeling nervous. Two squadrons of superdreadnoughts could rip her ships apart with ease, if the enemy got lucky. And they might well manage to get lucky, if she made a single mistake . . .

Then you'd better not make one, she told herself, firmly. *As long as you pick your targets with care, they shouldn't be able to guess your next destination.*

She sighed, then brought up the intelligence reports. They now knew more about the sector, enough to pick the next target. And there were several possibilities . . .

"Ringer might be the best bet," she muttered after a moment. "And it might hurt the enemy quite badly if we struck a handful of blows, then vanished."

◆ ◆ ◆

"These weapons are awesome, sir," Jean-Luc said.

"They're pieces of crap," Sergeant Dervish said. He was from a refugee family, he'd explained; Jean-Luc had been disappointed to discover that none of the refugees attached to the squadron had come from Verdean. "This is an assault rifle broken down to the bare basics, designed for illiterate baboons who can't shoot for toffee. I was playing with one after we captured the convoy and the aiming is appallingly bad."

Jean-Luc smiled. "At least you're pumping bullets in the general direction of the enemy . . ."

"The enemy is likely to be the safest person on the field," Dervish said. He sneered down at the rifle. "Accuracy goes to shit outside a few meters, young man; you'd need to spray and pray just to have a reasonable chance of hitting something. If I didn't know better, I would have thought they were unloading older pieces of crap onto planetary militia and other local defense forces."

He shook his head. "There were a handful of sniper rifles," he added, "but nothing I'd consider satisfactory. I've seen better weapons coming off private workbenches or locked away in museums, weapons that might actually *hurt* the enemy."

"It's still better than anything we had before the invasion," Jean-Luc said.

"Better than anything *we* had too," Dervish admitted. "Or so my father says, when he's in his cups. He spent all of his courage and determination just getting his family off-world before our new masters clamped down on us. If we'd spent money on weapons . . ."

He snorted. "Aragon wasn't a spacefaring power," he added after a moment. "If we'd spent money on weapons, we would probably have been crushed anyway."

Jean-Luc frowned. "What was it like? Going to the Commonwealth, I mean?"

"I was four years old," Dervish said. "We spent a couple of years in a refugee camp, then Dad got his papers and started to work. I went to school when I was five, then joined the cadet force at seven. By the time I went to boot camp, I was pretty much identical to everyone else. I don't really remember life before the Commonwealth at all."

"Oh," Jean-Luc said.

Jean-Luc looked down at the weapon in his hands. He'd been offered—they'd all been offered—the chance to stay with the squadron and eventually return to the Commonwealth, once the starships had completed their mission. He had to admit he'd been tempted—after a year on a penal world, his enthusiasm for continuing the fight had dimmed—but he was damned if he was abandoning his homeworld as long as there was something he could do. Besides, it wasn't as if he had any useful skills. He hadn't been training to be a starship pilot or an engineer even before the Theocracy had interrupted his education. There was no way he could justify remaining with the starships to himself, let alone to anyone else.

Dervish had been lucky, he suspected. He'd escaped early enough that he had no emotional tie to his homeworld. The Commonwealth was his home now. But Jean-Luc? To run from his homeworld would be the act of a coward. And besides, Perrier and the others were going back too, ready to try to make contact with what remained of the resistance or set up a new one. The attack on the system would prove to the population that the Theocracy could be beaten . . .

Assuming it comes off as planned, he thought. *If the starships have to retreat, we will be unable to land.*

The Marine cleared his throat. "Did you read the textbooks?"

"I tried," Jean-Luc said. "I wish I had more time to practice."

"Us too," Dervish said. "Six months of training didn't feel like enough when I went into combat for the first time."

Jean-Luc shrugged. He'd barely known which end of a gun to point at the enemy when *he'd* gone into combat, although—to be fair—it hadn't been planned that way. The Theocracy had launched a kill-sweep for insurgents and overrun his training base, forcing him and his fellow recruits to fight and run. All things considered, he'd been lucky his career as a daring resistance fighter hadn't ended there and then. Instead, he'd survived a year before finally being captured.

"I meant to ask," he said, "why do *you* have all these manuals?"

"We had a few insurgencies of our own to handle," Dervish said. "And we knew we were likely to lose worlds to the Theocracy, so we set up stay-behind units and issued training on guerrilla war. It was one of the many compromises that went into effect when the Commonwealth was actually founded. Just about everyone receives *some* form of firearms training."

"You said," Jean-Luc recalled, "that it would have made a difference if everyone was armed?"

"On your homeworld?" Dervish asked. "I think it would have resulted in a great many more dead on both sides, but would it have made a *real* difference? I don't know. The Theocracy might have decided that keeping you alive was too much trouble and blasted your world back to bedrock. Or they might have just kept piling on the rocks until you surrendered. As long as they held the high orbitals, you would have been fucked."

"Then we need to wait for you to return," Jean-Luc said despondently.

"Yes," Dervish agreed. "But you will have time to make preparations and wait."

◆ ◆ ◆

The spy lay on his bunk, staring up at the ceiling.

There didn't seem to be any way out of the trap. The longer he delayed, the clearer it would become that he *was* delaying . . . and then his handlers would kill his sister, perhaps betraying him to the CIS as well. He'd hoped that something would happen that would save him from having to commit treason, but nothing had materialized. Maybe a missile would strike the ship, killing him and him alone, or he would be reassigned to a department where there was no hope of getting a message out without being detected. Nothing had happened . . . and now he was trapped.

It was easy enough to skim through the ship's datanet, once one was allowed through the firewall . . . and, as a tactical officer, he was permitted access to almost every part of the ship's computers. He knew where the captain intended to attack, he knew where she wanted to go next; he even knew where the fleet train was waiting, safely away from the squadron. And getting that information to the Theocracy wouldn't be difficult . . .

Damned if I do, he thought. It would be the first step into outright treason; no, he'd made that choice the moment he'd decided not to report the contact to the CIS. *And damned if I don't.*

He closed his eyes in bitter pain, then opened them and reached for his datapad. Maybe someone would stumble across his work before it was too late . . . but he knew it wasn't going to happen. He'd erase all evidence of his tampering as soon as his work was done. And then . . .

They find a use for the data, he thought. *And hopefully everything will end.*

CHAPTER EIGHTEEN

"You know," Midshipwoman Grace Hawthorne said, "one could say this system has potential."

"I suppose one could," Lieutenant Lars Rasmussen said. "But you'd have to get rid of the occupying forces first."

He nodded to himself coldly. *Mermaid* had probed the system carefully, very carefully, hunting for signs of enemy activity. Verdean wasn't exactly Tyre or even Cadiz, but it wasn't a groundhog system by any definition of the word. A handful of industrial nodes dating back to the UN, he thought, orbited Verdean itself, while an old-style cloud-scoop drew HE3 from the gas giant. Judging by the handful of freighters orbiting the structure, Verdean produced much of the HE3 for the sector as well as its own requirements. He was mildly surprised the Theocracy had even left it intact, but maybe it wasn't too surprising.

They'd be able to keep a cloudscoop isolated from the remainder of the system with ease.

"Then set up a larger asteroid mining operation," Grace added. "You could probably have a small-scale shipyard within five years, then start producing your own ships and start expanding further."

"No doubt," Lars agreed. "But that does still leave the problem of a large and powerful occupation force."

He peered down at the passive sensors, frowning. There was nothing on Verdean I, as far as he could tell, but Verdean III—a Mars-type world—had a dozen radio sources on the planet's surface and a small network of satellites orbiting it. An industrial base, or penal camp, or what? It didn't *look* as though the Theocracy was attempting to terraform the world, but they might simply be choosing to use one of the longer ways to turn a dead world into a decent place to live. Or they didn't *want* to terraform the planet. It wasn't as if it would help the war effort.

"There's relatively few signals coming from Verdean itself," Grace added. "The dark side of the planet is . . . well, *dark*."

She was right, Lars realized. A spacer looking down on Tyre's dark side would have known the planet was heavily industrialized, if only because he or she saw the planet's lights blurring into a glowing mass. But Verdean was dark; only a handful of lights could be seen, concentrated around the major cities. He hadn't seen anything like it, outside a pastoral world where anything more advanced than the spinning jenny was banned; it suggested, strongly, that the Theocracy was crushing the life out of the locals. The sight sent cold shivers running down his spine.

"Make a note of all the sources," he ordered. He swore under his breath as two fast-moving icons appeared on the display, zipping around the planet on patrol. "Gunboats?"

"Looks that way," Grace said. "No idea what they're doing here."

"Causing trouble," Lars muttered. The Theocracy needed to work up its ships and squadrons, just like the Commonwealth, but he wouldn't have expected them to do it in an occupied system. Maybe they had been having problems with pirates and wanted to make a show of strength. "That's an unexpected complication."

"I can't see a carrier," Grace said after a moment. "They must be based on one of the orbiting stations."

"Probably," Lars said. It wasn't common to use gunboats for system patrol, at least in the Commonwealth, but the Theocracy might have evolved a different doctrine. "One large orbital station, a number of automated weapons platforms, and now a gunboat squadron."

"Maybe more than one," Grace said. "We don't know anything about their deployment patterns."

Lars frowned. "True," he conceded, finally. If the Theocracy had copied the UN's doctrine, they'd have somewhere between nine and twelve gunboats assigned to a squadron. On the other hand, the UN hadn't fought a proper war until the Breakaway conflict and it had lost so comprehensively that it had never had a chance to reevaluate its doctrine. "We'll have to assume the worst."

He took a long look at the planet, then sighed. "Take us back out of the system," he ordered after a moment. They hadn't picked up any hint of early-warning satellites, but passive sensors probably *wouldn't* until it was too late. "We'll slip back into hyperspace once we're out of sensor range."

"Aye, Captain," Grace said.

◆ ◆ ◆

"Home," Jean-Luc said.

Looking at the holographic image, he couldn't help feeling a trace of awe. He'd never seen his homeworld from orbit, not even when he'd been taken prisoner and transported to the penal colony. The Theocracy had shoved him and his fellow prisoners into boxes and left them there until they'd finally reached their new home. Several of them had died along the way, too weak or hungry to last long enough to survive. Now, he was back . . .

Perrier coughed. "Can you break through the defenses?"

"Yes," Captain Falcone said. "We'll have to lay waste to the system's industry, though."

Jean-Luc swallowed. "We *need* that industry!"

"The Theocracy controls it," Captain Falcone said. Her voice was gentle, but there was no *give* in it at all. "We'll help you to rebuild after liberation, I promise. But until then, we cannot allow the Theocracy to continue to use it against us."

"And there's no hope of preventing them from retaking control of the high orbitals," Perrier added. "There would be no time to build up our defenses before we lost control, again."

He sighed. "Do what you need to do, Captain," he said. "We'll send you the bill later."

The captain smiled. "We'll leave the freighters back here," she said. "The clock will start ticking the moment we enter the system, so have your people ready to move in and disembark as soon as possible. I estimate we will have less than three days before the Theocracy responds to the attack."

Jean-Luc swallowed. He'd thought himself ready to return to the fray, but now . . .

"I understand," Perrier said. "We will be ready."

"Good," the captain said. "We'll transfer you over to the freighters, then jump into the system; we'll come back to get you once the battle is over. Good luck."

"Thank you, Captain," Perrier said.

◆ ◆ ◆

"*Thundergod* is to take out the cloudscoop and any freighters within range," Kat ordered as she took her command chair. "Inform Captain

Bannister that I want her to time her attack so that it goes in at the same moment as ours."

"Aye, Captain," the XO said.

"There is to be no attempt to capture the cloudscoop," Kat added. "I just want it smashed. If she can take out the freighters first, without compromising her ability to deal with the cloudscoop, she is to do so, but the cloudscoop is her priority target."

"Aye, Captain," the XO said again.

Kat nodded, then settled back in her command chair. They'd gone through everything *Mermaid* had brought back with a fine-tooth comb and she knew they *should* have the advantage, but it was quite possible that something had been missed. Perhaps there was an enemy cruiser squadron lying doggo, ready to spring a trap, or even a whole formation of gunboats. Kat knew, from bitter experience, that gunboats were less effective against ships and squadrons that were prepared for them, but they'd still be a nasty opponent. Her formation's point defense datanet simply wasn't up to modern standards.

She pushed the thought aside, savagely. "Mr. XO," she said formally, "is my command ready for operations?"

"Yes, Captain," the XO said. "All stations report ready."

Kat sucked in a long breath. She'd considered sneaking up on Verdean, just as she'd done to the penal colony, but too much could go wrong. Verdean had too many starships in orbit, too many sensors probing space for her to feel comfortable about slipping into point-blank range without being detected. No, she'd have to launch a more conventional attack and hope it was sufficient to brush the enemy's defenses aside before they could be turned on the planet and slaughter the civilian population.

"We will proceed with Attack Pattern Delta," she said firmly. "Inform the squadron."

"Aye, Captain," the XO said. "Attack Pattern Delta, confirmed."

Kat nodded, feeling the tension rising within her chest. "Helm," she ordered. "Set course for Verdean."

"Aye, Captain," Weiberg said.

They were already holding station within hyperspace, a bare handful of light days from the system itself. They'd be on their target within minutes, slamming out of hyperspace . . . and, perhaps, coming under fire the moment they showed themselves. Hell, it *was* vaguely possible that they'd *already* been detected, thanks to the oddities of hyperspace and the sheer number of ships making their way in and out of the system. *Mermaid* had reported no obvious attempt to prepare for an attack, but the Theocracy could be trying to lure them into a trap.

"Opening gates in twenty seconds," Weiberg reported.

"Stand by all weapons," Kat ordered sharply. "Fire on my mark."

The gateway blossomed open in front of the flotilla, revealing a blue-green world surrounded by tactical icons. Kat stared, watching the stations rapidly taking on shape and form; the world looked surrounded, trapped by a web of steel. But it was an illusion, she knew; it was unlikely that more than a couple of the orbiting stations were armed. The dangers of a serf revolt were just too great.

"Fire," she ordered.

Lightning belched missiles: a dozen targeted on the orbital weapons platforms, the remainder aimed at the largest orbital station. The enemy had more time to prepare this time, even if it was just scant seconds; the Theocracy's electronic servants took control of the point defense and hastily opened fire, trying to swat down as many missiles as they could before they reached their targets. Kat smiled coldly—the orbital weapons platforms were aimed at the planet, not threats coming in from outside—as her missiles started to strike home. A dozen orbital platforms died in the first few seconds of combat.

"Enemy station is launching missiles," Roach snapped. "They're targeting the patrol boats."

"Cover them with point defense, but keep firing," Kat ordered. It was smart of the enemy to target her smaller ships, the ones lacking any real defenses. They might not know it, but they were weakening her ability to scout out new targets. "If any of the other stations open fire, target them too."

"Aye, Captain," Roach said. New icons flashed up on the tactical display. "Gunboats inbound; I say again, gunboats inbound."

"Target them as soon as they enter range," Kat ordered. There was no hope of evading them, not when they were easily twice as fast in real-space as any of her ships. Memories of them slamming antimatter missiles into 7th Fleet rose up in front of her eyes, chilling her to the bone. But 6th Fleet had been ready for them. "Continue firing . . ."

The enemy station's shields flickered, then died. A missile punched through the hull and detonated inside the structure, destroying its integrity and blowing it into a cloud of debris that scattered in all directions. Most of the debris would eventually be pulled into the planet's atmosphere and burn up, but some of the pieces were large enough to survive the fall through the atmosphere and hit the ground, doing real damage. She made a mental note to ensure they were broken into smaller pieces before time ran out, then looked back at the display. Seven gunboats were bearing down on *Juno*, firing constantly. They didn't seem to be armed with anti-matter missiles, she noted, but nuclear warheads were quite bad enough.

"*Juno* is taking heavy damage," the XO reported. Two gunboats died, picked off by the point defense, but the remainder kept firing. "Captain . . ."

Kat winced as *Juno* vanished from the display. Seventeen officers and crewmen, some reservists, some conscripted from civilian life, some volunteers hoping to get on the fast track to command . . . they hadn't stood a chance. There was no hope of picking up survivors, not when the Theocracy had a habit of taking potshots at lifeboats. All they could do was avenge the dead.

"*Juno* is gone," Roach reported.

"Continue firing," Kat ordered harshly. One of the automated weapons platforms was swinging back to cover the planet, readying itself to target population centers. Another launched a spread of missiles at *Lightning*, all of which were swatted out of space before they could strike the heavy cruiser. The platform itself died a moment later. "Take out the remaining weapons platforms, *now*."

"Aye, Captain," Roach said.

"*Henry Crux* is under heavy attack," the XO warned. "She's taking a beating."

"Move up *Mermaid* and *Max Mercury* to cover her," Kat ordered. Only three gunboats were left, but their crews were good. They'd even bolted missiles to their hulls . . . had they expected an attack, or had they merely sought to increase their mobile firepower? She would have to ask, assuming they took any prisoners. "Order *Henry Crux* to prepare to jump out if she cannot hold her position."

The last gunboat flickered, then vanished from the display. "All enemy gunboats have been destroyed," Roach reported. "The final weapons platform is under attack now."

Kat nodded, then watched—feeling a cold wellspring of delight—as the last platform exploded into atoms. Maybe there were nuclear warheads on the surface, concealed within the cities, but at least the occupation force would no longer be able to call down fire from heaven. Unless, of course, any of the remaining stations were armed. None of them had actually fired a shot, at least not yet, but she knew better than to take that for granted.

"Picking up a gateway here," Roach said, sharply. "Tactical computers think it's a courier boat, leaving the system."

"Understood," Kat said, grimly. The clock had always been ticking, but now she knew the enemy would be alerted soon. Courier boats were the fastest things in hyperspace for a reason. It would be nice to hope that something unfortunate would happen to her in transit, but she knew better than to count on it. "Put a timer on the main display."

"Aye, Captain," Roach said.

Kat thought fast. The enemy presumably knew that help would be on the way, but would they try to hold out? If they thought they didn't have a hope of escaping their own superiors, they might fight anyway, even though the battle was hopeless. Better to die quickly than slowly at the hands of the Theocratic Inquisition. Kat had seen a couple of their files detailing the precise way to handle sinners, defeatists, and traitors, and she had to admit they *did* tend to discourage surrender. But she had to try.

"Send the surrender demand to the orbital stations," she ordered. The demand did include an offer to take future POWs back to the Commonwealth, well away from any possibility of recapture, but she had a feeling it wouldn't be believed. "Refine targeting solutions for enemy bases on the ground."

"Aye, Captain," Linda said.

"I've identified several hundred enemy bases on the ground," Roach said. New icons popped up as the display centered on the planet itself. "Most of them look like military fortresses, Captain; there doesn't seem to be much else."

"Target them with KEWs, then open fire," Kat ordered. Perrier and his men had told her about the Theocracy's attempt to open schools to teach their religion, but she was damned if she was dropping KEWs on a school. There would be too much collateral damage merely from targeting the military bases. "Take as many of them out as possible."

"Aye, Captain," Roach said. The squadron wasn't set up for planetary bombardment, but it had enough KEWs to shatter the Theocracy's grip on the world below. "Bombs away."

"Picking up a message from the orbital stations," Linda said. "There's been an uprising, Captain. Most of the overseers are dead. The crews would like to surrender."

"Inform them that Marines are on the way to take control," Kat ordered. The crews would have to be taken away from the planet, unless they were determined to stay. She hoped not, if only because they had skills the Commonwealth needed. "They are to prepare themselves for transport once the orbital stations are under control."

"Aye, Captain," Linda said.

"A number of freighters are also making their escape," Roach said. "They're fleeing in all directions."

Kat shrugged. "Target any that come within range and destroy them if they refuse to surrender, but otherwise let them go," she ordered shortly. She would have liked to capture or destroy every freighter in the system, yet it would be impossible to take them *all* out without causing too many problems. "Dispatch *Mermaid* back to the freighters. It's time for Perrier and his men to return home."

"Aye, Captain," Roach said.

"We fired off sixty percent of our missiles," the XO said over the private channel. "Two of the light cruisers practically shot themselves dry."

"We'll have to reload," Kat said. She doubted the enemy would only send a couple of destroyers to deal with her, not when they had two superdreadnought squadrons on hand. It was unlikely her own squadron would be able to defeat whoever turned up to investigate. "Send the empty ships back to the RV point to reload, then return here."

"Aye, Captain," the XO said.

Roach cleared his throat. "Captain, I have the first reports," he said. "Eighty percent of our targets on the ground were smashed. The enemy command network is in tatters."

And the planet will be falling into chaos, Kat added mentally. She couldn't help thinking of Cadiz and the chaos that had run loose in the hours between the Commonwealth's retreat and the Theocracy's invasion. *Unless the resistance manages to establish some order before it's too late.*

"If you detect any more enemy concentrations, hit them," she ordered. "However, if you make contact with any of the resistance leaders, warn them we cannot stay in the system indefinitely. The Theocracy *will* be back and they *will* want revenge."

"I could broadcast a message on an open channel," Linda offered. "They'd be sure to be monitoring the channels, even if they're not daring to broadcast."

"Do it," Kat ordered. "Everything else will have to wait for the freighters to arrive."

CHAPTER NINETEEN

"The cloudscoop and seven freighters were destroyed, Captain," Captain Minford Bannister reported. She was a short woman with an aggressive temperament that had already cost her a chance at a more normal command. "I picked up a handful of escape pods, but the passengers were quite violent and had to be sedated."

"We'll keep them on the freighters once we get back to the RV point," Kat said. "Were there any other issues?"

"None, Captain," Minford said. "There were a handful of small settlements on the moons, but I didn't regard them as being worth destroying. They may have been established before the Theocracy rolled into the system."

"Local files would seem to agree," Davidson said. "The Theocracy didn't seem to think they were worth considering a potential threat."

Kat nodded. "Thank you, Captain Bannister," she said. "And please extend my compliments to your gunnery crews."

"Thank you," Minford said. "Do you still intend to remain in orbit until the enemy counterattack?"

"For the moment," Kat said. "We will see."

She tapped the console. Minford's face vanished from the display.

"I doubt we hurt the Theocracy that much," Davidson said. "By any reasonable standards, the industrial nodes here are a tiny percentage of what they have to have, if they're facing us on even terms. But losing them may cause problems in the future."

Kat nodded. The intelligence teams had swarmed over the captured stations, discovering that they'd largely been keyed to producing farming and life support equipment for a dozen nearby colony worlds. A minor matter, with the possible exception of the cloudscoop, but it would cause them headaches in the future. Who knew *what* would happen if smaller colonies could no longer feed themselves? Or, more likely, if there were problems fueling the ships traveling from system to system?

At the very least, they will have to start supplying the fuel from Aswan, she thought coldly. *It might just hamper what they have available for supporting the offensive.*

She ran a hand through her long hair, dismissing the thought. "And the captured personnel?"

Davidson took a breath. "As you suspected, Captain, most of them came from Verdean," he said. "They were conscripted into the workforce, their families held on one of the colonies on Verdean III. We've captured the bases and reunited families, but most of them don't want to leave their homeworld. We may have to drag them off world by force."

Kat winced. Tools and equipment were useful, but they were largely useless without a trained workforce to operate them. The Theocracy had to be short on the latter, which meant that removing the workers permanently—by force, if necessary—would hamper their war effort. But she didn't *want* to take them and their families by force.

"See if Perrier can convince them to depart," she said. "If not"—she took a breath—"they'll have to come with us anyway, as prisoners. They will be treated well, and we will return them when it's safe to do so, but they cannot be left behind. They'd be put back to work for the enemy."

"Or shipped off somewhere else, now that there's no point in keeping them here," Davidson offered. "I'll see to it personally, Captain."

Kat nodded, relieved.

"We also captured a dozen additional freighters," Davidson added. "Unfortunately, there was very little war material in the system and most of it was expended on us. I don't think we have any realistic hopes of setting an ambush."

"Understood," Kat said. She *had* had hopes, but she knew better than to rely on capturing something useful from the enemy. "And the resistance fighters?"

"They're on their way to the ground," Davidson said. "I don't think they're going to have a very pleasant time of it, Captain."

"I know," Kat said. Verdean had taken a battering; the Theocracy had ruthlessly purged any traces of the old order, then she'd smashed the Theocracy's military and government bases herself. Most of the planet's cities were in chaos, a state that would last until the Theocracy returned and hammered any visible centers of resistance from orbit. "Is there anyone on the surface we should consider evacuating too?"

"Not as yet," Davidson said. "We do have an open offer for anyone related to the resistance fighters, or anyone with useful skills, but so far no one has come forward and requested pickup. They may feel it's a trap . . ."

"Or that we're no better than the Theocracy," Kat finished. No one had said so, but she was sure a number of innocent civilians had been killed in the bombardment. "Or that we won't be staying long enough to pick up anyone."

"True," Davidson said. He cleared his throat. "What do you want to do with the freighters?"

"Put the former industrial personnel onboard, then send them to the RV point," Kat said. "Under the circumstances, we can probably risk sending them straight back home, even if they *do* have to fly through the Reach. Admiral Christian will be pleased, I hope, with the reports of our success."

Davidson nodded. "Of course," he said. "I . . ."

He broke off as the console chimed. "Brilliant," Kat said, glancing at it. "Rose MacDonald would like to speak with me."

"We're in the middle of a war zone," Davidson pointed out. "You could refuse . . ."

"I may as well speak to her," Kat said. She tapped the console, then nodded. "Go see to the industrial workers, Pat. Try and get them to come willingly, if possible."

Davidson nodded, then left, the hatch hissing closed behind him. She sighed and gathered herself as best as she could before the door buzzed loudly, announcing the arrival of the observer. Kat brought up the near-orbit display so she could keep an eye on it—the timer, hovering over the planet, counting down the seconds until enemy forces could reach Verdean from Aswan—and then keyed a switch. The door hissed open, revealing the grim-faced observer.

"Captain," she said, "why *are* we sending thousands of resistance fighters into a hopeless battle?"

"They want to return to their homeworld and make the Theocracy miserable," Kat said as the door hissed closed. She waved the observer into a chair, then glanced at the display. "Who are we to stand in their way?"

"Most of them will be dead by the end of the week," the observer said coldly. "I am no stranger to the power of orbital bombardment, Captain."

"Nor is the Theocracy," Kat sighed. "I would agree with you, Miss MacDonald, but anything that delays the Theocracy works in our favor."

"Call me Rose," the observer said. She met Kat's eyes, unflinchingly. "Do you really believe the resistance here can make a major difference? Or are you just using them for your own aims?"

Kat kept her face expressionless. She knew, from her XO, that Rose had a political agenda, but the question was a fair one. On the face of it, the resistance on Verdean was doomed; the Theocracy would crush them from orbit, as the observer knew. And yet, they might have their uses when the Royal Navy took the offensive. Who knew *what* the future would bring?

"The Theocracy is likely to start scorching worlds when we take the offensive," she said finally. "They'd want to deny us the chance to liberate them, let alone make use of whatever resources those worlds could offer us. Having a resistance force on the planet might make the difference between successfully saving their world and watching helplessly as it burns to ash."

Rose frowned. "Do you think the Theocracy will destroy Hebrides?"

Kat felt a sudden flicker of sympathy for the older woman. Tyre had been attacked, but the attacks had been comparatively minor: a handful of commando attacks, viruses inserted into computer systems, and a couple of bombings. Hebrides, on the other hand, had been invaded and occupied, with the Theocracy crushing all resistance from orbit. It was quite likely the enemy would scorch captured worlds, if there was a strong chance of them being liberated, if only to force the Commonwealth to choose between letting the worlds burn and leaving them in enemy hands.

"I don't know," she said. "But I do know that leaving the captured worlds in enemy hands will be just as destructive."

Kat sighed. "It's easy to make these choices from a distance, from a detached perspective," she added. "But when it comes to reality . . . the choices we make have consequences."

"They always do," Rose agreed. She looked down at the deck for a long moment, then back at Kat. "Do *you* feel the Commonwealth always makes wise decisions?"

"I think it has a habit of making the best decision it can, at the time," Kat said. "And sometimes those decisions cause problems, which have to be solved, but those solutions tend to cause other problems . . . and so on, and so on."

Rose smiled. "Like fighting the war?"

"It takes two people to stop a war, but only one to start it," Kat said. "The Theocracy was gobbling up worlds for decades before we even knew it had survived the Breakdown, let alone started an advance towards us. I don't think we had much of a choice, but to prepare for war. The refugees alone should have warned us the enemy was far from friendly."

"They did," Rose said. She frowned tightly. "What happened at Cadiz?"

Kat hesitated, suddenly aware of dangerous waters surrounding her. The truth—that Admiral Morrison had been an idiot—wasn't very well known, not when it might have demoralized the Commonwealth at the worst possible moment. But no one could look at the facts, even the handful of elements in the public domain, and think that *someone* hadn't blundered. In the long term, the truth would come out and, when it did, it would be devastating.

"We were caught by surprise," she said. She normally used a cruder expression, but there was something about Rose that made it hard to swear in front of her. "And they drove us away from the planet."

Kat shrugged, then nodded to the display. "We will have to leave here too," she added, warningly. "But we will return."

◆ ◆ ◆

"This is supposed to be *home*," Jean-Luc protested.

He'd been *born* in Filose City. His parents had met in the city, they'd married in the city, and they'd raised three children in the city. It hadn't been a bad place to grow up either, until the Theocracy had arrived. After that . . . it might have been a nightmare, but it was still largely intact. Now, large parts of Filose were in ruins, hundreds of buildings were nothing more than piles of rubble, and there was a giant crater in the heart of the city where the Theocracy had established their government base.

And there were bodies everywhere.

He shuddered as he stared down at the corpses. Many of them were enemy soldiers or clerics—their captors had been very inventive in devising unpleasant ways for them to die—but countless others were civilians: men, women, and children who'd fallen on their enemies, no longer scared to raise a hand against them. A young man lay on the ground, his head gone; beside him, a young woman had bled to death from three bullet wounds in her chest . . . he swallowed hard, barely able to keep his gorge from rising as he saw the remains of a child lying on the ground. The corpse was so mutilated that he honestly couldn't tell if it was a boy or a girl. Probably a boy, he told himself, although he could have been wrong. Most families had learned, very quickly, to keep their young women indoors at all times.

Because otherwise they might be raped, he thought, feeling bitter hatred curdling in his heart. *It would remind them of their place, they were told, if they were caught outside by the janissaries . . .*

He peered into the distance, trying to match the ruined city with the mental image he'd clung to for a year. The Black Tower had been there, he thought—the home of the city's military commander. Rumor had it that he'd committed the most awful crimes; he'd raped and killed hundreds of people personally, just to satisfy his hellish lusts. Jean-Luc had no idea how many of the rumors were true, if *any* of them were true, but no one had dared go near the Black Tower. Anyone who went inside as a prisoner was never seen again.

And they claimed to be telling us the true way to live, he thought. The religious classes had been hard, with whippings for anyone who forgot even a single word. And the mere accusation of heresy could kill. *We lived in fear, and hatred, and desperation.*

He looked back at Perrier. "Sir?"

"Most of the remaining civilians have headed for the hills," Perrier said. His face was bleak; he'd been away for five years, not one. To him, the devastation had to seem far worse. "We'll be falling back to join them there."

"As you wish," Jean-Luc said. There was no point in staying. He'd hoped to find traces of his relatives, even though his immediate family was dead, but it was clearly futile. The city was too badly damaged for anyone to remain, unless they were capable of finding food and drink among the wreckage. "How . . . how many people do you think died here?"

Perrier shook his head sadly. "I wouldn't care to guess," he said. He studied the bodies for a chilling moment, then looked up. "How many people lived here before you were captured?"

Jean-Luc frowned, trying to recall if he'd ever been told. "At least a few hundred thousand," he said, finally. Filose hadn't had the population density of Cherbourg or New Paris, but it had been a reasonably large city. "They can't *all* be dead."

"Maybe." Perrier continued to gaze at the wreckage and the bodies. "People taken off the streets and shot for looking suspicious, people press-ganged into worker teams, people moved into controlled environments to make it harder for the resistance to influence them . . . people killed in the final moments when the rocks rained from overhead and the population went mad. And everyone who survived might be heading for the hills."

"Where there won't be enough food," Jean-Luc said. He stared into the distance. A plume of smoke was rising from a former enemy base. The nasty part of his mind hoped the enemy soldiers had lasted long enough to be brutally murdered by their former victims. "They won't last the winter."

"The ration packs are being dropped to us," Perrier reminded him. "And we will have a chance to set up new base camps before the enemy return. They'll probably focus their attention on the larger cities. There are more human resources there."

Jean-Luc nodded. "Now what?"

Perrier rubbed his hands together. "Now we go to ground," he said. "Let them return, let them get complacent, and then we will come out of the hills."

◆ ◆ ◆

"They want what?"

"A number of the collaborators started signaling for help," Davidson said, "offering everything they knew in exchange for a ticket off the planet. What do we do with them?"

William sighed. "Captain Falcone is getting some long overdue sleep," he said. He resisted the temptation to add *alone* to the statement. They *had* to know he'd noticed they'd shared a cabin from time to time, even though it was technically against regulations. It didn't seem to be interfering with their duties, so he wasn't inclined to make a fuss about it. "Do they know anything useful?"

"They certainly know a great deal about how the Theocracy treats the conquered populations," Davidson said. "However, they're reluctant to say anything else without guarantees. They want us to lift them out before their fellows capture them or the Theocracy returns."

"Because both of them will kill the assholes, either for collaborating or failure," William said curtly. Were there any collaborators on Hebrides? Patriotism told him no, but cold logic suggested otherwise. There had been collaborators on Cadiz, despite the occupation force's general incompetence; there was always *someone* who wanted power, or revenge, or safety . . . or merely enough cash to be able to relax for the rest of his life. "Are they worth taking?"

"I don't think so," Davidson said. "But if we allow a massacre, it could have political implications."

"They'll be less willing to surrender to us later," William muttered. "*And* people will say we allowed, even encouraged, the slaughter."

He shook his head. "Tell them that if they surrender to us, we'll take them—but only if they cooperate completely without any attempt to lie to us," he said firmly. "If they are caught out, the deal is off and they will be treated as collaborators."

Davidson frowned. "You *do* realize that some of these individuals are guilty of the most awful crimes?"

William glowered at him. "Do you have a better suggestion? We either take them now, which will at least allow us to drain them of useful intelligence, or leave them to be slaughtered. I don't see any alternative."

"Me neither," Davidson admitted. "But it will seriously piss off the resistance."

"We can drop them on a penal world," William suggested. "It wouldn't be much of a problem for us, even if it's one of *our* hellholes rather than an enemy penal camp we liberate. If they're guilty of more than just trying to keep their families alive . . . well, we can punish them ourselves."

He looked at the display for a long moment. "And I think the captain will say the same," he added. "There's a time for emotional reactions and a time for pragmatism."

"I hope you're right," Davidson said. "But this looks very much like a no-win situation to me."

William shrugged. "It always was," he said. "Because when the enemy arrives, we're going to have to put our tail between our legs and run."

CHAPTER TWENTY

"Admiral?"

Admiral Junayd jerked awake, muttering curses under his breath. "What?"

"This is Ali, in Tracking," a voice said. He sounded alarmed. "A courier boat just jumped in from Verdean. The system is under attack!"

"Sound a general alert," Admiral Junayd ordered. He swung his legs out of bed, then stood. "Get me a tactical download as soon as possible."

"Aye, Admiral," Ali said. There was a pause while Admiral Junayd grabbed his trousers and jacket, pulling them on over his underclothes. "Tactical download available now."

"Route it to my terminal," Admiral Junayd ordered. "And then copy it to my staff."

He frowned as the terminal lit up. A fleet—no, a small squadron— of starships had entered the Verdean System and engaged the orbital defenses, blowing them into flaming debris before they could either repel the attackers or turn their firepower on the planet below. By the time the watchdog jumped out, heading for Aswan, the defenses were in tatters and the planet was sure to fall, either to the newcomers or the local resistance. The final emergency report suggested that several other locations within the system were *also* under attack.

This squadron may have captured or destroyed the convoy, he thought as he watched the download for the second time. The watchdog's sensors weren't up to scratch—no one had considered the Verdean System important enough to receive a modern ship—but they had picked up enough detail for him to make educated guesses about the attackers. *And then they headed directly to Verdean . . .*

He paused. *No, the timing doesn't work out*, he told himself. *They went somewhere else first, somewhere . . . but where? Unless they were just scouting for potential targets.*

"Inform my staff," he ordered. "The 23rd Superdreadnought Squadron is to ready itself for immediate departure. I shall be shuttling over in"—he glanced at the chronometer—"twenty minutes. Commodore Malian will remain in command of the base."

"Yes, Admiral," Ali said.

"And order Commodore Malian, Captain Haran, and Cleric Peter to meet me in my office in five minutes," he added. His steward appeared from a side door, carrying a large mug of coffee and a tray of biscuits. "They are *not* to be late."

The coffee was scorching hot, but he drank it anyway, nibbling on a couple of biscuits as he walked through the corridors to his office. He'd had time, thankfully, to replace the comfortable furniture with something more befitting a Theocracy commander, although traces of the office's former owner could still be seen if one looked carefully. Thankfully, Peter—his cleric—was so depressed over his assignment that he spent most of his time in his quarters rather than making a nuisance of himself. Admiral Junayd had a sneaking suspicion he was actually bending the rules in other ways, but so far he had no proof. If he had something he could hold over the cleric's head . . .

He smiled at the thought as he stepped into the office and took his seat behind the desk. A large star chart was already showing the distance between Aswan and Verdean, reminding him that it would take at least two days to get the superdreadnoughts to Verdean, even if they pushed their drives to the limit. Admiral Junayd wouldn't have cared to risk it, not given the near-complete lack of maintenance, but there was no choice. He *couldn't* leave an enemy force in possession of an occupied system for long.

"Admiral," Malian said. "Is it wise for you to take command of the squadron yourself?"

"I have more recent combat experience," Admiral Junayd said shortly. It was true—and besides, the thought of *staying* on the station was driving him mad. "It isn't up for debate."

He nodded to the commodore as Captain Haran, his chief of staff, and the cleric hurried into the room. The captain looked alarmingly efficient, as always, but the cleric looked as if he had been woken from a very sound sleep. There would be a chance for him to catch up on his sleep once they were on the superdreadnought, he was sure; besides, it would keep the cleric from poking around on the naval base while he was gone.

"I will take command and lead the superdreadnoughts to Verdean," he said in tones that brooked no dissent. "Commodore Malian, you will assume command of the base in my absence; whatever happens, do *not* send away the second squadron of superdreadnoughts. The attack may be a diversion to convince us to weaken our defenses here."

"Yes, Admiral," Malian said.

"Transmit a signal to home, informing them of the attack and that a squadron of enemy ships is loose in our rear," Admiral Junayd added. "Request both reinforcements and personnel to turn this base into something more useful. Warn them that Verdean's industrial base will be destroyed, if it hasn't been already. We may expect fuel shortfalls in this sector at the very least."

He looked at the cleric. "You and the captain will accompany me," he added. "I expect you to spend your time ministering to the ship's crew and praying to God that we manage to trap the enemy before they can retreat."

"Yes, Admiral," Peter said. He seemed to lack the fanatical mien of most clerics, somewhat to Admiral Junayd's relief. A fanatic would be a major headache, questioning everything at precisely the wrong time. "I will accompany you."

"Good," Admiral Junayd said. He rose to his feet. "Commodore, the station is yours. Try not to let it be attacked before I return."

"Aye, Admiral," Malian said.

Admiral Junayd smiled, then headed for the shuttlebay, his two officers following in his wake. The rest of his staff would already be on their way; once they arrived, they would start running through tactical simulations. Admiral Junayd had a feeling they were wasting their time—nothing short of a squadron of superdreadnoughts would try to stand up to *his* squadron of superdreadnoughts—but it didn't matter. He would show his zeal in responding to any threat to his command— and also give his crews some much-needed training before they had to cope with a *real* threat. Commodore Malian and his officers had let standards slip way too far.

Two days to get there, he thought. *Two days for the enemy to wreak havoc, then retreat before we can arrive. They won't stick around and wait for us.*

◆ ◆ ◆

"They'll be here at any moment," the XO said.

Kat nodded. The timer had reached zero thirty minutes ago, warning her that she could expect an enemy fleet to arrive soon. It was possible, she had to admit, that *something* had happened to the enemy messenger, but she dared not count on it. There were too many things that could go wrong if she started assuming the best, rather than preparing for the worst.

She glanced at him. "Have the shuttles returned from the surface?"

"Yes, Captain," the XO said. "We have the prisoners, and the volunteers, and the workers on the ships."

"Then order the rest of the squadron to slip into hyperspace and head to the RV point," Kat ordered. "Inform Captain Millikan that he is to send the freighters back through the Reach, then give us five days. If we fail to return, he is to declare himself commodore, open the sealed orders in his safe, and then proceed as he sees fit."

"Aye, Captain," the XO said.

Kat swallowed, feeling a lump settling in her stomach. Standing here, just *waiting* for the enemy to attack . . . she hadn't felt so vulnerable since the hasty return to Cadiz, after her cross-border mission. She'd *known* that the enemy superdreadnoughts were on the way; now, she knew the Theocracy would be straining every sinew to get a fleet out to Verdean before she could escape. And, unless she wanted to jump out now and abandon the system, she could do nothing but wait.

The tactical display flickered, then updated. "Captain," the XO said. "The squadron has entered hyperspace."

And let's hope they don't run into the enemy fleet, Kat added silently. Encounters in hyperspace tended to be dangerous for all involved, but the Theocracy wouldn't hesitate to try to run the squadron down if they thought they could. Their pride—and their reputation for being invincible—would have taken a severe dent, thanks to her. *They'd want revenge as well as the mere destruction of my ships.*

"Deploy the ECM drones," she ordered. "And then take us away from the planet, as planned."

"Aye, Captain," the XO said.

She forced herself to relax, studying the latest reports from her tactical staff. Verdean might not have had a military-grade industrial base, but its workers *had* known a great deal about the local sector before the Theocracy arrived. The intelligence staff had done their work well. Four other potential targets had been identified, three of them promising enough to have her planning to detach the remaining patrol boats to scout their defenses. The fourth . . . might be nothing more than a waste of time, if the reports were to be believed. But it might confuse the Theocracy if she attacked . . .

"Gateways," Roach snapped. Alarms rang through the ship. "I say again, gateways!"

Kat nodded, feeling her heart starting to pound. Twelve gateways into hyperspace had opened, disgorging an enemy fleet. Nine superdreadnoughts led the way, flanked by two squadrons of destroyers and a handful of light cruisers. Her squadron wouldn't have stood a chance in a straight fight. But then, she would have been surprised if the enemy *hadn't* responded with overwhelming force. They needed to make a statement as much as she did.

"I have a tentative ID on the superdreadnoughts, Captain," Roach reported. "They're one of the squadrons located at Aswan."

"Good," Kat said. She frowned as the enemy fleet spread out, orienting itself. It wouldn't be long before they locked onto her ship and the false sensor images, even though she was boosting away from the planet. "Keep us on our current course, then jump out on my command."

◆ ◆ ◆

Admiral Junayd couldn't help feeling a sickly sense of defeat as his fleet emerged from hyperspace and started to scan the surrounding region of space. Verdean looked untouched, but the network of satellites, defense platforms, and industrial bases in orbit were gone and the handful of bases on the local moon had clearly been nuked. The bases on the planet, the ones charged with educating the locals in the true faith, weren't even *trying* to contact him. It suggested, very strongly, that they'd been destroyed.

"Admiral, the enemy squadron is pulling away from the planet," the tactical officer reported. "They're well out of engagement range."

Unless we want to risk wasting hundreds of missiles on ballistic trajectories, Admiral Junayd thought. It struck him as a pointless exercise, spitting in the face of the inevitable. *They've timed their departure very well.*

"Detach the light cruisers," he ordered. "They are to enter orbit and attempt to make contact with any forces on the ground."

"Aye, Admiral," the fleet coordination officer said.

"The remainder of the fleet is to go in pursuit," Admiral Junayd added. "Best possible speed."

It was futile, he suspected. He would be surprised if the enemy stuck around long enough for him to overrun their ships, let alone bring them to battle, but it had to be tried. *Someone* would have to take the blame for the failure, and he hadn't been so politically naked since before the war had begun. Besides, the officer in charge of the defenses—along with the forces on the ground—was probably dead. And if he wasn't, given the Theocracy's attitude to defeat, he would soon wish he was. He'd be hung, drawn, and quartered.

Long seconds passed as the fleet altered course, the ponderous superdreadnoughts advancing towards their foe. The enemy fleet held its course and speed; Admiral Junayd had to admire their nerve, even though it worried him. Were they planning to draw the superdreadnoughts into a trap? A minefield, perhaps? Or hidden missile emplacements? Or . . .

"Admiral, the cruisers have made contact with the senior surviving officer on Verdean," the communications officer reported. "His base was hidden, as per protocol; he reports that every base and formation on the planet was wiped out from orbit once the enemy took the high orbitals. Any survivors were picked off by the locals."

"Duly noted," Admiral Junayd said. It was important to reestablish control of Verdean, but for the moment he had other problems. "Is he in any danger?"

"No, sir," the communications officer said. "His bunker was designed to remain undetected."

"Then tell him to wait," Admiral Junayd ordered. "We'll be back for him once we've overrun the enemy squadron."

Or they've jumped into hyperspace and fled, he added silently, in the privacy of his own thoughts. *They have to know they can't match us in a straight fight.*

"The enemy ships will be within firing range in seventeen minutes," Roach reported. "I don't *think* they've seen through our ECM, but they're launching probes and it's only a matter of time."

Kat nodded shortly. "Take us into hyperspace in ten minutes, unless the situation changes," she ordered. She was mildly surprised the enemy had bothered to give chase, although if *she'd* been in the enemy CO's shoes she would probably have wanted to claim she'd done everything she could to catch the imprudent raiders too. "And launch a flight of our own probes back at them. I want a complete breakdown on that squadron before we leave."

"Aye, Captain," Roach said.

We could outrun the bastards with ease if it was just us, Kat thought sourly. *Lightning* wasn't the fastest thing in space, but she was certainly faster than a bunch of lumbering superdreadnoughts. The enemy destroyers were the only ships that could keep up with her and they'd be reluctant to tangle with a heavy cruiser on their own. *Of course, they might try to delay us long enough for the bigger boys to catch up and smash us into atoms.*

"Probes away," Roach said. He frowned. "Captain, the enemy probes are closing in sharply. I don't know how long the ECM will hold up."

"Hold our course and speed," Kat ordered. As far as the enemy could see, they were facing the whole squadron, not a single heavy cruiser and a handful of ECM-projecting drones. What would they do when they finally realized the truth? Push the destroyers forward? Give up? Something else? "And watch for the moment they burn through the ECM."

"Aye, Captain," Roach said.

The XO opened a private channel. "Captain, they may not tip us off," he said. "If they hold *their* nerve, they may try to slip into firing range without revealing that they know there's only one real starship present."

"I know," Kat sent back. It was frustrating; she could fire on the enemy probes, but that would reveal she had only one starship capable of mounting weapons. It wouldn't be hard for the enemy to guess the truth. "But I want to learn as much as we can about them before we have to take our leave."

"Captain," Roach said. "The enemy ships are picking off our drones. Their targeting is unfortunately good."

"So it would seem," Kat agreed. She'd hoped the enemy training schedules had suffered along with their maintenance cycles, but apparently not. Perhaps Verdean was a trap after all. Or, perhaps, their CO had been doing the best he could with the tools he had on hand. It didn't seem as though there was any point in sticking around. "I want to jump out in five minutes."

"Aye, Captain," Weiberg said.

◆ ◆ ◆

Lightning's tactical processors ran through the entire ship, a redundancy built into the system to make it hard for a single lucky hit to disable the datanet and cripple the ship's ability to fight. At worst, the designers had planned it that other elements of the datanet could abandon their regular tasks and assume control of the ship's defenses. It had never occurred to them that a program, slipped into the datanet in the tactical department, could make its way—undetected—into the communications system, then order a signal blister to send a single message to one of the enemy ships. But then, the human element had always been the weakest of any secure system.

The spy uploaded the program, then waited. It sent its message, then erased all traces of its passage before wiping itself from existence. And no one knew what it had done.

Kat took a breath as the enemy ships lumbered closer. "Jump us out," she ordered. "And then generate static as we go."

"Aye, Captain," Weiberg said.

A gateway blossomed to life in front of *Lightning.* The ship shuddered, then plunged forward into hyperspace, followed by the ECM drones. Kat braced herself, half expecting to run into an ambush, but there was nothing more than the flickering lights and energy storms of hyperspace waiting for them. The drones switched to static mode, generating tiny disruptions to make it harder for the enemy to follow their mothership, then started the countdown to self-destruct. *Lightning* picked up speed rapidly, looping around the nexus of gravimetric force representing the primary star, then headed away from the system on an evasive course.

Kat allowed herself a moment of relief. She had assumed the Theocracy would give chase, even through hyperspace, yet it seemed the enemy had other ideas. Perhaps they had a point. She knew, from bitter experience, just how easy it was to lose an advantage if one fought in hyperspace.

"We appear to have broken contact successfully, Captain," Roach said.

"Keep us on our evasive course, for the moment," Kat ordered. There was no point in taking chances. "We'll head around to link up with the rest of the squadron in a day or two."

"Aye, Captain," Weiberg said.

We gave the Theocracy a bloody nose, Kat thought, settling into her command chair. She couldn't help feeling torn between glee and a bitter helpless guilt. *But they'll take it out on the planet, now that we're gone.*

CHAPTER TWENTY-ONE

"The enemy fleet has escaped, Admiral," the tactical officer said. He sounded nervous, no doubt expecting the blame. "We could follow them into hyperspace . . ."

"That won't be necessary," Admiral Junayd said. Hyperspace would give a small squadron advantages against his fleet, advantages he would be foolish to ignore. "Reverse course and take us back to the planet, best possible speed."

"Aye, Admiral," the fleet coordination officer said.

"They sent us a message," the communications officer added. "It was encoded; standard intelligence protocols, identifying the sender."

"Route it down to the intelligence staff," Admiral Junayd ordered. He'd expected the enemy to taunt him, but an encoded message? Had God blessed them with a spy on the enemy ship or was it nothing more than an attempt to bait a trap? Intelligence scheming lacked the beautiful simplicity—and openness—of space warfare; it was quite possible that their spy had been turned, if he'd ever been theirs in the first place. "And then forget you ever saw it."

"Aye, Admiral," the communications officer said.

Admiral Junayd nodded curtly, then switched the display back to the live feed from the light cruisers. The Commonwealth ships *had* hammered the occupation forces on Verdean into the ground, he noted; he would have been impressed, really, if it hadn't been a major headache for him to solve. He didn't have the ground forces sufficient to regain control of the surface, nor could he reasonably slaughter the entire planet. They were, after all, potential believers.

"Get me a direct link to the bunker as soon as you can," he ordered. They'd be within effective communications range in twenty minutes. "And then see if you can raise anyone else."

He shook his head, knowing it was probably futile. The industries of Verdean had been smashed, along with the colonies on the outer worlds and the cloudscoop. There was literally nothing left, apart from the population—and *they* were largely useless. He had a feeling that the Commonwealth, which could be as ruthless as his own people, had either kidnapped the trained workers or simply killed them. It was what *he* would have done.

The planet won't starve, he thought, *but losing the cloudscoop will cause fuel prices across the sector to rise.*

It wasn't a pleasant thought. The Theocracy had used its monopoly of HE3 to keep planets under control, as well as supervising the handful of independent shippers allowed within its territory. Now, dozens of planets would suffer shortages, which would provoke unrest and even riots. In hindsight, it might have been wiser to copy the Commonwealth's practice of establishing a cloudscoop in every system, but that wouldn't have been good for keeping those worlds under control. The weakness of that policy had come back to bite them in the rear.

And it would be damn near impossible to establish a replacement cloud-scoop now, in wartime, he added mentally. *The technicians who would put one together have been diverted to support the offensive.*

He cursed inwardly. Years ago, he'd been taught an old rhyme about the loss of a nail. It was hardly significant in itself, but if the loss of a nail could spell the loss of a horseshoe, and if the loss of a horseshoe could spell the loss of a horse, and if the loss of a horse could spell the loss of a messenger, and if the loss of a messenger could spell the loss of a battle . . . he couldn't help wondering if the attack on Verdean would trigger a similar series of disasters that eventually led to the loss of the war. Or perhaps he was just panicking over nothing. HE3 was stockpiled; there *were* freighters that could ship fuel from Aswan to a dozen other worlds . . . a few worlds might go cold for lack of fusion power, but by then the war would be won or lost anyway. They could endure.

Our ancestors endured hardships when they first spoke the words of the true faith, he reminded himself sternly. *How can we endure any less?*

It's not a fair comparison, his own thoughts mockingly replied. *Your ancestors didn't have to keep the galaxy's mightiest military machine going . . .*

"Admiral," the communications officer said, "I have a direct link to the bunker."

"Put the CO through," Admiral Junayd ordered.

He groaned inwardly as a face appeared on the display. Bearded, unkempt—a sure sign of a fanatic or an Inquisitor. "Admiral," the man said shortly. A line of text under his image identified him as Inquisitor Frazil. "Bombard the enemy positions at once."

"I believe that *I* am the sector commander," Admiral Junayd said. It was hard to keep the surge of anger from his voice, but he kept his tone under firm control. "And we have yet to locate any *enemy positions*. There seems to be a lack of tanks or mobile guns or anything else that might draw the eye."

The Inquisitor glared at him. "It is your duty to reassume control of this world so that the great work may continue," he snapped. "Years of patient work have been destroyed overnight. Many believers have been lost to unbelief."

"We will target enemy positions when they are located," Admiral Junayd said firmly. "However, I do not have the manpower on hand to replenish the occupation force. I will merely take control of the high orbitals, then wait for my superiors to dispatch reinforcements."

"There's no time," the Inquisitor insisted. "I will not see our work wasted!"

"I am in command here," Admiral Junayd said, feeling his temper snap. "You are under my orders. If you refuse to obey, place yourself under arrest on the charge of disobeying orders in the face of the enemy. I *suggest*"—he allowed his voice to harden—"that you do as you're told. We do not have the resources to engage in a bloody pacification campaign and I will not waste what little I have without reinforcements. Do you understand me?"

There was a long pause. An Inquisitor *might* get away with disobeying orders . . . but *someone* would have to take the blame for the disaster. Admiral Junayd waited, his dark eyes daring the younger man to cross the line. The Inquisitor scowled, then lowered his eyes, conceding the point.

"I understand you," he said. "But the believers on the surface will probably be killed!"

"We will do what we can to protect them," Admiral Junayd said. "Now, once we enter orbit, I will send a shuttle for you. I expect to see you on my ship shortly afterwards. Bring with you a complete report and a tactical breakdown. Both of them will be added to my report."

He closed the channel without waiting for a reply, then sighed. "Captain Haran?"

"Yes, Admiral?"

"I want a full report within an hour," Admiral Junayd ordered.

"And make sure you put it together independently of our friend below. He will not hesitate to try to make himself look good."

"Yes, sir," Captain Haran said.

Commander Amman was a slight young man, too thin and effeminate for Admiral Junayd's tastes. Or, perhaps, that was a reaction to his life-long disdain for intelligence analysts; they either got it right, in which case they would brag about their cleverness until he just wanted them to shut up, or they would come up with excellent excuses for getting it wrong. But Commander Amman came with good references, including some from one of Admiral Junayd's old comrades. It made him won-der why the commander had been assigned to Aswan in the first place.

"The message was designed to identify the originator, Admiral," Amman said. "Any intelligence section could decrypt the message, but only the person with the private key could have encrypted it. However, we lack access to the files that would do more than identify the spy as one of ours."

"Of course," Admiral Junayd said. Intelligence officers had a ter-rible habit of telling him things he already knew. Had he not worked closely with intelligence assets during the planning stage of the attack on Cadiz? "Do you know if this spy is a true believer, someone under threat, or an enemy agent?"

"No, Admiral," Amman said. "There was no warning in the files that this particular private key might have been compromised, but that may be meaningless. The enemy would not wish to advertise that they have turned one of our spies."

"Not if they wished to use him against us," Admiral Junayd mut-tered. "And what are the odds of one of the spies being assigned to a deep-raid mission?"

"Impossible to say," Amman said. "We know nothing of how the mission was put together, or what criteria they used to choose personnel. The spy might have engineered his transfer to put himself somewhere useful."

"Or his handlers might have put him there so he can mislead us," Admiral Junayd commented. "And without knowing much about the spy, we cannot guess if he may have been turned or not."

"No, sir," Amman said.

Admiral Junayd shrugged. "All right," he said. "What did the message actually say?"

"Very little," Amman said. "I think there wasn't much time to compose and send the message without risking detection. It basically warned us that the enemy squadron intended to hit Ringer next . . ."

"I see," Admiral Junayd said. He tapped his console, bringing up the star chart. Ringer was nothing more than a bunch of asteroid settlements; indeed, if they hadn't built up a small industrial base of their own, the Theocracy might have either ignored the settlements or transferred their population to an occupied world. "A logical target, would you not say?"

"Yes, sir," Amman said. "Ringer has very little in the way of defenses, beyond a handful of ancient destroyers. However, they do play an important role in providing support to commercial activities throughout the sector. They also have a standing agreement to help train our technicians in exchange for largely being left alone."

"Which means they are vulnerable," Admiral Junayd said. "But they could also be a diversion . . ."

He looked up at the star chart and groaned inwardly. It hadn't been hard to isolate a number of potential targets, but guarding them all was going to be sheer hell. If only he had a dozen StarComs . . . hell, he'd be happy with a couple of dozen additional courier boats! And if he spread his forces too thinly, there was a very real risk of the enemy concentrating their forces, then bringing them to bear against his dispersed units. *And if they launch a major attack on Aswan itself,* he added, *we might lose the base and its facilities before anyone outside the sector knows it's under attack.*

His terminal bleeped. "Admiral, this is Captain Haran," a voice said. "Inquisitor Frazil has come aboard and is waiting in Briefing Room A."

"Understood," Admiral Junayd said.

He looked at the intelligence officer. "We have a chance to set an ambush here," he said, "but we don't dare disperse our forces unless we *know* the spy can be trusted."

"Yes, sir," Amman said.

"I'll detach a couple of cruisers and a courier boat," Admiral Junayd said after a moment. "It would make sense to check on Ringer, particularly after the attack here. They can take up station there and wait. If the enemy shows up on schedule—or within a reasonable space of time—our forces are to engage or retreat, depending on the situation. We would then know, wouldn't we, if the spy was to be trusted?"

"Yes, Admiral," Amman said.

Admiral Junayd nodded, then rose to his feet and walked through the corridors to Briefing Room A. The Inquisitor was sitting at the table, looking grim; beside him, Cleric Peter looked surprisingly alert and Captain Haran was expressionless. Admiral Junayd waved them back into their seats as they started to rise, then sat down facing them.

"Captain," he said. "Your report?"

"Every base on the planet, save for the hidden bunker, has been smashed," Captain Haran said. "The devastation is quite extensive. I believe that collaborators, converts, and others who sided with us have either been killed or removed from the planet. In short, Verdean has returned to its pre-conquest state."

"There will be converts who have hidden their faith," the Inquisitor insisted. "We must protect them . . ."

Admiral Junayd held up a hand. He hadn't expected any change, not given the sheer scope of the enemy bombardment, but he'd had to check.

"I will detach a couple of destroyers and a regiment of janissaries," he said firmly. "They will be charged with securing the capital city, nothing else. Once reinforcements arrive, the remainder of the planet can be secured. I see no reason to waste my limited resources trying to fix a broken world."

"The world is not broken," the Inquisitor insisted. "It has been battered, but remains unbowed."

"It doesn't matter," Admiral Junayd said. "Verdean is no longer important. There are no longer any industries here to be guarded. Nor is there a major force that requires orbital bombardment support. I do not believe the enemy will return and, even if they do, it will make no difference. It will not have an impact on the war if we control every last square inch of the planet or not—or if we surrender control to the resistance. There will be time to deal with the local unbelievers later, once the war is won."

The Inquisitor stared at him in shock. "Admiral . . ."

Privately, Admiral Junayd felt a surge of elation. It was an article of faith, among the Theocracy, that territory, once occupied, could not be surrendered. The mere act of taking it made it theirs; abandoning it, even for tactical purposes, was a challenge to their faith. He felt an odd sense of liberation at accepting the concept, even though it might get him into more trouble. There was truly no *need* to keep Verdean.

"This world is unimportant," he said firmly. "What matters, right now, is an enemy fleet in our rear. It is going to do a great deal of damage before it can be stopped. Captain Haran?"

"Yes, sir?"

"Liaise with Commander Amman," Admiral Junayd ordered. "I want to dispatch a pair of cruisers and a courier boat to Ringer. After that, copy a full set of reports to a courier boat and send it back to Aswan. I will be requesting reinforcements from the homeworld, both starships and ground troops. The latter can be dispatched to Verdean when they arrive."

"Yes, sir," Captain Haran said.

Admiral Junayd nodded, then turned to the Inquisitor. "I will detach a couple of ships, as I said, but no more," he said. "You are under strict orders, which I will give you in writing, to merely hold your position and nothing else. The world will not be *truly* abandoned as long as we maintain a presence on the surface. These orders will not change until the reinforcements arrive."

Unless we get ordered to flatten the planet's remaining cities, if only to remind everyone else of just what happens to rebels, terrorists, and insurgents, he thought. *And then the entire planet will be largely depopulated.*

"My tactical staff will locate a handful of targets for punishment strikes," he continued. "I believe those should cow the enemy, at least long enough for reinforcements to arrive."

And hopefully slake the urge for bloody revenge, Admiral Junayd added silently. *If the Inquisitor manages to convince the Speakers to authorize a general bombardment . . .*

"You will return to the surface and assume command," Junayd concluded. "My fleet will move in two days; less, perhaps, if we receive word of another attack. Until then, I will be in position to support you, if necessary."

"Yes, Admiral," the Inquisitor growled.

Admiral Junayd would have felt sorry for the man if he hadn't been a complete bastard who was willing to bathe the planet in blood just to compensate for his mistake. Hell, it wasn't even *his* mistake. He'd been *twelfth* in the chain of command when the Commonwealth forces had attacked; his commander had died in the opening seconds of the battle and everyone else had died when the enemy had started hitting targets on the ground. Logically, he couldn't be blamed . . .

. . . but logic meant nothing when the Speakers were searching for a scapegoat.

"Good," Admiral Junayd said. "Go."

He looked at the cleric, motioning for him to remain behind. "I assume you've had a chance to speak to the crew?"

"They're very motivated," Peter assured him. "But there is one problem."

Admiral Junayd's eyes narrowed. "A problem?"

"I asked them not to mention it until you and I had a chance to discuss it personally," Peter said. "We managed to get an ID on the heavy cruiser. It's *Lightning*."

"I see," Admiral Junayd said. Somehow, he wasn't too surprised. The commanding officer who'd been tapped for the first known covert probe into Theocratic space would be an excellent choice for the first deep-strike raid. "And this is a problem . . . ?"

"The defenders were beaten by a *woman*," Peter insisted. "A *girl*!"

"Disastrous," Admiral Junayd said dryly. "We already knew that some women from the Commonwealth were very unwomanly indeed."

He wanted to roll his eyes in exasperation. The vast majority of his crew would find the concept of being beaten by a woman embarrassing . . . and there could be no pleasure in *beating* a woman, because she was only a woman. But Admiral Junayd knew better; he'd spent enough time monitoring the Commonwealth to realize that, in many ways, the Commonwealth made far better use of its manpower than the Theocracy. Female spacers could be just as deadly as their male counterparts—and being able to use female labor gave the Commonwealth a far greater pool of trained workers.

"I suggest we keep this to ourselves," he said. Stupid or not, the cleric had a point. It *would* affect morale. "And if the issue is raised, make it clear she is only a puppet, with her strings pulled by men."

"Of course," Peter said. He sounded as though he had solved a complicated puzzle to his satisfaction. "And it would be true."

No, Admiral Junayd thought, coldly. *It wouldn't. But if you want to cling to a delusion . . . then cling to it. But it won't make any difference at all.*

CHAPTER TWENTY-TWO

"There is no greater honor, so we are told, than that earned by those who put their bodies between their homeworlds and the devastation of war," Kat said softly. A third of the cruiser's crew stood in front of her, in the shuttlebay, but the remainder were listening through the intercom. "The crew of HMS *Juno* died in battle, fighting to defend the liberties we take for granted, the liberties that would be stolen from us if we lose this war. They died as heroes and, as such, we salute them."

She took a breath, feeling a sudden ache at her throat. *Juno's* crew had been reduced to atoms; there weren't any coffins to be launched into space, or to be shipped back home to their grieving families. They'd deserved better, she thought, than to die at the hands of the Theocracy, but they hadn't been able to choose the time and place of their deaths. And all she could do was remember them, to speak in their honor and fight on in their name.

"We are from many different worlds," she continued, "and we have many different ways of honoring the dead. But all that matters today is that they were part of our band of brothers and sisters, men and women who fought beside us to hold the line against the enemy. We do them honor, and pledge that their lives and deaths will be neither forgotten nor pointless. We will not forget them."

There was a long pause, then she started to list the dead. "Commander Alum Roebuck, Lieutenant Commander Angelica Ossa, Lieutenant Gage Mosher . . ."

She finished the recital, then bowed her head. "Let us not forget them," she said, quietly. "Dismissed."

The crew saluted, then headed for the hatches. Kat waited until the last of them was gone, then looked down at the list of dead men and women again. She'd watched people die before, knowing there was nothing she could do to save them, but this was different. She was the squadron commander, the commodore, even though she wouldn't hold the rank in anything more than name, and those deaths were on her hands. Maybe she hadn't killed them herself, maybe she hadn't fired the missile that had blown their ship to dust, but she couldn't help feeling as though she'd murdered them personally. They had died following her orders . . .

"Captain," the XO said gently. "It never gets easier."

"That's a good thing, I suppose," Kat said. She didn't want to think about the number of innocent civilians who were dead on Verdean, either through her bombardment or the retaliation she knew the Theocracy would launch. Their deaths, too, were on her hands. "But I can't help feeling responsible."

She shook her head, tiredly. What sort of mind would cold-bloodedly plot a war? Or deliberately launch a surprise attack on an enemy world that would be sure to make the war completely merciless? Or even crush prospective allies because there could be no room in the galaxy for two competing belief systems? It was absurd, she sometimes thought; how could anyone accept a single religion dominating the entire galaxy? And yet, she'd studied the Theocracy's past. Their enemies had tried to strangle their religion in the cradle. They had good reason for wanting to secure their position by all means necessary.

"You cannot help it," the XO said. "Everyone on the squadron understands the dangers, Captain. We all know we may die out here, with no one to recover our bodies, but we accepted the risks when we donned the uniform. The universe is not a safe place at the best of times."

"No," Kat agreed morbidly. "It isn't."

She cleared her throat, pushing her doubts, fears, and all-pervading guilt to the back of her mind. "I assume you spoke to the observer?"

"She wishes to remain on the ship," the XO said. "Her mission, apparently, has not yet been completed."

"Brave or foolish," Kat said. "What do you make of her?"

"She has a job to do," the XO said. "And it wouldn't sit well with her superiors if she took the easy way out, or you kicked her off the squadron. My homeworld expects one to roll with the punches, not waste time denying they ever happened. She might not have *expected* to end up here, but . . . well, she did. My people wouldn't respect her for not making lemonade out of the lemons someone handed her."

Kat took a breath. "Then she can stay here," she said reluctantly. It would be easy enough to contrive an excuse to send Rose MacDonald home, but it would be obvious that it *was* nothing more than an excuse. "As long as she isn't causing trouble."

"I don't think she'd earn respect by causing trouble, not in the middle of a war zone," the XO said drolly. "And you'd have every excuse to put her in the brig until the ship returned home."

"True," Kat agreed. She gave him a sidelong look. "Assemble a meeting of the command staff in the briefing room, twenty minutes from now. Ship commanders can attend via hologram. I'll be here until then."

The XO frowned, then saluted and walked through the hatch, leaving her alone. Kat held herself steady until she heard the hatch close, then sat down in front of the dais and stared down at the black coffin. It was symbolic, nothing more than a place to center one's prayers, yet it was important. Humans needed something to represent the dead.

"I'm sorry," she said quietly. She'd barely known *any* of *Juno's* crew. Sure, she'd had dinner a few times with Commander Roebuck, but there hadn't been time for more than a handful of exchanged words. They'd spent more time planning the operation than getting to know each other. "I wish I'd known you better."

But was that actually true? Perhaps it was easier to plan a war, or even a military operation, when one regarded the officers and crew as nothing more than numbers, statistics entered in the red ledger of the dead. A single death was a tragedy—she knew she would weep for her XO, or Davidson, or even Emily Hawking—but a million might be a statistic. Perhaps there would come a time when she looked upon the death of a dozen worlds, with populations numbering in the billions, and feel that they were a worthy sacrifice, their lives meaningless when weighed against the greater good.

And if that happened, she asked herself silently, would it make her a stateswoman—or a monster?

She looked down at the black coffin for a long moment, wondering if there was anything out there. Tyre had no organized religion, unless one counted the earning of wealth and the acquisition of political power. Who cared *what* someone chose to worship when they could be trading with you? She hadn't been raised to worship anyone, or anything; the whole concept seemed odd to her. And yet, there was a certain consolation in believing that there was an afterlife, that the dead hadn't simply blinked out of existence. She wanted to believe it was true . . .

But how can I, she asked herself, *when humanity has used such beliefs as an excuse to slaughter?*

The Theocracy had soured her on the concept of organized religion, but it was only the most recent offender. It hadn't been *that* long ago that the Church of Quantum Life had murdered over thirty thousand people on Terra Nova, convinced that the planet's beliefs were warping the universe and killing everyone. And then the UN had battled jihadists, Earth Firsts, Green Power, and too many strange and terrible sects to number. And then the pre-space world had seen millions slaughtered in the name of religion, all the way back to the start of human history itself.

She shook her head, then rose and headed for the hatch. There would be time to sort through her doubts later, perhaps even discuss the matter with someone she trusted. For now, she had a mission, one she could not afford to abandon. And if others died . . .

. . . she would just have to cope with the guilt, once the mission was over. There was nothing else she could do.

William knew he would never say it aloud, but he understood precisely what the captain was feeling. She was young, lacking in the seasoning that had taught him that shit happened, no matter what one did to prevent it. He knew she'd acquitted herself well, as commanding officer of *Lightning*, yet this was her first experience of squadron command. Losing a whole ship had to hurt, even though it hadn't been her fault. Only a fool or a politician could seriously expect to go to war without losing ships or lives.

He couldn't help feeling a flicker of relief as she walked into the briefing room, looking composed. Maybe she'd stopped off in her cabin long enough to wash her face if she'd shed private tears, or maybe she'd lost the habit of crying years ago, but it didn't matter. All that mattered was that she looked presentable and determined to carry on the mission. Anything less would have undermined crew morale and threatened their future successes.

"Be seated," she ordered flatly. She tossed an ironic look at the holograms floating at the rear of the compartment, then took her seat at the end of the table. "Commander?"

William cleared his throat. "We have successfully transferred the prisoners, liberated workers, and others to the freighters," he said. "They will be departing to the Reach within the hour, taking with them a copy of our findings so far. Admiral Christian and his intelligence analysts will be happy, no doubt, with the chance to finally start putting details into our charts of enemy space."

The captain nodded. "If any of you have messages you wish to send, bearing in mind that they will be read by the censors first, feel free to add them to the datacores being transferred to the freighters," she added. "Make sure your crews have the same opportunity. It will be several months, at least, before we return home."

If we ever do, William thought. He'd heard enough, during his detachment from *Lightning*, to know just how bloody-minded and vindictive the Theocracy could be. Commonwealth forces had singed the enemy's beard and the enemy would want revenge, something horrific and ghastly enough to make anyone else think twice about trying to raid behind the lines. *The plan was to force them to send ships after us, rather than press the offensive against Admiral Christian, and now they have all the incentive they need to do just that.*

His lips quirked. Being chased by half the ships in the enemy's fleet had sounded like a good idea when they'd thought of it . . .

He glanced at the captain, then pressed on. "We have also reloaded our missile tubes, having expended a considerable number in the recent battle," he continued. "So far, we don't have a serious shortage, but we should probably be careful when it comes to expending more missiles than strictly necessary. We may be able to capture enemy weapons, but firing them from our tubes is simply impossible."

"Not that easy to do, in combat," Commander Kent pointed out tartly. "Weapons usage has always been well over prewar predictions and that's something we have to bear in mind."

"True," the captain agreed. "However, I would prefer not to enter energy range if it could be avoided. The enemy ships will quite likely have better armor than most of our squadron."

William nodded in agreement. "The engineering crews are considering ways to alter enemy missiles so we can use them, but it comes with a great many risks," he said. "For the moment, be careful."

The captain smiled thinly, then leaned forward, resting her elbows on the table. "The enemy knows we're here now," she said. "They may know we hit the convoy, they may know we hit the penal world . . . but they definitely know we hit Verdean. Right now, warnings are probably echoing across the sector, telling their planetary defenses to beware of an enemy fleet."

"If they're willing to admit that something's gone wrong," Commander Jackson offered. "It would make them look very bad to have us running around in their rear."

"They'd have to be idiots to just let us get on with it," William said sharply. "And while they may be ruthless bastards, they're *not* idiots. We have to assume the worst."

The captain nodded. "Which means we don't have time for elaborate raids any longer," she added. "Get in, smash the targets, and get out again. They will attempt to position their ships to catch us; statistically, the odds are in our favor, but they only have to get lucky once. I don't think I need to remind you that a single enemy superdreadnought is more than capable of reducing this entire squadron to dust and ash."

She took a breath, then pushed on. "I intend to hit Ringer, as planned," she said. "The industrial base there is smaller, but it's a vital part of the sector's economy. However, it's quite likely that they'd put it right on the top of suspected targets, which is why we need to move fast."

William nodded, then watched as she keyed the star chart and focused it on Ringer.

"Three days from here to Ringer . . . we can get there, if we're lucky, before word reaches them. That said"—she brushed her hand through her hair—"we will scout the system, as always, and if the defenses have been augmented we will fall back, hopefully without revealing our presence. *Mermaid* will, as always, serve as our spy."

Commander Yale leaned forward. "Commodore," he said, "attacking Ringer will cause a considerable amount of hardship for the locals."

"That's not our concern," Captain Bannister snapped. Her hologram glowered around the compartment. "The locals are working for the Theocracy; willing or unwilling, we cannot allow it to continue. If we offer to take them with us and they accept, that's fine; if not, we cannot allow our concern for them to hamper our operations. We are at war."

"They're not Theocratic civilians," Commander Yale pointed out. "They are, at best, citizens of an occupied state."

"Then they're either working at gunpoint, in which case they should be relieved to have us liberate them, or willing collaborators," Captain Bannister said firmly. "I don't think I need to remind you that the penalty for collaboration is death. There is a reason for that beyond the simple desire to punish them for their crimes."

"No, you don't," the captain said. She tapped her fingers on the table, then leaned forward decisively. "We take them alive, if we can, and if not . . . we won't allow sentimentality to stand in our way."

She paused. "After that . . . we will need to consider our next target carefully," she added. "I want you all to study the data, then pick a target that is unlikely to be defended—and, at the same time, somewhere worth hitting." She smiled rather sardonically. "If, of course, such a place actually exists."

William frowned. He had his doubts. So, it seemed, did the captain.

"We will depart within the hour and pause at a new waypoint, a light year from Ringer," the captain concluded. She waved a hand at the star chart, banishing it. "That will give us time to decide on the next target, then plan a coordinated strike. We may need to divert the enemy by attacking several targets at once—it's a shame they don't have StarComs—but it can be done."

She paused. "Dismissed."

The holograms saluted, then blinked out of existence. One by one, the officers left the compartment until only William and the captain remained.

"There won't be many targets that fit the bill," he said softly. "Quite a few of the worlds here are useless, at least as far as the war effort is concerned. Hitting a purely farming world is nothing more than pointless spite."

"Then we will have to hope that kicking the Theocracy off a planet is a worthwhile goal in itself, as well as forcing them to keep reasserting control," the captain said. She sighed. "It will be costly, but we have no choice. Aswan is too heavily defended to take out without a battle squadron of our own . . ."

"We do have a number of their freighters," William said slowly. An idea had occurred to him. "If we were to capture some antimatter or mining nukes, we could turn one of the ships into a suicide craft. Get through the defenses, dock at the central station, and *BOOM*."

"They'd have to be insane to let the ship dock," the captain said. She cocked her head, thoughtfully. "Even Admiral Morrison wasn't that stupid. They wouldn't let the ship dock without checking her out thoroughly first. We take such precautions ourselves."

"Yes, but they don't *know* there's a threat," William said. "Even a complete failure, with the bombs detonating harmlessly, would force them to spend as long as it took examining every freighter in the sector. It would be costly as hell."

"True," the captain said. She smiled at him. "God knows we had problems after the first raids on Tyre."

William nodded. The commandos had been down for months, perhaps years, before the wars had begun, but the War Cabinet had been forced to order every freighter entering orbit to be carefully inspected before it was allowed to dock. Nothing had been found—nothing from the Theocracy, at least—yet it had caused everything from minor delays to contract defaults and colossal expenses. If there hadn't been a war on, there would likely have been a riot by now.

"See what we can find at Ringer," the captain said. "And until then . . . thank you."

"You're welcome," William said. "It's what I'm here for, Captain."

CHAPTER TWENTY-THREE

"Reminds me of home," Lieutenant Lars Rasmussen said. "Only *my* home colony had a giant planet far too close to us."

"And a place where you could get what you needed, if you couldn't make it for yourself," Midshipwoman Grace Hawthorne pointed out. "Ringer had no contact with anyone until the Theocracy arrived, the poor bastards."

Lars nodded. Quite a few of the first asteroid settlements had been founded by people seeking political or religious freedom, a tradition that had continued ever since the first scoutships had ventured into hyperspace in search of new places to live. Ringer, according to the scant details in the files, had been settled by a group that had wanted to completely isolate itself from the rest of humanity and, to make sure it was left alone, had carefully picked a system that was of little interest to anyone else. A handful of asteroids, a couple of comets, and little else;

it was a closed system in more ways than one. No one had visited the system, as far as anyone knew, until the Theocracy had arrived.

And the locals must have been horrified, he thought, *when they realized just who had found them.*

He pushed the thought aside, then examined the sensor readings. Ringer was a combination of old and new technology, some dating all the way back to the pre-space era, others clearly produced within the last decade. It wasn't uncommon for asteroid settlements to go back to the basics, which were easier to repair, but Ringer had to have received help from outside to keep up with the times. He couldn't keep himself from wondering if the locals had experienced *some* contact with the rest of the sector before the Theocracy arrived, even though the files suggested otherwise. Asteroid settlers tended to be technically proficient—they had to be, just to keep their settlements alive—and Ringer's settlers probably had skills the sector needed. The *Theocracy* certainly wanted them.

"Two cruisers," he muttered. The bright red icons were impossible to miss; it looked, very much, as if the enemy starships were making it clear they were there. "And a handful of defense platforms."

"They may have weapons mounted on the asteroids themselves," Grace reminded him. "I think they'd definitely have point defense, even if they didn't have any long-range missile tubes."

"True," Lars agreed. Asteroid dwellers tended to be of two minds about mounting weapons on settled asteroids. On one hand, they needed point defense; on the other, it drew fire from enemy starships. A single nuclear-tipped missile could shatter an asteroid and kill everyone inside. "I make ten freighters in the system, either docked with the asteroid or waiting in a holding pattern. Do you concur?"

"Confirmed," Grace said. "They may be forming up a convoy."

Lars nodded, slowly. The Commonwealth's shipping lines hated to see freighters docked when they could be moving between star systems and making money, but the Theocracy had always taken a different view of it. They preferred to keep their freighters under control, which, he had to admit, made a great deal of sense if they knew there were prowling raiders in the sector. The two cruisers might be the convoy escort, waiting patiently for all ten freighters to be loaded so they could be on their way. If the squadron could arrive before it was too late, they'd have a chance to capture or destroy a number of freighters *and* a pair of cruisers.

"Back us out, very slowly," he ordered. There was no way to know just how advanced the asteroid's sensors were, but it was quite possible that the locals were preternaturally attuned to the space surrounding them. They might pick up something, the merest flicker, that would reveal his ship's presence. "Commodore Falcone will want to hear about this."

"Aye, sir," Grace said.

"Two light cruisers, Captain," the XO said. "It seems like an easy target."

"And ten freighters," Kat added. "It seems a very *tempting* target."

She studied the star chart, silently calculating vectors in her mind. The enemy *could* have gotten a warning to Ringer by now, if they regarded the handful of asteroid settlements as a priority target. Or they might have enough courier boats to make sending a warning easy without draining their resources. It was just possible that her opponent might have gambled and stationed a small squadron of its own at Ringer . . .

Two light cruisers, she thought. It was unlikely they could do more than delay *Lightning* alone, unless the Theocracy had invented a whole new weapons system. And, oddly, seeing them there was reassuring. If someone had planned an ambush, they'd probably prefer to keep the light cruisers under cloak, just to prevent her taking fright. *We could take them both out and weaken the enemy.*

She nodded slowly. "We'll advance towards the system and jump in here," she said, tapping a location on the display. Close enough to the asteroids to allow her a clean shot at the freighters, far enough from the enemy cruisers to allow her to check they *weren't* supported by an entire superdreadnought squadron before it was too late. "We'll hit the cruisers, then the freighters, if they refuse to surrender."

"Aye, Captain," the XO said. "And our next target?"

Kat sighed. She'd debated it endlessly during the voyage, first with the XO and then with the other starship commanders. No matter how she looked at it, any reasonable targets were likely to be heavily guarded . . . unless, of course, she attempted to divert the enemy's attention through a feint. If the enemy had had a StarCom network, she knew, it would have been a great deal easier as the enemy concentrated resources in threatened systems while she struck elsewhere.

And if we could send signals back to the Commonwealth at FTL speeds, she thought ruefully, *Admiral Christian and the War Cabinet would be peering over my shoulder all the time.*

"Morningside is probably the best target," she said. "But I want to make a feint at Aswan first, just to keep them confused."

"Aye, Captain," the XO said. "I'll have the tactical staff start looking at options now."

"Good," Kat said. She took a breath, studying the final records from *Mermaid*. Ringer might pose complications, but it should be an easy target. Unless, of course, it was a trap. "We move in twenty minutes."

Captain Ruthven ground his teeth together in irritation as the janissaries dragged the two offending crewmen into his office. It hadn't been a good week; first, he and his ship had been assigned to cover a handful of asteroids populated by unbelievers and then, if that hadn't been enough, he'd been given strict orders to withdraw if confronted by overwhelming force. There was no way he could make *that* look good on his service record, no matter his orders; he'd be lucky to have a hope of being assigned to the front before the war was won and all chances of glory faded into nothingness.

He scowled at the two crewmen, who cringed under his gaze. His brothers had both written letters from the front, telling him of the infidels running from their missiles and how they'd brought countless worlds under their thumb. To hear them talk, they'd won the battles personally; they'd certainly made it clear that they'd played a major role in the coming victory. It wouldn't be long before the Theocracy was firmly in control of Tyre and the war came to an end. Ruthven would have no real chance of glory . . . at least until the next war.

"Well," he said angrily. "Do you have anything resembling an explanation?"

The two crewmen exchanged glances. "It was just a spot of fun, sir," one protested. "She was asking for it."

"Aye, she was," the second said. "Wearing sluttish clothes and walking down . . ."

Ruthven nodded to the janissaries, who stabbed the two men with shockrods. They screamed in pain, but somehow managed to remain standing. Clearly they knew better than to show weakness when they were in deep trouble. He sighed in irritation—like their commanding officer, his crew deeply resented their posting to the rear—and then leaned forward, allowing his anger to show on his face. It was well within his authority to have them executed out of hand and they both knew it.

"Let me explain something to you," he said calmly. "The inhabitants of this asteroid cluster bent the knee to us. They *submitted* to us. We allow them to maintain their beliefs, their way of life, as long as they serve us. And they *do* serve us. The items they produce are a vital component of this sector's economy."

He sighed, again. It was unlikely the two crewmen really understood what he was telling them. They'd probably had nothing more than a basic education; they would have learned to recite the holy words from memory, but not to actually think. He would have been surprised if they could even read more than a few words.

"They submitted to us," Ruthven repeated. "And, because of that, they are granted protection as long as they obey. We *swore* we would grant them protection, and safety, in order to keep them working for us. And part of that, as I believe you were informed, is that their women are *not* to be touched. It would upset them."

He glowered at the crewmen, who looked back at him as if he'd started speaking in tongues. They didn't understand, of course; to them, women who were believers were kept under firm control, while any other women were fair game. The concept of certain societies being left alone, in exchange for submission, was probably beyond them. They certainly hadn't taken any of the warnings to heart before they'd dragged a woman off the streets and raped her until she was bleeding. No doubt they expected nothing more than a pat on the back . . .

"We cannot be seen to break our word," he warned. "When a society bends the knee to us, we must grant protection in exchange for submission. You chose to ignore the warnings and harm someone under our protection. For this, you will both be flogged to within an inch of your lives."

He nodded at the janissaries, who dragged the two men out of his office. The sentence would be carried out, of course, and then the men, if they survived, would be reassigned to the punishment units, where they would be given suicidal missions to complete. If they survived for six months, their record would be wiped clean, but he hadn't heard of anyone surviving more than a couple of months. Even outside wartime, there was no shortage of suicidal tasks that needed warm bodies.

Idiots, he thought. But perhaps it wasn't surprising, given their upbringing. *Idiots who shouldn't be allowed to breed . . .*

The ship's alarms started to howl. Ruthven jumped to his feet, then practically ran through the hatch and onto the bridge. Red icons were shimmering into life on the display, enemy starships jumping out of hyperspace gateways and advancing towards the asteroid cluster. He didn't need the lines of text below the starship icons to know that they were the same ships that had attacked Verdean. The size and composition of the flotilla was identical.

"Red alert," he snapped as the enemy fleet oriented itself on his ship. "Prepare to engage the enemy!"

He thought fast. His orders admitted of no ambiguity. If the enemy had superior firepower, enough to make his defeat certain, he was to withdraw at once. But there were ten freighters in the system . . . he'd be blamed for their loss, even though he'd only been following orders from his commanding officer. He'd be lucky to keep his head, let alone his command, once word spread. Any hope of being sent to the front before the inevitable victory would vanish faster than a snowflake in hell.

"The freighters are to cast off and jump into hyperspace," he ordered. Some of them hadn't finished loading, but there was no help for it now. "Freighters that don't have hyperdrives are to follow ships that do. They're to head straight to Aswan and inform the admiral that this system is under attack."

"Aye, Captain," the communications officer said.

Maybe I can salvage something from this after all, Ruthven thought coldly. Saving the freighters might be enough to save his career. The Theocracy didn't have anything like enough bulk freighters, not when they tended to have the worst and least-motivated crews in space. *Protecting the freighters is more important than protecting the unbelievers.*

"Target the lead enemy warship and open fire as soon as they enter missile range," he added, addressing the tactical officer. "Helm, I want you to hold the range open as long as possible."

"Aye, sir," the tactical officer said. "*Bringer of Word* is moving up to support us."

Ruthven nodded. He knew better than to think he could do more than delay the enemy, not if he had to preserve his command, but at least he could *try* to give them a few lumps before his inevitable withdrawal. And if he actually hit one of their ships . . . maybe, just maybe, he would emerge looking good after all.

"Fire as soon as they enter missile range," he repeated. "And then prepare to withdraw once the freighters are on their way."

◆ ◆ ◆

"Enemy ships are almost within engagement range," Roach reported. "Freighters are casting off from the asteroid now."

"Target the enemy ships and open fire as soon as they enter range," Kat ordered. Someone on the other side was reacting coolly, very coolly, to her arrival. There didn't seem to be any panic as far as she could tell; they were calmly trying to get the freighters out before her ships could fall on them like wolves on sheep. "And broadcast the surrender demand, all frequencies."

"Aye, Captain," Linda said.

"Entering missile range," Roach said. He paused as new icons flashed to life on the display. "Enemy ships have opened fire; I say again, enemy ships have opened fire."

"Return fire," Kat ordered. The enemy broadsides matched what she'd expected from a pair of light cruisers. It wouldn't be enough to break through *Lightning's* point defense, although her smaller ships might have problems if the enemy focused on them. Luckily, the brief and violent battle over Verdean had exposed flaws in her point defense datanet. "Repeat the surrender demand, then prepare to target the freighters."

She watched, coolly, as the enemy missiles flew into her point defense network and flickered out of existence. There just weren't enough of them to pose a threat, even if they'd been fitted with the latest penetrator aids. Her own missiles, on the other hand, were overkill; one of the enemy cruisers staggered out of formation, spewing air and debris, while the other altered course, hoping to bring more of its point defense to bear. She smiled coldly, remembering the nightmarish seconds when 7th Fleet had been caught like a rat in a trap, then muttered a command. A second spread of missiles roared towards its target . . .

"Two of the freighters are offering surrender, Captain," Linda said. "A third is charging a vortex generator, preparing to jump out."

They can't have been expecting us, Kat thought with heavy satisfaction. If they'd been expecting a raid, they'd have kept their vortex generators powered up, even though it would have shortened the life of the components by months. *They certainly weren't ready for us.*

"Target that freighter and take it out," she ordered. If the crew wasn't prepared to surrender, there was no point in trying to board the ship. They'd probably try to self-destruct when the Marines arrived. "And then target any other freighter that looks like it's trying to run."

"Aye, Captain," Roach said. He keyed his console. "Missiles away."

Kat smiled. The freighter didn't stand a chance. Two missiles slammed into its puny shields and it vanished into a brilliant fireball. The remaining freighters hastily started to power down their vortex generators, signaling surrender. All she had to do was destroy the cruisers . . .

◆ ◆ ◆

"Captain, the enemy is targeting us," the tactical officer warned.

"I can see that," Ruthven snarled. *Bringer of Word* was dead—or close enough to dead that it made no difference. Captain Zed had always been enthusiastic about closing with the enemy, which was suicidal against a much larger ship. "Open a gateway and get us out of here."

The helmsman swallowed audibly, but nodded. "Aye, Captain," he ordered. A gateway blossomed to life in front of the cruiser, allowing them to lunge forward and dive into hyperspace. It closed behind them seconds later. "We're clear."

"Set course for the edge of the system," Ruthven ordered. They'd observe the enemy formation for as long as they could while the courier boat hastened back to Admiral Junayd to make its report. The admiral wouldn't be pleased about the loss of *Bringer of Word*; Ruthven knew he needed something—anything—to make up for that failure. "Best possible speed."

He leaned forward, cursing under his breath. They'd failed; they'd lost the freighters, unless the enemy decided to be exceptionally foolish, and they'd lost the asteroids. The locals *might* remember who had looked after them, ever since they'd offered their submission, or they might remember the rape and decide the Theocracy's promises weren't worth anything. And if *that* happened . . .

The admiral issued the orders, he thought. *But the admiral might choose to disavow them if he feels I acted wrongly. And then I will be blamed . . .*

He shook his head. He'd done the best he could. Everything else, including his life, was now in God's hands. And God helped those who helped themselves.

CHAPTER TWENTY-FOUR

"Admiral," Captain Haran said. "A courier boat has just arrived from Ringer. The system was attacked."

"Download the tactical report to my console, then call a staff meeting for one hour from now," Admiral Junayd ordered. "And inform the fleet to be ready to move at a moment's notice."

"Aye, sir," Captain Haran said.

Admiral Junayd nodded, then studied the tactical display thoughtfully. Verdean had been quiet since the fleet had entered orbit . . . which hadn't stopped Inquisitor Frazil from calling down fire on a hundred targets over the last couple of days. In the absence of orders from any higher authority, Admiral Junayd hadn't raised any objection. At least it looked as though they were doing something, even though it was largely pointless. The enemy resistance had faded into the country-side, just waiting for outside forces to liberate the system and reclaim the high orbitals. As far as Admiral Junayd was concerned, they could wait forever.

He pushed the thought aside, then frowned as the tactical report appeared on his console. The mystery spy, it seemed, had told the truth; the enemy had attacked the Ringer system and, as of the last report from the courier boat, had engaged both light cruisers. It hadn't looked good, although Admiral Junayd was hopeful that the cruisers would have followed orders and evaded the enemy rather than sacrifice themselves in a display of futile heroics. And if the last update from Captain Ruthven was accurate, the locals might have a very good reason to sign up with the Commonwealth.

So the spy was telling the truth, he thought. *And that means . . . what?*

He scowled, rubbing his goatee thoughtfully. Spies could never be trusted fully, not when they'd betrayed their own side for money or power or whatever else made sense to a moronic spy. The fact the enemy *had* attacked Ringer was a point in the spy's favor, but the enemy could be carefully trying to manipulate him into believing the spy, just so the crushing betrayal would be even more of a shock. Or the spy might grow frustrated with risking his life for nothing and give up if Admiral Junayd didn't make a show of believing him. It was hard enough to guess at the actions of someone he knew, at least from the files, but harder still to guess which way a spy would jump. If only he knew the man . . .

There were just too many possibilities, starting with the simple fact that the enemy had launched another attack and would presumably be moving on to the next set of targets. As long as he was perpetually caught off guard, without ships in position to intercept, they could practically run wild throughout the sector. There was no reasonable chance of ever being able to catch them *without* the spy, but that was what bothered him. The spy was precisely what he needed, at just the right time. It suggested, very strongly, that it might be a trap.

But I don't have a choice, he thought. *I have to rely on the spy.*

He keyed his console. "Order a squadron of light cruisers to prepare for departure to Ringer," he said. It would take at least three days to
get the squadron there, more than long enough for the enemy to finish
destroying the system's industries and pull out. But he couldn't leave the
enemy in place, not when Ringer held so many discontented citizens.
Who knew what they could do if they had time and willing help? "And
then start working up a sphere showing where the enemy might be."

"Aye, sir," Captain Haran said.

It was the same enemy flotilla, according to the reports. There had
been no attempt to disguise *Lightning*, let alone her older compan-
ions. That suggested, very strongly, that there was only *one* squadron of
enemy ships behind the lines. Quite apart from the logistics issue, he
was sure the Commonwealth Admiralty would be reluctant to cut entire
squadrons of modern ships loose for raiding missions, not when they
needed them for screening elements and convoy escorts. God knew the
Theocracy had the same problem. And that meant . . .

He activated the star chart and considered the matter, carefully.
Commonwealth ships weren't any faster in hyperspace, as far as he knew,
than anything from the Theocracy. Logically, assuming the enemy had
departed just after the courier boat, they had to be somewhere within a
sphere centered on Ringer. It looked good, but the sphere covered over a
dozen light years, an area of space so vast as to be completely impossible
to search. Every ship in the combined navies of the entire settled galaxy
could hide within that sphere and remain completely undetected, save
by the most extraordinary stroke of luck. But it did offer one possibility, at least. He could say which worlds might come under attack next.

Aswan is probably out, he thought. *But there are other targets . . .*

His intercom chimed. "Admiral," Captain Haran said, "the staff
meeting will start in ten minutes."

"I'm on my way," Admiral Junayd said.

He rose, then copied his conclusions to his terminal and left the
office, walking through the corridors to the briefing room. This time,

thankfully, the Inquisitor was taking his spite out on the planet's inhabitants rather than Admiral Junayd or any of his staff. He wouldn't have had anything to contribute, Admiral Junayd was sure, but he knew from bitter experience that anything resembling a "secret" meeting would be reported to his superiors, who would take a jaundiced view of the whole affair. No doubt the fact he had a cleric and several intelligence officers attending the meeting wouldn't be good enough, if his enemies caught wind of it.

Good thing we invited the bastard, he thought, as he stepped into the briefing room. *He can't complain he wasn't invited now.*

He smirked at the thought, then sat down as the steward served coffee before withdrawing into a side room. Captain Haran closed and locked the hatch, then put the reports from the courier boat on the main display. The staffers, none of whom had seen them, watched with grim expressions. There would definitely be enough blame to go around if their ultimate superiors decided so.

"The enemy has struck again," Admiral Junayd said when the recording had finished. "This time, however, we may have an advantage."

He keyed a switch, displaying the expanding sphere centered on Ringer. "We know they have to be somewhere within this region of space," he said. "Every red world"—he tapped another switch, altering the display—"must be considered a possible target. Therefore, it is my intention to move the squadron to a position where we can respond quickly to any attacks within this sphere."

And be ready to set an ambush if the spy gets back to us, he added mentally. He didn't want to share any information concerning the spy with anyone who didn't already know about him, not when it might lead to trouble. *Even if he doesn't, we will be in position to respond.*

"We're going to move to here," he said, tapping a location on the display. "I want courier boats to head to each of the suspected target systems to inform them of our current intentions and to be ready to summon us, if the enemy attacks. Another pair of courier boats is to be dispatched to Aswan. Commodore Malian will need to be prepared to support our deployment, if we do run into the enemy."

He paused. "Are there any points that should be raised before we continue?"

"Yes, Admiral," Commodore Isaac said. "If we leave Verdean, we may miss a message from Aswan or any other systems that come under attack."

"I will be leaving two courier boats here," Admiral Junayd said. "There is nothing else we can do about the problem."

He sighed, inwardly. It was a valid concern, unfortunately, even though he was fairly sure that Isaac was buttressing his position in case their superiors took a dim view of his decisions. In the time it took for his couriers to inform Commodore Malian of his movements, the enemy *could* attack another system or he could receive new orders via the StarCom. However, there was nothing he could do about it, save for remaining in orbit and not bothering to respond to any of the attacks. Even the Theocracy couldn't change the tactical realities that had bedeviled humanity since the first scoutships had ventured into hyperspace.

"I have requested—again—reinforcements from home," he added. "I do not believe they will be forthcoming. Therefore, I intend to consider ways to set traps for the enemy. We do not have any armed freighters in the sector, but we may be able to modify several bulk freighters to serve as makeshift Q-Ships. It may be possible to lure the enemy into attacking a convoy. We do know they destroyed one convoy and they will certainly want to target others."

There was a pause. "We may also be splitting up the squadron," he warned. "In that case, the superdreadnoughts will be operating independently."

Commodore Isaac cleared his throat. "Admiral," he said. "Tactical doctrine clearly states . . ."

"Tactical doctrine assumes that it is we, not the enemy, who are perpetually on the offensive," Admiral Junayd snapped. It hadn't been a bad bet, back when the Theocracy had started its conquests, but they'd never actually had to fight a real war. A multistar political system had space to trade for time and ships that could be deployed to actually strike deep into Theocratic space. "I understand the dangers of parceling out our superdreadnoughts in penny packets, but we have no choice. Unless one of you is concealing a fleet of cruisers in your pockets, perhaps?"

He pushed on before anyone could say a word. "We will depart in one hour," he said. "If you have deployed additional crew or janissaries to the system, recall them. I will not tolerate further delays. Dismissed."

The compartment emptied quickly, leaving Admiral Junayd alone. He shook his head, then looked at the display. In truth, unless he got very lucky, he had to pray the spy came through and told him where to place his ships. Because if he didn't . . .

. . . it could cost him all that remained of his career.

It wasn't a pleasant thought, but it was one that had to be faced. Someone always had to take the blame. God granted victory to the deserving, the Theocracy preached, and if victory was not granted the loser had to be undeserving. Admiral Junayd knew he'd been lucky to escape the first defeat—if Princess Drusilla hadn't committed a staggering act of treason, he might well have been brutally executed for failure— and a second failure would kill him. Never mind that he didn't have half the ships and crew he needed to protect the sector, never mind that the enemy could choose her targets with impunity . . . never mind that the locals had every reason to hate the Theocracy. It would be his fault.

He considered, briefly, defecting. If a lowly woman could do it, why couldn't a man with thirty years of naval experience under his belt? It wouldn't be *that* hard to come up with an excuse for boarding a courier boat and taking control, once he was deep in hyperspace. He could steer the boat to the Commonwealth . . .

. . . and then his family would be executed.

The Commonwealth had tightened up its security considerably since the war had begun, according to intelligence reports, but it still leaked. Admiral Junayd had no illusions; sooner or later, someone would figure out that he'd defected and take it out on his family. No, nothing short of walking to his execution with the proper attitude—the supplicant willing to pay with his life for his sins—would save everyone related to him. He was trapped, a helpless prisoner of his own society . . . a society he was starting to loathe.

And you hate it now, his own thoughts mocked him. *Did you hate it when you were feted as the great naval hero who would carry the flag to Tyre and beyond?*

He was too honest to deny it. He'd had a good career, right up until the moment planning met reality in the skies of Cadiz. His family connections had ensured he made it into the naval academy; his gift for memory had ensured he wasn't held back for failing to recite his prayers perfectly . . . and, since his graduation, he'd risen steadily in the ranks. He'd even learned to handle religious functionaries who knew nothing about military matters, yet held the power of life and death over every officer and crewman on his ships. But he'd been blamed for Cadiz and only sheer luck had saved him from becoming the scapegoat for a simple failure of imagination. War was a democracy, after all, and the enemy got a vote. If the plans couldn't handle a surprise like Princess Drusilla's defection, what good were they?

And we did manage to hammer 7th Fleet, he reminded himself firmly. *We jumped ahead of schedule, because we knew they couldn't ignore a war fleet so close to their borders, but we nearly won. And we did batter the fleet into near uselessness. If they hadn't had a fleet of reinforcements nearby . . .*

He shook his head. The latest news from Tyre mocked him—and the entire Theocracy. It was impossible to fault Admiral Christian . . . but if he'd served the Theocracy, he would have been executed for his failure to destroy the enemy fleet. Charging right at the enemy formation, even if one was hideously outgunned, was regarded as a good thing, no matter if it was pointless and stupid. The idea of a tactical withdrawal was beyond the imagination of most of his officers . . . and if they did have the wit to conceive of the concept, they immediately buried it before they could be accused of defeatism. How could anyone win a war by retreating? And yet, preserving one's ships instead of fighting a hopeless battle might lead to overall victory.

His terminal buzzed. "Admiral, the courier boats have been dispatched," Captain Haran informed him. "Cleric Peter wishes to speak with you at your earliest convenience."

Admiral Junayd had to bite down a sneer. What was he supposed to tell the cleric? The truth? He wasn't a child, indoctrinated to believe that clerics had a direct line to God . . . and that they would keep anything they were told to themselves, respecting the privacy of the confessional booth. No one with any wit believed that clerics kept secrets. A person who had doubts about God, about the Theocracy, about *anything*, would take his life in his hands if he dared speak to a cleric. There was no one Junayd could confide in who would not betray him.

"Inform the cleric that he can meet me in my cabin in ten minutes," he said, standing. There was no point in hiding in the cabin, not when there was work to do. "Have the ships earmarked for Ringer been dispatched?"

"They're being prepared now," Captain Haran said. "Commodore Isaac insisted on choosing the squadron personally."

I'm sure he did, Admiral Junayd thought nastily. *He probably thinks he will be my replacement if the Speaker relieves me of command.*

"Then have them dispatched as soon as they're finally ready," he ordered. There would be a chance to push the blame onto Isaac, if he wished . . . but the last thing the fleet needed, really, was a struggle over command authority. Besides, he had a feeling the light cruisers would discover nothing more than drifting wreckage and dead bodies. "Was there any message from the surface?"

"No, sir," Captain Haran said.

"Good," Admiral Junayd said. "I'll see the cleric in ten minutes."

He closed the channel, then pasted a cold expression on his face. There was no point in showing weakness, not when the wolves were already gathering. Commodore Isaac might be the first to take a step, to try to push himself forward as a potential replacement for his superior officer, but he wouldn't be the last. A failure had no friends or loyal subordinates for fear it would rub off. It was just another thing he found himself envying in his nation's enemies.

Gathering himself, he stepped through the hatch and walked down the corridor. The cleric was no doubt already inside his cabin, perhaps checking to see if there was anything incriminating hidden under the bed. Admiral Junayd wondered, absently, if Commonwealth officers had to put up with a glowering political watchdog, then shrugged, dismissing the thought. He had to make do with the system that had birthed him, no matter how much he envied his opponents.

He opened the hatch. The cleric was seated in a hard-backed chair, his fingers pressed together in prayer. He looked up as Admiral Junayd entered, then waved him to a chair . . . as if it were his own cabin, rather than the admiral's. Admiral Junayd sighed inwardly, recognizing the power play, then took his chair. There was no point in irritating a cleric for nothing.

"I must say I'm quite concerned," Peter said shortly. "This is the second major system to come under attack."

"The enemy can choose targets at random," Admiral Junayd said smoothly. It sounded as though he was making excuses, but it was the literal truth. "They can concentrate their forces against one world; we have to spread ours out to cover two *dozen* worlds."

"That would appear to be true," Peter agreed. "However, it is not particularly reassuring."

Then we should have built better defenses instead of lavishing resources on the fleet, Admiral Junayd thought. *But I can't tell you that, can I?*

Pushing the thought aside, he leaned forward and began to explain his plan.

CHAPTER TWENTY-FIVE

"The locals *claim* they can provide transport for all ten *thousand* civilians," William said as he stepped into the captain's office. "However, with only a handful of freighters, it's going to be a very tight squeeze."

"Almost certainly," the captain agreed. "Can we bring in the captured freighters to give us some extra capacity?"

"If we have the time," William said. "We might be better off taking them in the freighters, then transferring them into the other ships once we reach the RV point."

The captain didn't hesitate. "Do it," she ordered. "Are the inhabitants willing to go?"

"They don't expect the Theocracy to be merciful once they return," William said. "I think they were hoping for a way out before we arrived. They've actually got quite a few ideas on how to expand life support capability so we can take them all."

He looked at the near-space display and frowned. A handful of asteroids with *very* limited living space and a sealed environment. The locals, it seemed, had strict rules on breeding; each couple could only have two children, unless they were lucky enough to win the breeding lottery and have a chance to get a third child. He'd been told that the population had remained remarkably stable for seventy years, even after the Theocracy had annexed the system. But then, the Theocracy had been more interested in using the locals than converting them. It had still been a hair-raising existence.

There was very little overt horror, he thought. *But there were a great many implied threats.*

"That cruiser is still out there," the captain said, thoughtfully. "They're watching us."

"They probably want to try and track our exit vector," William said. It was unlikely the Theocracy's sensors were good enough to make any real headway, but they'd set off on a diversionary vector, just in case intelligence was wrong. "Do you want to try and chase them down?"

"It would probably be a waste of time," the captain said. "Did you manage to pull anything useful from the remains of the other cruiser?"

William shook his head. "Their surviving datacores were completely wiped and powdered, Captain," he said. "It looks as though the ship was so badly damaged that it activated automated scuttling codes. They might not have managed to trigger the self-destruct, but it sure as hell wiped out anything *useful*."

"The teams may still find *something*," the captain mused. "But it probably won't be anything particularly useful."

She shrugged. "Once they have the freighters loaded, rig the asteroids with nuclear demolition charges," she added. "Maybe we can arrange for them to explode in their face when they return to the system."

"Aye, Captain," William said. He paused. "It might be better, however, if we left the habitat asteroids alone."

The captain raised her eyebrows. "The enemy could still make use of them."

"We do have to destroy the industries," William said. He'd been impressed, then alarmed, by just how much the locals had managed to do with such a limited supply of raw material. If the Theocracy had actually tried to learn from them, it would have been disastrous. "But the habitat asteroids belong to the locals. There's no profit in destroying them when the destruction serves no useful purpose. And one day, the locals may be able to return."

"The Theocracy may destroy them," the captain said.

"Then at least the Theocracy will get the blame," William said. "We're taking ten thousand people away from the only home they have ever known. The very least we can do is refrain from smashing their homes into dust. They may be able to return after the war."

"If their culture survives contact with the rest of the Commonwealth," the captain said. She looked up at him. "Very well; mine the industrial platforms, but not the habitable asteroids, as long as there is nothing there the enemy can use for war material."

"I will see to it personally," William said. "The locals *do* have every reason to cooperate."

He shuddered. The Theocracy, for whatever reason, had allowed the locals to keep their culture and society, provided they made themselves useful. Indeed, they'd even enjoyed a certain amount of legal protection . . . which hadn't stopped enemy spacers from harassing their women and occasionally going a great deal further. William made a mental note to ensure that the story was turned into propaganda, aimed at anyone who believed it was possible to coexist with the Theocracy. Even when an entire population surrendered and submitted, it wasn't enough to keep them safe.

That must be deliberate policy, he thought. *They're more interested in converts than putting together a multicultural polity.*

"Good," the captain said. "Of course, the *real* question is when will they launch a counterattack?"

"I wish I knew," William said. They were five days from Aswan. Assuming a courier boat had jumped out the moment they arrived, it would probably have reached the enemy base by now . . . but if the enemy fleet they'd seen at Verdean had remained there, it was a day or two closer. "I'll start the loading immediately."

◆　◆　◆

Kat watched the XO go, then returned to her contemplations. There had been relatively little on Morningside in the captured datacores, but her intelligence officers had interrogated the locals and discovered that it was a relatively large colony, settled directly from Ahura Mazda itself. Cross-checking with the UN's files, they'd noted that there *had* been a previous colony from Earth, but for some reason it had never succeeded. Kat, reading between the lines, suspected it meant that the original settlers had been wiped out by pirates or absorbed by the Theocracy. However, unlike Verdean, it wasn't regarded as occupied territory, but a loyal settlement.

Which makes it an obvious target, she thought coldly. *And certainly one that would be very embarrassing to the enemy, if we happened to raid it.*

She closed her eyes in silent thought. It was difficult to say which worlds the enemy would consider worth protecting, now that they knew she was in their rear, yet Morningside was definitely high on the list. Maybe Morningside didn't have much in the way of industry—the planet didn't even have a cloudscoop—but it did have a fairly large population, one that presumably had strong ties to the Theocracy's homeworld. And it probably supplied food to the enemy forces, as well as manpower.

Going there is a gamble, she told herself. *But if we feint at Aswan first, we should upset them long enough to leave a space for attacking Morningside.*

It wasn't a comfortable thought. She couldn't launch a serious attack on the fleet base without far more starships than she had, while feinting at the system ran the risk of running into superior firepower. On the other hand, raiding the system would force the enemy to concentrate their minds on their defenses and she might have a chance to take a shot or two at an enemy convoy while she was there. It would be worth the risk.

She brought up the report from *Mermaid* and skimmed through it again. Aswan was heavily defended, although she was fairly sure she could deal with the system's defenders if she had a couple of superdreadnought squadrons of her own. Like most fleet bases, it was divided into a naval base, orbiting a rocky world, and a cloudscoop orbiting a gas giant. It would have been more efficient to base everything near the gas giant, but the enemy probably had long-term plans to terraform the rocky world. The Theocracy didn't appear to care about its personnel—it certainly didn't seem to waste money supplying entertainment for them—yet it had to understand the value of shore leave unless they genuinely believed that crewmen spent their days working and their nights studying religion.

Her lips twitched in genuine amusement. There had been a woman—Kat hadn't bothered to remember her name—at Admiral Morrison's party. She'd moaned about spacers using the brothels and bars at the spaceport, even nagged the admiral to try to shut them down. It had never crossed her mind that spacers might *need* somewhere to relax and unwind . . . no doubt the Theocracy's religious leaders felt the same way too. They'd probably be shocked to discover just what spacers did when they were off duty . . .

And I wonder what happened to the silly cow, she thought. There had been no time to evacuate Cadiz before the enemy superdreadnoughts had come rolling in, thanks to Admiral Morrison. The woman was probably dead. Or, if she'd been taken alive, wishing she *was* dead. *Some people have no idea of just how the universe works.*

She pushed the thought aside, then kept working. Perhaps if they used decoy drones to pin the enemy against the planetary defenses . . .

♦ ♦ ♦

"Keep moving," Davidson ordered. "Leave those bags behind; keep moving."

William stood beside him and watched, as dispassionately as he could, as a line of humanity flowed through the asteroid and into the giant freighter, where Marines handed out tranquilizer drinks and stacked the sleepy refugees into the holds. Men, young and old, were trying to look composed as they walked into an unknown future; women were glancing around nervously as if they expected to be attacked at any moment . . . and children, their faces pale and wan, clutched stuffed animals as they hurried onto the ship. William felt a stab of bitter guilt for uprooting their lives, even though he knew there was no choice. The Theocracy would take a terrible revenge when it finally reclaimed the system.

"I need to take this with me," a man insisted. "It's everything I've done . . ."

"Leave it here," Davidson ordered, stepping forward. "There's no room for anything larger than stuffed toys."

"But it's my work," the man protested. "I need to keep it!"

"Put it on the datacore, then upload it to the ship," Davidson snapped. "Or drop it here, with the rest of the bags. We may have time to pick it up."

The man glared at him, then realized he wasn't going to get anywhere and threw the bag up against the others. William sighed inwardly—there was always someone who seemed to think that the ban on anything more than the clothes on his back didn't apply to him—and watched as the bag rolled down the pile and landed on the ground. Maybe there *would* be time to pick up the luggage, although he doubted it. The real problem would be sparing a freighter long enough to return to the colony.

"Commander," a voice said, "are you sure you can get everyone out?"

William turned to see Mayor Gregory Yu, feeling an odd twist of dislike mixed with sympathy. By any reasonable standard, Yu was a collaborator—and yet, as anyone could argue, he really hadn't had a choice. The Theocracy wouldn't have hesitated to remove him and put someone else in his place if he'd stood up to them; he'd fought hard to preserve something of his people's culture, even as he bowed the knee to the enemy. It was easier, a great deal easier, to condemn people who swore allegiance to the enemy before the war was actually lost.

"I hope so," he said. Yu wouldn't be treated with great respect in the Commonwealth, but he'd keep his life. His people too would survive and prosper. And who knew? They *might* get to return home one day. "Time is not exactly in our favor, but we can probably take everyone before we run out of space."

Even if we have to put them on the warships, he added mentally. Most of the warships were over-engineered, easily capable of carrying hundreds of additional souls without straining their life-support unduly. The real problem would be refugees blocking the corridors when the crews were rushing to battle stations, but it could be endured. *We can do more than that, if necessary.*

"Thank you," Yu said, seriously. "This was a nightmare."

William looked at him and understood, suddenly, just how his homeworld's governors had to have felt back when the pirates had been raiding at will. There had been no choice but to sacrifice lives . . . no, not to send people to die, but to a fate worse than death. He shook his head, no longer able to feel anything but pity for the man in front of him. Death was easy, perhaps, when it was just his life at stake . . . yet, what would *he* do if there were thousands of lives, including children, under threat? Would he truly choose to condemn them all to death?

"The Commonwealth will take care of you," he said. It had been good at absorbing refugees, even ones who were largely useless. *That* wasn't something that could be said of *anyone* from Ringer. Their innovations might be very useful as they integrated into Commonwealth society. "Do you happen to know if they took anyone back to their homeworld?"

"A handful of teachers," Yu said slowly. "They even *paid* for them."

"They must have wanted willing servants," William said. Slaves could do brute labor, where it was easy to keep an eye on them, but technical skills required a certain degree of freedom. *He* wouldn't have cared to fly in a starship maintained by a slave, particularly one in a position to do a little subtle sabotage that might bear fruit a few months afterwards. "I wonder . . . what did they teach?"

"Maintaining closed environments," Yu said. "What we do here, all the time, to survive."

"The intelligence staff will probably want to talk about that," William said. It wasn't *that* different from constructing the bare bones of a starship, but starships included hyperdrives and weapons as well as crew quarters. Maybe the Theocracy chose to allow its own personnel to concentrate on the former. "How long do you think you could have survived here, without them?"

"Centuries," Yu said. There was a hint of pride in his voice. "We would have remained stable for years, if the Theocracy hadn't arrived."

William shrugged. Ringer *was* an impressive, if limited, achievement . . . but he had a feeling that it would have run into trouble, sooner or later. If societies, cultures, or religions could evolve in ways that would surprise their founders, why not a closed system? It would be worse, he suspected, if dissidents had nowhere else to go. There had been quite a few settlements, in the past, that had run into civil unrest and collapsed into chaos.

"You'll have your chance to rebuild, after the war," he promised. "And when the Theocracy is gone, maybe you can rejoin the galaxy."

♦ ♦ ♦

Kat looked down at the report and sighed. The asteroids had been evacuated, save for a handful of older inhabitants who had flatly refused to leave. Her XO had explained to them that the Theocracy wouldn't treat them very well, but they were determined to stay. In the end, Kat had shrugged and given up. She didn't have time to have her Marines drag them off the asteroids and hold them in the brig until the squadron fled the system.

"Captain," Roach said. "I'm picking up multiple ships jumping into the system."

"Understood," Kat said. Given the timing, the ships probably came from Verdean. "I'm on my way."

She rose to her feet and hurried through the hatch, onto the bridge. Red icons were flickering into existence, each one marking the location of a light cruiser. It didn't look as though they were accompanied by any superdreadnoughts, although that proved nothing. The larger ships could easily be lurking in hyperspace, plotting an ambush or waiting for their smaller escorts to get a precise lock on her ships.

"I make nine light cruisers, Captain," Roach said as Kat took her seat. "They're sweeping us with long-range sensors, but not making any move."

Scouts, Kat thought. "Have the industrial platforms been mined?"

"Aye, Captain," the XO said. He glanced at his console. "All of the away-duty personnel have returned to the ships. We're free to leave."

Kat briefly considered fighting—the odds were even, at least on paper—and then dismissed the thought. The Theocratic ships were presumably modern, probably worth two or three of her ships apiece. And besides, they *could* be preparing an ambush . . .

"Open a gateway," she ordered. There was no point in procrastinating. "Take us out of here."

"Aye, Captain," Weiberg said.

◆ ◆ ◆

The spy gritted his teeth as the squadron slipped back into hyperspace. It didn't look as though the Theocracy had picked up his first message, unless the two cruisers the squadron had engaged when they'd arrived had been sent to Ringer in response to his signal. Now . . . he'd programmed the communications grid to send a second message, despite the increased risk of detection. But was it really worth the risk when the Theocracy seemed to be ignoring him?

He sighed inwardly as he gazed at his console. He'd told them precisely where Captain Falcone intended to go after her feint at Aswan. He'd told them everything they needed to know to set a trap. But were they paying attention to him? Two cruisers hadn't been anything like enough to stop a single heavy cruiser, let alone the entire squadron. Had they been trying to test him? Or was he risking his life for nothing?

If nothing happens at Morningside, he thought, *I will send no more messages.*

It was a risk, he knew. He was *sure* he'd wiped all traces of his work, yet he knew all too well that he might have missed something. It was quite possible that he would be caught, having failed to help the Theocracy or save his sister. And if that happened, she would probably be killed. Everything he'd done would have been for nothing . . .

And yet, he asked himself bitterly, *what choice do I have?*

CHAPTER TWENTY-SIX

"So the spy showed himself again," Admiral Junayd mused.

"Yes, sir," Commander Annam said. "His latest report states that the enemy intends to attack Morningside. It seems an odd target."

"Not if you wanted to disrupt us," Admiral Junayd said. "It's a great deal easier to ignore threats to planets crammed with unbelievers than a colony settled directly from the homeworld."

He studied the star chart thoughtfully. Morningside made very little sense from a tactical perspective, but from a strategic perspective it was ideal. If word got back to his enemies that he'd *allowed* a Commonwealth attack on a population of believers to go ahead, it would spell the end of both his career and his life. *And* it would rub the Theocracy's nose in its failure to protect its citizens. Faith in the ultimate victory of the Theocracy would be badly weakened.

"Very well," he said. "Call a staff meeting—twenty minutes from now. I have a plan."

Commander Annam nodded. "Admiral," he said. "The existence of the spy . . ."

". . . must be revealed now," Admiral Junayd said firmly. "My command staff is beyond reproach. They are all committed to victory over our enemies."

And victory over me, he added privately. *They'd be quite happy to blame me if I insisted on preparing a trap without providing them with any real evidence that the enemy intends to attack, particularly if we* are *being conned.*

He smiled coldly, then spent the next fifteen minutes working his way through a list of possible waypoints for the fleet to hide. There was no point in putting the fleet within the target system itself, not when it was quite possible the enemy already had the system under covert observation. They might not deduce the spy's existence from the arrival of the superdreadnoughts, but there was no point in taking chances. By the time Junayd needed to head to the briefing compartment, he had the bare bones of a workable plan.

"We have been blessed by God," he said once the compartment was sealed. "Thanks to one of our brave intelligence operatives"—it still galled him he had no idea who was spying for them—"we now know the enemy's presumed next target. They intend to hit Morningside."

He ran through a brief outline of what the spy had sent and his own conclusions, then leaned forward, resting his hands on the table. "The fleet will move to here," he said, pointing to a location on the star chart. It was within five minutes of Morningside, yet far enough from the system that they'd have to be very unlucky to be detected when the enemy fleet arrived. "We will wait, maintaining a covert observation of the system, until the enemy arrives. When they do, we will jump in behind them and attack. Our objective will be the destruction or capture of the enemy ships."

There was a long pause. "Are there any questions?"

"Yes, Admiral," Commodore Isaac said. "Should we not inform the authorities on Morningside that the system may come under attack?"

"It would only upset them," Admiral Junayd said breezily. "More to the point"—he added, before Isaac could object—"they do not have the firepower to make a difference, while any visible precautions they take would be noticeable. The enemy may back off without ever entering engagement range."

"They would be foolish *not* to take precautions anyway," Isaac pointed out, clearly unwilling to let the matter pass. "Everyone in the sector should know, by now, that an enemy fleet has attacked Verdean."

"And Ringer," Admiral Junayd reminded him, although word of *that* little disaster probably hadn't reached Morningside yet. His light cruisers hadn't reported back either. "Still, we will be forced to leave that to God. We will *not* notify the system authorities that they should expect an attack."

He sighed, inwardly. If everything went according to plan, Isaac's objections would be ignored by a grateful Theocracy, but if something went badly wrong it would provide more ammunition for the admiral's detractors. Hell, if Junayd hadn't known that Isaac had been sent to Aswan a year ago, he would have wondered if it had been arranged for the commodore to be assigned there to keep an eye on his superior officer. Even if he hadn't been, it wouldn't be hard for Isaac to realize the advantages of building a case against Admiral Junayd. His superior already had a black mark on his record.

"We will depart in twenty minutes," he said. The spy hadn't given a timetable. It was all too easy for Admiral Junayd to imagine his fleet arriving too late, with the enemy ships already withdrawing from Morningside. "Once we're underway, I expect you to start reviewing potential tactical scenarios for the upcoming engagement. It is vitally important that we make the most of this opportunity. We may not get a second chance."

Because they will certainly smell a rat, he thought. *Two squadrons of superdreadnoughts, fifty-odd possible targets . . . even if they assume I sent out both squadrons on patrol duties, the odds of them being caught are alarmingly low. They'd be fools not to suspect the truth.*

"I will organize prayers for our victory," Cleric Peter said. "I am sure that God will not snatch the victory from us, when our people's lives are at stake."

"A sensible use of your time," Admiral Junayd said, smoothly. It was; the longer the clerics spent at prayer, the less time they could spend harassing his crew. "Dismissed."

He watched everyone leave, then looked down at his hands. God *had* granted them an opportunity, he knew, but it was no *more* than an opportunity. They would have to capitalize on it themselves if they wanted a victory. And if it failed . . .

I'll just have to make sure it doesn't fail, he thought grimly. *And do everything I can to make sure it's a success.*

◆ ◆ ◆

"The freighters are on their way to the Reach," the XO reported. "The entire population of Ringer, save for the handful of holdouts, are heading to their new homes."

"Good," Kat said. She didn't know what had happened to the holdouts after the Theocracy had discovered that the system's industries had been smashed, but she doubted it was anything good. Their relatives would have a chance to forge new lives in the Commonwealth and, eventually, go back home. "And the squadron itself?"

"Ready to depart for Aswan," the XO said. "We'll link up with *Mermaid* at the RV point near the system."

"Even better," Kat said. Attacking an enemy fleet base, even as a feint, was risky . . . but part of her looked forward to the challenge. If nothing else, there would be no risk of harming innocent civilians in the crossfire. "Inform the bridge. We will depart at once."

"Aye, Captain," the XO said.

Kat nodded. Two days . . . two days to reach the RV point and check with *Mermaid*, then they could feint at Aswan. And then . . . Morningside. And then . . . maybe they could go deeper into enemy space. The Theocracy might already have redeployed units from the front lines to help hunt her squadron down, but if they hadn't . . . raids closer in towards their homeworld would be bound to draw attention. Who knew what sort of problems the Theocracy would have if she raided one of their older conquests?

"Take us out," she ordered quietly. "By the time we reach the RV point, I want to be ready to go on the offensive."

◆ ◆ ◆

"The courier boats have returned from Morningside," Captain Haran said ten minutes after the fleet reached the waypoint outside the system. "There's no sign of an enemy attack."

"Good," Admiral Junayd said. They'd beaten the enemy to the target system. There would be time to plot his ambush properly. "Maintain two courier boats on watchdog duties at all times. I want to be notified the moment the enemy arrives."

"Aye, sir," Captain Haran said. "We also received a new set of updates from Aswan."

"Download them to my console," Admiral Junayd said. "I'll review them now."

He watched the younger man go, then keyed his console. The first set of messages consisted of orders to hunt down the enemy ships and destroy them, without mercy; the second set, clearly written by someone with more understanding of the tactical realities, told him to guard the industries and forsake the rest of the sector if necessary. It seemed unlikely the writer had known that both Verdean and Ringer had come under attack. The third set of messages promised a handful of reinforcements, but warned that very little could be spared from either the war front or the home guard. If the Commonwealth managed to attack the shipyards near the core, the war would be within shouting distance of being lost.

So they want me to catch the enemy, but they don't want to give me any reinforcements, he thought sourly. *How am I supposed to cover every possible target without breaking up my superdreadnought squadrons?*

It was a tempting idea, in many ways. Nothing he'd seen from the enemy had suggested they were able to take on a single superdreadnought, let alone an entire squadron. He could leave three superdreadnoughts at Aswan, as a reserve, and parcel out the remaining fifteen ships to fifteen out of fifty possible targets. The enemy would be deterred, he was sure, from attacking a world covered by a superdreadnought. But it would make it impossible to concentrate his units in a hurry if he needed to send a squadron forward to the front lines. He'd be damned whatever he did.

And they're sending me a new set of StarComs, he thought as he read the next set of messages. It wouldn't have been a bad idea, if he'd been sent reinforcements as well, but now . . . all he had was the chance to watch an enemy raid in real time. Hadn't they *read* his report? The basic problem hadn't changed at all! He simply didn't have the ships to cover every prospective target without spreading his forces too thin. *Do they want me to fail?*

The thought sent ice shivering down his spine. There were failures, petty minor failures, and disasters that could easily cost them any remaining chance at victory. Surely, no one would risk the war effort just for a puny political advantage? He'd already been disgraced; it was unlikely, incredibly unlikely, that he would be allowed to return to the front lines. But if someone hated him enough to sabotage his career still further . . .

He shook his head. It didn't matter. All that mattered, here and now, was ambushing the enemy and destroying their ships before it was too late.

♦ ♦ ♦

"Gateway opening," Weiberg said. "Returning to realspace . . . now!"

Kat braced herself. Aswan was the most heavily defended system they'd visited, even if she had no intention of going within range of any of the fixed defenses. The display rapidly started to fill with red icons: a squadron of superdreadnoughts, a handful of smaller ships, a dozen industrial nodes, and repair yards . . . Aswan might be tiny, compared to Tyre, but it was clearly a formidable part of the enemy's war machine.

"They're scanning us," Roach warned. "They know we're here."

"I would have been disappointed in them if they didn't," Kat said dryly. The squadron wasn't even *trying* to hide. "Launch drones, then hold position."

"Aye, Captain," Roach said.

Kat smiled, then watched the display, feeling her heart starting to race in her chest. The enemy would do . . . what? They'd worked their way through a dozen simulations, but experience had told her time and time again that the enemy would come up with something new and unexpected. She rather suspected the enemy commander would try to send his superdreadnoughts up after her, if they were in working order, but he had to know they wouldn't catch her. It would only make him look good to his superiors.

"The superdreadnoughts are being surprisingly slow at bringing up their drives," the XO said through their private link. "They may be in worse condition than we assumed."

"Probably better to give them a wide berth anyway," Kat sent back. "They might still have all their launchers armed, ready to fire."

"Enemy cruisers are altering course," Roach reported. "They're coming up after us."

"Plan Beta," Kat said. "Launch external missiles as planned, then prepare to jump back into hyperspace."

"Aye, Captain," Roach said. He worked his console for a long moment. "Missiles away; I say again, missiles away."

Kat nodded, never taking her eyes off the display. Missiles were normally impossible to hide; they blazed brightly as they roared towards their targets. But missiles launched on unpowered vectors, as if they were nothing more than meteors, were a different matter. It was quite possible that even *active* sensors would miss their presence if they had something brighter to track.

"Drive powering up now, Captain," Weiberg said. "We can jump back into hyperspace on your mark."

"Hold it," Kat ordered. It would put a great deal of wear and tear on the vortex generator, but she wanted to see the results of her plan for herself. As long as the enemy didn't get into firing range, it was perfectly safe. "Stand by . . ."

The missiles went active. Half of them lanced towards the cruisers, locked onto their targets and angling towards them with deadly force. The other half went after the orbital facilities—Kat had targeted everything apart from the StarCom—with the intention of wreaking as much havoc as possible. Enemy point defense units went active at terrifying speed, targeting the missiles and trying to kill as many of them as possible before time ran out. Kat smirked to herself, coldly, as three missiles made it through the defenses and slammed into the industrial nodes. The cruisers might have survived unscathed—she couldn't help a flicker of reluctant admiration for the enemy's point defense—but at least she'd left a mark on the base itself.

"The cruisers are accelerating, Captain," Roach reported.

"Helm, take us out of here," Kat ordered. The Theocracy would have to stomach the damage she'd inflicted—and the fact they hadn't managed to even target her ships, let alone destroy them. "Best possible speed."

"Aye, Captain," Weiberg said. "Gateway opening . . . now."

Kat smiled coldly as they slipped into the welcoming lights of hyperspace, then high-tailed it away from the enemy base. It was just possible the enemy had managed to coordinate an ambush, but hyperspace was clear. The squadron picked up speed, altering course so sharply that the enemy would find it hard to track them even if a ship had followed them through the gateway. By the time the enemy recovered, they would be well on their way to the next target.

"Good work, all of you," she said. They'd hurt the enemy—and they'd collected valuable new pieces of data on enemy sensor networks. It would be easier, next time, to program missiles to slip through the defenses and strike their targets. "Adjust course for Morningside."

"Aye, Captain," Weiberg said.

Kat rose to her feet. "Mr. XO, you have the bridge," she said. "I'll be in my office."

"Yes, Captain," the XO said.

◆ ◆ ◆

"We need to redeploy our ships to Aswan at once," Commodore Isaac said. "Admiral, the enemy took out two small industrial nodes . . ."

"Through using a trick that won't work twice," Admiral Junayd said coolly. The report from Aswan hadn't made comfortable reading, but it had confirmed his belief that the enemy fleet didn't have the firepower to take on a heavily defended world. There was no way they would have passed up the chance to destroy Aswan and an entire squadron of superdreadnoughts if they'd had the arms. "This is not the time to lose our nerve."

"Lose our nerve?" Isaac repeated. "Admiral, with all due respect . . ."

"They want us to panic," Admiral Junayd said. He keyed the star chart, highlighting the distance between Aswan and Morningside. "They want us to concentrate our forces at Aswan, defending a world that is already armed to the teeth. In the meantime, they pick another target for themselves and attack, relying on the confusion of their first assault to leave us unable to stop them. No, this is no time to lose our nerve."

"Unless the spy was a plant all along," Isaac said. "They might have used him against us . . ."

"The attack on Aswan was annoying and embarrassing, but it was not a significant victory for them," Admiral Junayd said. He found it hard to keep his voice under control. None of his subordinates had dared to question him before, had they? "We can easily replace the nodes they hit, nor will a second such attack do any more damage. More to the point, if that spy is actually a plant, they could have used him to manipulate us to move *everything* back to Aswan. We have good reason to believe he is working for us."

"Unless it's an elaborate trap," Isaac said.

"Only a fool would come up with a plan that depends on the enemy doing *precisely* the right thing," Admiral Junayd snarled. "We could have moved the entire fleet to Ringer"—and he knew people on the homeworld would be asking precisely why he *hadn't*—"and trapped them there. Instead, we waited . . . but they could not have *known* we would wait."

He tapped the table, sharply. "We will wait here," he added shortly. "When the enemy arrives, we will engage their ships and destroy them. Do you understand me?"

Isaac held himself steady. "Yes, sir."

And you will ready the knife for my back if the enemy is delayed, Admiral Junayd thought coldly. *Do Commonwealth commanders have someone ready to stick a knife in their backs too?*

"Good," Admiral Junayd said. "Now prepare your squadron for battle. We would not like to be unready for the enemy now, would we?"

CHAPTER TWENTY-SEVEN

"*Mermaid* has returned, Captain."

Kat nodded, shortly. "Has there been any major change?"

"No, Captain," the XO said. "The only problematic issue is unusual distortions of hyperspace surrounding the double star."

"As expected," Kat said. "Do they pose any danger?"

"Probably not, unless we do something stupid," the XO said. "There don't seem to be any actual *surprises* . . ."

"Good," Kat said. "I'll be on the bridge in a moment. We'll move in immediately afterwards."

She closed her terminal and then rose to her feet. Morningside was odd; a binary star system that had managed to produce a habitable world. The primary star was G2, like Sol; the secondary star was a red dwarf. Kat had a feeling, judging from the amount of debris that had gathered at the barycenter between the two stars, that the *reason* the first colony had failed had been because the combined gravity wells of two stars and several large planets pulled showers of asteroids in towards the larger worlds. A spacefaring colony wouldn't have any problems deflecting or destroying a rain of death, but a colony without any orbital defenses would be in deep trouble.

And it makes it harder to reach the system through hyperspace, she thought grimly. *It may not stop anyone from getting here, but it does make it more difficult to see what might be waiting for us.*

She gathered herself, then walked through the hatch and onto the bridge. The XO, sitting in the command chair, rose as she entered, then nodded towards the display. *Mermaid's* report was waiting for her, focused on Morningside itself. There was little else in the system save for a handful of tiny facilities at the barycenter. Below the report, lines of text from the intelligence analysts warned that the planet seemed to be producing five or six times as much food as the population needed, even assuming each person ate more than the average citizen on Tyre or another Commonwealth world. Judging from the presence of no less than three orbital stations, it was quite likely that Morningside sold food to the rest of the sector.

Odd, she thought as she sat down. *It's rarely economical to ship food outside a single star system.*

"Mr. XO," she said, putting the question aside for later consideration. "Is the squadron ready to move?"

"Yes, Captain," the XO said. "The squadron is fully at your command."

"Then take us in," Kat ordered.

Lightning quivered gently as she passed through the eddies in hyperspace caused by the binary star, just enough to make Kat nervous, then advanced towards the planet at high speed, her crew watching carefully for unexpected threats. It didn't look as though there was *anything* in hyperspace save for random flickers of energy that might mark the birth of later energy storms. Kat watched the countdown rapidly tick down to zero, then braced herself as the starship plunged through the gateway. They had arrived.

"Enemy defenses are scanning us," Roach reported. "Their planetary defense network is going online."

Such as it is, Kat thought. *She* would have considered Morningside an ideal location for a cloudscoop and a small industrial base, but the Theocracy seemingly disagreed. What more did they want? They had a loyal population, a gas giant just waiting to be mined, and a large cluster of asteroids for raw materials. Her father would have considered it to be a sure thing and happily invested in the system for a small share of the return. *They didn't seem to care about building up either the industry or the defenses.*

"Engage the automated weapons platforms," she ordered. "Target long-range missiles on the stations, then transmit a warning. The stations will be fired on within ten minutes."

"Aye, Captain," Roach said.

Kat nodded as her squadron opened fire, targeting the weapons platforms. It was unlikely the Theocracy's servants would abandon their posts, but she owed it to her conscience to at least *try* to avoid killing them. Morningside simply didn't have the firepower to stop her and they both knew it.

Her terminal bleeped. "Captain, this is Parkinson in Tactical," a voice said. "We believe we have located a handful of spaceports and space-related facilities on the planet's surface."

"Mark them for destruction," Kat ordered after a brief glance at the display. None of the spaceports seemed to be located near the cities, which was odd, but if the Theocracy was more concerned about control than economics, it did make a certain kind of sense. "Upload the targeting coordinates to tactical, then have them taken out once we're in orbit."

And there's little chance of hitting a civilian base, she thought. *Everyone we kill will be working directly for the enemy.*

"I'm picking up a response from the stations," Linda said. "It isn't polite."

Kat smiled, unsurprised. "Tactical, take out the stations when the deadline runs out," she ordered. "Smash them into as many pieces as possible."

"Aye, Captain," Roach said.

◆ ◆ ◆

"Admiral," Captain Haran reported, "the enemy is attacking Morningside!"

Admiral Junayd grinned savagely. "Inform Commodore Isaac that he is ordered to take us into the system," he said. The hyperspace eddies surrounding the system would make life difficult, but the enemy would be equally disadvantaged. "And drop us out as close to the enemy as possible."

He grabbed his tunic, then hurried onto the bridge. The report from the courier boat was already playing in front of him: fourteen enemy starships, led by a heavy cruiser that was becoming alarmingly familiar. He saluted the enemy commander mentally—woman or not, it was clear she had nerve—and then took his command chair. Dull rumbles echoed through the giant superdreadnought as she prepared to advance.

"All ships are reporting ready, Admiral," Commodore Isaac reported.

"Take us in," Admiral Junayd ordered. Was Isaac delaying matters in the hopes the enemy would escape, spiking his superior's career? There was no way to know. "As soon as we arrive, open fire."

"Aye, Admiral," Isaac said.

◆ ◆ ◆

"Gateways!" Roach snapped. "Enemy gateways!"

Shit, Kat thought. Nine vortexes appeared, right behind her squadron. The trap—it had to be a trap—had been carried out very well. *They knew we were coming.*

"Evasive action," she snapped as the first superdreadnought lumbered out into realspace and started to scan for enemy targets. "Launch missiles at the stations, then take us away from the planet!"

"Aye, Captain," Weiberg said.

Kat swore under her breath as the enemy fleet emerged, its gateways flickering out of existence behind it. Nine superdreadnoughts, twenty-seven smaller ships . . . an overwhelming force by any reasonable standard. The enemy had either had a remarkable stroke of luck or someone had betrayed the squadron. She closed her eyes in pain, then forced herself to run through the tactical situation. There was no point in continuing the attack, not now. She'd be lucky to get out of the system alive.

"Deploy drones," Kat added. The enemy ships flashed red as they locked on, then opened fire. "Ramp up our speed as much as possible, then start repowering the vortex generators."

"Aye, Captain," Roach said.

"Captain," Lynn said through her implants. "I should warn you that powering up the generators so rapidly . . ."

"We'll die if we stay here," Kat said. The enemy might have opened fire at extreme range, but they'd fired so many missiles it was unlikely to matter. Her point defense and ECM couldn't hope to stop them all. The only upside was that they didn't seem to be deploying gunboats to help steer their missiles towards their targets. "Keep powering up the drives; prepare to take us out as soon as possible."

"Point defense online, ready to fire," Roach reported. "Datanet online; we'll fight as one."

It won't be enough, Kat thought. The wall of missiles was rushing closer, far too many to be stopped even if everything worked perfectly. *We're in deep shit.*

"Deploy shuttles with targeting packs," she ordered. The enemy would catch on quickly, once they realized what had happened, but she should get at least one shot in. "And prepare to fire a full barrage. Can you ID the enemy flagship?"

"Negative, Captain," Roach said. "They must be using lasers to coordinate their ships."

They learned from Cadiz too, Kat thought. She looked at the enemy formation, nothing more than a crude hammerhead. Where would she put the flagship, if she were in command? There was no rear, no place of safety . . . and only a fool would place the flagship in the position where it would be most likely to draw fire. *The superdreadnoughts to the left or right of the lead ship?*

"Designate Enemy Number 5 as priority target, lock missiles on her hull," she ordered. It was a potential candidate for the enemy flagship and she might just get lucky. "Scatter a set of ECM drones among the missiles and disrupt their targeting as much as possible."

"Aye, Captain," Roach said.

"Fan out the second barrage, targeted on the smaller vessels," she added. "And use the shuttles until they die."

Roach hesitated, noticeably. "Aye, Captain," he said finally. "Missiles away; I say again, missiles away."

Kat winced, inwardly. She'd just sent the shuttle pilots to certain death, just to keep her own ships alive a moment longer. And the hell of it was that she didn't know if it would be worth it or not.

The wave of enemy missiles entered attack range and closed in on their targets, a handful burning out their drives and going ballistic before vanishing from the display. Kat watched, bracing herself as best as she could, as hundreds of missiles died . . . but hundreds more made it through, lancing down towards her ships. The datanet wove all fourteen of her warships into a single unit, ensuring that not a single moment of effort was wasted or duplicated, yet it wasn't enough. She gritted her teeth as the missiles reached their targets . . .

Lightning shook violently. Red lights flared up over the ship's status display, then faded slowly as the datanet caught up with the results. A second missile slammed into the rear shields, sending more shock waves running through the vessel. Kat gripped hold of her command chair and prayed, silently, that they survived long enough to open a gateway and get out. There was no other hope.

"*Armstrong* and *Mother's Milk* are gone," the XO reported. "*Checkmate* is streaming debris after taking heavy damage. *Mermaid's* drones drew off the missiles closing in on her . . ."

"Understood," Kat said. Deploying so many drones wouldn't please the bean counters, but under the circumstances she found it hard to care. The fact that the enemy would probably learn more about Commonwealth ECM from the encounter was more of a concern . . . she shook her head, dismissing the thought. She would worry about that later, if they survived long enough to escape. "Deploy a second flight of drones."

"We hit Enemy Number 5 nine times," Roach reported. "No appreciable damage. Enemy fleet is launching a second barrage of missiles."

"Continue firing," Kat ordered.

She sucked in her breath sharply. Clearly, the ships they'd seen at Aswan had been the worst in the sector. The force bearing down on her had plenty of experience swatting missiles with its point defense. Their timing wasn't perfect, and she could see the datanet was nowhere near as sophisticated as her own, but the weaknesses weren't glaring enough to matter. She really needed ten times more missiles and launchers.

"Seven minutes to vortex activation," Weiberg warned. "There are power surges on *Henry Crux*. She may not be able to open a vortex in time."

"Prepare our generator to open one for the entire squadron," Kat ordered. It was another risk—and sooner or later she would run out of luck—but there was no choice. The enemy had trapped her quite neatly. "And alter course. Take us towards the primary star."

"Aye, Captain," Weiberg said.

The XO gave her a sharp look but said nothing. Kat didn't blame him. The closer they got to an immense gravity well, the harder it would be to slip into hyperspace and make their way through the eddies to escape. On the other hand, it would be a great deal harder for the *enemy* to track them through hyperspace, assuming they were willing to give pursuit. The odds would still be in their favor, but she'd have a reasonable chance of either escaping or giving them a bloody nose before they killed her.

"Picking up a signal," Linda said. "They're ordering us to surrender and promising fair treatment if we surrender now."

Kat shook her head. She knew, all too well, just what she could expect if she fell into enemy hands. The Theocracy would know, of course, that she'd been hailed as a heroine—the *woman* who'd escaped their attack on Cadiz and led a counterattack that had blasted the occupation forces off the surface of the planet and recovered thousands of civilians and soldiers before falling back again. She'd be raped, publicly humiliated, and then slowly killed, the recordings distributed across the Commonwealth in the hopes of weakening morale. Maybe they'd backfire, maybe they'd just make the war more savage, but she'd still be dead . . .

. . . and the rest of her crew wouldn't have it any better. The men would be interrogated, then killed or dumped in a POW camp; the women would be raped, then killed or forcibly brought into the Theocracy. She'd heard too many horror stories to believe there was any hope of surrendering peacefully. The Theocracy simply spat in the face of common decency.

"Ignore it," she ordered. She glanced at the timer, then cursed under her breath. Time was not on their side. "Continue firing."

◆ ◆ ◆

"The enemy is not responding," the communications officer shrugged.

"They refuse to face the light," Cleric Peter said. "We must bring them to heel."

They know better than to surrender to us, Admiral Junayd thought. He'd urged, as strongly as he dared, the First Speaker to rule that POWs were to be treated decently, but the Speakers had not listened. It wasn't a surprise—no one had been decent to the Theocracy's POWs, back on Earth—yet it had come back to bite them. The enemy would sooner fight to the death, trying desperately to take a bite out of his ships, than surrender. *They know what they can expect.*

"Continue firing," he said instead. Perhaps, if he'd won outright at Cadiz, he could have changed things . . . or perhaps he wouldn't have *wanted* to change things. He angrily pushed the thought out of his head a moment later. There was no point in wishing for things he couldn't have. "Do not stop until they surrender or die."

He shook his head, studying the display. The enemy ECM drones were far better than he'd realized, good enough to keep convincing his missiles to waste themselves on the drones rather than their targets. One of the enemy ships had fallen out of formation—another flight of missiles was on their way to blow it into atoms—but the remainder of the ships had maintained a surprisingly decent formation despite their surprise at being caught in a trap. Their ships were taking damage, yet not enough to slow them down . . .

And they're heading right towards the star, he thought. He couldn't help another flicker of admiration. *Clever bitch.*

The superdreadnought shuddered as it unleashed another wave of missiles, launching them towards the enemy. Admiral Junayd sat back in his command chair and forced himself to relax. It wouldn't be long now.

"*Peter Blair* is gone," the XO reported. "They overwhelmed her, once she fell out of formation."

Kat nodded, then swore as another missile slammed into *Lightning*. The cruiser's shields were still holding, barely, but damage was starting to mount. A few more shocks like that one and her ship would start coming apart at the seams, if she didn't lose a shield generator or a drive node first. Several of the former were already starting to overheat. And if she lost more than a couple of drive nodes, her ability to escape the enemy would be badly compromised.

"Vortex generator online," Weiberg snapped. "We can jump out!"

Maybe we should get closer to the star, Kat thought. It would be worth trying, if the enemy hadn't been breathing so closely down their necks. *No, there isn't any time to be clever.*

"Open the vortex," she ordered. "And hold it open long enough for the squadron to escape."

"Aye, Captain," Weiberg said. The lights dimmed as nonessential power was rerouted to the vortex generator. "Vortex opening in three . . . two . . . one . . ."

"Admiral, the enemy is opening a vortex gateway," the tactical officer yelled.

"I can see that, fool," Admiral Junayd snapped. It changed everything. Taking his fleet into hyperspace so close to a star was asking for trouble. "Continue firing!"

It was too late. One by one, the remaining enemy ships—some so badly damaged they were bleeding plasma—slipped into the gateway and vanished. The gateway closed as soon as the last ship had gone, leaving behind no trace of its existence. Admiral Junayd mentally saluted his foe—she'd held her nerve like a true warrior—then smiled to himself. She might have escaped, but her confidence would have taken one hell of a beating.

"Stand down from battle stations," he ordered calmly. Six enemy ships destroyed, the remaining eight damaged . . . it might not have been a complete success, but it was hardly a complete *failure*. "Damage report?"

"Minimal," Commodore Isaac said. "Their missiles were unable to penetrate our shields."

"Then a victory," Admiral Junayd said. He turned to the cleric. "You will prepare a prayer of thanksgiving."

"Of course, Admiral," Peter said.

I can spin this into a victory, Admiral Junayd thought. The Theocracy needed a victory and he'd delivered, even if it was a very minor achievement indeed. *But what will I do with it?*

CHAPTER TWENTY-EIGHT

Kat hung in the inky darkness of space, looking down at *Lightning's* hull.

The shields had held, barely, but some energy had leaked through the protections and left her ship's hull scorched and pitted. A number of weapon and sensor blisters had been wrecked; the ship's name, painted black against the white hull, had been completely eradicated from the hull. Her crew was already at work, swapping out the destroyed systems and replacing them from the stockpile of spare parts she'd brought with her, but it wouldn't be enough to restore her ship to full capacity. She'd have to go back to a shipyard to complete the job.

Which isn't an option at the moment, she thought bitterly. Assuming they headed straight back to the nearest shipyard she knew to be in friendly hands, it would still take at least a month. *Our mission isn't complete.*

She gritted her teeth, then took control of the spacesuit and guided it slowly back towards the airlock. She'd always loved EVAs as a cadet, when it had been possible to indulge herself in the belief that she was completely alone in the universe, but now . . . now, she couldn't help feeling stranded, as if there was no hope of rescue. The airlock opened ahead of her, allowing her to return to her ship, yet she still felt alone. Too many lives had been lost in the brief, aborted attack on Morningside.

At least we got their stations, she told herself unconvincingly. *It wasn't a total loss.*

She shook her head as the airlock repressurized, allowing her to remove her spacesuit and pass it to the airlock officer. Six ships were gone, three more so badly damaged that it was unlikely she could get them home, let alone take them back into combat. That gave her four ships, not including *Lighting*. Attacking the enemy had suddenly become a great deal harder, even if the enemy didn't set another ambush. The more she thought about it, the more she realized that something had gone *very* wrong. There was no way the enemy should have been able to isolate them so precisely.

"Thank you, Captain," the officer said. "Will you be needing it again?"

"Just place it on the rack," Kat ordered. "I'll let you know if I want to return outside."

She shook her head, then walked back to her cabin and stepped through the door. A large mug of coffee had been placed on her desk, waiting for her. She smiled tiredly, then sat down and took a sip while bringing up the latest reports from the repair crews. *Lightning's* repairs would be completed, as much as possible, within a week, but the other ships were far harder to restore. One report even stated that *Henry Crux* had been so badly damaged that her bridge consoles had exploded, something Kat had *never* seen outside poorly maintained pirate ships . . .

But it happened to us, she thought. *And logically it shouldn't have.*

She put the report aside, then brought up the records of the battle. They'd been in the system less than ten minutes before the enemy fleet had arrived . . . post-battle analysis had suggested the presence of a courier boat or a watchdog, but no trace of an enemy fleet. Hell, if the fleet had already been in the system, Kat would have expected them to sneak up on her and open fire at point-blank range. It would have been utterly devastating. Instead . . . they'd jumped out of hyperspace and attacked.

They couldn't have gotten word so quickly unless they were lying in wait, she thought. *If they'd been in the nearest system, it would still have taken them much longer to redeploy to Morningside, assuming they were ready to go. No, they must have been lying in wait . . . but why?*

Her buzzer chimed. "Enter."

The hatch opened, revealing the XO and Davidson. Both men looked tired; the XO was too exhausted to hide it, while Davidson's pose would have fooled anyone who didn't know him very well. Kat keyed her console, calling her steward to bring coffee for both of them, then rose and nodded to the sofa. She sat down facing them as the steward appeared with more coffee.

"*Henry Crux* is a write-off," the XO said flatly. "She's too badly damaged to be worth trying to repair, at least without a major investment."

"Reassign her remaining crew to the personnel pool and slot them in when you find a convenient place," Kat ordered. The shortage of personnel had finally come back to bite them in a big way. Repairs that could have been made in the heat of combat hadn't been made, allowing the damage to get worse and worse until entire ships had been lost. "Inform Commander Kent that he's assigned to the tactical department for the moment."

"Aye, Captain," the XO said. "I recommend he be allowed at least a day of rest first, though. He's not in a good state."

Kat nodded. Kent hadn't been expected to gain a command for another three years, at least until he'd been offered a chance to transfer to Operation Knife. Losing a ship would hurt, but it would be far worse to be reassigned to what was, to all intents and purposes, a desk job until the squadron returned home. And then . . . losing a ship, even an ancient heavy cruiser, would be enough to cripple his chances of receiving a new command.

We could have him sent for psychiatric evaluation on Tyre, she thought morbidly. *Here . . . all we can do is keep an eye on him.*

"Do as you see fit," she said. "If there is another slot that might suit him better, feel free to reassign him."

The XO nodded curtly.

"This leads to another question," Kat said. "How did they catch us?"

"We were betrayed," Davidson said flatly. "How *else* could it have been done?"

Kat visibly winced. She hadn't wanted to consider the possibility.

"They knew where we were going in advance," the XO said. Clearly, he'd been thinking along the same lines. "They had an ambush prepared, one that caught us by surprise; they could only have done that if they'd been warned, somehow, that we would be going there. And they didn't respond to the feint at all."

"As far as we know," Kat said slowly. "They might have refused to panic when we attacked Aswan, or they might have called reinforcements from elsewhere."

"They would have been fully justified in calling for help if they believed a major assault on Aswan was likely," the XO said. "No, the only reason they *didn't* was because they knew where we were going *next*. And they were right."

"We have a rat onboard," Davidson said. He leaned forward. "How many people knew we were going to Morningside?"

Kat frowned. "Before or after the attack on Aswan?"

"If they had time to plot an ambush, I'd bet they knew after we attacked Ringer," Davidson said. "That squadron of superdreadnoughts wasn't the one we confronted at Aswan."

"The crews were much better trained, for a start," Kat muttered. She cleared her throat. "If you're correct, if we have an enemy intelligence agent onboard, how did they get a message off the ship?"

The XO looked embarrassed. "It isn't unknown for crewmen to tap into secondary communications nodes and use them to signal their friends on other vessels," he said. "If the spy was careful, he or she could have transmitted a signal from a communication node and then wiped it from the records. They'd have to isolate the node from the main datanet, but they're practically *designed* to keep functioning if they lost their connection to the rest of the ship. There are so many redundancies built into the nodes that they could lose half their functionality and keep going."

"There wouldn't be any acknowledgement, either," Davidson added. "As long as they didn't try to send orders back, there would be no way to know the spy exists."

Kat groaned, inwardly. She knew a little about industrial espionage—her father had made sure she knew the basics, even though it was unlikely she'd ever take up a senior role with the family business—but she didn't know much about interplanetary espionage, apart from what they'd been taught at Piker's Peak. Most of their lessons had been dreadfully unspecific: she'd been told not to leave data unsecured, not to talk about the details of her assignments, postings, and operations, and to make damn sure she kept her security codes under wraps. The only notion she remembered well had been the warning that raw midshipmen, newly minted as *very* junior officers, might be targeted by enemy spies. A recruitment attempt might not be recognized until it was far too late.

And then you would be hopelessly entangled in a spider's web, she thought, recalling the warnings they'd been given. *Once you are compromised, you will always be compromised.*

She pushed the thought aside. Either the Theocracy had invented a completely new way to track ships through hyperspace—and send messages at FTL speeds without StarComs—or they'd somehow managed to place a spy on board. But how? Had the covert attempt to recruit potential commanding officers for her ships interested an enemy operative? Or . . . or had the enemy simply had an incredible stroke of luck? Or . . .

"Fuck it," she said crossly. "Where do we start looking?"

"The enemy had to have been warned about the planned attack before we actually attacked Aswan," Davidson said. "I think that only a relative handful of crewmen might have known our planned destination."

Kat nodded. "The tactical staff," she said crossly. "And anyone the other commanders might have told."

She shook her head. "The spy might be dead," she said savagely. "And we wouldn't even *know* about it!"

"The other commanders knew not to discuss it," Davidson said.

"It might not have mattered," the XO countered sharply. "There are few secrets on a starship, Major. Rumors spread faster than light. Someone bragging to impress his bunkmate, someone engaging in pillow talk with their lover, someone just unable to keep his mouth shut after a few drinks . . . there's no reason to restrict our search to the tactical staff."

Kat would have liked to disagree, but she knew he was right. Rumors spread through starships very quickly, growing more inflated or outrageous with each retelling. The enemy had a genuine seer on the command staff. The enemy had an angel whispering secrets into their ears. The enemy had made a pact with the space demons . . . and, compared with some of the absurdities she'd heard, talk about the next target was almost nothing.

"It's still the best place to start," Davidson said. "High enough to be involved in tactical planning, low enough to pass unnoticed." He looked at Kat. "With your permission, Captain, I would like to interrogate everyone in the tactical department."

"Regulations strictly forbid using any form of enhanced interrogation without due cause," the XO pointed out.

"We are at war," Davidson snapped. "Regulations can be put aside at the captain's discretion."

"It would also cause a great deal of resentment," the XO added.

"They can suck it up," Davidson snarled. "They're grown adults, not little boys whining because everyone's been told to turn out their pockets after the church crown went missing."

Kat held up her hand. "Calm down, both of you," she said, keeping her voice as level as she could. Both of them were at the very edge of their endurance yet forced to concentrate on a major problem. The XO was meant to defend the crew if necessary; Davidson had no priority other than the hunt for the spy. "Do we have any likely suspects?"

"None," Davidson said. He'd probably already looked at the files. "Anyone who couldn't pass a basic vetting would not have been attached to this operation."

"Senior officers do get vetted more thoroughly," the XO said. "I was . . . *asked* . . . a great many questions after my homeworld was overrun."

"They wouldn't send an obvious spy," Kat said slowly. What would Sherlock Holmes and Doctor Watson do? They'd set a trap . . . but after the ambush, she knew she didn't have time to play games. Besides, the next ambush could easily cost her all of the remaining ships. "A refugee?"

"There are no first-generation refugees outside the groundpounders," Davidson said coldly. "Anyone marked as a second-generation refugee would have been either thoroughly vetted or simply excluded from anything sensitive. I don't think we'll find *Theocratic Spy* listed in their personnel file . . ."

"*Major*," the XO hissed.

"This is what we are going to do," Kat said before the two men could start fighting. "We are going to remain here anyway until the remaining ships have been repaired, so the spy will have no further opportunity to get a message out to the enemy. You two are going to get some rest, then you can start looking for evidence before doing anything else.

If you *cannot* find any evidence"—she took a breath—"I will authorize the use of truth drugs and lie detectors."

"Captain, that could cost you your career," the XO said.

"Yes, it could," Kat said. Technically, naval personnel were excluded from the legal protections laid down in the Commonwealth Constitution, but it would still hamper her career if the effort proved fruitless. No one liked the thought of what were effectively random strip searches, even if there was no alternative. Legal, perhaps; moral, certainly not. "I do not see any alternative."

She glanced at Davidson. "Start with Commander Roach," she added. "He's in charge of the department; he may have noticed someone behaving oddly, or acting in a suspicious manner."

"Lieutenant Parkinson has been handling personnel issues for tactical," the XO put in quickly. "Commander Roach has spent far too much of his time on the bridge."

"Check with her too, then," Kat ordered. She'd have to have a word with Roach if he'd been neglecting his duties. But then, half the tactical staff that *should* have been assigned to them never had been. "And see if she merits a brevet promotion if she's handling matters above her station."

Her eyes narrowed in sudden recognition. "Lieutenant Parkinson . . . wasn't she the girl with the gambling problem?"

"I have kept an eye on her, Captain," the XO said. "I believe she has largely recovered from that misstep. And she *did* handle herself well during the battles around Cadiz."

"Good," Kat said. She knew all too well just how hard it was to recover from a youthful mistake, particularly if it was one that could have had nasty consequences. "Get some sleep, then check with both of them."

"Aye, Captain," the XO said. "With your permission, I will check in on the bridge and then go to my cabin."

"Granted," Kat said. She hoped that meant he would actually *sleep*. "Whatever else happens, we need to sit down in a couple of days and plot our next moves."

The XO nodded and rose. "We need to make sure the enemy knows we're not cowed," he said. "Right now, they're probably gloating over their victory. Even a small raid would give them a nasty fright."

He saluted and then headed for the door.

"He's a good man," Davidson said once the hatch had closed. There was nothing but genuine affection in his tone. "Looking out for his people, despite knowing that one of them is a rat."

"I know," Kat said. The best XO she'd known had offered good advice to junior officers even though he'd ridden them hard. Davidson made a better XO, she thought, than she'd ever been. "Can we find the spy?"

"If worse comes to worst, we can interrogate everyone on the ship," Davidson said. He yawned, suddenly. "It may not get us anywhere, if the spy has already been killed, but . . . at least we'd know the survivors were innocent."

"Or that there's another explanation," Kat said.

Davidson looked at her tiredly. "Like what?"

"I wish I knew," Kat said. She yawned herself, fighting down the urge to just curl up in her chair and go to sleep. "Any technological explanation . . . if the enemy could track ships through hyperspace, Pat, they'd have won the war by now. Unless they somehow managed to get a rogue program into our datanet . . ."

"It would have been found," Davidson said. "The techheads who do the work are among the most stringently vetted people in the Commonwealth."

Kat nodded. It was an unpleasant fact that certain agencies within the Commonwealth were allowed to discriminate, refusing to accept applicants who had items in their background that might—*might*—make them a security risk. Anyone who had relations on the other side of the border had to be considered a potential danger, even though it was unlikely they'd serve the Theocracy willingly. The refugees from Verdean and Ringer would never be allowed to rise to the very highest levels, no matter how loyal and faithful they were. And they would *never* be allowed anywhere near a starship's datacores.

"Then we must proceed on the assumption we have a spy," she said curtly. "Get some rest, then start hunting for the bastard."

Davidson gave her a stern look. "You need to sleep too," he said. His voice softened before she could take offense at his tone. "Get some rest yourself."

"I will," Kat said.

She hesitated, then reached out and pulled him into a kiss. It was the wrong time and place, but she wanted—needed—to feel alive. His lips felt hard and demanding against hers . . . she moaned slightly as his tongue slipped into her mouth, his hands reaching down to stroke her breasts through the uniform.

"Come with me," she said, standing. "Please."

Davidson grinned, then followed her into the bedroom.

CHAPTER TWENTY-NINE

William was *not* pleased.

He'd been raised to believe in loyalty. As a child, one was loyal to one's parents; as a grown man, one was loyal to one's group; as a starship crewman, one was loyal to the rest of the crew. There was room for dissent, even for active disagreement, but not for outright disloyalty. The glue that bound a ship's crew together could not survive treachery. It would undermine the faith and trust the crew needed in order to work together. A spy—someone who had deliberately betrayed his fellow crew to the enemy—was the worst of all. He had tried to get them all killed.

He hadn't slept very well. He'd kept thinking, wondering just who would betray his or her shipmates—and why. As XO, he was responsible for supervising the crew; had he, somehow, missed the signs of a budding traitor? Or had he overlooked something that had started a person down the road to treachery? Or had he simply ignored the traitor, dismissed him as unimportant and never even *considered* the possibility of treachery? By the time he'd finally drifted off to an uncomfortable sleep, his head was echoing with anger and bitter pain. Someone was going to pay for betraying their shipmates . . .

But it wouldn't be enough. How could it be? The crew would be broken and scattered by the news, when they needed to pull together. Their faith in one another would be shattered. It wouldn't be easy for them to bond again after such a betrayal. And yet he needed to make them work as a group once more. Maybe, just maybe, they could isolate the spy— even keep news of his or her existence a secret. But it wouldn't work unless they caught and removed the traitor before it was too late.

William pulled himself out of bed and stumbled into the shower, then turned on the tap and washed his body down with cold water. The cold shocked him awake; he cursed under his breath, then forced himself to look in the mirror. He'd terrify anyone who saw him, he suspected; his face looked as if he hadn't slept for days, let alone hours. He washed his face *thoroughly*, then turned up the temperature and concentrated on relaxing. If things had been different, he might have declared himself unfit for duty and asked the doctor for a sedative, but it was unthinkable when the ship was in deep trouble. He stepped out of the shower and dressed quickly, then glanced at the status update on his terminal. *Lightning* was still several hours from being ready for action, while the remaining four ships were days away. It might be better, he thought, for *Lightning* to set out on her own, while the other ships were repaired.

Once we have the spy in the brig, he told himself firmly, *then we can start making some proper plans.*

He checked his appearance in the mirror, then walked out of his cabin and down towards the tactical compartment. He'd run through everyone's file in the department last night before his meeting with the captain, and none of them had stood out as a potential spy. Not, he had to admit, that he'd expected anyone to have *spy* written in his or her personnel dossier. The Theocracy wouldn't use someone without a background that would stand up to scrutiny, particularly given how much sensitive information flowed through the tactical department. It practically *had* to be someone from Tyre . . .

. . . which, he hoped, meant an unwilling spy rather than a willing traitor.

It struck him as odd, but he'd been an officer long enough to know that everyone had their pressure points. If someone had offered him command, he knew, it would have been hard for him to refuse whatever they demanded in exchange. Or if they'd offered him something he wanted . . . who knew? If someone desired something badly enough, the mere prospect of getting it would be enough to weaken their resistance. Money? Forbidden pleasures? Or even a chance to live life high on the hog after the war?

Or resentment, he added, mentally. *Someone might have been passed over for promotion enough to want revenge on the entire system.*

It wasn't a comfortable thought. If someone had started to compile a list of officers and crew who had good reason to be resentful, they would have to put William himself at the top of the list. Sixty years old, forty years in the Navy, a career that hadn't been blighted by any ghastly failures . . . and he hadn't been offered a command, while a young girl in her late twenties had been promoted ahead of him. If Captain Falcone hadn't proved herself, he wondered, would he have resented her badly enough to betray the Navy? Once, he would have considered it unthinkable; now, he knew it was a very real possibility.

He sighed inwardly as he stepped into the tactical department and surveyed the thirteen officers working at their consoles, replaying everything that had happened at Morningside, from the moment they'd entered the system to the moment they'd fled back into hyperspace, losing six ships and hundreds of lives in their wake. None of them *looked* like obvious traitors—William chided himself for thinking that any of them *would* look evil—but one of them was the most likely suspect. Unless, of course, something *had* been leaked and the spy was in a different department. It wouldn't be the first time someone seemingly insignificant had proven themselves a deadly threat.

"Commander," Lieutenant Cecelia Parkinson said. She looked older, more mature, than he remembered, although her short red hair and freckled face still made her look young. She'd lost some of her innocence, he noted; her mistakes on her first cruise, even if they hadn't been fatal, had left scars. "What can I do for you?"

"I need a word," he said. He didn't think Cecelia was the spy, but she *did* have a black mark in her record. "Your office, now."

Cecelia hesitated, then turned and led him through a hatch into a small office. It was barely large enough to swing a cat: a desk, a couple of chairs, a computer terminal . . . really, it was nothing more than a status symbol. Technically, it should have belonged to Lieutenant Commander Roach, but he'd passed it to Cecelia when it became clear she would be largely running the department. William made a mental note to have a few words with him about the issue, then sat down and faced the younger woman. Cecelia was clearly trying to keep her expression under control, but it was easy to tell she looked worried. She just didn't have the experience to hide her emotions from him.

"Lieutenant," William said, "how *are* things in your department?"

"A little shaken up, sir," Cecelia said. "The enemy caught us by surprise and no one's quite sure how they managed to do it."

"I'm sure," William said dryly. He looked her in the eye. "Have you been having any more problems with gambling?"

Cecelia flinched. "No, sir," she said. "I've been too busy to do anything other than my duties."

William nodded slowly. Crewman Steadman, who'd lured Cecelia into his gambling network, had been transferred off the ship when *Lightning* returned to Tyre, along with most of his cronies. The notes William had put in their files should ensure they were never assigned to any frontline ships, although the demands of war might overrule his wishes. Cecelia would have a chance to grow out of her mistakes, if she had the determination. She seemed to be doing fine.

"Someone leaked," he said flatly. "The enemy knew where we were going in advance."

Cecelia looked relieved. "Yes, sir," she said. "That was my conclusion too."

"Good," William said. He felt a flicker of pity for her. She had to know that the leak had almost certainly come from the tactical department, her command. On the other hand, if she'd had concerns, she should have brought them to him. He'd have to give her a stern lecture later. "Do you have any suspects?"

"No, sir," Cecelia said. She took a long breath. "There doesn't seem to be anyone with a valid reason to support the Theocracy."

"There *aren't* any valid reasons to support the Theocracy," William growled. A young woman like Cecelia would have to be utterly insane to support the Theocracy, which would—at best—regard her as a brood mare. "But someone else might disagree."

He closed his eyes for a long moment. The thought of having everyone in the department interrogated was horrific. It would undermine the bonds of trust between officers and crewmen as surely as the spy's existence would undermine the glue binding the ship's crew together. No one, absolutely no one, liked the idea of being drugged, then having to answer questions . . .

"I think we need to go through the files again," he said, keying his wristcom. Davidson could start making preparations to carry out the interrogations, one by one. "Let me see whom you have under your command."

Cecelia nodded, then tapped her terminal, calling up the files. *Lightning* had fifteen tactical officers in all, ranging from officers on the command track to analysts who weren't expected to rise any higher in the service. William marked the latter as potential suspects, particularly if one of them had been pushed into becoming an analyst rather than remaining on the command track. Resentment *could* be a powerful motivator, after all . . .

But we need officers and men, he thought. *There's a bloody war on. They could probably reapply to the command track and no one would try to stop them. It isn't as if any of them are super-users from Tyre.*

He scowled. The more he looked at it, the more he wondered if the only viable suspect was Cecelia herself. *She* had a past, after all, and while it was a very *minor* past it would be enough to damage her promotion prospects beyond repair. There might be no alternative, but to put a young officer through enhanced interrogation . . .

Damn it, he thought. *They're all from decent families with naval backgrounds . . .*

He stopped as a thought occurred to him, then started cross-referencing the dossiers with other naval files. If the officers were members of naval families, it was quite possible that one or more of them had a relative who had been captured by the enemy. It should have sufficed to have the officer removed from any sensitive position—the prospect of blackmail couldn't be ignored—but maybe there had been a glitch in the system. Or, perhaps, something had been overlooked.

"Bingo," he said, delighted. "Look what I've found."

Cecelia frowned. "Lieutenant Aloysius Parker," she said. "Newly minted; command track . . . with a sister who was listed as missing in action after the Battle of Cadiz. Not a confirmed POW . . ."

"No," William mused. There were times when he really *hated* bureaucracy. "And because she wasn't listed as a POW, there was no red flag in his file."

He gritted his teeth in rage. There had been so much confusion during the first battle that quite a few officers had been listed as MIA, even though they were probably either prisoners or dead. The Theocracy hadn't bothered to open negotiations regarding POWs; they certainly hadn't even shared the details of captured officers and men with the Commonwealth. No doubt they'd calculated that refusing to swap POWs hurt the Commonwealth more than the Theocracy. He had to admit that they were probably right.

"It doesn't prove anything, sir," Cecelia pointed out carefully.

"He should have declined the assignment," William said. He opened the next set of files, just to check to see if there were any other possible suspects. "If you can be forced into betraying your planet, you are supposed to take it to your superiors and ensure you are not posted to anywhere harmful. There are *procedures* in place for that."

"Yes, sir," Cecelia said.

"Stay here," William ordered once he'd finished skimming the remaining files. He had no faith in Cecelia's ability to dissemble, not when he needed to round up the Marines and make the arrest. Maybe he didn't have *proof*, but at least he had solid grounds for carrying out a formal interrogation. "I'll deal with the matter personally."

"Yes, sir," Cecelia said. "What . . . what are you going to do to him?"

William sighed. It was easy to feel sorry for Parker—and, no doubt, when the case finally came to trial, the defense lawyer would spin a sob story for the jury. But Parker had managed to get several hundred crewmen killed and a number of ships destroyed or put permanently out of commission. There couldn't be mercy . . .

"It would depend on just how cooperative he's feeling," he said finally. The Theocracy might not realize the spy had been caught . . . assuming, of course, that Parker *was* the spy and he wasn't following a wild goose chase. "But that will be up to the captain."

"Yes, sir," Cecelia said.

William rose, headed out of the office, and walked through the tactical department. Parker didn't *look* any different, even though he was certainly guilty at the very least of concealing the fact he could be blackmailed. But the XO hadn't really expected horns growing out of his skull. He *did* look tense, but that proved nothing. Half the crew looked tense when they had a moment to think about just how impossibly unlikely the ambush had been.

He keyed his wristcom as soon as he was out of the department. "I have a suspect," he said shortly. "Set up to receive him in tactical chamber five, then have Roach call him into the compartment."

"Aye, Commander," Davidson said. He sounded disgustingly fresh and alert, although William had a suspicion he'd spent the night in the captain's cabin. On the other hand, anyone who'd lived through boot camp would be able to survive on three to four hours of sleep a day. "I'll meet you there in five minutes."

And hope to hell we got the right one, William thought. Technically, the captain had the authority to order an interrogation on weak—or even nonexistent—grounds, but it wouldn't look good when the ship returned to port. *Because if we didn't, we'll have to interrogate the entire tactical crew.*

Tactical chamber five was really nothing more than a small briefing compartment, used to demonstrate tactical concepts to the crew and rehearse operational plans before showing them to the commanding officers. The Marines took it over quickly, then called Roach and asked him to send Parker to the chamber. It wouldn't alert the suspect, William hoped. The tactical staff were often asked to go through minor concepts by their superior officers; now, after the squadron had been ambushed, there was good reason to go through everything with a fine-tooth comb. Moments later, Parker stepped through the hatch and was promptly grabbed by two Marines.

Davidson stepped forward. "Lieutenant Parker, we have strong reason to believe that you have been working as an enemy intelligence agent," he said formally. "By authority of the War Powers Act, it is my duty to subject you to an enhanced interrogation procedure. I am obliged to warn you that your normal rights and legal protections have been placed in abeyance and the captain will stand in judgment over you. However, if you cooperate, the case will be placed in front of a court-martial once we return to Tyre."

He nodded to the Marines, who cuffed Parker to a chair. "Do you have anything you want to say for yourself before we begin?"

"I didn't mean to," Parker said. "I wasn't given a choice!"

"I see," Davidson said. He gentled his voice, slightly. "Tell us everything, starting from the beginning."

William listened, carefully, as the whole story slipped out. Parker's sister had been captured on Cadiz. The Theocracy had then contacted him on Tyre and told him to spy for them if he didn't want his sister brutally raped and murdered. He'd requested assignment to the squadron in the belief it would be going somewhere safe, somewhere where he would have an excuse for not being very useful, but instead he'd discovered himself in enemy space. And they would have known if he hadn't done anything to help them . . .

And he betrayed the entire crew, William thought coldly. *We cannot let him live.*

"How did you send the messages?" Davidson asked. "What tricks did you use?"

"Reprogrammed the communication nodes," Parker explained. "It was the only way to get a message out without it being logged."

William sighed, then drew Davidson aside for a brief consultation. "Drug him and verify as much of the story as possible, then transfer him to the brig as secretly as possible," he ordered. It wouldn't be easy to conceal the fact they'd taken a prisoner, but with so many crewmen moving around it should be possible to conceal just what had happened to Lieutenant Parker. "Captain Falcone will have to decide his fate."

"Yes, sir," Davidson said. "We might be able to use him."

"I think so," William said. They'd have to sit down and go through everything with Parker, but there wasn't any strong reason why that couldn't be done. "Send them a piece of information to misdirect them . . . you never know."

He sighed. The only upside to the whole affair, at least, was that they'd found the spy. But were there any others? Even if there were none, and Parker probably wouldn't know if there *were*, the crew's trust had been broken. The long-term consequences could be disastrous.

"I'm going to report to the captain," he said. "Write out a full report, then forward it to both of us."

"Of course, sir," Davidson said. He looked at Parker. "A weak man, at the end."

"Yeah," William agreed. "But at least he can't do any more harm."

CHAPTER THIRTY

"Captain?"

Kat glanced at the hatch, then muttered a curse under her breath. "Come in!"

The door opened, revealing the XO. "You didn't answer the buzzer," he said. "I was worried."

"I'm fine," Kat said, crossly. She glanced down at the datapad in her hand. "I was reading the personnel files."

"We caught the spy," the XO said. "Or one of them, if there is more than one."

Kat nodded slowly. "Did you know that Midshipwoman Toni Jackson was in a band? That she had a handful of friends who played in bars on Tyre, when they had a chance to meet up? That she turned down a music deal to remain in the Navy?"

"No, Captain," the XO said.

"Or that Lieutenant Sally Pagan loved old books," Kat added. "She was a reservist; she worked at the Planetary Library after retiring from the Navy the first time and is credited with restoring a very old copy of *Foundation*. There's even a copy of an article she wrote on pre-hyperspace science fiction and how it predicted the future—and what it managed to get wrong."

She shook her head tiredly. "I didn't know either of them."

"But they're both dead," the XO said. "It doesn't get any easier to lose people, Captain."

"I know," Kat said sourly. "But I can't help feeling guilty about not knowing them. They're names and faces in files, nothing more. I never heard Midshipwoman Jackson play; I never read Lieutenant Pagan's articles . . . I never really even knew they existed. And there are hundreds more just like them, hundreds of people who are now dead."

She looked back at the datapad, picking names out at random. "Senior Crewman Thomas Throne had a drinking problem," she said. "He was fine onboard ship, according to his mates, but when he was on shore leave he would get drunk and spend his time battling the redcaps. Crewwomen Laura Adams was caught having an orgy with three other crewwomen two years ago, apparently. Crewman Lesley Morse had three children, all of whom are only just entering their teens. What do I tell them when they ask why they had to grow up without a father?

"I need to write a letter for each and every one of them," she added bitterly. "And I didn't know any of them well enough to say anything."

The XO frowned. "You might have to send them a form letter, Captain," he said. "There isn't *time* for you to write out five hundred separate letters."

"I *should* write them each a personal letter," Kat insisted. "It's the right thing to do."

"There's a department back home that handles such matters," the XO reminded her. "You would not be responsible for taking care of the families."

"These people died under *my* command," Kat insisted. "It's something I have to handle personally."

She glared down at the datapad, then put it on the table. It had been easier when she'd been a junior officer; she'd known everyone in her department, as well as most of the rest of the crew. Now . . . she didn't know everyone on *Lightning*, let alone the remainder of the squadron. There simply hadn't been time to walk through her ship and meet her crewmen, even though they were under her command. And now far too many of them were dead.

"We're going to hold a proper funeral in an hour," she added curtly. "And maybe even a remembrance ceremony."

"Those are private gatherings," the XO said. "You cannot *order* one to take place."

Kat glowered at him. He was right.

"Yes," she said finally. She ran her hand through her hair, then looked at him. "What did the spy have to say for himself?"

"Basically, he was forced into spying for the enemy after his sister was taken prisoner, Captain," the XO said. "They provided proof she was still alive and reasonably safe, as long as he followed orders. In short, the bastards got lucky."

"Very lucky," Kat muttered.

"Parker tried to get himself assigned to somewhere harmless," the XO added. "He just happened to find himself here."

Kat had to laugh. "Shot ourselves in the foot, didn't we?"

"In more ways than one," the XO confirmed. "The sister wasn't listed as an official POW, so his file wasn't flagged . . . hell, Captain, the CIS let us down pretty badly."

"In hindsight, I should have walked into Admiral Morrison's office and shot him out of hand," Kat said tartly. She would have been executed for murdering her superior officer—not even her father could have saved her from the gallows—but it might have preserved thousands of lives. "There's no point in wishing to change the past."

She took a breath. "They know the spy is trustworthy now," she added after a moment. "We could use this, somehow. Misdirect them."

"It'll only work once," the XO warned. "They'd assume the worst after we used the spy against them."

"I know," Kat said.

She looked back down at the datapad. It was hard to think straight, not when so many lives had been lost, not when she felt terrifyingly guilty. How could she feel that it wasn't her fault? She'd been the one who'd made the mistake of sharing too much information with her junior officers, unaware that one was planning to betray her. And the enemy had given her a bloody nose, restoring their own morale. She'd embarrassed them and hurt them, she knew, but it wasn't enough.

"We need to go back on the offensive," she said. "But most of the significant targets are too well defended for our weakened forces, particularly now."

"Then we find a weak point," the XO said. "They can't guard *everywhere* against a sneak attack."

Kat shrugged, then tapped her console, bringing up the star chart. The easy targets were largely insignificant, unless she wanted to bombard civilian populations from orbit. It would annoy the Theocracy, but it wouldn't significantly hamper them. The handful of more viable targets were risky as hell, given her shortage of warships. And the enemy might have started parceling out superdreadnoughts to cover them.

"We have a choice," she said, finally. "We can either head deeper into enemy space, where we might be able to find more significant targets, or we can return to the Commonwealth. I don't think we have the resources to risk more attacks in this sector."

The XO hesitated. "There's another possibility," he said. "Actually, there are two of them."

Kat looked up. "Go on."

"First, we scout around Aswan and wait for a convoy to depart," the XO said. "And then we attack it in hyperspace."

"Battles in hyperspace are notoriously unpredictable," Kat reminded him. "A single explosion could whip up an energy storm that would force us *all* to crash back to normal space."

"That might not be a bad thing," the XO said. "We could take a crack at them while they were disorganized, or back off if we were outgunned."

Kat nodded, slowly. "And the second possibility?"

"There's a smuggler base in the sector," the XO said. "I go there, get intelligence, and come back. We might learn something useful."

"You might also be betrayed," Kat said. She considered the possibilities for a long moment, then frowned. "I doubt the Theocracy is unaware of their presence."

"My brother's files say the *local* Theocrats know about it," the XO said. "The base really isn't that far from Morningside. However, they turn a blind eye in exchange for certain . . . considerations."

"Bribes," Kat said. She shook her head in disbelief. "How does that even *work*?"

The XO smiled. "Tyre isn't the most democratic state in human history," he said, "but it is reasonably transparent and the way to climb the ladder to power is well understood. The civil service is not corrupt, any malefactors are dealt with promptly and people trust the government to leave them alone when they're not doing anything wrong."

Kat nodded. "Because playing moral guardian is *so* inefficient," she said. "My father used to say there were certain issues that should never be touched."

"Exactly," the XO agreed. "But if you grow up in a society which is rotten to the core, where you can cheerfully ignore the rules if you have power and status, where your superiors will screw you over if they happen to need a scapegoat . . . you wind up with very little respect for those rules. Why should you show any respect when your superiors show none? And hell, you *need* power to protect yourself from anyone else."

He shrugged. "I'd be surprised if every bureaucrat in the Theocracy isn't a corrupt little bastard trading favors just to survive," he added.

"Get bribes from the people you're supposed to supervise? Why not? Want a harem? Why not collect a few women as tribute and add them to your household? Your superior might pitch a fit? Offer him one of the women as a gift. Dealing with smugglers? Why not?"

Kat looked at the star chart, thoughtfully. "And you think the smugglers will know something we can use?"

"I'd be surprised if they weren't collecting data constantly," the XO said. "Information is power in their world."

"They'd notice if we took *Lightning*," Kat said. "How do you intend to travel?"

"I'll take *Mermaid*," the XO said. "She's old enough to be a smuggler vessel without raising too many eyebrows. We'd be fucked if someone got a look inside, but if we run into a warship we'd be fucked anyway. I can dock with the asteroid and go inside, if we take something to barter. Those captured enemy spare parts should raise a nice price."

He smirked. "After what we did to Verdean, Captain, I imagine the price has skyrocketed."

Kat nodded in agreement. It would be blindingly obvious just *where* the spare parts had come from, but she knew from bitter experience that no one would care. If a colony world on the rim of explored space refused to ask too many questions about something that *had* to have been stolen by pirates, she couldn't see desperate enemy officials caring either. It *did* raise the issue of accidentally aiding the enemy, but under the circumstances she didn't see any other choice. The only *real* concern was losing her XO if the enemy caught them before they could escape.

"You'll have to be very careful," she warned. "This isn't your brother's territory."

"They'll let anyone dock, as long as they're not blatantly hostile," the XO assured her. "And the data . . . well, we can use it to formulate a proper plan."

"Good," Kat said. She glanced at her chronometer, then sighed. "It's time for the funeral, Commander. When will you be able to leave?"

"*Mermaid* was largely untouched," the XO said. "I imagine I can leave thirty minutes after the funeral."

"We'll set up an RV point before you go," Kat said. "No, we'll stay here; the rest of the squadron can wait elsewhere, with the fleet train. I may have a use in mind for the scrapped ships."

"Good luck," the XO said.

"I should be wishing *you* that," Kat said. She half wished she could go with him, or go in his place, but she knew that was impossible. A starship commander could not risk her life on a smuggler's asteroid, or lead a mission down to a dangerous planet. *That* only happened in bad movies. "Just take very good care of yourself."

"I will," the XO said. "I'll be back before you know it."

◆　◆　◆

The captain looked . . . *different*, somehow, as she read out the second set of names. William listened, holding his cap in his hand, as she recited each and every one of the dead, her voice lingering for long moments as she recalled what she'd read in the files. It was never easy to say good-bye to the dead, he knew, but it was harder when one felt guilty. Everyone who joined the Navy knew the risks, yet far too many of them were just faceless names and notes in the files. Even *he* didn't know *everyone* attached to the squadron.

And I never will, he thought numbly. He'd come to terms with it long ago; his homeworld, for all its faults, had never tried to convince its children that they could be safely wrapped in cotton wool. Death came for everyone, no matter how much engineering one tried to splice into one's genetic code. Even hiding in a perpetual stasis chamber was only a way to hide from the Grim Reaper. Death came for everyone and the only thing a person could do was accept that, one day, he or she too would die. But the captain felt guilty.

He didn't blame her. She'd had very little time to whip her command into shape before leaving; hell, he had the feeling that someone else had been intended for the command before the king had intervened. She had had very little time to get to know her personnel, even if she hadn't had the enforced distance of being their commanding officer. To feel guilt over their deaths was one thing; to feel guilt over not knowing them was quite another. William had served under men who hadn't cared about their subordinates and they could be dangerous, but there was a fine line between caring for one's subordinates and being unwilling to risk their lives.

I'm sorry, he thought. The captain was young, perhaps too young. *But there will be many more deaths to come.*

The captain reached the end of her list, then tapped a button. Tractor beams picked up the coffins—this time, at least, there were bodies— and carefully propelled them out into the vacuum of space. They'd drift forever, William knew; they were so far from any star that it was highly unlikely the coffins would ever be captured and drawn to a fiery death. It was possible to believe, as many spacers did, that their ghosts would haunt the void forever, influencing the affairs of the living. There were even religions built around the concept . . .

But there won't be if the Theocracy wins the war, he thought, grimly. *They'll smash anything that looks like an enemy religion.*

He shook his head as the last of the coffins drifted out into space, then watched the crew slowly filing out of the shuttlebay. The captain was looking down at the black coffin, a grim expression on her face. William chivvied the remaining crewmen out of the shuttlebay, then headed towards the bridge. The captain needed time to say good-bye to her fallen crewmen in private.

"Commander," Roach said as he stepped onto the bridge. "Can I have a word?"

William eyed him for a long moment. The tactical officer hadn't been hauled in for interrogation, but he had to know he was in some trouble. Parker had been in *his* department, after all, and it was *Roach's* job to review the personnel files and spot any discrepancies. On the other hand, like everyone else, Roach had been overworked right from the start. In hindsight, they might have been lucky that there had only been one major problem on the squadron.

"One moment," he said. He looked at the communications officer. "Linda, contact *Mermaid* and inform her commander that they are being detached for a specific mission. I shall be shuttling over as soon as possible."

"Aye, Commander," Linda said.

"Come with me," William said to Roach. "Lieutenant Weiberg, you have the bridge."

"Aye, sir," Weiberg said. He barely looked up from his console. "I have the bridge."

William led the tactical officer through the hatch and down to his cabin. There was no dedicated office for the XO, although he had blanket permission to use the captain's office if necessary. This time, however, he had a feeling this discussion was better held elsewhere.

"Right," he said, once the hatch was closed and locked. "What can I do for you?"

"Commander," Roach said. "I should have been consulted on Parker . . ."

William felt his temper start to fray. "You *should* have been supervising the tactical department, as well as handling your bridge duties," he said sharply. "If you *had* been doing your job, perhaps Parker would have been caught *before* we were ambushed!"

Roach clenched his fists, then visibly forced himself to relax. He was tired; they were *all* tired and demoralized after the ambush and retreat. William silently cursed the staffing problems again, then reminded himself that they had plenty of spare personnel now that a handful of ships were being scrapped. The only problem would be working up the handful of remaining ships before they had to go back into battle.

"With all due respect, sir," Roach said, "I . . ."

"No," William said. He held up a hand before Roach could say another word, then forced himself to keep his voice calm and level. "I understand your feelings on the matter, both your outrage and your embarrassment"—*and your sense it wasn't your fault,* he added silently—"however, I do not have time to deal with the matter. I do not believe you deliberately covered up anything, merely that you didn't have the time to handle *all* of your responsibilities. There will, of course, be an inquest when we get home, but until then I expect you to do your duty."

He took a breath. "Do you understand me?"

"Yes, sir," Roach said.

"Good," William said. He studied the younger man for a long moment. "I will be leaving shortly. During my absence, I expect you to work hard to rebuild your department and prepare it for the next challenge. Once I return, we will discuss any other matters. Do *not* let me or the captain down."

"Yes, sir," Roach said.

"Good," William said, again. He sighed inwardly. Roach would either blame himself or blame everyone *but* himself. The entire crew really needed a rest, but they weren't going to get one. "Very good. Dismissed."

CHAPTER THIRTY-ONE

"It looks like yet another boring system," Lieutenant Lars Rasmussen observed.

"Set course for the asteroid cluster, then broadcast the signal code I gave you," William ordered. "There should be a response within seconds."

"Aye, sir," Rasmussen said.

William concealed his amusement with an effort. Rasmussen was in command of the vessel, but William outranked him. In theory, Rasmussen had the legal authority to give orders to admirals and even politicians; in practice, it would be a brave or foolish junior officer who tried. He seemed to have compromised; he paid attention to William, but steadfastly held to his command. William would have been impressed if he'd had time to care.

"That's a response," Midshipwoman Grace Hawthorne said. "They're pointing us towards a large asteroid, then demanding payment in advance."

"How unsurprising," William observed. "Remember: none of you are to leave the ship without my permission. If I don't return or contact you within five hours, cast off, return to the RV point, and report to Captain Falcone."

"Aye, sir," Rasmussen said.

William nodded, then watched grimly as the asteroid slowly came into view. He'd seen quite a few hidden settlements, but this one wasn't really hidden at all. It emitted enough betraying radiation for the enemy to have no trouble finding it if they bothered to look. He'd had doubts, no matter what he'd said to the captain, but now . . . now he realized he'd been correct all along. The Theocracy knew the base was there and turned a blind eye.

"Take us towards the docking port," he said as the asteroid turned slowly, revealing a handful of ports cut into the stone. Several starships were clearly visible, including two old warships and something that *looked* like an early model pleasure yacht. The remainder were freighters of various designs, one of which was a complete unknown. Something the Theocracy had produced? Or something from the other side of the settled universe? "I'll pay when the hatch opens."

He picked up his carryall as the ship docked, then made his way down to the airlock and stepped through. A pair of grim-faced men were waiting for him, one with his arms removed and replaced by a set of very visible combat augmentations. William refused to show any reaction—it was a childish attempt to intimidate him—as he held out their payment, a handful of Commonwealth credit chips. They would be worthless in the Theocracy, of course, but smugglers were no respecters of borders. Besides, the crown was worth more than anything the Theocracy used for money.

"That would be suitable," the first man grunted after checking the chips carefully. "You have the right to use this airlock and docking port for two days. Fuel, energy, and anything else is extra."

"Thank you," William said dryly. "Can you point me towards the market?"

The man nodded. "Down in Section C," he said gruffly. "Be warned that you may not offer insult, aggression, or violence towards anyone else within the rock. Any offenders will be put outside the airlock without a protective suit."

He turned and strode off, followed by his augmented companion. William frowned after him—that level of visible augmentation was unusual—then headed down towards Section C. The layout of the asteroid looked to be fairly standard; there didn't seem to be many differences between this location and the handful of other smuggler bases he'd visited, although the population here seemed to be smaller. It probably had something to do with their location, he reasoned; the chance of making a fortune off corrupt officials versus the prospect of being brutally killed if the Theocracy's enforcers got hold of them. He shrugged, then stepped through the door into the marketplace, looking around with interest. It was smaller than his brother's asteroid, but almost as well-appointed.

"I have spare parts to sell," he said once he found a prospective reseller. He held out a datapad containing the manifest, then smiled. "Make me an offer."

The reseller—a dark-skinned woman who seemed to have been slimmed down until she was hellishly thin—eyed the manifest sourly. "I'll give you ten thousand credits, five thousand joys, or one thousand crowns the lot."

William frowned. "Credits?"

"You can only use them here," the reseller said. She smiled, revealing very sharp teeth. "Useless anywhere else, I'm afraid."

And no doubt rigged to benefit the asteroid's managers, William thought. "You can have the lot for ten thousand crowns."

The woman snorted. "I'd give you ten thousand *joys*," she said. William puzzled over it for a moment, then realized it had to be a slang term for the Theocracy's currency. "You don't have anything like enough here for ten thousand crowns."

They haggled backwards and forwards for a long moment, then settled on seven thousand crowns. William took the advance payment, called the ship to arrange for delivery, and then settled on a time to pick up the rest of the payment. The reseller, having melted slightly, offered him a handful of items from her selection, although she admitted—with another toothy smile—that times were hard. William guessed the Theocracy was buying up everything it could, as well as redirecting production towards the war. There would simply be much less to steal.

"I need to speak to an information broker," he said, finally. "Can you recommend one?"

"Quietus over there is the best on the rock," the reseller said. She giggled, a high-pitched sound that put William's hackles on edge. "Not that that's saying much, out here."

William nodded, thanked her, and headed over to the information broker. He looked very much like the others he had met while he'd been on a quest for his brother—short, very composed, and clearly augmented heavily. One of his eyes had been replaced by an implant; the other looked normal, but flecks of gold were clearly visible. William sat down facing him and waited until the man had activated his privacy generator.

"I need information on shipping movements through Theocratic space," William said, calmly. The man would probably take him for a pirate, but it hardly mattered. "What do you have?"

Quietus looked thoughtful for a long moment. "I have shipping charts, but nothing more detailed," he said. "The convoy details I have are subject to change without notice."

Which is an excellent excuse for scamming me, William thought. "Can you get anything more authentic?"

"My sources might be reluctant to share such details," Quietus said. "It would get them in trouble. You would need to make a *very* good offer."

William considered it. "A thousand crowns?"

"Not good enough, given what is at stake," Quietus said. "They wouldn't live long enough to spend it."

"I can take someone onboard, then transport him and his money out of the Theocracy," William offered. He supposed if he had to work for the Theocracy he'd want out too. "I think that would constitute suitable payment."

Quietus smiled. "And where would you take him?"

"One of the border worlds or asteroid settlements," William said. "I could give him a couple of thousand crowns, if his information pans out. That would be enough to get him started."

"Might be doable," Quietus said. "What would you want from him?"

"Everything," William said simply. "Ship schedules, charts of Theocratic space, locations of naval bases . . . everything he can bring, in short. And I would pay you two thousand crowns for arranging it."

Quietus lifted his eyebrows. "*Three* thousand crowns, considering the risk."

"Two thousand," William said. "That's enough for *you* to set up somewhere else too."

"Very well," Quietus said. "You will pay me one hundred crowns for trying to recruit someone who wants out. If I find a possible candidate who fits your requirements, I will arrange for him to be smuggled here, at which point you will pay me the remaining one thousand, nine hundred crowns. It will take at least five days to accomplish those tasks. Do we have a bargain?"

"We do," William said.

"I may also request transport myself," Quietus said. "Would *that* be acceptable?"

"If you wish," William said. He had a feeling the CIS would want a few words with Quietus before he was allowed to go, but that was Quietus's problem. "I may have to place you in stasis until we reach our destination, but you would be allowed to leave once we arrive."

"Very good," Quietus said. He cocked his head, sending a contact code into William's implants. "You will be informed if I succeed or fail."

William rose, then spent the rest of the hour exploring the market-place and looking for anything that might prove useful. It was odd; star-ship components seemed to be very expensive, while personnel weapons were surprisingly cheap. He couldn't help wondering if the smugglers were selling them to insurgencies on occupied worlds, then dismissed the thought. No matter the number of corrupt officials involved with the smugglers, they'd have to be insane to allow the smugglers to sup-ply weapons to their enemies. Unless, of course, they were so far gone they hardly cared.

"They came for the supplies, sir," Rasmussen said, when he returned to the ship. "We handed them over, as you ordered."

"Good," William said. It would be at least an hour before he could collect the rest of the cash, but he could wait. "I have some new orders for you."

It was seven days before Quietus finally got back in touch with him, seven days during which William grew more and more paranoid about possible betrayal. Whoever Quietus had tapped to serve as a defector might be having second thoughts, or taking part in an elaborate sting operation. Maybe they'd brought an entire enemy squadron with them, or a handful of armed janissaries who would try to capture *Mermaid*. But, when Quietus called him to a private office, he discovered that matters were more awkward than he'd realized.

"This is John," Quietus said. He waved a hand at a one-way mir-ror, which looked into another office. A pale-skinned man sat at a table, looking nervous. "He is—he *was*—a mid-level official on Aswan. Commodore Malian, his former superior, used him as a go-between, but their new commanding officer is a bit more of a hard-ass. John felt it might be safer to leave, so he took the bait. It was very hard to get him, his two wives, and their five children out of the system without sounding any alarms."

William blinked. "There are *seven* of them?"

"Eight, if you count John, and nine, if you count me," Quietus said. "I do want to go too."

Idiot, William told himself. *Just because I have no wife and children doesn't mean that everyone else is equally free to leave at a moment's notice.*

"I will need to check the data first," William said. If John really *had* worked at Aswan, he would know enough to keep the intelligence staff happy for months. "And then we can transfer them to my ship."

"Of course," Quietus said. He produced a datapad and held it out. "A sample can be found here."

William scowled at him, then peered down at the datapad. It certainly *looked* authentic. A handful of updated starship schedules, a couple of outlines of the defenses of various systems . . . it was either authentic or a very good fake. And the latter would be easy to spot, once the analysts went to work. There would be an opportunity for revenge on John, Quietus, and John's family afterwards, if necessary. They would certainly be reluctant to cheat him if they believed he was a pirate.

"Very well," he said. "I will require the full data once everyone is on my ship."

"Of course," Quietus said. "Shall I tell him to prepare?"

"Yes," William said. "Tell him we will leave in twenty minutes."

He keyed his wristcom and sent a few orders, then waited impatiently for John to return with his family. The two wives were veiled, their faces hidden behind black robes that robbed them of all individuality; two of the children, both girls, were veiled too, although he could see their brown eyes. All three of the boys wore long robes; he couldn't help reminding himself to be careful, recalling just how fanatical young men could be. They might not understand why their father had taken them from their home and, when they realized they were actually going to the Commonwealth, they might do something stupid.

John's voice was strange, oddly accented. "You are the one who will take us all?"

"I am," William confirmed. "If you will come with me . . . ?"

He frowned as he led the way down the corridor. The women brought up the rear; the young girls at the very back, hiding from the boys. There was something about such blatant inequality that sent chills down his spine; his homeworld had prided itself on breeding tough-minded men and women, where one's strength and determination meant more than one's gender. To be treated as chattel because of one's birth . . . it was a repulsive historical nightmare. But it was one that had to be endured until the Theocracy was crushed. If a *princess* could gain the nerve to escape, no doubt other women had the same sparks of independence glowing within them too.

"Do *not* touch anything within the ship without permission," William warned as they reached the airlock. "This is not a safe environment."

The hatch hissed open, revealing two crewmen. Both of them had clearly taken the instructions to wear something piratical to heart. The red shirts and black trousers, with several weapons hanging from their belts, made them look like characters out of a bad romantic play rather than real pirates. William sensed Quietus having second thoughts, but it was far too late. He led the small group through the hatch and into a medium-sized cabin that was easy to secure.

"You are not to leave this compartment without an escort," he said as he waved the women and children inside. "We will get you somewhere safe as quickly as possible."

One of the boys glanced at his sister, then said something in a language William didn't recognize. John snapped at him, raising a hand as if he intended to strike the child; the boy cowered back, then glowered at his younger sister . . . as if, somehow, it was all her fault. William felt cold; it looked, very much, as if John kept his family in line with a rod of iron. What had the boy *said*? Had he objected to sharing a cabin with the girls? Or what?

"It . . . it would be better if you could put the girls in a separate cabin," John said. "Is that possible?"

"Perhaps," William said darkly. Although, judging by the expression on the boy's face, it would probably be safer for the girls to keep the two sexes apart. "I will try and make arrangements."

"Thank you," John said.

William sighed and closed the hatch. "We'll be casting off in five minutes," he said once he showed Quietus to his cabin. "I need that data now."

"Here," Quietus said. He gave William a sharp look. "You're not pirates or smugglers, are you?"

"No," William said. "But we *will* keep our agreement, believe me."

He closed the hatch, then keyed his wristcom. "Lieutenant, you may cast off when ready," he said. "Take an evasive course back to the RV point."

"Aye, sir," Rasmussen said.

William smiled to himself, then sobered as he remembered the two women. Princess Drusilla hadn't been so submissive, but she'd been a *princess*. Was that the fate awaiting every woman in the Commonwealth, if their homeworlds were occupied? He remembered everything that had happened on Cadiz, before the counterattack, and shuddered. Any woman who dared show an independent streak had been savagely punished.

"When you have a moment, clear a cabin for the girls," he ordered. "And see if your XO can talk to them. They may respond better to another woman."

"Aye, sir," Rasmussen said.

William carried the datachip to his tiny cabin as he felt the patrol boat cast off, then plugged it into his isolated terminal. There was a pause, then long streams of data started to flicker up in front of him, everything Quietus had promised and more. He couldn't help smiling in relief as he realized it had all been worthwhile, once the data was carefully examined. They now knew enough about the Theocracy to start hammering it apart, piece by piece.

Most of their shipyards, even their repair yards, are concentrated around their core worlds, he thought slowly. *Even a naval base like Aswan has only a handful of repair facilities. Their ships have to limp all the way home for major repairs . . .*

It made no sense, from a practical viewpoint, but the Theocracy was more interested in social control than building a formidable military machine. William was no expert, yet it seemed to him as though the enemy's industrial base was already running hot. They'd practically bankrupted themselves just to build the military they had, let alone keep it going. And, without a network of repair yards, they couldn't cope with increasing numbers of damaged ships.

His wristcom buzzed. "Commander," Rasmussen said. "We are now in hyperspace. No sign of pursuit."

"Good," William said. He made a mental note to thank Scott when he next saw him, then nodded to himself. "Make sure our guests remain reasonably comfortable until we rejoin the squadron, Lieutenant. I want to keep them in a good mood."

"Aye, sir," Rasmussen said. He hesitated, noticeably. "Do you think we succeeded?"

William looked at the data unfolding in front of him. "I think so," he said. "But we may not know for several weeks, at best. And one other thing?"

"Yes, sir?"

"Not a word about this mission, not to *anyone*," William warned. "This secret must remain secret for the nonce."

"Yes, sir," Rasmussen said.

CHAPTER THIRTY-TWO

"The younger of the wives has been . . . *treated*," Doctor Katy Braham said. There was more than a little distaste in her voice. "Not to put too fine a point on it, she follows orders. *All* orders. She quite literally has no will of her own."

Kat swallowed, tasting bile in her mouth. Princess Drusilla had explained, back when she'd defected from the Theocracy, that her father had intended to turn her into a Stepford Wife, but Kat had found it hard to believe that *anyone* could be so cruel. Kat's father might have been exasperated with her from time to time, yet he'd never set out to steal her free will. But the evidence was right in front of her—a woman, barely out of her teens, who was helpless to resist any commands. Someone had rewired her brain to make her an obedient slave.

It was worse, she suspected. The woman *knew* what had happened to her—knew it, hated it, and yet was unable to resist. There was a helpless fury in her eyes that sent chills down Kat's spine, the fury of a slave trapped in unbreakable bonds. She couldn't so much as block her ears to prevent the commands from reaching her mind, let alone refuse to obey them. It was a chilling presentiment of what might be in store for Kat if the Theocracy won.

The XO looked pale. "Is there any way to reverse the treatment?"

"I'm not sure," the doctor admitted. "These procedures were originally developed for patients who had serious mental problems; later, some very wealthy people on Earth used them to create a cadre of loyal servants before the whole practice was banned. In this case . . ."

She sighed, studying the medical readouts. "In this case, the brain might have adapted to the modifications," she said. "This is far more complex than a simple conditioning—and a conditioning, while it can be removed, might well leave the victim in a state of shock for years to come. I suggest putting her in stasis until we get back to Tyre, then sending her over to a medical crew that specializes in brain injuries. There's nothing more I can do for her here."

Kat nodded slowly. "What else can you tell me about them?"

"The boys are healthy, if arrogant," the doctor said. "They had some problems being examined by a female doctor, although I'm not sure if that was out of misogyny or a form of misplaced modesty. The girls, on the other hand, are too thin for their age; the senior wife, too, has not had enough to eat. She's quite a piece of work herself, I might add. She didn't hesitate to tell me I should have a husband and kids rather than be working as a doctor."

"I see," Kat said. "Is she conditioned too?"

"No," the doctor said. "But I think she would be very unwise to disobey her husband, at least openly. My honest opinion, Captain, is that we should hang on to the women; the defector, if he wishes, can go to one of the independent colonies."

"He'd want to take the boys with him," the XO said. "It sounds like they need a healthy dose of boarding school."

"That attitude would be knocked out of them pretty quickly on one of the independent worlds," the doctor said, firmly. "Or they'd be killed by someone when they gave offense."

Kat held up a hand. "Keep them separated for the moment," she said. She couldn't help thinking the doctor was right, but her brothers had been arrogant little shits when they'd been young too. On the other hand, they hadn't been raised in such a poisonous atmosphere, nor had they been taught that their sisters were automatically inferior. "We can sort out their disposition later."

"The Child Protection Service would not hesitate to remove the girls, at least," the doctor warned. "This isn't a typical case, but we have had other problems concerning immigrant children who were mistreated by their parents."

"By your standards," the XO said.

The doctor rounded on him. "I hardly think that programming a young woman into a life of helpless servitude and half starving young girls is acceptable by *anyone's* standards," she said. "Not to mention the sheer disgusting loss of potential this represents. The Theocracy is a cancer on the face of the galaxy, a perversion of everything we stand for. It has to be destroyed."

She slapped the table hard. "*Fuck* cultural sensitivity," she hissed. "There are some things we should refuse to fucking tolerate."

Kat blinked in surprise. She'd never heard the doctor swear before, not even after the escape from Cadiz or the ambush at Morningside. But the doctor was right. There was no way that anyone could leave the girls with their father and brothers, not when they would be treated like dirt. It would be easy enough to arrange for them to be slipped into Commonwealth society, with foster families, while their mother was deprogrammed.

"Take care of them," she said softly. "Mr. XO?"

She turned and led the way back to her office, then sat down on the chair. "It's going to be a headache explaining this to your friend," she said. "He's going to think we're stealing his family from him."

"I think we don't have a choice," the XO said bitterly. "But it's still going to come back to haunt us."

Kat looked into his troubled eyes. "Why?"

"Intelligence is a murky field," the XO reminded her. "A defector, someone who can tell us a great deal about the enemy's intentions, is a pearl beyond price. Treating them well, giving them money and places to stay—and making it publicly clear that that's what we have done—helps to encourage other defectors. I have a feeling the CIS will complain, loudly, if the message we send is something else. Like, for example, come to the Commonwealth and have your family taken from you."

"No," Kat said flatly. "There are some lines we will not cross."

"You might be surprised," the XO said. "They had me making deals with smugglers—and some of the people I spoke to might have been pirates, the murderers and rapists we execute on sight. I don't find it hard to believe that the CIS might make deals with people who are even worse, at least by our standards."

Kat looked down at her hands. She didn't want to believe him, but she had a feeling he might well be right. There was idealism . . . and then there was politics, and the demands of fighting and winning a war that could not be lost. She knew more than she wanted to know about the endless tussle for supremacy in Tyre City, the willingness to stoop to new lows just to gain a temporary advantage. Maybe the CIS would insist that the girls be returned to their father, even though they would be abused.

I'll adopt them if that happens, she thought darkly. Technically, that would require her father's permission, but she had a feeling she could make it hard for him to deny her. *Let them try to take the girls from me, if I added them to the family. The bad publicity alone would be disastrous.*

"We'll cross that bridge when we come to it," she said finally. "I understand you learned a great deal about our enemy?"

"Indeed," the XO said. "And Davidson's team of interrogators are learning a great deal more."

He tapped the terminal, bringing up a star chart. "The enemy," he said, as the display centered on their current location. "For the first time, we have a detailed outline of enemy space."

Kat nodded slowly. The defector had definitely brought enough information to make the risk of smuggling him out of Aswan more than worthwhile. Now, she knew where the enemy based their major shipyards, although they were clearly too heavily defended for her remaining ships to attack. It wouldn't be hard to slip more scoutships through the Reach and get hard data, then plot a major attack. Convincing the Admiralty to cut loose enough superdreadnoughts to mount an offensive would be a great deal harder.

But we're already ramping up our production levels, she thought. The intelligence analysts had already calculated that the enemy couldn't have more than a hundred superdreadnoughts at most, despite the terrifying scale of their military buildup. *Give us a couple of years and we'll have them outnumbered three to one.*

"There's something else of considerable interest in the Aswan System, something we missed earlier because none of our sources were in the know," the XO said. "This place here."

Kat's eyes narrowed. The naval base orbited a Mars-type world that was slowly being terraformed, and there was a gas giant, but none of the other worlds in the system seemed anything other than utterly unremarkable. She'd glanced at the old files, dating back to the UN, yet nothing had stood out. But the XO was pointing to the fifth planet from the star . . .

"This planet is called Redemption," the XO said very quietly. "Apparently, there's a POW camp there."

"*Mermaid* will need to take a look at the planet," Kat said. It *could* be a trap . . . but Aswan was in a good location to serve as a clearing-house for POWs: far enough from the front to make it unlikely a rescue mission could be launched, close enough to allow the enemy to sort through their prisoners and pick out anyone who might be useful. "If there's a POW camp there . . ."

"If," the XO said. "There's at least one squadron of superdread-noughts on guard at all times, Captain. Getting in would be a major headache if we had a battle squadron of our own."

"Which we don't," Kat said slowly. She briefly considered attempting to get word to Admiral Christian, then realized he probably couldn't spare the ships to mount an offensive so far behind enemy lines. *Her* ships were expendable; *his* superdreadnoughts were not. "If we could lure those superdreadnoughts away, somehow . . ."

"It might not be possible," the XO said. "They'd be fools to leave Aswan uncovered."

"True," Kat agreed. She looked at the star chart, thinking hard. Could she *use* the spy's communications codes, now that the enemy knew they could trust him? But unless he told them that she'd picked up reinforcements from somewhere, they wouldn't deploy both squadrons of superdreadnoughts. "We could sneak a team of Marines down to the surface."

"But then we wouldn't be able to get the prisoners out without bringing in the squadron," the XO countered. "They'd have ample time to intercept us."

Kat nodded slowly. The enemy superdreadnoughts they'd sighted at Aswan might not be fully combat-capable, but they could lumber to Redemption and intercept her ships before they managed to pick up the POWs and retreat. She ran through a handful of possibilities in her head, yet nothing seemed to work. There was no way they could do more than attack the POW camp's defenses before they were forced to run for their lives.

And that would tell them we knew about the camp, she thought. *They'd either improve the defenses or move the prisoners to a different location.*

"We will need to take a careful look at that planet, under stealth," she said. Redemption didn't appear to be as heavily defended as Aswan—that would have tipped off her scouts that there was something there worth guarding—but it would certainly be surrounded by a handful of passive sensors. "Have *Mermaid* prepared for a deployment there."

"Aye, Captain," the XO said. He keyed his wristcom briefly, then smiled. "We do also have the convoy schedules. There's a large convoy passing through Aswan in four days and another one, apparently an important convoy, passing through UNAS-G2-6585 in two weeks. I don't think we've any hope of capturing the first convoy, but we could certainly have a go at *destroying* it."

Kat accessed the file, then frowned. "It might easily be a trap."

"In that case, our defector friend is a liar," the XO pointed out. "But . . . if that's the case, we'd know about it by now. The Marines were careful to make sure he was given a full-spectrum interrogation. If he was conditioned to resist interrogation, Captain, we'd know about it by now."

"Because his brains would be leaking out of his skull," Kat said. "We could slip into Aswan with *Mermaid,* then lurk in ambush while *Mermaid* prowls around Redemption, hunting for the POWs. If the convoy arrives as expected, we can launch a full spread of missiles and then drop back into hyperspace. There would be no time to engage the defenders . . ."

"Just a smash-and-run mission," the XO said. He studied the convoy timetable, thinking it through. "It should be doable. And it will knock the enemy back over, after their success earlier."

Kat nodded. The enemy's morale had to have skyrocketed after their successful ambush, even if they hadn't managed to destroy her entire squadron. She'd hoped her string of attacks had started to demoralize the Theocracy's forces, even if it hadn't convinced them to redeploy ships to hunt her down, but their victory would have reversed all that. Pulling off another ambush, right in the heart of their naval base, would hopefully send their morale back into a downward spin. Who knew? It might even lead to the death of the commanding officer who'd plotted the successful ambush in the first place.

There's something unpleasant about hoping the enemy will off one of their own officers, she acknowledged in the privacy of her own thoughts. *But if it gets rid of a dangerously competent enemy officer, it might be worth it.*

"We'll depart in two hours, if *Mermaid* is ready," she said. An idea crossed her mind and she smiled. "I want you to speak to our spy and put together a message for the enemy. Tell them . . . tell them that we're getting reinforcements and we intend to resume full-scale offenses as soon as possible."

"I'm sure that will worry them," the XO said after a moment. He didn't sound convinced. "Do you have something in mind?"

"I have a vague idea," Kat said. It wasn't something she wanted to discuss, not until it had jelled into something useful, but she might as well start laying the groundwork. "They had a good idea of our strength from Verdean, saw the same number of ships at Ringer, and then they kicked our asses at Morningside. They know they inflicted enough damage to put some of our ships out of commission permanently."

She smiled. "Let them think we're getting reinforcements," she concluded. "They'll stop being reluctant to send ships away from Aswan if they think we have a serious chance at ripping away the defenses of another planet."

The XO frowned. "You plan to lure them away?"

"It's something to consider," Kat said. No matter how she looked at it, there was no way her squadron could beat eighteen superdreadnoughts. It would be a minor miracle if she managed to scratch their paint, let alone inflict any real damage. "They won't lower the defenses of Aswan enough for us to attack the naval base, but we might be able to do something to the POW camp."

"Understood," the XO said. "But they'll be doing their best not to dance to our tune."

"I know," Kat said. She met his eyes. "Prepare the message. Let them *think* we have reinforcements. And then we can see what we can do with it."

"We do have a handful of decoy drones left," the XO said. "But will they be enough to fool the enemy?"

Kat shrugged. "We'll find out," she said. It was quite possible that the enemy would refuse to allow her to lead them by the nose. Or perhaps they would be *too* convinced by the drones and decline the opportunity to do real harm. "I'll see you on the bridge just before we depart."

She watched him go, then looked up at the star chart. POWs! That changed everything. She knew she couldn't leave POWs in enemy custody, not after the horror stories from Cadiz and the other occupied worlds. Leaving them in enemy hands would be a betrayal of everything the oath she'd sworn stood for. But the enemy would have their own plans for the POWs . . . and they would probably have taken precautions to ensure that escape was impossible. If there were prisons on Tyre where prisoners were implanted with a device just to knock them out if they ever left, why couldn't the Theocracy do the same? Or worse? Give the prisoners explosive collars to make sure they couldn't leave without permission?

And if we try to take them by force, she thought, *they might kill the prisoners.*

She shook her head as she rose and headed for the hatch. There was no way she could talk herself into abandoning the POWs, not as long as there was a slight chance they could be rescued. *Mermaid* would sweep around Redemption; Davidson and his men would take a look at the records and determine if there was any way to pull off a rescue. And if it was possible, Kat would move heaven and earth to carry it out.

"Set course for Aswan," she ordered as she stepped onto the bridge. They were only a couple of days from Aswan, although the remainder of the squadron would have to reposition again. They'd meet up once they'd completed the raid on Aswan and slipped away from any pursuit. "Mr. XO?"

"*Mermaid* has her orders, Captain," the XO said. "She's ready to depart with us. The remainder of the squadron will move to the next RV point, after we depart."

"Good," Kat said. She looked at the status display, then cleared her throat. "Helm, take us to Aswan."

"Aye, Captain," Weiberg said.

CHAPTER THIRTY-THREE

"I have the report for you here, Admiral."

"Thank you, Captain," Admiral Junayd said. "Rather odd, don't you think, that a base such as Aswan would suffer a malfunction that destroyed an entire shuttle in transit?"

Captain Haran frowned. "I wouldn't know, sir."

"Did they have a maintenance issue that finally caught up with them," Admiral Junayd asked, "or was it something more sinister?"

He smiled to himself, then took the datapad and scanned the report. It wasn't very informative, but the investigative team—if only to escape the charge of being lax when a valuable shuttle had been lost—had managed to write fifty pages that boiled down to a simple observation that they didn't know *how* the shuttle had been lost. Seventeen people were dead and, while most of them had been civilians, it was still inconvenient. The best maintenance crews had all been for-warded to the front.

"Have the remaining shuttles examined, just in case," he ordered finally. An explosion when the shuttle was entering atmosphere smacked of a maintenance error, suggesting the crews were lazy or incompetent or both. "I wouldn't want this to be held against me."

"No, sir," Captain Haran said. "I'll get right on it."

He saluted and then walked out of the hatch. Admiral Junayd smiled thinly, then turned his attention to the star chart. The victory against the raiding squadron had been a success—and the propagan-dists back home had turned it into a truly staggering victory against overwhelming force—but he knew, all too well, that it wasn't perfect. A number of ships had escaped and some of them, he was sure, would be repaired quickly. And then the raiders would start raiding again.

And my superiors were already talking about cancelling the planned supplies, he thought sourly.

It was a galling thought. The higher authorities had been forward-ing everything *but* reinforcements to him, yet now they were talking about cutting back. There was no shortage of demand, after all, and only a limited supply. Maybe Admiral Junayd no longer *needed* resup-ply now that he'd given the enemy a bloody nose. But he knew the enemy hadn't been beaten, certainly not completely. It was frustrating, incredibly so, to realize that the victory had safeguarded his personal position—even Commodore Isaac had been quiet since the enemy had been forced to flee—but not secured the sector. He needed to capital-ize on his victory, to prepare defenses for the time the enemy showed themselves again, yet he lacked even the bare bones of war material to do it. And when the enemy struck, they would undermine his position, even if their offensive did nothing more than annoy him.

He looked at the timetables, then sighed. One convoy due to arrive within hours, several more, including two sent to Aswan itself, due over the next few weeks. Perhaps the enemy would wait long enough for him to do *something*, but what? The best idea he'd had, so far, was stripping Aswan of its fixed defenses to give the rest of the sector additional protection, yet he knew he'd be executed if he tried. Aswan could not be left undefended.

But it will have a squadron of superdreadnoughts to protect it, unless they get called to the front, he thought savagely. There were already reports that the front might well start demanding his mobile units, even though he desperately needed them himself. He'd heard rumors, whispered from officer to officer, that the officers in command were plotting a major offensive against the Commonwealth. *But if they take my superdreadnoughts, I won't have a hope of stopping even a minor attack on a weakly defended world.*

"I'll just have to pray," he said to himself. God could help him, if He would, but no one else could. "And see just what happens."

Kat couldn't help feeling cold as *Lightning* slipped towards Aswan, protected by her cloaking device and distance from the enemy defenses. It didn't look as though the enemy had expanded their fixed defenses, although the presence of two squadrons of superdreadnoughts was a powerful argument against attacking the planet directly. The swarming activity around one of the squadrons—and the repair yard—worried her more than she cared to admit. If the defector had been telling the truth, if the Theocracy truly had too few repair yards, it was possible the enemy was seeking to expand its facilities. And that would only make them more dangerous, in the future.

From a practical point of view, the Theocracy's internal structure seemed absurd. Kat had been half inclined to dismiss some of what she'd heard because it was unbelievable, before she'd recalled some of the lessons from her youth. There had been no shortage of business models that had called for massive expansion, concentrating on a single core competency and trying to snatch as much of the market share as possible before their debts and overextension caught up with them. Sometimes it worked; often, far more often, the business collapsed into chaos and failure, the best of its facilities and staff snatched up by other businesses or its creditors. The Theocracy had, quite literally, mortgaged its future to establish itself as a serious galactic power.

But they don't have the staying power for a long war, she thought grimly. *If we can hold on long enough to get our industrial might into play, we can kick their ass from here to the other side of the universe.*

It was a tempting thought. Wait a year, then launch another series of raids into enemy territory, using modern ships and improved weapons. The Theocracy's industrial base, already tiny, could be hammered down to nothing, cutting off their lines of supply. Their fleets would grind to a halt for lack of supplies, allowing them to be picked off at will; their occupied worlds, already seething with unrest, would overthrow their tormentors and declare independence. And the Commonwealth, powered by a mighty industrial base, would sweep through the enemy systems and invade their homeworld itself.

Sure, her own thoughts mocked her. *And what will we do with the spoils of victory?*

"Captain," Weiberg said. "We have reached our destination."

"Hold us here," Kat ordered. Like most worlds, Aswan had a dedicated emergence zone for starships, although, unusually, it was some distance from the planet itself. She wasn't sure if it was a sign of paranoia—Tyre's emergence zone had been put back after the first attacks on the planet's surface—or a simple acknowledgment that the Theocracy's navigation was far from perfect. "Passive sensors only. I don't want anything that might betray our presence to the enemy."

She settled back in her command chair and forced herself to wait. Assuming the convoy hadn't been delayed, there would be no more than an hour before they dropped out of hyperspace, but even a rigid structure like the Theocracy had to know that convoys could easily be late. There was no point in killing someone for a harmless mistake, was there? But if some of the stories from the defector were accurate, it was quite common for the Theocracy's officers to kill their subordinates if they needed a scapegoat. The prospect of being executed to cover his superior's dealings had prompted the defector to plan a successful escape.

And now he's going to lose his wives and children, Kat thought. It was hard to feel any guilt, even though she knew it would be a problem. She'd prepared adoption papers for the girls, just in case, but she had a feeling the matter would be settled out of court. *I would feel sorry for him if he hadn't arranged for his wife to be stripped of her free will.*

She'd rarely had nightmares after Piker's Peak, even after the first time she'd been at true risk of losing her life. But she'd had nightmares after looking into the poor woman's eyes, nightmares in which she too was a slave, trapped by her own mind . . . nightmares in which she was shattered by her friends and family. Whatever happened, Kat promised herself, the story would not be lost. The entire galaxy would hear about what had happened, about what the Theocracy was prepared to do to an innocent girl. Maybe then the morons who thought it was possible to make a just peace would shut up . . .

Calm down, she told herself, firmly. *Calm down and prepare yourself for the coming battle.*

The tension slowly rose on the bridge as the timer ticked down the final minutes before the convoy was due to arrive. Kat forced her breathing to slow to a steady pace as she concentrated her mind, keeping herself as calm as possible. The timer reached zero and began to count up again, reminding her that the convoy was late. She smiled inwardly as Weiberg let out a frustrated sound, as if he'd built up as much anticipation as she had, then shook her head. It wasn't as though she'd pegged *everything* on the enemy arriving on time.

"Gateways," Roach snapped. "I say again, gateways!"

"Red alert," Kat ordered quietly. Five gateways were opening up in front of them, revealing seventeen freighters and five destroyers. None of them *looked* particularly alert, but coming out of hyperspace with readied weapons was generally considered a sign of hostile intent. "Lock weapons on target."

"Aye, Captain," Roach said. "Weapons locked."

Kat smiled. "Fire," she ordered. "Drop the cloak, raise shields!"

Lightning shuddered violently as she unleashed a full spread of missiles. The enemy had no idea she was there until it was far too late; the missiles, launched from well within engagement range, zoomed towards targets that had barely any time to react. A handful of point defense crews managed to spit off a shot or two before the first missiles slammed home, ripping into weak shields and undefended hulls. She felt a brilliant surge of excitement as the first freighter died, exploding into a fireball as her missiles ripped it apart, smashing everything it carried in its holds. Three more died in quick succession, followed by seven more. The remaining freighters were lucky enough not to draw the attention of her first barrage.

"Retarget the second spread," she snapped. "Take out the remaining freighters!"

"Aye, Captain," Roach said. "Enemy destroyers are bringing their weapons to bear on us!"

"Ignore them," Kat ordered. "Deal with the freighters!"

Admiral Junayd hadn't expected anything to happen, so he'd left command of the system in Commodore Malian's hands while he'd composed a message for his superiors, explaining why he should be sent additional reinforcements. He was on his feet, running for the command core, before his mind had *quite* realized that alarms were howling through the massive station. By the time he reached the command core, it was clear that all hell had broken loose in the space near the planet. The icons representing the freighter convoy were in disarray, while a large red icon was systematically tearing them apart.

"Admiral," Commodore Malian said, "the system is under attack!"

"The *convoy* is under attack," Admiral Junayd snarled. The enemy ship, damn her to hell, had singlehandedly smashed an entire convoy. Five destroyers didn't stand a chance against her, but she could evade anything he dispatched from orbit. And yet he had no choice. "Dispatch the cruisers now!"

The last of the freighters died in a colossal fireball, followed by one of the destroyers. Their crews, no doubt anticipating the execution they'd face for allowing the entire convoy to be destroyed, were angling their ships towards the enemy cruiser, but they simply didn't have the firepower or defenses to stand up to her weapons. Maybe they'd be able to get close enough to ram, yet he rather doubted it. They simply couldn't hope to survive long enough to slam their hulls into the enemy.

"The enemy ship is pulling back from the planet," Commodore Malian said. "You scared her off, sir!"

"They did what they came here to do," Admiral Junayd snapped. The attack had been perfect—perfectly timed, perfectly carried out . . . why stick around and risk throwing it all away? He'd already been humiliated in front of the entire sector. The commanders at the front wouldn't hesitate to use it against him, if only to make him take the blame for their future failures. "They're not scared at all."

A second destroyer vanished from the display. "Contact the destroyers," Admiral Junayd ordered reluctantly. "They are to fall back and wait for the cruisers. Repeat the order if they fail to comply at once."

"Aye, sir," the coordination officer said.

Admiral Junayd cursed under his breath. It was unlikely the destroyers *would* obey orders . . . unless their commanders believed there was a reasonable chance they would escape execution. It would be better to die quickly, trying to make up for their failure, than to die slowly at the hands of the Inquisition. And their crews would be under a cloud too. It wasn't impossible, given the scale of the failure, that they would *all* be executed.

And this is the system you are pledged to serve, he reminded himself. *How can a commander and crew learn from their mistakes if they are killed out of hand?*

He shook his head sadly as a third destroyer died, the remaining two falling back on the planet. He'd have to argue that the true failures had already died, scapegoating the dead, if he wanted to save their commanders . . . but he had no choice. The Theocracy didn't need more dead officers, not when too many had died in the war. It needed people who could learn from their mistakes . . .

"Put a lock on the StarCom," he ordered. He needed to make the case to his superiors personally, before Commodore Isaac or someone else started muddying the waters. "Until I countermand the order, the only messages going out of the system will be ones I personally authorize."

"Yes, Admiral," Commodore Malian said. "But what are we going to do?"

"Do?" Admiral Junayd asked. "We're going to do our duty."

◆　◆　◆

"The remaining destroyers are falling back to the planet," Roach reported.

"Good," Kat said. The cruisers would be within engagement range in two minutes, when she would have to run, but there was enough time to complete the second half of the mission. "Send the signal."

"Aye, Captain," the XO said. He keyed his console. "Done."

And let's hope that fools the bastards, Kat thought. Parker was cooperative—and he was being watched carefully, after a less-than-gentle interrogation—but she knew better than to rule out a last attempt at betrayal, even though he had to know his sister would probably never be returned to the Commonwealth. *And if it fools them, there are options here.*

She shrugged, then looked at Weiberg. "Open a gateway," she ordered. "Take us out of here."

"Aye, Captain," Weiberg said. The vortex spiraled open in front of *Lightning* and then sucked them through its giant maw. "We're clear."

"Take us to the first RV point," Kat ordered. "And watch for any possible pursuit."

She smiled coldly as she leaned back in her chair. Seventeen freighters and their cargo smashed . . . it wasn't as good as capturing the ships, but it was good enough to give the enemy a bloody nose. And three destroyers were a bonus. The Theocracy would need to start assigning more and heavier escorts to their convoys, now they'd had a warning that their current precautions were nowhere near enough. Even if she never hit another convoy during the mission—and she intended to hit at least one more before the enemy realized they'd had a leak—they'd need to redeploy more of their units. It would have a baleful effect on their ability to take the offensive.

"We'll meet up with *Mermaid*, then proceed to UNAS-G2-6585," she said, as it became clear the enemy hadn't risked a pursuit. "By then, we should have a better idea of just how to proceed."

"Aye, Captain," the XO said.

Kat felt her smile grow wider. The crew had been demoralized . . . but no more, not after a textbook-perfect ambush. And there was a second one to follow . . . once *that* had been completed, they'd be at the top of their game.

If we can take out the POW camp, she thought, *it might be time to fall back and gather reinforcements.*

"We did get a message from the spy," Commander Amman said. He sounded as if he was trying hard to put a positive gloss on the disaster. "He tells us that the enemy is getting reinforcements."

"Not that they need them," Admiral Junayd said. He wasn't sure if it was sheer luck or careful planning that had put the enemy so close to the emergence zone, but he had to admit they'd made good use of what they had. A heavy cruiser couldn't have stood up to the superdreadnoughts, yet it had had no difficulty in shredding the freighters before making its escape. "They just struck us a mighty blow."

He looked at the star chart, thinking hard. The emergence zones would have to be changed, of course, but no one in transit would get the word before it was too late. If the enemy had plotted out other emergence zones . . . he shook his head. The only system with regular convoys passing through was Aswan itself. They wouldn't be able to hit any other convoys unless they had inside information. And if they did . . .

No, he told himself. *That is unthinkable.*

"Get me a list of everything they destroyed," Admiral Junayd ordered finally. He'd have to work hard to find a silver lining to this cloud, or his career would come to an abrupt and fatal end. "And next time, Commander, you'd better hope your damned spy brings us something *useful*."

And maybe, he added to himself, *it might be time to start considering contingency plans of my own.*

CHAPTER THIRTY-FOUR

"Getting in won't be hard, Kat," Davidson said. They lay together on her bed, studying the report from *Mermaid*. "I'd go so far as to say we could probably get all the prisoners up and out within thirty minutes. However, will we *have* thirty minutes?"

Kat frowned. Redemption wasn't *far* from Aswan; assuming the enemy sent a radio message instead of a courier boat, it would take twenty minutes for Aswan to get the message and scramble a response. The superdreadnoughts would jump through hyperspace and be on her head within minutes. And if the enemy sent a courier boat, she'd be lucky to have time to scramble her shuttles before the superdreadnoughts arrived.

"We might end up repeating Second Cadiz, only without 6th Fleet," she said slowly. No matter how she looked at it, there didn't seem to be any way to distract *all* of the superdreadnoughts, let alone keep them from responding to a distress call. "Five ships couldn't stand up to them long enough to get the POWs out."

She looked at the report and scowled. The POW camp wasn't very complex; it was nothing more than a large dome covering a handful of barracks clearly designed for military personnel. Her intelligence staff had run the calculations and concluded that, as long as there weren't a number of underground bunkers, no more than a thousand prisoners could be held at the complex. But it would still take time to deal with the handful of paltry defenses, load the prisoners onto the shuttles, and make a run for orbit. By the time they got there, the enemy fleet would have arrived.

"Then the fleet needs to be lured away," she said. She was sure she could use Parker to convince the enemy to send one of the superdreadnought squadrons somewhere else, but that would still leave the *other* superdreadnought squadron. Hell, even a relatively small squadron of cruisers would be enough to put a major crimp in the operation. "We managed to do that at Cadiz."

"There's enough defenses around the cloudscoop here to make it practically invulnerable," Davidson pointed out. "They wouldn't panic and send everything after you."

Kat nodded. "Is there any alternative?"

"We could try a covert orbital insert," Davidson suggested. "That would at least get us down on the ground before the shit hits the fan."

"We'd still need to get the shuttles down to you," Kat said. "And if they got a message off before you took the guards out, you'd be screwed. I wouldn't have a hope of recovering you, let alone any of the prisoners."

"I knew the job was dangerous when I took it," Davidson said cheerfully.

Kat poked him in the stomach with a finger. "There's a difference between a dangerous but practical mission and an outright suicide mission," she said. "We're not at the stage where I have to send you and your men to die *yet*."

"I love that *yet*," Davidson said.

Kat rolled her eyes at him. She loved him, really she did, but there were times when his "live for the moment" attitude gnawed at her. It made her wonder just what sort of life they'd have when the war ended, when they probably would be demobilized as the Navy cut back to a peacetime establishment. Would they stay on Tyre? Or buy a ship and head out to live a life of independent trading?

"Me too," Kat said. "I think we need something more cunning."

"Use the drones," Davidson said. "Make them think we have an entire squadron of superdreadnoughts under your command?"

"They'd call our bluff," Kat said, shaking her head. "One failure to unleash a full Weber of missiles and they'd know we were conning them."

She sat upright, crossing her hands under her bare breasts. No matter how she looked at it, she couldn't see a way to get in, snatch the prisoners, and get out. Second Cadiz hadn't been an easy ride, even *with* 6th Fleet backing her up; repeating it, *without* the superdreadnoughts, would be asking for trouble. No doubt the enemy had studied the battle as intensely as her own people. They'd *know* what she was doing and react accordingly.

"We could ask for support from Admiral Christian," Davidson said. "A POW camp . . ."

"They'd need to cut loose at least two squadrons of superdreadnoughts," Kat said. There was something to be said for eighteen superdreadnoughts slicing through the enemy rear, but not if it came at the cost of the Theocracy breaking into the core worlds. "I don't think he could spare them even for a short while—and it would take at least a month before they could be returned."

"Crap," Davidson said. He sat up next to her, his expression grim. "We can't just leave them there."

"I have no intention of leaving them there," Kat said shortly. She leaned into his embrace, feeling herself totally devoid of ideas. "I just don't know how to get to them without getting us all killed."

The intercom bleeped. "Captain, we will be at UNAS-G2-6585 in thirty minutes," Weiberg reported. "We're still ahead of schedule."

"Assuming *they* keep *their* schedule," Kat muttered. It had been risky, mounting the first convoy attack, but necessary. And yet, there had been no choice. She *had* to remind the enemy that she existed, that she could still make a difference. "We can't stay here forever."

She cleared her throat. "Understood," she said, replying to her lieutenant. "I'll be on the bridge in twenty minutes."

"Fight you for the shower," Davidson said.

Kat smirked, then leapt off the bed and dived into the tiny shower. Whoever had designed the captain's suite, she'd often thought, had never bothered to consider what would happen if the captain had a partner. But then, it was rare for captains to be allowed to take their partners onto their ships. The only time it happened regularly was on exploration starships, which often spent months or years away from their homeworlds. She assumed *their* commanding officers had larger cabins.

She washed quickly, then pulled on her uniform while he showered. There was no time for anything other than a quick good-bye, then a run to the bridge. She forced herself to calm down as she stepped through the hatch and took her seat, checking the displays as *Lightning* grew closer to her destination. UNAS-G2-6585 wasn't a particularly interesting star, save for one detail. It had no planets at all.

Which wouldn't be so unusual, she thought, *if it had been anything other than a G2.*

It must have frustrated the UN's explorers when they'd passed through the system, she thought, although the scant file contained nothing more than a bare-bones summary of the lone star. A G2 star held the promise of life-bearing worlds, or worlds that could be terraformed, but *this* one was all alone in the night. They'd surveyed the system briefly, found nothing, and headed onwards to their next target. UNAS-G2-6585 was useless to everyone, save as a navigational waypoint. The Theocracy, it seemed, agreed on that point.

They may not have realized we killed the first convoy, she thought, as the gateway opened, allowing them to slip back into realspace. *Or they thought there wasn't a hope of us lying in wait at* every *possible waypoint.*

She smirked. The Commonwealth randomized its navigational waypoints as much as possible, choosing to allow independent freighters or convoy commanders to pick their own, rather than sticking to a preselected menu. It was a wise security precaution, all the more so after discovering a handful of spies within the Commonwealth. But the Theocracy, it seemed, disagreed. *They* liked their ships to run on time, following hyper-routes that might as well have been set in stone. Didn't they realize it made their courses predictable?

They might not have had a problem with pirates before the war, she thought coldly. *They were too busy paying them off to go after us instead.*

"Transit complete, Captain," Weiberg said.

"Cloak, then hold us here," Kat ordered. "All we can do now is wait."

She glanced at the timer grimly. They had three hours, assuming the enemy stuck to their schedule. She shook her head in amused disbelief, then forced herself to concentrate on the latest reports from engineering and tactical. The former reported that they'd done all they could to repair the damage from the ambush, but the latter warned that they were running out of missiles. There were only a handful left on the freighters . . .

We'll need to resupply, Kat thought sourly. She'd had the disabled ships stripped of weapons and then cannibalized for spare parts, but there was no way to avoid the fact she was running out of all *sorts* of things she needed. *Whatever happens, after this, we may need to go home anyway.*

It was a bitter thought. She'd hurt the enemy, she *knew* she'd hurt the enemy, but she would still have to fall back and leave their sector. There would be a return, of course, with more firepower, yet she still felt as if she was running away. No, she told herself firmly; it was a withdrawal to resupply. She *would* be back . . .

An alarm sounded. "Vortexes, Captain," Roach snapped. "Nine gateways!"

"Red alert, stand by all weapons," Kat ordered. The gateways were farther away this time, disgorging seven freighters, two destroyers, and a light cruiser. "Move us into attack position."

"Aye, Captain," Weiberg said.

"Target the cruiser, then the destroyers," Kat added. The cruiser would pose the greatest threat, but the destroyers couldn't be ignored. "Fire on my command."

"Weapons locked," Roach said. "Entering attack range in ten seconds; I say again, entering attack range in ten seconds."

Kat smiled coldly, readying herself. "Fire!"

Lightning fired a full spread of missiles, targeted on the light cruiser. The enemy ship swung around sharply, bringing up her shields and point defense, but it was already too late. Kat felt a flicker of sympathy—the enemy commander must have the reactions of a cat—yet he didn't stand a chance. There wasn't enough time to evade the missiles, ready his defenses, or jump back into hyperspace. Seventeen missiles slammed into his shields, battering them down and blowing his ship into vapor. There were no survivors.

"Enemy destroyers launching missiles," Roach warned.

"Continue firing," Kat ordered. "Stand by point defense."

Her eyes narrowed as she studied the freighters. Six of them were turning away, trying to buy time to recycle their vortex generators to escape before they were destroyed, but the final freighter was turning *towards* her. The commander was either insane or had something hidden up his sleeve.

"Designate Freighter Five as a potential target," she ordered. "Prepare to engage her if she refuses to cut her drive and surrender . . ."

She sucked in her breath as the freighter launched a spread of missiles at *Lightning*. Roach reacted immediately, firing a salvo back while Weiberg altered course so the point defense could sweep the missiles out of space before it was too late. Kat smiled coldly—the enemy crew had clearly wanted to get into the battle, rather than bide their time until *Lightning* came too close to escape a spread of missiles—and then watched as the freighter's shields collapsed, leaving her hull bare. An antimatter warhead wiped her from existence, followed by the sole surviving destroyer.

"All targets destroyed," Roach reported.

"The freighters are surrendering," Linda said. She sounded perplexed. "Captain, I didn't even send them the surrender demand."

Odd, Kat thought. *Are they trying to trick us or . . . or what?*

She looked at the display, thinking hard. No Theocracy warship had *ever* surrendered, as far as she knew, and no freighter had offered surrender without a formal demand. Was she attacking smugglers or renegades working for the Theocracy? It didn't seem likely—the freighters looked uniform, rather than the hodgepodge of different designs she'd come to expect from independent shippers—but she made a mental note to bear it in mind. Having shippers willing to work for her might be useful.

"Order them to stand down all systems, save for essential life support," she ordered. If they were hoping she'd come within range, allowing them a free shot at her hull, they were going to be disappointed. "Deploy the Marines . . ."

She bit down on a warning she knew Davidson and his men didn't need. They'd rehearsed boarding tactics ever since they'd returned to the ship, working with the other military units to get it as close to perfect as possible. They would even know the interior of the ships from previous encounters . . . they'd get in, take control of the vessels, and secure the crews. And then they could determine what they'd actually managed to capture . . .

"Hold our position, but keep them covered," she ordered quietly. "Inform me the instant there is any change."

"Aye, Captain," Roach said.

Kat watched, grimly, as the shuttles closed in on their targets. The freighters didn't so much as twitch as the shuttles docked, armed and armored Marines spilling into the ships and hunting for potential targets. She followed them through the datanet, listening to the messages they snapped backwards and forwards as they rounded up the crew, feeling the tension only continuing to rise as nothing happened. Something was wrong, but what? Had they stumbled across a POW convoy? Or had they missed something significant . . . ?

"All ships secured, Captain," Davidson reported. "Their self-destruct systems were not activated; I say again, their self-destruct systems were not activated. They didn't even try to dust the computers."

Kat shook her head in disbelief. Surely, if the enemy crew were loyalists, they would have made sure the freighters were unusable. Unless they thought they'd be killed out of hand if they wrecked the ships.

"Understood," she said. "Are they enemy crewmen or renegades?"

"Enemy crewmen, as far as I can tell," Davidson said. "They've certainly got the language and accents down pat."

Kat frowned. Just *what* had they stumbled over?

"We're just checking the manifests now," Davidson added. "I . . ."

He broke off. "Captain," he said. He sounded as if he were trying very hard not to laugh. "I think you're going to want to see this."

"Show me," Kat ordered, swinging her console around so she could access her private datacore. "Upload it to me."

She frowned as the manifest appeared in front of her. A handful of spare parts, identified only by ID codes, a small selection of weapons . . . and a *StarCom*?

"They're carrying a StarCom?" she asked. "A *working* StarCom?"

It seemed impossible. The structures orbiting the Commonwealth's planets were huge, easily four times the size of a superdreadnought. Breaking one down and transporting it to another world would require at least two bulk freighters, unless something the size of an old UN colonist-carrier ship was used. None of the freighters in front of her were anything like large enough to carry a full-fledged StarCom. Had the Theocracy managed to make a miniature version? It didn't seem possible.

"I'm no expert, but it looks as though they stripped one down to the bare essentials," Davidson said. "The engineering crew will need to take a careful look at it."

He paused. "I think that explains why they surrendered so quickly," he added. "They probably had strict orders to keep the StarCom intact, rather than blowing up their own ships to ensure it didn't fall into enemy hands."

"Probably," Kat said. Her mind churned, coming up with ideas for using this completely unexpected stroke of luck. "What's in the other ships?"

"Weapons, mainly," Davidson said. "Missile pods, automated weapons platforms . . . I think this was a resupply convoy for the entire sector."

Kat smiled. An idea was starting to flower into life in her mind. "Prepare the ships for a hasty return to the RV point," she ordered. "Before we leave, take a team of engineers and see if they can get the StarCom up and running. I may have a use in mind for it."

We could always send a report from enemy space back home, she thought. It was easy enough to tune one StarCom to link into another, if one had the correct codes. But she had another idea in mind. *I wonder if we could use this to mislead them . . .*

"Understood, Captain," Davidson said.

Kat looked down at her hands as her crew scrambled to work. Maybe, just maybe, there was a way she could get at the POW camp, if everything went according to plan. She had the files from the defector, the StarCom and its database of communications codes . . . and Parker, who was willing to do anything to make up for his mistakes. If she was lucky, she could undermine the enemy . . .

. . . and even if it didn't work, she knew they wouldn't know what she was actually doing. Or what she was actually trying to do. The

POW camp should remain unmolested until a much larger fleet could be assembled and sent to Aswan, rather than have the prisoners moved elsewhere. As long as the enemy remained in ignorance . . .

Well, she told herself, *they won't know until it's far too late.*

She glanced at the XO. "Once we return to hyperspace, meet me and Major Davidson in my office," she added. "We have a mission to plan."

"Aye, Captain," the XO said.

Kat looked at the star chart, hastily running through a set of calculations. The convoy was due to reach Aswan in two weeks, assuming it stayed on schedule. There would be some leeway, she was sure, although the base commander would probably take a dim view of any lateness. She might *just* have enough time to lay her plans, make her preparations, and ready the remainder of her squadron.

And, at the very least, we can ask for reinforcements, she told herself. *And share what we've learned about the Theocracy with Admiral Christian.*

CHAPTER THIRTY-FIVE

"This is the situation," Kat said. She tapped a switch, bringing up a holographic chart of the Aswan System. "The enemy's naval base, along with most of his mobile forces, are gathered in orbit around Aswan itself. They have a smaller patrol force stationed near the gas giant and a handful of automated weapons platforms orbiting Redemption. Given the importance of the planet, we must assume they also have a watchdog keeping an eye on things under stealth."

"They should," the XO said. "Why don't they keep the prisoners on Aswan itself?"

"I suspect it has something to do with interservice rivalry," Davidson offered. "Whoever is in charge of taking care of POWs probably wants a base of their own, rather than put them anywhere near the naval base. We used to have similar disagreements with the army."

Kat shrugged, dismissing the matter. "We're going to unload the freighters and mount those missile pods to their hulls," she said. "The engineering crews should be able to handle it, particularly if we just dump the rest of their cargos into space rather than trying to ship them all back home. *Then* we're going to rig up a slave control system and send the freighters into the Aswan System, ready to fire on the defenders as soon as they come into range."

"The freighter convoy will be overdue," the XO warned.

"Not by more than five days," Kat said. She'd run the calculations as best as she could, using the data they'd recovered from the defector and checked against the datacores on the freighters. There *was* some leeway, as she'd expected, and, given what the freighters were carrying, the Theocrats would probably be too relieved to see them to ask too many questions. "We can put together a cover story if necessary. Maybe one of the ships had a drive failure and they had to slow to take the convoy in tow."

"They'll also be missing their defenders," the XO added. He looked at the star chart for a long moment. "They'll smell a rat."

"We're going to use drones to pose as their ships," Kat said. "It shouldn't be too tricky to get an ECM drone to pretend to be an enemy ship, rather than one of ours. By the time they get close enough to tell the difference, they'll already be under fire."

She looked at Davidson. "*Lightning* will have to accompany the freighters, under cloak," she added. "While we're busy making a mess, you and your men will have to get down to the POW camp and snatch the prisoners. Commander McElney"—she glanced at the XO—"will take command of the remainder of the active squadron. You should have enough time to complete the evacuation and jump out, heading for the first RV point."

The XO cleared his throat. "There are still two squadrons of super-dreadnoughts there," he said. "It won't be hard for them to detail one squadron to deal with you and the other to come after the rest of the squadron. That would be overkill for each of us."

"If everything goes to plan," Kat said, "those superdreadnoughts will no longer be there."

She tapped the display. "We're going to raid Porcupine," she said, pointing to a system seven light years from Aswan. "It will look like we jumped into the system, took one look at the defenses, and ran for our lives. However, it will give us a chance to send them one more fake message. We'll tell them that the *next* target on the list is Salvation."

"And they'll detach one of their superdreadnought squadrons in hopes of mounting a second ambush," the XO said. "They'd be too far from Aswan to intervene once we attack."

"So I hope," Kat said. "The other squadron of superdreadnoughts . . ."

She met his eyes. "We have one of their StarComs," she said. "We're going to send orders for those ships to go to the front."

"Admiral Christian is going to kick your ass," Davidson remarked.

"They'd never fall for it," the XO said. He shook his head in sheer disbelief. "They should check their orders, shouldn't they?"

"Perhaps," Kat said. "However, I was reading through the debriefings very carefully. Aswan has been *expecting* to receive orders to send one of the squadrons forward, so they won't be too surprised to finally *get* them. We have the codes to make them *look* convincing and . . . well, questioning orders isn't exactly encouraged in the Theocracy. If we make it sound as though the superdreadnoughts are urgently needed, they won't have *time* to work up the nerve to ask for clarification."

"Tell them there's been a major counteroffensive and the front lines are being pushed backwards," Davidson said.

"It's a minimum of two weeks from Aswan to Cadiz," the XO said slowly, playing devil's advocate. "No matter how hard they push their drives, they're not going to get there any faster. They might be concerned that they'd get there in time to be smashed . . . if, of course, there *was* an offensive."

Kat looked down at the display. "Their senior officer, according to the defector, has a habit of commanding the squadrons sent out to intercept us," she said. "If we lure him away first, his subordinate may be reluctant to ask questions. He might just dispatch his remaining squadron and hope his smaller ships, and the fixed defenses, are sufficient to handle any threats until his superiors return."

"He *might*," the XO said. "Captain, I can see the plan working, but it depends on too many factors outside our control."

"We can mount a covert watch on the system," Kat said. "If the superdreadnoughts don't depart as ordered, or they recall the other squadron first, we back off. Hell, we can use the StarCom to signal Admiral Christian and update him on our status. He might be able to spare us a handful of modern warships."

"If nothing else, it would certainly expose the flaws in their society," the XO mused thoughtfully. "They'd have to become like us to beat us—and that would probably destroy them."

"Probably," Kat agreed. "Major?"

Davidson took a breath. "It has the advantage of audacity," he said. "But it could also go horrendously wrong."

The XO smiled. "Forgotten your testosterone pill today?"

"It isn't just me at risk," Davidson said, irked. "It's all of us."

"If there isn't a reasonable window to carry out the plan, we'll fall back and break contact completely," Kat said. She hated the idea of leaving the POWs in enemy hands a moment longer, but freeing them wasn't worth the total destruction of her squadron. It would be better to round up a squadron of battle cruisers and then return to Aswan. "Yes, there is a risk, but we take risks in our stride each and every day."

"Yes, Captain," the XO said.

Kat took a breath. "Mr. XO, put together a plan to arm the freighters and the crippled ships the moment we return to the RV point," she ordered. "Then prepare yourself to transfer to *Oliver Kennedy*. You'll have overall command of the remainder of the squadron once we enter the system. Take as many tactical officers as necessary to handle the task."

"Aye, Captain," the XO said.

"Major Davidson, you and your men will transfer to *Oliver Kennedy* and the other ships," Kat continued. "I want you to put together a plan to get in, grab as many prisoners as you can, and get out. There is to be *no* attempt to hold the planet or set up stay-behind units, merely a prison break. Use all of the remaining shuttles if necessary, rather than just the Marine shuttles. In the event of everything going to hell, improvise."

"Yes, Captain," Davidson said. "What happens if your ship gets boarded?"

"I doubt that will be an issue," Kat said. "But the crew will be carrying sidearms, just in case."

She frowned. The Theocracy *had* tried to board a handful of ships by force, rather than compelling them to surrender, but it had always ended badly. Either the boarding parties were wiped out by armed crewmen—they hadn't seemed to anticipate resistance from anyone other than the Marines—or the victims had a chance to trigger the self-destruct before it was too late. *She* wouldn't have kept trying a tactic that had failed spectacularly several times over, but the enemy seemed to be remarkably bloody-minded about some things.

"Don't worry about it," she added. "We'll be fine."

"And the cripples will draw fire," the XO pointed out. "Are you planning to try to ram them into the enemy ships?"

"More likely their fortifications," Kat said. "I would be surprised—very surprised—if we were allowed to get a ship into ramming position."

She tapped her console, deactivating the display. "There's no way to keep the details of the operational plan a secret, at least not without causing problems, so I want you to keep a very close eye on *any* way that a message can be smuggled off the ship," she concluded. "We cannot afford another leak."

"Aye, Captain," Davidson said.

He smiled. "One way or the other, Captain, this will definitely go down in the history books."

"Sure," the XO said pessimistically. "Right under the heading of how not to do it."

Kat laughed. "It's something they will never expect," she pointed out. "And really, just who would be stupid enough to carry out an attack with a handful of freighters and crippled warships?"

She shrugged. "We'll test the StarCom by sending back a full report," she concluded. "The Admiralty will know everything we know, even if we don't return."

◆ ◆ ◆

Although he would have hated to admit it, William was a naturally conservative person. He disliked the thought of taking a wild jump into the unknown, let alone charging right into a system that was so heavily defended that at least two squadrons of superdreadnoughts would be required to flatten the defenses in a single attack. And yet, in the privacy of his own mind, he had to concede that the plan might work. It was the hint of insanity that would drive it forward, he was sure, along with the enemy's belief that their communications networks were unbreakable. Hell, they *were* unbreakable. William didn't have the clearance to know more than rumors about the CIS's attempts to spy on the enemy's StarCom network, but he'd heard that they'd proven fruitless. By the time the ships reached the RV point and work began, he'd decided to trust in the captain's plan.

"This isn't *really* a mobile StarCom," Lynn said as William stepped into the engineering department. The chief engineer sounded torn between fascination and dismay. "They've miniaturized a few things, Commander, but I wouldn't expect this unit to last more than a couple of years at most, once they spin it up. I think they'd probably also have problems with oscillating harmonics that will tear the thing apart given time. They'd need some pretty heavy-duty computer programs to control the system and I don't think what they have is up to the task."

"I see," William said. "Can't we duplicate and improve on the concept?"

"Oh, we probably could," Lynn said. "I tell you, Commander, most of the savings here are false savings. Someone probably sold the enemy leaders a bill of goods. In the short term, they have a cheaper StarCom network; in the long term, they will have to work hard to keep the system up and running, when they could have made a much bigger investment on day one and saved themselves a great deal of cash. The system just keeps running into the cold equations and the realities of engineering."

"They probably think they can replace them in the long run," William said.

"No, they don't," Lynn said. He rubbed his hands together with mischievous glee. "I've seen this type of thinking before, sir. They buy a cheap system, then keep wasting their resources on upgrades, throwing good money after bad, rather than admit they made a mistake. My word, sir; heads would roll if someone made a mistake . . . and in the Theocracy, that's probably literal."

He shrugged. "The bottom line, sir, is that we *can* send messages into their network, but the whole system probably won't last very long," he admitted. "We simply don't have the power to keep it up and running. I wouldn't expect a *superdreadnought* to be able to keep the singularity in existence indefinitely. Another cost-cutting measure, sir, that's going to bite them hard in the ass. It's quite possible that wherever they intended to put it wouldn't be able to *use* it. I've seen that happen before too."

William frowned. "Really?"

"Oh, yes," Lynn said. "There was a planet thirty-odd years ago that suffered a major disaster and needed help, so people all over the Commonwealth pitched in to send them emergency supplies to tide them over until they recovered. However, there was no attempt to *coordinate* the assistance, so half of the material they sent was completely useless. I believe a lot of it got put back on the market and sold, in exchange for funds that they could spend to get what they actually *needed*."

He shook his head. "A *proper* StarCom would be able to control the collapse of the singularity so the StarCom itself wouldn't be affected and a new singularity could be spun up afterwards," he said. "This one? When the singularity collapses, it'll take most of the StarCom with it. We may have done the idiot who put the design together a major favor, sir. He'll have more time to make his escape before his superiors recognize that they've been conned."

"I'm sure that the propaganda department can turn him into a hero," William said dryly. "How long will it take you to put the system together?"

"Couple of days," Lynn said. "I've got every trained engineer in the crew—and even a handful of people who have some experience without qualifications—out there bolting missile pods to hulls, shoring up everything we can, and generally making sure this ragtag squadron can deliver one last punch. I just hope we don't have to fight a long battle, sir; none of these ships were actually *designed* to be slaved to another, not even the freighters."

William nodded, slowly. The captain had insisted that the Theocracy wouldn't be too surprised if the convoy was overdue, but they *were* control freaks. It was quite likely that there would be a *lot* of questions for the crew, particularly after *Lightning* had wiped out an enemy convoy right under the enemy's nose. And many of the questions would be impossible to answer; hell, if the Theocracy took no more precautions than Tyre before the war, the veneer disguising the freighters and crippled warships would still fade very quickly.

And let's hope they don't want to talk to the cruiser CO, he thought. *That would ruin the plan beyond repair. The bastard is dead and gone.*

"I hear you're going to have squadron command," Lynn said, changing the subject. "And you *never* had a formal command of your own."

"I know," William said. The captain hadn't realized it until he'd pointed it out, but if someone squinted at regulations the right way, they could make a fair case for the captain facing a court-martial board. Giving command of an entire squadron to someone without command experience was forbidden, even though he'd served watch on *Lightning* and had over forty years of experience in the Navy. "But the captain didn't have a choice."

"Enjoy it," Lynn said. He shrugged, again. "I'd be surprised if you didn't get tapped for a command of your own in the next couple of years. I've heard they're going to be rushing many more starships into commission now that the gloves are off. We'll have more ships than we have commanding officers."

"I hope so," William said. "It'll please the observer too."

"Ah, yes," Lynn said. "She was poking around here awhile back; I asked her to leave and she just left without ever looking me in the eye."

"She was probably embarrassed," William said. He made a mental note to check in with Rose MacDonald before the squadron departed on its final mission. Maybe she should transfer to one of the other ships, one that might be able to make an escape if the plan went horrendously wrong. "That's how people on my homeworld act when they realize they crossed the line."

"Well, tell her she can have a tour while we're on the way home," Lynn said. "I wouldn't mind showing her around, sir."

"I'll tell her," William said. "But we have to survive the battle first."

"You know," Davidson said. "This could be our last night together."

Kat laughed. *Lightning* had nipped in and out of Porcupine, as planned, taking the opportunity to broadcast propaganda into the data-net before allowing a squadron of light cruisers to drive them away.

Hopefully, the enemy would realize she hadn't fired a shot and draw the conclusion that she had few—if any—missiles left. But as long as they picked up the message she'd sent, using Parker's codes, she didn't care. It would convince the enemy to prepare another ambush for her.

"That was *far* too hackneyed a line," she said. They'd spent five days laboring to put everything in place for the attack on Aswan. Tomorrow, they'd know if the plan would work or if the enemy would refuse to take the bait. "You could just try to pull me into bed."

Davidson shrugged. "I thought bad romantic lines were funny," he said. He looked past her, at the display. "You might have made a good Marine."

"I doubt it," Kat said. "I never liked crawling through mud."

She smiled, remembering her childhood. It might have been lonely, but it hadn't been *bad*. There had been the estate, a private garden easily large enough for a hundred children, and countless trees to climb. But she'd rarely seen her parents . . .

And if we don't manage to survive the action tomorrow, she thought as she turned and took him in her arms, *I won't see them ever again.*

CHAPTER THIRTY-SIX

"Admiral, a courier boat has arrived from Porcupine," Commander Annam said. "The spy sent another message."

"That's nice," Admiral Junayd growled. It was hard enough coming up with excuses for not reporting the loss of the convoy, not when he didn't have anything to balance the scales. "And what did your spy have to say?"

"The enemy intends to make one final attack, on Salvation," Commander Annam said. "They're going to be hitting the planet in just under two days, then returning to the Commonwealth."

Admiral Junayd blinked in surprise. Salvation? The planet wasn't heavily defended because it was largely worthless, the population sullenly bowing the knee to the Theocracy and ignoring them wherever possible. It would get a full settlement of Theocrats soon enough, he was sure, but until then the system could be ignored. And yet . . . an enemy attack would be embarrassing, particularly after the loss of the convoy.

He keyed the terminal, bringing up the star chart. It would take a day, at best speed, to reach Salvation, just long enough to get there first and set up an ambush. This time, he was sure, there would be no mistake. They'd get into point-blank range and overwhelm the enemy's defenses by sheer weight of fire. And the complete destruction of their fleet would be enough to make up for the convoy. He could report a victory to his superiors and bury the bad news at the back of the report.

"Inform Commodore Isaac that the squadron is to ready itself to depart in an hour," he ordered. "Commodore Malian is to remain in command of the base."

"Aye, Admiral," Commander Annam said.

"And tell Isaac to attach three flanking squadrons to his ships," Admiral Junayd added. "This time, we're going to be ready for them in hyperspace too."

Commander Annam looked doubtful but nodded. "Aye, sir."

Admiral Junayd dismissed him with a wave of his hand, then started to close down his terminal. He'd save his work, board the superdreadnought, and head off to Salvation, accompanied by enough mobile units to chase the enemy down if they fled back into hyperspace. It was a risk, but he *needed* a victory. Another defeat would mean the end of him.

He keyed his communicator thoughtfully. "Captain Haran, ensure that a courier boat is attached to the squadron," he ordered. "I have an idea."

And that, he thought quietly, *is very true*.

◆ ◆ ◆

"That's them on their way," Grace said. "Nine superdreadnoughts, twenty smaller ships . . . vector suggests a direct-line course to Salvation, although they might change course."

"I see them," Lars said. On the display, one by one, the enemy ships jumped into the vortex and vanished. "And the base itself?"

"Still got another squadron of superdreadnoughts and a dozen smaller ships," Grace said. "They're even deploying a handful of armed shuttles."

Lars stroked his chin thoughtfully. The shuttles weren't gunboats, but if gunboats weren't available, shuttles would have to suffice. Someone was either clever or desperate . . . mounting weapons and sensor packs on shuttles wouldn't make them harder to hit, yet it *would* give the defenders some additional warning if there were more cloaked ships skulking around.

"Pull us back," he ordered. "Prepare to slip back to the squadron."

"Aye, sir," Grace said.

"The enemy ships have departed," Linda said. "*Mermaid* reports that an entire fleet of ships has left the system."

"Show me," Kat ordered. It felt odd to be going into battle without her XO on the bridge, but there was no choice. "Put them on the main display."

She watched, grimly, as the enemy ships slipped into hyperspace. They *might* be trying something clever, but she doubted it. Salvation wasn't anything like as important as Aswan, not to them. They'd be insane to risk leaving the planet's defenses weakened if they believed the system was going to come under attack.

"Very well," she said. It was important that the enemy didn't have any time to think. "Order *Mermaid* to return to the system, then raise Commander Horsham. He is to send the message in one hour; I say again, he is to send the message in one hour."

"Aye, Captain," Linda said.

Kat sucked in her breath. They'd done everything they could to make the message look authentic, to make it clear that the local commander had no choice but to comply as quickly as possible, yet she knew that far too much could go wrong. If the enemy questioned orders, if the enemy sent back a demand for clarification, the entire plan would fall apart. She wanted to send the message immediately, but the enemy would have a chance to recall the second squadron of superdreadnoughts. All she could do was wait for them to put enough distance between themselves and Aswan before she tried to trick the defenders into sending away their remaining ships.

At least we know the StarCom works, she thought. She'd linked to Admiral Christian and sent a complete report, including everything they'd learned and the coordinates for the enemy superdreadnoughts. Maybe, just maybe, he'd have a chance to set a trap. *Whatever happens, the intelligence is already on its way home.*

"*Mermaid* has jumped out," Roach said quietly. "They're on their way."

Kat felt sweat trickling down her back as she waited for the hour to tick away. She hadn't been so nervous at Cadiz, had she? Not when the enemy had attacked the crippled system and not when the Navy had mounted a counterattack . . . ? But she hadn't had time to be nervous during the first battle and she hadn't planned the second battle herself. This time, the glory of victory—or the shame of defeat—would fall squarely on her head. The XO had been right. Too many things could go wrong.

"Commander Horsham is sending the message now," Linda reported.

Here we go, Kat thought.

"Hold the fleet at ready stations," she ordered. They would need to give the second squadron a chance to move away from the system too. "We jump in thirty minutes."

Or fall back, her thoughts added, silently.

Commodore Malian knew he wasn't considered a zealot, not like the senior officers who commanded the attack fleets that were clawing their way into the Commonwealth. Indeed, he'd been surprised to receive promotion at all, even if it had been to a naval base that had long since lost most of its importance. No one had seriously considered the prospect of the enemy raiding behind their lines, even though in hindsight it was blindingly obvious. He had expected to spend most of his time doing as little as possible while enjoying the fruits of his links to the smugglers. Being on the front lines hadn't been part of his plans.

"Commodore," his aide said. "We picked up an urgent message from the front."

Malian took the datapad and read the message, feeling his eyebrows lift in surprise. It was direct, straight to the point; he was to send his superdreadnoughts and any ships that could be spared to an RV point within occupied space, where they would receive further orders. He'd had a feeling he would have received such orders, sooner or later, but getting them now was unfortunate. Admiral Junayd had taken the other superdreadnought squadron with him and regulations strictly forbade cutting the defenses of a naval base any further.

But it's an order from the front, he agonized bitterly. It had been made clear, back before the war, that the demands of the front took priority. He'd be lucky if he was *only* executed if he refused to send his superdreadnoughts upon demand, despite the risk. And yet, if he *did* send the ships, he'd be in trouble for breaking regulations. Damned if he did, he thought, and damned if he didn't. *What do I do?*

He stared down at his hands helplessly. Admiral Junayd would be furious to discover that he'd lost his second superdreadnought squadron, and he might take it out on Malian, but orders were orders. He considered, briefly, asking for clarification, but Admiral Junayd had ordered him to keep the StarCom under tight control. *Nothing* was allowed out without the admiral's permission. The only way he could please both of his superiors was to let the superdreadnought squadron go, then send a courier boat after Admiral Junayd. He could bring his ships back to fill the holes.

"Contact Commodore Perkin," he ordered slowly. A tap on the datapad uploaded the navigational data into the superdreadnought's datanet. "His ships are to depart immediately for the preselected RV point."

"Aye, sir," his aide said.

"And dispatch a pair of courier boats," Malian added. "One to fly directly to Salvation; one to follow the admiral's track in hyperspace. They are to inform him of this development."

And he can decide what to do, Malian thought. *He can take the blame if things go wrong.*

◆ ◆ ◆

Grace let out a harsh bark of laughter. "That's the superdreadnoughts gone, sir," she said. "I didn't think it was possible!"

"Have a little faith in the commodore," Lars advised. He peered down at his scanner, then smirked. "We'll give them a few moments, just to make sure they're not trying anything clever, then slip back and jump out. And then all hell can break loose."

"Aye, sir," Grace said.

◆ ◆ ◆

Kat looked down at the report, feeling cold ice congealing in her stomach. "Sound red alert," she ordered. One way or the other, the die was cast. "Force One will advance and engage the enemy, as planned. Force Two will remain here for five minutes, then advance itself."

And hope to hell we don't screw up the timing, Kat thought as she forced herself to relax. *If Redemption manages to get out an alert before we attack Aswan, we may be in some trouble.*

"Captain," Roach said. He'd effectively taken over the XO's job, although there was relatively little for him to do. "The makeshift squadron is ready to depart."

"Then open the vortex," Kat ordered. "Take us to Aswan."

She braced herself as the eerie lights of hyperspace flickered around the freighters and the crippled warships. Her engineering crews had worked for days rigging their ECM, if only to make them *look* like enemy ships, but she knew they wouldn't stand up to a close examination. A single shuttle flying past the squadron would let the cat out of the bag. She closed her eyes as shudders ran through the cruiser, then opened them as the gateway blossomed to life in front of her. The squadron streamed through, back into realspace.

"The lead freighter is sending the codes now," Roach reported. "They should be up-to-date."

Kat nodded. They were entering the danger zone, the moment when they could neither retreat instantly nor lunge forward in a suicidal attack. Commonwealth doctrine placed most emergence zones in that region, if only to prevent smugglers and raiders from doing anything stupid; looking at Aswan, Kat saw no sign the Theocracy disagreed. But then, they had fewer shipping concerns than the Commonwealth. Their spacers probably hadn't noticed any additional security measures . . .

"Receiving confirmation now," Roach said. "They're trying to raise the cruiser."

Shit, Kat thought. They'd gone through every scrap of recovered data, but there simply hadn't been enough to fake a convincing message from the destroyed ship. Perhaps it would have been wiser to claim the convoy had been attacked, that the escorts had died saving the freighters, yet it would have forced the Theocracy to inspect the ships before they managed to get anywhere near a sensitive target. *Now what?*

"Hold the ships on course," she ordered. The enemy shuttles were already departing the repair yard, heading towards the freighters. Even assuming the ECM held, and that was doubtful at close range, it wouldn't be enough to stop the Mark-I Eyeball. "Send them back a message suggesting communications problems."

"Aye, Captain," Roach said. "I could have the freighter CO inform them that the cruiser lost most of her communications arrays."

"Do it," Kat ordered. The enemy wouldn't be fooled for long, if at all, but it might just win them some additional seconds. "Do you have passive locks on your targets?"

"Yes, Captain," Roach said. "Enemy facilities, not enemy ships."

◆ ◆ ◆

"Commodore," the tactical officer said, "Freighter Number 5 is claiming that *Holy Word* has lost her communications arrays."

Malian hesitated. The freighters were important, immensely so. They *needed* the weapons and equipment they carried, particularly the StarCom. Being able to coordinate their activities across the sector would make it easier to hunt down the raiders. But, at the same time, the freighters were behaving oddly and their escorts were showing a complete disregard for regulations. They'd sent their IFF pulses to the defenders, as they should, yet they hadn't bothered to send anything *else*. He didn't like it.

"Open direct links to the destroyers," he said. If the cruiser *had* lost her communications arrays, he could at least speak to her escorts. And if he couldn't . . . it suggested a number of unpleasant things, none of them reassuring. "I want to speak to their commanders personally."

"Aye, sir," the tactical officer said.

◆ ◆ ◆

"Captain," Roach said, "the enemy CO is demanding to speak to the destroyer commanders."

"That's torn it," Kat said. She'd hoped to get closer before the enemy smelled a rat, but if they weren't already suspicious, they would be the moment the destroyers also claimed to have communications problems.

She glanced at the timer, then back at the main display. A dozen shuttles were closing in on the formation, their sensors probing at the ECM. "Are the missile pods online?"

"Yes, Captain," Roach said. "They're ready."

"Fire," Kat ordered.

It wasn't common to bolt orbital missile pods to freighters, let alone warships. The pods rarely survived the launch sequence, while the missile drives could do considerable harm to the starship's hulls. Indeed, Kat had seen several concepts for towing missile pods that had come to grief on the simple fact that any interaction with the starship's drive field would be utterly disastrous. But if she didn't care about losing the motherships, she could bolt hundreds of missile pods to their hulls and fire at will.

"Missiles away, Captain," Roach reported. His voice turned darkly humorous. "I think the shuttles flinched."

"Ramp up the drives, as planned," Kat ordered. Her unmanned ships were unlikely to reach the orbital facilities before they were destroyed, but they'd give the enemy a fright. "And take out the shuttles before they get into engagement range."

"Aye, Captain," Roach said.

◆ ◆ ◆

Commodore Malian stared in horror at the display, unable to move or speak. One moment, the convoy had been advancing into orbit; the next, hundreds—perhaps *thousands*—of red icons appeared, each one representing a missile heading towards his facilities. Most of them would burn out before they could enter terminal attack range, but there were so many missiles that it was unlikely his facilities would remain unharmed. And even if they went to purely ballistic trajectories, without a hope of altering course, they were *still* certain to hit the planet.

"Commodore," the tactical officer said. "Request permission to engage with point defense."

Malian had to fight to compose himself. "Granted," he said. He'd never been in combat before. Was it always like this? "Take as many of them out as possible."

He watched, grimly, as the red icons roared closer. Most of them appeared to be targeted on the repair yards, although a handful were definitely aimed right at his station. That made sense, he reluctantly admitted; wrecking the yards and the industrial nodes would render Aswan completely unimportant, in the grand scheme of things. His handful of ships was forming up into a single unit, but it was too late. The only good news was that none of them appeared to have been targeted.

"The shuttles are being engaged, sir," the tactical officer said.

Malian glared at him. Compared to the storm roaring down on his facilities, bringing with it certain death for him personally, who cared? Admiral Junayd would order his immediate execution once he heard the news. If he'd kept the superdreadnoughts an hour longer . . .

But I sent the courier boats after the admiral, he thought. It was something to cling to, even as his command was ripped apart. *At least he might make it back in time to take revenge.*

◆ ◆ ◆

"The cripples are engaging the enemy ships," Roach reported. On the display, one of the cripples vanished, followed rapidly by a second. "I don't think any of them are going to get through."

"It doesn't matter," Kat said. *None* of the ships were manned, save for *Lightning* herself, and she had no hope of getting them back home. And even if she did, they were too old and expensive to repair. Better they soaked up a handful of missiles rather than being scrapped or sold to poorer worlds. "Just keep watching the missiles."

She smiled coldly as the stolen missiles homed in on their targets. The enemy point defense crews were good, she had to admit, and her missiles were starting to go ballistic, which made them easier to hit, but there were just so *many* of them. If only she had antimatter warheads, when even an intercepted missile could be deadly.

"The repair yards are taking hits," Roach reported. Brilliant explosions flashed up on the display as the nukes started to detonate. "The enemy command station is under attack, but defending itself . . ."

He broke off. "The repair yard has been destroyed, Captain," he added. A handful of icons winked out of existence. "Seventeen industrial platforms have been smashed."

And, no matter what happens, they will know what we've done, Kat thought, feeling cold hatred pulsing through her mind. It was a shame the command post was likely to survive, but it would be immaterial with the system's facilities destroyed. *They'll never feel safe behind the lines again.*

CHAPTER THIRTY-SEVEN

"Jump completed, sir."

William nodded. It wasn't *easy* being in command of a squadron—he'd had no time to work out a relationship with Commander Millikan—but he had no choice. He'd told the younger man that he was still in command of his ship while William would command the overall squadron. If Commander Millikan had a problem with that, and William rather figured he would, he'd been professional enough not to let it contaminate their working relationship.

"Engage the enemy defenses," William ordered. "Scan for any traces of watchdogs."

"Aye, sir," the tactical officer said.

William rubbed his forehead. If it had been hard enough to command an entire *fleet* from *Lightning*, it was a great deal harder commanding six ships—four warships and two freighters—from a badly outdated light cruiser. There was no flag deck, no CIC; he'd had to take a console on the already-cramped bridge and prepare himself for either resentment or confusion. But there was no choice.

"Enemy defenses turning to engage us," the tactical officer reported. "We're taking them out now."

"No trace of a watchdog," another officer added, through the data-net. *Oliver Kennedy* didn't have a proper tactical compartment either, so they'd had to improvise. "We seem to be clear."

"That proves nothing," William snapped. "Continue firing."

"Aye, sir," the tactical officer said.

William nodded, then studied Redemption as it appeared on the display. The icy world was right at the edge of the life-bearing zone, its atmosphere too thin to support human life without spacesuits or heavy genetic enhancement. It was unlikely that anyone would *want* Redemption, which was probably why the Theocracy had turned it into a POW camp. Even if the POWs managed to get out of the dome, they wouldn't be able to get anywhere before they suffocated to death.

And they can blow the dome if the prisoners riot, he thought grimly. *If we time this wrong, everyone in the complex is going to wind up dead.*

"All orbital defenses destroyed," the tactical officer reported.

"Good work," Commander Millikan said.

"Deploy the Marines," William ordered. "And prepare to launch the shuttles; I say again, prepare to launch the shuttles."

He studied the planet in the display for a long moment. There were no settlements, save for the POW camp itself; there were no active defenses, save for a couple of scanners positioned near the camp. It struck him as odd, but it was quite possible that whoever operated the camp cared more for secrecy than active defenses. Or, given the Theocracy's economic weakness, they simply didn't have the money to defend the POW camp. He smiled at the thought, then watched as the Marines plummeted through the planet's atmosphere. If they failed . . .

◆ ◆ ◆

Captain Patrick James Davidson braced himself as he plummeted through the thin atmosphere, surrounded by his comrades. He'd practiced skydiving from orbit into the teeth of enemy defenses, or even sneaking through gaps in the enemy's sensor network, but the enemy didn't seem to be watching for incoming threats. They seemed to have relied completely on the orbital defenses, all of which were now gone. Patrick gritted his teeth, then triggered the antigravity system moments before he would slam into the ground. His fall stopped, allowing him to drop the last few inches to the icy surface.

"Over that ridge," he snapped as the Marines fanned out. There was no incoming fire, which was both good and bad; he had time to deploy his forces, but at the same time, he knew the enemy might be keeping some forces in reserve. "Advance!"

The Marines advanced forward, weapons at the ready, until the POW camp came into view. It looked like a bubble, a dome of glass surrounding a handful of barracks; Patrick couldn't help wondering just who had decided that such an insecure place was actually a good idea, even though it did have its advantages. Anyone who felt like running away would be able to get an eyeful of the unprepossessing terrain surrounding the prison camp. He led his men towards the small installation near the shuttlepad, then charged forward as a pair of enemy guards came into view. The guards had no time to react before they were knocked down and flattened to the ground.

"Get through the hatch," he snapped.

A Marine leaned forward, hacked into the control module, and took command of the system. The hatch hissed open, revealing a processing center that looked as though it belonged in a prison. A handful of guards were running forward, carrying projectile weapons that wouldn't have a chance of getting through Patrick's body armor. Patrick lifted his rifle, switched to stun, and started to mow the guards down before they could react. Their stunned bodies tumbled to the ground, waiting for pickup. Patrick strode over them and led his team through the small complex, towards the other set of hatches. Despite his fears, he had to admit it didn't *look* like a torture chamber.

He opened the second hatch and stepped into the dome. A handful of prisoners stared at him, their faces widening with shock. Did they think he was an enemy soldier? It was possible, he had to admit; the black armor carried no logos or insignia. He hesitated, then cracked open his suit. The POWs relaxed, very slightly, when they saw his face.

"I'm Captain Davidson," he said, using the suit's systems to boost his voice. "We're here to get you out of this shithole. Get into lines and ready yourselves for the shuttles."

The prisoners broke out of their trance and hurried towards the hatches, several dozen more pouring out of the barracks. Patrick glanced at a man who looked like a soldier, probably someone from one of the planetary militias, then motioned for him to join the Marines. He'd need to pick the man's brain, if only to find out just how many people there were in the camp.

"Get the shuttles down to the hatches now," he ordered.

He sucked in his breath as he glanced at the time. Twenty minutes before Aswan could pick up a radio signal from Redemption—assuming, of course, that there hadn't been a watchdog in orbit. It wasn't going to be easy to evacuate the complex. Unless he'd missed something, he hadn't seen any spacesuits in the guard complex, save for the two worn by the guards on the outside. It might be hard to get the POWs into the shuttles unless the two airlocks could be mated, a depressingly effective security precaution none of them had considered until it was far too late. They might have to take the risk of cutting through the dome, praying it wasn't rigged to shatter if the atmospheric integrity was broken.

"All right," he said. "Name, rank, serial number?"

The POW looked badly shaken. "Corporal Wallis, Highland Brigade," he said. "Planetary Militiaman M-482762."

"Very good," Patrick said. "Now tell me, how many prisoners are there in this complex and how many of them can move under their own power?"

"Twelve hundred," Wallis said, after a long moment. "Some of the prisoners in the final barracks can't move, sir; they were kept in isolation. They were never allowed to mingle with the rest of us."

"We'll deal with them," Patrick promised. Lines of prisoners, male and female, were forming in front of the hatches. Thankfully, despite his nightmares, the guards didn't seem to have molested any of the women. Come to think of it, he hadn't seen any sex slaves in the guard complex either. "Was anyone planning an escape?"

"I don't think so, sir," Wallis said. "I heard when I arrived that the complex is bugged to the nines. There was no way to plan anything without them hearing of it."

A POW's duty is to escape, Patrick thought. He'd been taught that, back at boot camp, and it had always stuck in his mind. *But these POWs had nowhere to go.*

He pushed the thought aside as the first shuttle came in to land. "Get in line," he ordered as he keyed his communicator. "Platoon One: with me. Platoon Two: sort the prisoners and get them into the shuttles."

Platoon One fanned out around him as they jogged towards the final barracks. It looked pretty much identical to the others, save for the sign on the front barring anyone from entering without special permission. Patrick checked the door, then smashed it down with one kick from his armored suit. Inside, it was dark, illuminated only by red lights positioned in the metal ceiling. Patrick switched his visor to night-vision mode, then advanced forward. Instead of a set of bunks, as he'd been expecting, there were a handful of doors, each one firmly locked. It was a set of prison cells within the prison.

"Open that door," he ordered, picking one at random. A Marine wrenched the door off its hinges, allowing him to peer inside. "Who are you?"

A brown-skinned man looked back at him, blearily. It was clear, given the number of bruises on his skin, that he'd been beaten repeatedly before being shoved into the cell. Patrick winced, then muttered commands. The prisoners in the barracks would be freed, then transported back to orbit. There would be time to sort them all out later.

"Roger," the man croaked. "Roger Mortimer."

The name was completely unfamiliar. Patrick considered it for a second, then checked the name against the files. His suit found nothing, but it relayed the request to the ships in orbit and came back with both an answer and an ID file. Lieutenant-General Roger Mortimer had been an officer in the Commonwealth Army, stationed on Cadiz. He'd been listed as missing, presumed dead in the chaos that had overwhelmed the planet when the Theocracy attacked. No one had considered the possibility that he'd survived.

The Theocracy separated the prizes from the common herd, Patrick thought as one of his Marines assisted Mortimer to leave the cell. *They wanted to use Mortimer for . . . for what?*

He shook his head. "Get the next shuttle in ASAP," he ordered as he called for reinforcements. If Mortimer was any guide, it was quite likely that most of the remaining prisoners in the barracks couldn't walk for themselves. "We need to get them off the planet as quickly as possible."

The first shuttle took off, rocketing into the sky above the dome. A second one was already landing, extending its airlock towards the hatch. His men were well trained, thankfully; they hadn't had any time to practice. He watched as two more prisoners were helped into the light, then half carried towards the waiting lines. They'd be taken onto the next shuttle and boosted to orbit, where they would be put in stasis.

The next thing most of them would know, he hoped, was that they were back home.

He glanced at the timer. Seven minutes left . . .

"Get a move on," he snapped. Another shuttle landed, ready to take the next consignment of former POWs. "Time is not on our side."

"The Marines report that some of the prisoners were high-value targets," the tactical officer said. "So far, they've recovered two colonels, a commodore, and a general. None of them are in good shape."

"Get them into stasis tubes when they arrive," William ordered. He suspected the Theocracy would have wanted to interrogate the prisoners, but most senior officers were equipped with implants designed to counter the effects of interrogation or, as a last resort, to kill them. "I don't think we have time for a complete breakdown."

He scowled as he looked at the near-space display. It was empty, but he knew that could change at any moment. Even if Captain Falcone had managed to distract the enemy, they could still spare a ship or two to respond to a distress call. There were five minutes left before they ran out of time.

"Tell them to hurry," he ordered, finally.

William forced himself to relax, thinking hard. There was something about the whole system that didn't make sense, not to him. If the POWs—or some of them, at least—were high-value targets, they should have been kept somewhere with more security. Or had the Theocracy assumed that no one knew where Aswan was? Or would dare to attack it if they did? He fretted for a long moment, then tried to push the thoughts out of his mind. The puzzle would be solved, sooner or later, perhaps after the prisoners were interrogated. Their captors might have had good reasons for wanting to keep them near the front lines.

But anything they knew would be outdated quickly, William thought. *We'd deactivate their command codes from the datanets, even if we thought they were dead. Trying to use a deactivated command code would sound the alarm.*

The timer bleeped. "Commander," the tactical officer said. "We're out of time."

"Keep moving the shuttles," William ordered. There was little else they could do, not when they needed to wait for the Marines. "And see how many more shuttles there are to come."

◆　◆　◆

"Three more," Patrick said. "I've got fifty-seven prisoners still to move, then the guards and us."

He cursed under his breath. The broken and battered prisoners had been moved onto the shuttles, thankfully, but many of the remainder were still waiting for a slot. His men had searched the entire complex, finding very little of any use. The Theocracy hadn't mistreated anyone who had not been in the last barracks, as far as he could tell, but they hadn't been very accommodating either. Even Commonwealth POWs were granted books and other forms of entertainment.

At least we took the datacores from the guard complex, he thought. He had a feeling they would be next to useless, but intelligence might be able to produce *something* interesting from them. *And the guards themselves may be able to shed light on the complex and its purpose.*

He watched the remaining prisoners depart, then motioned to his Marines to transport the guards into the final shuttle. None of the guards had recovered; they were secured, tossed into the shuttle, and finally latched to the deck to keep them still. Patrick took one final look at the POW camp, then followed his men into the craft. Moments later, the shuttle's drives surged and the craft threw itself into the air.

"Mission accomplished," he said, keying into the datanet. "All POWs recovered, sir; the POW camp is empty."

♦ ♦ ♦

"The POW camp is empty, Commander," the tactical officer said.

"Smash it," William ordered, shortly.

"Aye, sir," the tactical officer said. "KEWs away; I say again, KEWs away."

William nodded. The last of the shuttles was climbing through the atmosphere now, racing to catch the tiny squadron before it withdrew. Everyone else had already docked with their motherships; teams of medics and volunteer crewmen were helping to move the POWs into pre-prepared holds or sickbays depending on their condition. He smiled to himself—he hadn't expected everything to go so well—then swore out loud as two gateways appeared in high orbit. A pair of destroyers dropped back into realspace, their weapons already searching for targets.

Too late, he thought triumphantly. The destroyers were modern; they might be able to give his squadron a very hard time, even though he had two light cruisers and a destroyer under his command. But he had no intention of standing his ground, let alone allowing them to enter engagement range. *You're far too late.*

"The final shuttle is coming into dock now," the tactical officer said.

"Jump us out as soon as she's latched on," William ordered. "Signal to *Mermaid*; she is to jump back to Aswan and inform Captain Falcone that the mission has been completed. The remainder of the squadron is to make its way to the first RV point."

"Aye, sir," the communications officer said.

"Enemy vessels are launching missiles," the tactical officer reported.

Too late, William thought again. *We're already on the move.*

"Gateway opening," the helmsman said. On the display, it seemed to lunge forward and swallow the flotilla, dragging them into hyperspace. "We're gone, sir."

"Then set course for the RV point," William said.

He forced himself to watch the display as the squadron swept away from the planet, knowing he was leaving his commanding officer behind. Her orders were inflexible, yet . . . yet he felt guilty for daring to abandon her. He wanted to loop back around the star and come to her aid, even though he knew it would be futile. She'd escape . . .

"Commander," Davidson said through the intercom. "I've unloaded the prisoners from the shuttles, sir; we're currently checking them against the records."

"Good," William said. Busywork would keep Davidson from pestering him about his commanding officer—and his lover. "Make sure you keep a sharp eye on them. Some of them may have been conditioned."

"Yes, sir," Davidson said.

William nodded, then closed the channel. For better or worse, he'd completed his half of the mission. Now . . . all he could do was wait and pray that Captain Falcone escaped.

"Captain," Linda said. "*Mermaid* has jumped out of hyperspace. Mission complete; I say again, mission complete."

Kat smiled, relieved. She had only two warships left, both badly damaged. The enemy ships were on their way, picking up their courage to confront the squadron . . . and, perhaps, guessing that some of the ships on their sensors simply didn't exist. If the POW camp had been raided successfully, the mission was now complete and . . .

"Captain," Roach snapped as alarms howled through the ship. "Nine gateways; I say again, nine gateways!"

Kat sucked in her breath as an entire superdreadnought squadron slid back into normal space, escorted by a handful of smaller ships. She glanced at the text in the display; it was the enemy squadron that had been lured to Salvation, not the one heading to the front lines. And while they seemed surprised to see her, they were already charging weapons . . .

"Evasive action," she ordered. "Charge the generator. Prepare to get us out of here."

CHAPTER THIRTY-EIGHT

Admiral Junayd stared in horror at the nightmare unfolding in front of him. He'd pushed his ships to the limit from the moment the courier boat had caught up with them, but it had been too late to prevent the enemy from attacking Aswan. The facilities had been smashed, the giant orbital fortress was damaged . . . and the enemy ships were already falling back from the planet.

"Contact Commodore Malian," Admiral Junayd ordered. He was dead. He *knew* he was dead. This failure would guarantee his execution. But maybe, just maybe, there was still a chance to catch the enemy. "Get me a full tactical download, *now!*"

Admiral Junayd glared at the helmsman's back. "And set a pursuit course," he added. "I want them under our guns before they can escape!"

"Aye, sir," the helmsman said.

It wouldn't be fast enough, Admiral Junayd thought. Some of the remaining enemy ships were clearly damaged—unless they were ECM drones posing as starships—but they could still break free and jump into hyperspace before he caught them. He'd have to follow them out of realspace if he still wanted to intercept them . . . and he had no choice. Besides, it might be time to concede defeat and put his contingency plans into operation.

He cursed under his breath as the tactical download appeared in front of him. They'd been tricked, somehow; the enemy had captured the StarCom convoy, then turned it against the defenders. He couldn't understand how they'd done it, unless someone had deliberately tipped off the enemy, but his orders had backfired on him. He'd told the convoy crews to do nothing, absolutely nothing, that might damage the StarCom and, clearly, they'd taken the orders to heart. If they'd blown their ships instead of surrendering . . .

It doesn't matter, he told himself as the download came to an end. The enemy had attacked Redemption too, landing shuttles and liberating the Inquisition's prized prisoners. That mistake, at least, couldn't be blamed on him, although he had no doubt the Inquisition would try. They'd been determined to refuse anyone else access to their captives. *And now their secret compound has been discovered and raided. They'll need a scapegoat too.*

"Admiral," Captain Haran said. "The enemy ships are preparing to leap into hyperspace."

Of course they are, Admiral Junayd thought bitterly. *How like a woman to fight and run.*

He shook his head. The enemy commander had carried out a brilliant plan and accomplished her objectives . . . even though he'd overloaded his drives trying to get back in time. Male or female, such an accomplishment deserved respect. Not that she'd get it, of course, from the Theocracy. The propaganda departments would probably work overtime to either erase her from the record books or turn her into a puppet, handled by her XO.

"Take us in pursuit," he ordered flatly.

"Admiral . . ." Commodore Isaac said. He stood, clasping his hands behind his back. "I must remind you of the dangers of pursuing an enemy fleet in hyperspace."

Admiral Junayd drew his pistol in one smooth motion. "And I must remind *you* of the dangers of questioning your superior's orders during a combat situation," he said. The commodore might already be measuring his back for the knife, but Admiral Junayd was damned if he was going to let him get away with it. "Return to your station and handle your duties or die, right here and now."

He smiled inwardly as the commodore paled, then sat. Had he forgotten, so quickly, that the commander of any task force had the right to execute his subordinates for questioning or disobeying orders? Admiral Junayd might be in deep trouble as soon as word got back to the homeworld, but he hadn't been stripped of his authority *yet*. No one would raise a fuss if he blew Isaac's brains over the bridge.

"Take us in pursuit," Admiral Junayd ordered, resting his gun in his lap. After that little play, no one was likely to side with the commodore against him until orders arrived from their superiors. By then, the issue would be settled, one way or the other. "And order the squadron to prepare to spread out once we're in hyperspace."

He tapped his console. The enemy hadn't gone after the Aswan StarCom, probably with the intention of ensuring that reports of the disaster—no, the debacle—got back to the homeworld and his superiors. Thankfully, some of his personal staff were still keeping the device in lockdown rather than allowing Commodore Malian to use it. He sent a string of orders, one commanding his staff to send a very important message back home, the others ordering them to wipe the system afterwards, burying their traces. If nothing else, his family would have a chance to go into hiding and survive . . .

It wasn't much, Admiral Junayd knew. But after this failure, after the second confirmation that God had withdrawn His favor, there was no chance that either he or his family would be granted mercy. They'd be tortured to death, slowly and painfully, in payment for their sins . . .

. . . and if he returned home, there would be no way to escape.

"Captain, the enemy superdreadnoughts are moving in pursuit," Roach reported. "I don't think the ECM will fool them for much longer."

"Direct the remaining automated ship to engage them," Kat ordered. There was no point in remaining where she was, not any longer. "Helm, open a gateway. Get us out of here."

"Aye, Captain," Weiberg said.

"Send the self-destruct code to the drones," Kat added. The drones couldn't pass through the gateway and she had no time to recover them. Besides, watching a dozen ships vanish like soap bubbles would humiliate the enemy still further. "They are to destroy themselves just after we enter hyperspace."

"Aye, Captain," Roach said.

Kat allowed herself a cold smile as the gateway spiraled open in front of her ship. The enemy would never forget this day. Nor would they trust their convoys, no matter what codes they had. They'd insist on inspecting them all before they reached attack range, adding further delays to their already overstretched logistics network. *Lightning* shuddered as she slid into hyperspace, then accelerated away from the planet's gravity well. If the enemy had the nerve to chase her into hyperspace, she would still have an excellent chance of escaping . . .

"Captain," Roach said. "The enemy ships have entered hyperspace."

Kat frowned. *Lightning* could easily outrun the superdreadnoughts, but the smaller ships would be a problem. The Theocratic vessels would have trouble locating her ship, given how easily hyperspace distorted even short-range sensors, yet it only took one of them getting lucky to slow her escape. And she couldn't exchange missile fire with a light cruiser, let alone a superdreadnought. She'd practically shot herself dry.

"Find a patch of distortion and steer us towards it," she ordered coolly. If they broke contact, even for a few minutes, she'd have a very good chance of evading them long enough to make her escape. Even if they didn't, they'd have to be insane to start a fight near a distortion. The resulting energy storm might destroy both sides. "And then take us onwards, towards the RV point."

She looked down at her display, thinking hard. The rest of the flotilla had steered a different course, assuming they'd broken contact; they'd go to the RV point, then make their way back to the Reach if Kat didn't meet up with them. No matter what happened to *Lightning*, they'd make their escape, taking with them the former POWs, a defector, the prisoners . . . and a working enemy StarCom. The operation, by any realistic standards, had been a great success.

And even if it costs the Commonwealth a heavy cruiser as well as the outdated ships, it would still be worth it, she thought. *With what we now know about the enemy, targeting future offensives and winning the war will be a great deal easier.*

She settled back in her command chair as the red icons grew closer. If they were caught, if they were pinned down, *Lightning* would give a good account of herself before the energy storms swept both sides out of existence. And if they escaped . . .

We'll be back, she promised herself. *And this time we will be here to stay.*

"They were drones, Admiral," the sensor officer said.

"So they were," Admiral Junayd said. The only explanation for twelve starships popping out of existence was that they'd never existed as anything more than false sensor images. "Take us into hyperspace."

He kept his face impassive as his squadron slid into hyperspace and spread out, searching for the enemy. It wasn't easy to track the ship, but she hadn't put *quite* enough distance between them before it was too late, even though hyperspace was producing a dozen alternate possibilities. Admiral Junayd nodded to himself as his ships altered course, feeling more and more confident as he realized the enemy craft was rocketing *towards* a distortion eddy. No one would take that kind of risk unless they felt they had no choice.

But it will be enough to save them, he thought bitterly. *I dare not take a full squadron of superdreadnoughts into the eddy.*

"Signal the smaller ships," he ordered. "They are to press the enemy closely, while the superdreadnoughts spread out and surround the eddy."

Commodore Isaac tensed, but said nothing, no doubt aware of the prospect of immediate death. Admiral Junayd smiled coldly, keeping his thoughts to himself. Spreading the squadron out raised the possibility of friendly fire, of accidentally mistaking his ships for the enemy and opening fire, but there was no real alternative. Apart, of course, from using one of his contingency plans . . .

He keyed his terminal, uploading a specific set of orders into the datanet. Thankfully, most of the crewmen who'd get them were too junior to do anything more than follow orders, even if they *had* heard rumors of impending disaster. They'd do what they were told . . .

. . . and, in doing so, lay the groundwork for his final break with his superiors.

◆ ◆ ◆

"The enemy superdreadnoughts are spreading out," Roach reported. "But the smaller ships are still chasing us."

Kat nodded grimly. The enemy was taking a chance, but it might well pay off for them. If she kept moving through the eddy, their smaller ships might catch up with her; if she altered course, she might run into one of the superdreadnoughts. The distortion affecting her sensors, growing stronger with every moment she advanced towards the eddy, would keep her from seeing an enemy ship until she was right on top of it.

Or worse, she thought. *We'd see so many false sensor images that we wouldn't realize it when we ran into a real superdreadnought.*

She closed her eyes, knowing there was only one option left.

"Prepare to launch missiles," she ordered. "I want the warheads to detonate"—she tapped her console—"here, here, and here. As soon as the missiles are launched, ramp up our speed as much as possible."

"Captain," Roach said. "That will trigger an energy storm for sure."

"I know," Kat said. "They have nine valuable superdreadnoughts chasing us. I can't imagine they'd want to fly them into an energy storm."

She looked down at the console, biting her lip. No matter what she said, there was a strong possibility that the storm would overwhelm them too. It wasn't considered a wise tactic because it could threaten both sides. But she was badly outgunned . . . and besides, killing nine superdreadnoughts would only help her side. *Lightning's* loss would be barely noticed.

"Fire," she ordered quietly.

Lightning's drives hummed as the ship surged forward, her acceleration revealing her presence to the enemy hunters. Kat sucked in her breath, then smiled as the enemy ships hastily fell back. It was too late; the warheads detonated, energizing hyperspace and generating a whole new energy storm. It raged behind them, a primal surge of energy that would smash any starship to atoms if it were caught in the storm, throwing sheets of disruption and distortion in all directions.

And even if they manage to evade the storm, she thought, *they sure as hell won't be able to track us through the chaos.*

"Keep us moving," she ordered. Storms were notoriously unpredictable. It was quite possible the storm behind them would vanish as quickly as it had appeared. "And don't look back."

◆ ◆ ◆

"Admiral," the sensor officer said, "they deliberately triggered a storm!"

Commodore Isaac leapt to his feet. "Drop us out of hyperspace, now," he snapped. "I . . ."

Admiral Junayd shot him through the head.

"Belay that order," he said. It was the *right* order, but not the one he wanted to give. "Reverse course; best possible speed."

The helmsman glanced at the body, then did as he was told. Admiral Junayd watched, keying more commands into his console, as the super-dreadnought struggled to put as much distance between itself and the storm as possible. It didn't look as though it was working; the storm was exciting hyperspace, which was—in turn—reacting to the starship's drive fields. The remainder of the squadron had already dropped out of hyperspace, saving themselves from potential catastrophe.

"Admiral, the storm is disrupting our drive field," the sensor officer reported nervously. "It needs to be shut down, if we can't return to realspace."

"Then shut it down," Admiral Junayd ordered calmly. "Inform the crew that we are powering down all nonessential systems to preserve ourselves from the storm."

"Aye, sir," the security officer said.

"And urge them to pray too," Admiral Junayd added. Having all nonessential personnel gathering to pray would save time. "Order the Cleric to lead prayers in the shuttlebay."

He smiled to himself as the lights dimmed, then rose to his feet, striding casually over towards the rear of the compartment, where a large display showed the ship's current condition. The storm was causing power surges, but, thankfully, the redundancies built into the starship were preventing it from taking any serious damage.

Admiral Junayd turned, silently noted the position of everyone on the bridge, then lifted his gun and opened fire, targeting the security officer first.

Several crewmen jumped to their feet, but they were merely the next to die. By the time the clip was empty, everyone on the bridge, apart from him, was dead.

"May God keep you," he said as he reloaded his gun. He couldn't help feeling a flicker of regret, as if he'd crossed a line he hadn't known existed. He hadn't had any particular loathing for most of the crew—and Captain Haran had been a decent young man—but he couldn't leave them at his back, not now. "And may He take you to your final resting place."

He tapped a switch, triggering a ship-wide lockdown, then strolled off the bridge, making his way down towards the docking ports. Thanks to the command to pray, all personnel either would be making a show of their piety or manning essential stations, leaving the interior corridors deserted. He saw no one by the time he stepped through the hatch and into the courier boat. It was a tiny ship, with only two crewmen. They turned to stare at him as he stepped into their ship.

"Admiral," one said. "The boat is ready . . ."

"Good," Admiral Junayd said. He'd considered coming up with a lie, but there was no way he could take them with him. They'd know something was badly wrong the moment he ordered them to set course for the nearest Commonwealth fleet base. "And I thank you."

He lifted his gun and shot the first man through the head. The second stared, then jumped at him; Admiral Junayd shot him twice, then stepped aside and watched as the body crumpled to the floor. He hadn't hated them either, but they still had to die. Gritting his teeth, he dragged the bodies to the airlock, then linked back into the superdreadnought's datanet one final time. He couldn't trigger the self-destruct without Commodore Isaac or his flag captain, but he could do something almost as good. Destroying the ship's datacores would leave her drifting through hyperspace forever.

No way back now, he thought. He felt an odd urge to giggle, which he suppressed firmly. *I don't think they'd want me any longer.*

He stepped back into the courier boat, closed and locked the hatch, then took the command chair and brought the ship's drives online. The hyperspace storm was abating now, as he'd hoped; he said a silent prayer, then cast off from the superdreadnought. Unless someone was feeling very brave, none of the other ships would return to hyperspace for at least an hour, giving him plenty of time to make his escape. And it was unlikely they'd ever be able to locate the superdreadnought. They'd probably assume the worst and give the crew a hero's funeral.

And now all I have to do is wait, he thought as he triggered the drives. There wouldn't be much to do on the courier boat—he had no idea how the crews tolerated their lives—but he'd endured worse. *Wait and see if what I have to offer is enough to convince the Commonwealth to take me in.*

♦ ♦ ♦

Kat couldn't help feeling relieved as *Lightning* reached the RV point and linked up with the rest of the squadron. The engineers had already dismantled the StarCom, although they'd warned that it might not be possible to put it back together again, and readied it for transport back home. She'd have to read the reports later, Kat knew, but for the moment all she wanted to do was set off as quickly as possible.

"Captain," the XO said from *Oliver Kennedy*. There was something in his voice that chilled Kat to the bone. "There's a POW I'd like to bring back to *Lightning*. I think you have to see him personally."

"Very well," Kat said, slowly. "Who is it?"

The XO took a breath. "Admiral Morrison."

CHAPTER THIRTY-NINE

"You have *got* to be fucking kidding me."

"I wish I was," the XO said. Kat had met him, Davidson, and a Marine escort in the shuttlebay. "I had his DNA checked against the files, Captain, and it's definitely Admiral Lord Buckland Morrison, late of 7th Fleet and Cadiz Naval Base."

Kat stared at the man in disbelief. The last time she'd seen Admiral Morrison, he'd been at ground zero of a major attack on the Occupation Force HQ, on Cadiz. She'd honestly assumed he was dead, even though she hadn't seen the body. The Theocracy hadn't gloated about taking him prisoner, or offered to trade him for another prisoner, or even used his survival as a propaganda tool. It wouldn't have been *hard* to claim that Admiral Morrison had been a deep-cover agent all along, undermining the Commonwealth's faith in the Royal Navy at the worst possible moment. Hell, Kat knew there were people who believed that Admiral Morrison *had* been a traitor. He'd certainly been a fool.

And someone ensured he got the post, she thought, recalling her father's words. Someone important and powerful, powerful enough to use Admiral Morrison without leaving traces even someone as capable as her father could track. *Someone put him in a position where he could do a great deal of harm.*

She swallowed, feeling as though her mouth was suddenly dry. Her father had said that only one of the dukes, the most powerful aristocrats on Tyre, could have organized the placement and then successfully covered it up. If one of the dukes had done it, perhaps as an enemy puppet, perhaps with intentions of his own, it would be a major scandal. Faith in the aristocracy would collapse into rubble. She was seriously tempted to simply draw her sidearm and shoot, leaving the mystery forever unsolved. But she wanted to catch whoever had been behind him, wanted it very much. They had to be punished for their crimes.

"Captain," Admiral Morrison croaked, "I . . ."

Kat studied him, grimly. Admiral Morrison had been strikingly handsome, the product of both genetic tailoring and hours spent having his body reshaped in line with the latest fashions. Now, he looked ghastly; he'd lost weight, his eyes were haunted, and his voice sounded broken. The Theocracy couldn't have been running him as a deep-cover agent, Kat was sure; they wouldn't need to torture anyone working for them. She would have felt sorry for him, if she hadn't known what he'd done. For whatever reason, Admiral Morrison had lowered the defenses around Cadiz to the point the enemy had no difficulty in overrunning them when they finally crossed the border.

And we were damn lucky to save anything, she told herself sharply.

"I assume command," Admiral Morrison said. He made an effort to pull himself up to his full height. "I am an admiral and . . ."

"No," Kat said flatly. Even if it hadn't been against regulations to trust POWs until they'd been checked out, she wouldn't have handed command over to him. "You are in deep shit."

She had to fight down the urge to rub his nose in the impending court-martial. By the time it had finished, he might find himself wishing he was back in the POW camp.

"You will be taken to Sickbay," she added, "then placed in stasis until we return to Tyre."

She looked at Davidson. "Take him to Sickbay, then stay with him until he's in stasis," she ordered shortly. "I don't want him trying to assert authority or speaking to *anyone* apart from the doctor until we get him back home."

"Aye, Captain," Davidson said.

"Most of the POWs are unharmed," the XO said as the Marines escorted Admiral Morrison towards the hatch. "A handful of senior officers, male and female, were brutalized, probably in hopes of extracting information from them. Several of the victims were in quite serious condition when we recovered them. They're currently in stasis, waiting for medical attention."

"Good," Kat said, still distracted. Admiral Morrison—alive? A dozen fanciful explanations ran through her head, each one easily dismissed with a tiny flicker of rational thought. "How many people know about the admiral?"

"Only a handful of Marines and the medics," the XO assured her. "I was careful to keep him isolated from the rest of the former POWs, once I realized who he was. They didn't have any idea he was one of the . . . *special* prisoners."

"They'd want to lynch him," Kat muttered. She understood the impulse. "We'll keep everyone else in the dark as much as possible, at least until we reach Tyre."

"I've already told the medics to keep it to themselves," the XO said. "The Marines won't talk out of turn."

"No, they won't," Kat agreed. They started to walk back towards the bridge. "Overall, Commander, how did it go?"

"Very well, all things considered," the XO said. "They *did* send a pair of destroyers after us, but they were just a heartbeat too late. We got lucky."

"Very lucky," Kat agreed. She just hoped they wouldn't run into another enemy fleet as they crossed the front lines. The squadron didn't have enough missiles left to fire a full salvo, let alone fight a running battle. "And now we're heading home, crammed with former POWs, prisoners, a single defector and his family . . . and enough intelligence to really help the war effort. I think they'll rank it a success."

"If they muster the firepower to take advantage of it," William said. "The enemy will figure out we got a defector, I suspect. They'll change things."

Kat nodded. It wouldn't be *long* before the enemy's High Command compared notes and realized they'd been conned. They'd have to change all the codes, making it much harder to insert additional fake messages into the StarCom network. There were Rear-Echelon Motherfuckers (REMFs), she was sure, who would complain she'd thrown away a priceless intelligence scoop, but she knew better. It simply wasn't possible to insert fake messages on a regular basis.

"They can't move stars and planets," she said. "And I don't think they have the resources to move their facilities while fighting the war. There will be time to put a far stronger raiding force together and take it directly into the heart of the enemy fortifications."

"I hope so, Captain," the XO said. He looked at her, suddenly. "What does it mean for us that Admiral Morrison survived?"

Kat hesitated. There hadn't been a court-martial for Admiral Morrison, if only because there was no point in putting a corpse on trial. But now that they'd recovered him, there would *have* to be a court-martial . . . and, given what was at stake, it would have to be public. She found it hard to care if Admiral Morrison was systematically disgraced before he was marched to the gallows, but it might undermine the Commonwealth. No, she told herself. It *would* undermine the Commonwealth. Admiral Morrison was directly responsible for the loss of three worlds and countless ships. How many other officers would be smeared by his failures?

And if he was a spy, if there is the merest suggestion he was a spy, we'll tear our ranks apart looking for others, she thought dully. Admiral Morrison might be a fool, or a patsy, but he would have been vetted before he was promoted to captain, let alone admiral. *If he escaped the vetting, clearly our procedures are inadequate. They will need to be tightened up.*

"I don't know," she admitted. She briefly considered altering course, attempting to meet Admiral Christian and borrowing his StarCom, but she knew that would just set the cat among the pigeons earlier. "I honestly don't know."

She took a breath. "Is there any other news?"

"Possibly," the XO said. "We recovered Commander Sarah Parker too. Ironically, despite his . . . moral failures, Lieutenant Parker played a role in rescuing his sister."

Kat shook her head. "Have you told her . . . ?"

"Not yet, Captain," the XO said. "What *are* they going to do with Mr. Parker?"

"I wish I knew," Kat said.

It wasn't something she wanted to think about. Lieutenant Parker *was* guilty of treason—and his treason had led to the loss of three ships and hundreds of deaths. On the other hand, a competent defender could point out that he'd *tried* to avoid serving as a spy, even if it had backfired on him. And there was the very real fact that the bureaucracy had failed to flag him as a potential security risk, ensuring he would be stationed somewhere harmless until the end of the war.

And he did help us win the battle, damage the enemy, and save his sister, she thought numbly. *That has to count for something, doesn't it?*

"We'll see what happens when we get home," she said finally. There would have to be punishment, if only because of the dead. There was no way a mere dishonorable discharge would suffice. But maybe he wouldn't have to be dumped on a penal world. "Until then . . . let him meet his sister, if he wishes. It may be his last chance."

She cleared her throat. "We'll proceed home at best possible speed," she said. "I'm sure you will be speaking to the observer at some point, Commander. She is *not* to hear about Admiral Morrison, not at all. We're going to have enough problems dealing with this hot potato without having a second political crisis on our hands."

"I understand," the XO said. "And Captain?"

"Yes?"

"You were right," the XO said. "Attacking Aswan was the right thing to do—and it worked."

"Thank you," Kat said. She wasn't sure why his approval meant so much, but it did. "And Commander, I couldn't have done it without you."

◆ ◆ ◆

"It's good to know that so many prisoners were rescued," Rose said.

William smiled. "The Navy believes in looking after its personnel," he said. "If someone is taken prisoner, we do our damndest to free them."

"Even at a considerable risk," Rose added.

"It's part of the unspoken contract," William said. He looked her in the eye. "If someone is wounded, we do everything we can to save them; if someone is lost, we do everything we can to find them; if someone is killed, we do everything we can to get their body back home, or bury it in space if that was their wish. The Navy is, in many ways, a giant family. We're not perfect, but we try hard to look after our people."

"So it would seem," Rose said. "However, integration is still a problem."

"I think it's a problem that will fade," William said. "Like it or not, the member worlds of the Commonwealth started at different levels, in both technology and training. As the years go by, we will deal with those problems and even out the differences. We may lose a certain diversity, but we will gain a more integrated navy."

Rose nodded, slowly. "Do you think that's a good thing?"

"I think we cannot afford to rely on Tyre producing all our defenders," William said. "And besides, military training can be the key to a better life in the future. In the long run, it will be good for everyone."

"Assuming our homeworld is freed," Rose said pessimistically. "I was listening to some of the debriefings conducted before the attack on Verdean. The Theocracy tore that world's society apart."

William nodded, remembering Perrier, Jean-Luc, and the others. They had more supplies than they'd ever dreamed of before they'd been liberated from the penal world, but they were still hopelessly outgunned. Maybe they'd be crushed from orbit . . . or maybe they'd have the patience to wait, biding their time, until the Royal Navy returned in force. He couldn't help wondering what would happen to Hebrides if the enemy remained in control for several years. Would there be anything left of the homeworld he knew and loved?

Not that you loved it enough to stay, he thought savagely. *Scott had a point about neither of us staying where we were born.*

"And what will they do," Rose asked, "if they believe they will actually lose the war?"

"I wish I knew," William said. He'd discussed it, endlessly, with the captain and Major Davidson. Some enemy commanders might surrender, if they realized they wouldn't be murdered in cold blood once they put down their weapons, but others might start trying to take down innocents with them. "We can make promises, let them keep their lives, yet they may truly believe in their religion. Surrender, to them, is the end of the world."

He cleared his throat. "What do you intend to write in your report?"

"That integration needs to speed up," Rose said flatly. "It's the only way to prevent the Commonwealth from becoming a menace."

William hesitated. On one hand, he doubted the Common-wealth—or Tyre—*could* become a menace to the member states, not without altering its entire structure. Tyre was practically *designed* to allow talented newcomers to rise, even enter the power structure at quite a high level. But on the other hand, there was the nagging fact that he hadn't been offered a command—at least, until the captain had given him temporary squadron command. And then . . . what if the Commonwealth *did* start exploiting its member worlds? Tyre and a couple of other worlds were vastly more powerful than the rest of the Commonwealth put together.

"War will see to that," he said. "The demand for new spacers will bring in more and more officers and crewmen from all over the Common-wealth."

He paused. "But, for the moment, is it really wise to start another political crisis? We have too many of them already."

"Probably not," Rose said. "But it's vitally important we register our concerns now."

William sighed. "The war comes first," he said. "We can argue how to share out the spoils of war afterwards."

"If there are spoils," Rose said. "And if we survive long enough to take advantage of them."

She shook her head. "How long until we get home?"

"Five weeks," William said. The captain was determined to avoid a leak. "You'll have plenty of time to write your report."

◆ ◆ ◆

By the time the courier boat dropped out of hyperspace, Admiral Junayd was thoroughly bored. There was nothing to *do* on the tiny ship, save read religious texts, pray, meditate on the state of his soul, and worry about his family. Had they hidden themselves in time? There was no way to know.

Three days after his escape, he found himself half wondering if he should reverse course and seek forgiveness even though he knew there would be none; five days afterwards, he could have sworn he was seeing the ghosts of the men he'd killed staring down at him when he snapped awake. It wasn't uncommon for spacers to see things, he'd learned as a young cadet, but most stories were suppressed by the religious authorities. Now . . . now, there was no one to reassure him that he was imagining it. He honestly had no idea how the crewmen had managed to stay sane.

He glanced at the scanner as the courier boat approached the naval base. Three squadrons of superdreadnoughts were clearly visible, backed up by dozens of smaller ships and a *swarm* of hundreds of gunboats. He felt a sudden stab of envy—even on the defensive, the Commonwealth was a fantastically rich society—and then keyed a command into the console, slowing the starship to a halt. In theory, the Commonwealth wouldn't shoot at a courier boat—it might have been bringing messages from the enemy leadership—but in practice, he had no way to be sure. The Theocracy hadn't signed any of the agreements made between the major interstellar powers after the Breakaway Wars.

"I would like to defect," he said when he was challenged. A flight of gunboats flew past, so close he could see them with the naked eye. They wouldn't have any difficulty blowing him out of space if they saw something, anything, suspicious. "I'd prefer not to broadcast my name on an open channel. This system may well be under observation."

It damn well should be, he added silently. It was an irritating thought. He'd recommended the policy as part of the prewar preparations. *Unless they chose to ignore my recommendations, of course.*

He waited, patiently, until a shuttle arrived, latching onto the courier boat's airlock. Four Marines entered, weapons at the ready. Admiral Junayd raised his hands, then waited, as patiently as he could, for them to finish sweeping his body with sensors, looking for hidden surprises. He could endure any indignity as long as he was safe. The

Commonwealth wouldn't give him command of a fleet—the idea was laughable—but they'd take care of him.

It was nearly four hours—and a careful examination that had seemed to take forever—before he came face to face with Admiral Christian.

"Admiral," Admiral Junayd said. He would have preferred to deal with another officer, but there was no choice. "I would like to defect."

"So you said," Admiral Christian said. His voice was very cool. He'd faced Admiral Junayd in battle, over Cadiz, and might bear a grudge. "Might I ask why?"

"Because if I stayed, I would be killed," Admiral Junayd said. If he was lucky, the combination of the lost superdreadnought and his family going into hiding would be enough to muddy the waters. The Theocracy would have its chance to pretend he died bravely instead of being executed as a failure. "I can help you, if you don't broadcast my name."

Admiral Christian leaned forward. "Why?"

"My family will be killed," Admiral Junayd said flatly. He was too proud to lower himself to beg. The die had been cast the moment he'd shot Isaac on his own bridge. "I have gifts, if you want them, in exchange for your silence. Intelligence, tactical data, even starship design notes."

"We'll be delighted," Admiral Christian said. "And welcome to the Commonwealth."

"Thank you," Admiral Junayd said.

CHAPTER FORTY

"Admiral *Junayd* defected?"

"Yes, Captain," Grand Admiral Tobias Vaughn said. "Admiral Junayd defected. He seemed to believe his life was in danger, thanks to you."

Kat shook her head in disbelief. "They were prepared to kill one of their commanding officers?"

"It does explain some of the oddities about their system," Vaughn said. "We moved him to a high-security facility on Tyre and started debriefing him. He knows enough to make taking care of him for the rest of his life *very* worthwhile."

"Yes, sir," Kat said.

"The other piece of good news is that Admiral Christian managed to pull off the ambush you suggested," Vaughn continued. "Nine enemy superdreadnoughts were destroyed, in exchange for two of our own. Thanks to the defectors, we now know just how badly that will hurt them once they realize what happened. It's possible we will be able to go on the offensive sooner than we hoped."

"That's good, sir," Kat said.

Vaughn cleared his throat. "Overall, Captain, the operation was a complete success, despite the loss of a number of outdated ships," he said. "The damage you did will shock the enemy; the intelligence you gathered will allow us to target other raids in the future; and the contacts you made, on Verdean if nowhere else, will assist us in securing control of the system when we launch the big counteroffensive. You did very well."

"Thank you, sir," Kat said.

"Certain . . . *intelligence* officers have complained that you used the StarCom, rather than shipping it back home for study," Vaughn added. "They were most put out by their inability to put it together for a second time. However, His Majesty told them off in no uncertain terms. Recovering a number of POWs, as well as burnishing your reputation as one of the leading lights of the Navy, has been good for the public. I dare say civilian morale has improved tremendously."

He paused. "And Justin Deveron is no longer a problem," he added. "His patrons were not amused when the whole affair made them look bad, as it did. You shouldn't have to think about him again."

"I didn't think about him," Kat said coolly.

The admiral smiled, then met her eyes. "Your recommendations regarding promotions, Captain, will be taken into account," he said. "Commander McElney *will* receive a starship of his own as well as a knighthood, although it may be several months until he is firmly seated in the command chair. I'm afraid your rank of commodore cannot be made permanent, under the circumstances, but you will probably be able to choose your next assignment. Admiral Christian has put in a request for your services, as have a couple of other senior commanders. Still, you won't be allowed to leave the system until Admiral Morrison has been indicted."

Kat leaned forward. "Sir?"

"Admiral Morrison will be put in front of a public court-martial, once a full investigation has been carried out," Vaughn said shortly. "You may be required to testify in front of the court."

He paused. "Mr. Parker will pass into intelligence's custody," he added. "Under the circumstances, he will spend the rest of his life in an open prison or exile, rather than a penal colony, which is as lenient as we can be. Heads will be rolling, considering the scale of the security breach. Luckily, the news hasn't been made public or it would be impossible to avoid another court-martial."

"Thank you, sir," Kat said. She had expected less, no matter what strings she pulled. "I felt sorry for him."

"Emotions should not be allowed to rule us, Captain," Vaughn said sternly. "He was dealt a bad hand, I agree, but he made poor choices. It was sheer luck that recovered his sister, not anything he did."

"Yes, sir," Kat said.

"You're expected to attend the ceremony at the Palace," Vaughn said. "Until then, consider yourself on leave. *Lightning* will be returned—again—to the yard crews, who will no doubt complain bitterly about having to redo most of their work. I dare say your father wants a word with you."

Kat nodded. "I would like to attend Admiral Junayd's debriefing sessions."

"I suspect that will not be possible," Vaughn said. "Intelligence complained bitterly about your . . . promises to the female defectors."

"With all due respect, sir," Kat began. "I . . ."

"I understand your feelings," Vaughn said, holding up a hand. "And I have not seen fit to stand in your way. *However*, there will be consequences for your decisions. I strongly suggest you stay out of their way for a while."

Kat scowled. "Yes, sir."

"Dismissed, Captain," Vaughn said. "And, once again, well done."

◆ ◆ ◆

William looked down at the golden star, unable to quite believe it was his. Part of him had decided, long ago, that he would *never* be offered command, no matter how hard he worked or how much experience he gained. He had tried to remain optimistic . . . he shook his head, admiring the way his name had been carved into the star. A command, a genuine command . . . he wouldn't have minded, he told himself, if he'd been offered a garbage scow, if he'd been offered *something*.

"You will probably be assigned to a heavy cruiser," Admiral Young had said. "I cannot make promises, not yet, but I believe that would be the best use of your talents."

"Commander . . . *William*," a voice said.

"Captain," he said, before catching himself. Captains called each other by their first names. "*Katherine?*"

"Just Kat, please," Kat said. Even in her dress uniform, she looked way too young to be a commanding officer. "Katherine is what my parents call me."

She smiled. "And congratulations."

"Thank you," William said. He held up the star. "Your work?"

"I recommended you for promotion after our last voyage," Kat said. Thinking of her as anything other than *Captain* would be difficult. "They saw fit to deny my request until now."

William scowled. Had he been awarded a command because of his service, because of Kat Falcone's recommendation . . . or because of Rose MacDonald? Had someone felt that it was time to speed up integration, despite the risks? Or had someone decided he could be trusted to serve as an example of an integrated officer, *without* the risks? He considered, briefly, demanding an explanation, perhaps even refusing the promotion, but he knew it would be professional suicide. Promotions were rarely offered more than once.

"You'll do fine," she assured him. "Once you have a command, it will be back to the front lines."

"Or behind them," William said. "Do they have any plans to send another squadron behind enemy lines?"

"I suspect so," Kat said. "However . . ."

The door opened. "It's time," she said, reaching out and taking his arm. "Let's go."

William sucked in his breath as they walked forward—he couldn't help thinking they were walking to the altar—into the giant chamber. It was lined with nobility, ranging from dukes and lords who were household names to men and women who'd purchased their noble titles and taken their place among the planet's rulers. He wanted to stop, but iron discipline kept him moving forward until he was standing in front of the throne. The king looked down at him and, unbelievably, winked.

"Who brings this man before me?"

"I, Lady Katherine Falcone, do," Kat said. Her voice was clear, showing no hint she was intimidated by the massive gathering. But then, *she* was the daughter of a duke. "He is worthy of your recognition."

The king rose to his feet. "Captain William McElney . . ." he said. His voice was calm, but William thought he detected hints of uncertainty buried within the tone. A junior officer, perhaps, hopelessly out of his depth. William had mentored dozens of them in his long career. "You have served Us well. Kneel."

William hesitated, then fell to his knees. Kat dropped beside him, still holding his arm. The king drew his sword and stepped forward, holding the blade out until it was resting gently on William's shoulder. He tensed, despite himself; a single slash and his head would be rolling on the ground. But the king would never kill someone in front of the entire aristocracy.

"It is Our very great honor to invest you with a knighthood," the king said. "We welcome you to Our family, to those who serve Us and Our Kingdom. Arise, Sir William."

He drew back the sword. William rose, slowly, as the crowd cheered. A knighthood wasn't just an empty title, he knew; it was social acceptance, an open invitation to take up a place among the aristocracy. Kat gently tugged on his arm, pulling him around; he blinked in surprise as he saw Princess Drusilla standing amidst the throng. He hadn't expected to see her again, ever. But then, her defection had been a major point in the Commonwealth's favor.

"Come on," Kat whispered. "It's time to go."

William nodded and allowed her to lead him out of the room, into an antechamber. It was suddenly very quiet as the door closed behind them.

"Congratulations, Sir William," she said seriously. "You deserve it."

"Thank you," he said. "What now?"

Kat laughed. "Join me for dinner? Patrick should be back soon; we can go eat together and talk about the future."

William hesitated, then nodded. "Why not?"

"Katherine," Duke Falcone said, when Kat entered his office. "Have you heard the news?"

Kat frowned. She'd had dinner with her former XO—she knew she was going to miss him—and had been seriously considering a night on the town with Davidson before her father's message had arrived. It had been terse, ordering her to return to the mansion at once; she'd bid her friends farewell, then caught an aircar home. Her father wouldn't have summoned her if it hadn't been urgent.

"No," she said. "What news?"

"Admiral Morrison is dead," Duke Falcone said curtly. "There was, apparently, a tragic accident. His brain literally melted."

Kat blinked in shock. "What happened?"

"According to the reports, they were preparing to use a mind probe on him," Duke Falcone said. "They established the link, then there was a sudden surge of power, causing a colossal cerebral hemorrhage. His body was shoved into stasis at once, of course, while medics were called, but by the time they examined him it was far too late. They can keep his body alive, Katherine, yet the man himself is long gone. There isn't a hope of interrogating him."

"That wasn't an accident," Kat said.

"Almost certainly not," Duke Falcone agreed. "Units of the Special Security Force took everyone in the complex into custody, then checked them all out *thoroughly*. The mind probe itself was examined. Apparently, it was programmed to generate a power surge when linked to a specific brainprint. As of yet, Katherine, no one has been marked as a potential suspect."

Kat swallowed. "Someone reached into the heart of a top-secret detention facility and murdered the one man who might be able to explain what happened at Cadiz."

"Precisely," Duke Falcone said. "I don't think I need to explain to you the political consequences."

"No," Kat said. She'd seriously considered killing Admiral Morrison herself, before thinking better of it. Clearly, his unknown patrons had been thinking along the same lines. "Whoever was backing Admiral Morrison will remain unidentified."

"Quite," her father agreed. "They may have acted to cover the whole disaster up, Katherine, or they may have something darker in mind. And we *still* don't have the slightest idea who they are."

"Or why they promoted Admiral Morrison," Kat said. "We have no suspects at all?"

"There are thirteen dukes," her father said dryly. "Seeing I know I didn't do it, that leaves twelve possible suspects. All of whom, I might add, have enough political power to quash any accusations without solid proof."

He shook his head. "We have a war to fight, Katherine," he concluded. "For now, all we can do is watch, wait, and see if they reveal themselves.

And take precautions, in case this is more than a simple attempt to cover up a major blunder."

"I understand," Kat said.

"I hope so," her father agreed. "Because if they can reach into a top-secret detention facility and murder our single most important prisoner, without leaving any traces that point back to them, what else can they do?"

END OF BOOK TWO

ABOUT THE AUTHOR

 Christopher G. Nuttall has been planning sci-fi books since he learned to read. Born and raised in Edinburgh, Chris created an alternate history website and eventually graduated to writing full-sized novels. Studying history independently allowed him to develop worlds that hung together and provided a base for storytelling. After graduating from university, Chris started writing full-time. As an indie author, he has published eighteen novels and one novella (so far) through Amazon Kindle Direct Publishing. Professionally, he has published *The Royal Sorceress*, *Bookworm*, *A Life Less Ordinary*, *Sufficiently Advanced Technology*, *The Royal Sorceress II: The Great Game* and *Bookworm II: The Very Ugly Duckling* with Elsewhen Press, and *Schooled in Magic* through Twilight Times Books.

As a matter of principle, all of Chris's self-published Kindle books are DRM-free.

Chris has a blog where he publishes updates, snippets, and world-building notes at http://chrishanger.wordpress.com/, and a website at http://www.chrishanger.net.

Chris is currently living in Edinburgh with his partner, muse, and critic Aisha.